Heart of Stone

Book Four in the Fire & Ice Series

By

Karen Payton Holt

Copyright - Karen Payton Holt: 2018

All rights reserved

The story is a work of fiction.

All characters in this book are fictitious and any resemblance to real persons, living or dead, is purely coincidental.

Think 'Twilight' meets 'Game of Thrones', with a dark twist, and you are in the right mindset to enter the world of Fire & Ice.

AVAILABLE NOW:

BOOK ONE in the Series:

Fire & Ice: Awakening

Available in Paperback on Amazon
ISBN 978-1-9806710-4-6

Paperback and Hardback available in bookstores:
A5 Paperback ISBN 978-1-9996614-0-3
Hardback ISBN 978-1-9996614-1-0

FREE on Amazon Kindle Unlimited

BOOK TWO in the Series:

Fire & Ice: Survival

Available in Paperback on Amazon
ISBN 978-1-9830806-5-4

Paperback and Hardback available in bookstores:
A5 Paperback ISBN 978-1-9996614-2-7
Hardback ISBN 978-1-9996614-3-4

FREE on Amazon Kindle Unlimited

BOOK THREE in the Series

Fire & Ice: Earth Walker

Available in Paperback on Amazon
ISBN 978-1-7181294-5-0

Paperback and Hardback available in bookstores:
A5 Paperback ISBN 978-1-9996614-4-1
Hardback ISBN 978-1-9996614-5-8

FREE on Amazon Kindle Unlimited

This is **BOOK FOUR** in the series:

Fire & Ice: Heart of Stone

Available in Paperback on Amazon
ISBN 978-1-7915462-8-1

Paperback and Hardback available in bookstores:
A5 Paperback ISBN 978-1-9996614-6-5
Hardback ISBN 978-1-9996614-7-2

FREE on Amazon Kindle Unlimited

Fire & Ice Prequel: Death of Connor Sanderson

Available in Paperback on Amazon
ISBN 978-19831113-4-1

Paperback and Hardback available in bookstores:
A5 Paperback ISBN 978-1-9996614-8-9
Hardback ISBN 978-1-9996614-9-6

FREE on Amazon Kindle Unlimited

Watch This Space, up VERY soon,

BOOK FIVE: Invasion – coming out in 2019

For the latest news on the publishing dates visit my websites:

karenpaytonholt.com

Karen Payton Holt on Facebook.

@karenpaytonholt on TWITTER.

karenpaytonholt on Instagram

Our epic journey continues, and I hope you enjoy

Book Four in the Fire & Ice Series.

Please share your thoughts and feelings in reviews – this is my

fifth novel and I welcome your support.

I dedicate this novel to the people who believe in me.

They drive me forward, and, at times,
give me a much-needed kick up the posterior.

This is for my mum, Sylvia, and my friend of forty years, Steve.

The past year has been hard,
and support has become more and more important.

Thank you to those family members and loved ones
who have boosted my strength.

Thank you to friends who have showed they really care.

Chapter 1

A group of four horses galloped at breakneck speed across the open fields at the top of the cliffs. Three black stallions bore riders wearing dark capes, their garb flowing over their mounts' hindquarters like a river of oil. The impassive faces of the vampire jockeys remained hidden behind masks of soft leather. The horses' sides heaved as they fought to stay on the heels of the charcoal-gray gelding carrying the vampire commander.

The gusting wind snatched at the thin white leather cloak plastered to a body which hinted at the alluring shape of a woman. She shunned the use of a cloying mask. Her delicate white features were set, and ice-blue eyes glinted within the deep shadow of the cowl hood anchored to the gold coronet fitted tightly across her forehead. She smiled, and the curve of her blood red lips bared white teeth.

The walls of the imposing fortress up ahead wore the pink haze of the dying sun. The windows glowed orange as though the aftermath of the battle which had raged inside left embers of hatred smoldering in its belly. A gunmetal gray sea launched an unrelenting attack on the land. The crashing waves cascading up beyond the castle's foothold stained the walls in a dark skirt, with a petticoat of turbulent white froth beneath.

Shifting in the saddle, the commander guided her mount from the soft going of the pasture and onto the compacted stone of the road. The horse's hooves rang out over the granite causeway as they made the final approach to the castle and passed beneath the dull iron prongs of the raised portcullis.

The wooden doors of the gatehouse remained closed.

Reining in her mount, she waited, riding the skittering sidesteps and feeling every equine muscle ripple beneath her seat. As the horse's ears twitched, she absently reached out a gloved hand and patted his shoulder. "Steady, boy." Her lilting breathy voice drifted on the air. Injecting splintered glass into her tone, she lifted her eyes to the gates and said, "Birgitta, Regent of Scandinavia, begs entrance."

Tilting her head, she listened for the whisper of fabric brushing over stone-hard flesh which would signify a response to her command. She already knew it would not come. Her Earth Mother, Morrigan, had seen the fallen guardsmen and the jet-haired child in a vision. But, it was the pale woman with honey in her hair and warm brown eyes who Birgitta sought. When Sentinel Lars slipped under the spell of this enchantress, Birgitta's hold on him weakened.

She must be strong to have found her way into his cold heart. Birgitta's gash of red lips parted as she inhaled deeply, sampling the atmosphere. The calcium dust emulsified in the air seeped through the cracks in the portal. The crushed bodies scattered beyond the castle gates would not be a surprise.

Men are pawns with the mistaken belief that all female vampires are the same. Birgitta's clear-water gaze glittered. *With Morrigan's guidance, bending them to my will in order to thrive has been simple. This human, Rebekah, has our gift.* Doctor Heinrik had supplied the woman's name when he came, cap in hand, seeking an audience with the regent. Resentful when his own power over Sentinel Lars diminished, he begged Birgitta to witness her betrothed's *fascination* with this female at first hand.

Birgitta dispatched the doctor back to Lars' household, instructing him to bring samples of blood, hair and skin from mother and child. Heinrik had failed to return.

But I am too late.

At a wave of her gloved hand, a bondsman dismounted, approached the gates and pounded on the wooden surface with the hilt of a dagger. His mask creaked as his face registered surprise when the gates groaned slowly open. He pushed them both wide and moved out of the way, allowing Birgitta and her escorts to ride into the courtyard.

The horses whinnied as the heavy dead weight of the vampires slipped from their backs. Standing in the cool shadow within the castle courtyard, Birgitta's three bondsmen uncovered their blank faces, tucked the masks under the leather belts of their tunics, and silently lined up against the battlement wall.

Sweeping her cape back over her shoulders, Birgitta freed the hood from her coronet and unveiled long white-blonde hair. The platinum breastplate molded to her body flowed like mercury over each curve, clinging to her high full breasts and the hard ridges of a toned abdomen, before hugging the enticing flare of her hips. A short skirt of soft white leather clung to her thighs as she braced her feet and scanned the courtyard. Barely noticing the splendor of the lush gardens beyond the sculpted archway, she focused on the yawning black alcove of an open door in the curved wall at the foot of a stone turret.

After a second's pause, Birgitta exploded into movement and strode across the flag-stoned courtyard. Disappearing into the cool damp embrace of stagnant air, she entered the tower and followed the winding staircase up into the heart of the castle. Exiting through a door on the second level, where the gallery of the grand hall led around to Lars' private chambers, she stopped.

Overhead, the suspended wooden hoop of the medieval chandelier skewed at an awkward angle. One of the hefty metal chains, torn from its anchor point in the sweeping Gothic vaulted arc above, hung down, motionless, like a dead serpent. Birgitta's eyes were inevitably drawn downward into the belly of the cavernous space. Lars' magnificent 16th century banquet table bore a new set of scars. She squinted at the new, paler tracks scored deeply into its surface.

Striding to the edge of the forty foot drop, Birgitta stepped into the void. She crouched on landing, gracefully absorbing the impact. Circling the table, she ran her fingertips over the fresh gouges and her lip curled. The stone floor glinted where Lars' ax had hacked out splintered shards.

Morrigan was right. He fought hard to keep this Rebekah.

Returning to the gallery via the wide stone stairway, Birgitta entered Lars' private chambers. A wooden chest lay open with silk and brocade dresses spilling out in a kaleidoscope of color. They were not clothes Birgitta would be seen dead in. Her lips twisted with wry humor. *But this* warm *blooded Rebekah, Lars' saw fit to share remnants of his past with her. Fool.*

The ruby drapes of the four poster bed remained drawn, and Birgitta set her jaw before pulling them back. There he rested, Lars, her latest conquest, and her mate for the next hundred years, carefully chosen by the pagan binding ritual. Now, her plans lay in tatters. Despite the careful alignment of the body, the sturdy column of Lars' throat was a crumpled mass. A crust of thick brown blood discolored the edges of his golden breastplate.

Lifting the metal cover exposed the deep crater of a wound which had penetrated his ribcage, and cradled inside it, sat the crushed stone of his desiccated heart. *The woman has a fierce protector.*

Gently replacing the breastplate, Birgitta stretched out beside Lars. Pulling on a silver chain around her neck, she withdrew a filigree encased vial from its resting place between her breasts and unscrewed the lid. Pouring the thick paste of dried blood it contained into Lars' mouth, she studied his glazed stare.

The abyss of his blown smoky-gray pupils remained cloudy, confirming what she already knew. Lars had been without sustenance long enough for his brain to atrophy.

You'll never know I will avenge you. She sighed and laid her cold palm on his cheek. "Why could you not stay true to me, my love? I would have let you live a century before I sacrificed you to my Earth Mother's Gods." She kissed his lips. "Our coupling ceremony would have brought you everything you desired, if only you had stayed true," she whispered. "The Gods bless you, my prince. The one who has slain you will become your successor. Earth Mother tells it is so."

Rolling back up to her feet in a fluid movement, Birgitta closed the curtain once more. She replaced the silver vial beneath her body armor, turned, and left the room.

Excitement stirred inside her as she strode back through the castle. She relished the challenge of enchanting this ferocious warrior and taking him from Rebekah. *Finding him is easy.* What Doctor Heinrik could not tell them, she and Morrigan had gleaned from reading the portents of the spirits. "His name is Connor, his home is London, and I shall take his heart."

There was no doubt in her mind. For Birgitta, becoming a vampire offered great power. The blood flowing through her mortal veins divined potency from her Celtic ancestors, and from being a descendent of an Ovate Druid. The 'cunning' women in her family were otherwise known as witches – they were feared by all but the dull-witted. Immortality put paid to the ritual of reincarnation. But, The Otherworld, which lay between death and being reborn, became a place through which Birgitta could travel at will, leaving her body and projecting her image. Being immortal, the mystic realm welcomed her. It had served her well for seven hundred years.

Morrigan will foretell the means. The Druid's cauldron held the wisdom of the 'bright knowledge'. It would reveal the mysteries of life and death and guide their hands. "Yes, I shall bring this vampire to his knees and test the strength of Rebekah."

Birgitta swept back into the courtyard, mounted her horse, and lifted her face to the rapidly cooling air of dusk. Night crushed the sun into the horizon, casting a carpet of blood over the rippling black sea. Kicking her horse into action, her pale blonde hair streamed out behind her as she galloped back over the causeway and headed home. Her bondsmen spurred their steeds on as, following in her slipstream, they fought to match her pace.

Chapter 2

Rebekah kicked her motorcycle through the gears, her attention divided between avoiding potholes in the road and keeping Greg's broad back within sight. Her heart thudded and a cold sweat broke out on her skin as she took a bend too fast and the motorcycle twitched. *This is how to get myself killed. I'm going soft in my old age.* She ruefully acknowledged that daydreaming kept enticing her away.

There was a time when human survival occupied every space inside her brain. Behind her visor, Rebekah smiled. Now, Connor and Seren offered her a future rather than mere existence, but, having a protective vampire as her lover and partner certainly cramped her style.

Connor would go mad if he knew I was out here with Greg. But it had never been easy for Rebekah to stay home and wait. Seren was fully absorbed in Osiris, the love of her life, or her immortal life. Since the group's return to Kent four months ago, winter had been harsh, and now, at last, spring was in the air.

Rebekah found the hours alone hard to fill, with Connor in London so much. He was a vampire, but, first and foremost, he was a doctor. In his laboratory at the hospital, he had finally found the solution to the survival of both humans and vampires; a blood substitute that worked.

Beneath the glaring sun, sweat trickled down between Rebekah's shoulder blades as she throttled back, pulled the motorcycle up on the grass verge beside Greg, and eased off her crash helmet.

"Park up under the trees. The lake is a half hour trek through the forest."

She couldn't make out the expression behind his sunglasses, but Rebekah knew they both felt like naughty school children. She laughed gently. "C'mon Greg, we're going fishing to stock Oscar's freezer. Even Connor can't be mad about that."

Greg squinted up at the hazy sunshine and said wryly, "True, but we have to get back before he knows you were gone."

Rebekah snorted as she dismounted the motorcycle and hung her helmet over the handlebar. "It's not as though we haven't done this a million times before."

"No," Greg agreed, "but that was before Seren. So, no, we haven't done this without Connor or Julian knowing about it and watching our backs. We are outside the vampire exclusion zone."

"And how many times has Connor said he's glad you're not a vampire because you're as hard as nails?" wheedled Rebekah with a smile. "He trusts you."

Greg huffed, and his well-worn combat gear creaked. "I reckon running my platoon was a picnic compared to keeping you safe. Measured against what Connor will do to me, it would have been better if the pandemic had finished me off."

The pandemic which killed eighty percent of the human race and led to the rise of the vampires had been not quite twenty years ago, but it felt like they were talking of a mythical age neither of them could any longer believe existed. The twenty-five-year-old Greg had felt helpless when almost all his men either died of the disease or were killed or captured by the vampires.

Greg preferred death to becoming a captive on the human farm and having his blood siphoned to feed the enemy. So, when Connor turned out to be a man he admired, and a vampire to boot, he found the readjustment tough.

Being a terrified six-year-old when her mother died and Uncle Harry took her in, for Rebekah, human society within the city limits was merely a fairytale.

The twenty-mile ride to the largest of the Darenth Water lakes had passed without incident, and with the sunshine warm on her face, Rebekah felt happy. The eco-shelter inhabitants had still managed to fish in the lakes by staying under the radar of the vampires, but never without the constant fear of discovery. Of course, when Rebekah became the mother of Seren, the first and only vampire/human hybrid child, the entire vampire population of London had discovered the eco-community's existence. Their group of humans were no longer refugees, but protected species.

"But the sun is shining and, as long as we leave before dusk, we'll be fine."

"Unless it rains," Greg added, dramatically quirking a mock horror eyebrow. "This is England, and a lot of things have changed, but crappy weather ain't one of 'em," he said in his best East London cockney accent.

Rebekah laughed and thumped him on the arm. "There's not a cloud in the sky, so nice try."

Greg shouldered his backpack, jerked his head and turned away towards the densely packed trees. "Fall in, soldier."

Rebekah's hair lifted as a warm breeze rushed across the grass, transforming the meadow into an undulating green sea. Following Greg, she stepped into the glowering embrace of the dark woodland, and what began as welcome shade soon became an atmosphere thick with humidity. Breathing required more effort as they trudged along the path and deeper into the forest. Rebekah's honey blonde hair was longer than she usually wore it, and fifteen minutes later the heavy braid felt like a wet rope hanging down her back.

The lake came into view, and Greg pulled a key from his pocket when he spotted the wooden store house between the trees. Using the sleeve of his combat jacket, he rubbed the worst of the rust from the base of the padlock. Rebekah smothered a smile as he grimaced when no amount of brute force, spit, and wiggling of the key could shift the seized mechanism.

"Stand back and cover your face." With one swing of his blacksmith's mallet, he shattered the lump of metal.

The hinges of the door shrieked as Greg pulled it open. Leaning in, he grabbed a flashlight from a shelf and grunted as he swept the beam around the dusty interior. "Ah, there it is." Diving forward, he caught the handles of a sturdy holdall and pulled until the bulging canvas shifted and he could drag it into a clearer space.

"Here." Still crouching, he passed the flashlight over his shoulder to Rebekah. He shook most of the grit off the bag before opening it. He pulled out two sets of waders and flung them onto the grass. Moments later, he rejoined Rebekah outside, clutching fishing rods and a tackle box.

Rebekah inspected the waders and rubbed a wet thumb over the white mold staining the rubber.

"The waders are fine, that white stuff will wash off in the lake." Greg squatted and selected fishing line from the tackle box. Once he had polished the excess oil from the reels, they whirred, freewheeling when he spun them around. "We're good to go."

As they drew closer to the huge lake, the worn path disappeared and the going became harder. It took all Rebekah's effort to lift her rod clear as the ground became overgrown with reeds and long grass. She scrunched up her nose at the overpowering smell of rotting leaves. They picked their way down to the water's edge, where a light breeze brought the relief of fresh air.

The view took Rebekah's breath away. The water glittered with a carpet of diamonds and an ice blue sky framed the belt of emerald trees on the distant bank. Birds rustled in the canopy overhead, and it felt as though she and Greg were the only other living things on Earth.

Rebekah jumped when a fish broke the surface of the lake, its body glistening with light brown scales as it arced through the air and tumbled back into the water.

"Carp." Greg smiled. "And a big one. They grow to forty pounds, so don't be disappointed if you don't land one." He set to work on loading the reel of a six foot rod with 14lb mono and weighting his line with dough bait. "It will take a while. You have to wear them down before you try to reel them in."

Greg waded into the shallow water. The reel whirred and the fine thread danced through the air as he cast his line. On the fourth attempt, he appeared content. Shifting his stance, he settled in for the wait, fitting the end of the rod into the leather holder on his hip. His attention became fixed on where the lure bobbed on the surface. Casting a glance at his stern profile, Rebekah had the feeling she had become invisible. She loaded her own rod, trudged twenty feet along the bank and mimicked Greg's action, wading in until the water was just above her knees.

The afternoon trickled by, punctuated by explosions of frenzied excitement as Greg landed three fair-sized carp. The air became blue with expletives when he lost one. Rebekah landed one fish and kept checking the net to see if it was real.

The bright glitter on the lake melted away to a dusting of frost and as the dark shadow of the trees laid a chill down over Rebekah's skin she leaned forward to catch Greg's eye.

He nodded sharply and called out, "Time to go."

Reeling in her line slowly, she stopped when a gigantic carp leapt from the water in front of her. "The one that got away," she murmured gently, wondering if it was one of the 'forty-pounders' Greg had been hoping to land. *It would have been an entertaining battle of wits and brawn.*

Rebekah returned to her task. Gazing out over the lake as the bait dragged through the water, she froze and cold sweat trickled down between her shoulder blades when a distant arrowhead of ripples raced across the lake towards her. She instinctively began to wade backwards, the end of her rod whipping high into the air as her grip tightened and her movements jerked.

Squinting, she made out the details of a fierce white face rushing up from beneath the silver gray sheen of the water. A gasp lodged in her throat as a black mass hurtled out of the trees to her left and plunged into the depths. A tidal wave of heavy spray splattered her chest, and Rebekah staggered back as the vampire was forced back down beneath the surface.

She yelped, "Vampire." Falling onto her backside on the slippery bank, her heels skidded as she clutched at the slick wet grass and scrabbled backward.

Greg appeared, hooked his hands beneath her armpits and hauled her to her feet.

The lake erupted into a boiling cauldron of rolling black shadows, the thrashing movements not unlike the death throes of Greg's last carp.

"Run." Whisking Rebekah around, Greg shoved her in the back, hard. "Run." He swung around to face the lake, planted his feet wide and yanked his blacksmith's mallet from its anchor point on his belt.

Rebekah knew two things; Greg could run faster if he didn't have her to worry about, and she must get out into the sunshine.

The heavy waders made it feel as though she was struggling through molasses, but wasting precious seconds pulling them off was out of the question. Grabbing hold of tree trunks and hauling herself up the incline, she just kept going.

She listened for Greg's pounding stride. Not allowing the feeling of being alone space inside her head, she ran until her chest burned.

Gulping as her oxygen starved muscles tingled, moist air filled her lungs and refused to leave them again. As pinpricks of light crowding her vision made her head swim, the shadows lifted and rays of sunshine slanted across her hot skin. *Nearly there.* Relief weighed her down, but she pushed onward. The last tree she grabbed hold of felt warm beneath her palm, the sun bright on her fingertips. Suddenly, her collar yanked tight, choking her, and her feet left the floor as something hauled her backwards.

An iron grip closed in a band around her chest and she jabbed an elbow back, bruising her flesh as it grated over a wall of solid muscle.

"Ouch," a familiar voice growled.

Her boot ground into his foot and angry tears blurred her vision. She closed her eyes, not wanting to look when he turned her around, clasped her tightly against his body, and kissed her.

"Stop struggling," he murmured. His throat rumbled with satisfaction as her lips parted to let him in, and her gasp of surprise scalded his tongue.

Her thundering heart rocked against his chest, and he smiled against her lips. "Rebekah."

The cold sweat on her skin became a warm tide as anger engulfed her. Connor chuckled as she beat her hands against his rigid body and grumbled into his mouth, "You scared the shit out of me."

He leaned back, his hold anchored around her waist, and Rebekah wished he would kiss her again as his gray gaze hardened to flint. Water ran down the rigid planes of his uncompromising expression and it suddenly registered that she, too, was soaked through.

"You *should* be scared. Do you know how close you came to dying? That vampire was not out there for fun." Connor snorted. "Fishing? You might as well lay a trail saying 'come and get me'."

The color drained from Rebekah's face as shock hit. "You're right. It was stupid of us, I'm sorry, Connor." Dread stirred in the brown depths of her eyes as she muttered hoarsely, "Greg-"

"He's fine. I gave him a ducking, but a bruised ego is all he's suffering from." Connor grinned. "Ah, here he comes now."

Rebekah raised a brow. "I don't-" With a wry grin, she gave up. "No, of course I wouldn't." She tilted her head, listening intently. "Tell me, can you smell him? Hear him? What?"

Connor laughed. "All that, and more."

Rebekah's longing showed as she said, "I wish…"

Connor lifted her chin with a cold fingertip, tracing it over the flush of her cheekbone. "I haven't had enough of this yet." Resting his forehead gently on hers, he stroked a hand up from her waist and covered her breast. When her heart rate accelerated, he smiled. "Or this." His kiss enticed her as his tongue ran along her bottom lip and he begged her to kiss him back. "Uh oh, busted," murmured Connor as he withdrew.

Greg coughed up water as he sloshed his way to the tree-line. Catching sight of Connor, he stopped. Welt marks on his cheek flushed an angry red as he clamped his mouth shut.

"Sorry?" Connor offered, spoiling it with a grin.

"You're pushing it, mate."

Connor reached behind, into the belt of his pants, and withdrew the wooden handled blacksmith's hammer. "All I'm saying is... a shorter backswing gives less of a warning."

They both knew Connor was kidding. There was no mileage to be had in trying to surprise a vampire.

Levity melted from his face as Connor said, "That was a close call, Greg. Wait for Anthony or me to clear the area next time you need to go fishing."

Rebekah flushed and Greg shuffled uncomfortably as he took the hammer from Connor and shoved it into his utility belt.

"Ah, I see…" said Connor, as the penny dropped. Turning a disapproving eye on Rebekah, he added, "You know, Greg, she may be the mother of my child, but if you need to paddle her backside, feel free."

Rebekah's cheeks burned hotter and a salacious grin chased across Connor's face.

"Leave me out of the domestics. *You* can't talk her out of doing stuff, so how the hell am I supposed to?" grumbled Greg as he walked out of the trees and collected his motorcycle.

Connor chuckled ruefully, acknowledging the truth of that.

Greg grunted as he swung the nets filled with carp into the plastic-lined panniers on his bike and pressed the clasps home, sealing the rubber gasket and trapping the smell inside. "I better get these back. Oscar will need to put them on ice."

Standing within the confines of the shaded woodlands, Connor cast a satisfied glance at the dull sky. His favorite time of day approached. The waning sun sitting low on the horizon as dusk fell was the closest a vampire could come to walking in daylight. He still retrieved his greatcoat from where it hung over a tree branch, put it on and flipped up the collar.

Connor rested a hand at Rebekah's waist and guided her to the motorcycle, her warm perspiration creating an enticing reaction as Connor's mouth flooded with venom. Plucking the helmet from the handlebar, he turned to face her. Admiring the unconsciously sinuous movement as she wriggled free of the rubber waders, he waited until she looked up. His black hair fell forward, veiling his expression as he gazed down from his six foot three inch tall vantage point. His gray eyes stirred with currents of exhilaration as he said casually, "You're hot. We could stop off at the small lake on the way home."

Her heart turned a somersault and Connor's face tightened, his dramatic cheekbones blanching to the palest shade of white as his jaw muscle twitched. He tucked a strand of damp hair behind her ear and his fingertip drifted down to rest on the carotid pulse going crazy in her neck. His hooded gaze smoldered and animation drained from his body.

Rebekah could see the battle raging inside him as he swallowed hard and stopped breathing.

The blade of hunger burning through his center cut him open, and Connor locked every muscle down as he forced himself deeper into revival sleep.

Rebekah waited for his control to slot into place. She knew better than to touch him at that moment. She had only once seen his control crumble, and it had terrified her. Of course, she knew more now, about the compulsions vying for his attention. She had seen Seren combat them, too.

Connor explained it as having three personalities rattling at the cell doors inside his head. By releasing only one cellmate at a time, a vampire allowed blood to rehydrate a single compartment inside the brain. They mastered this skill or fell victim to vampire dementia – murderous rage which deteriorated into a comatose state, and then death. Not the suspended animation of vampirism, where feeding maintained your human state for all eternity, but *true* death, where the brain atrophied and the desiccated body hardened to marble. Connor still hoped to change all that. The solution? Synthetic blood, freely available.

Only releasing the persona of revival sleep made it possible for Connor to touch Rebekah and not break bones. The other two, the belligerent drunkard of rap-sleep and the psychopath of grave sleep, Rebekah had never met, and she suspected she would not survive it if she did.

Connor's love for her, and his suffering to endure it, was yet another reason she wanted him to turn her. He unveiled a pewter soft gaze, intent glinting in the depths, and taking a deep rumbling breath, he moved once more. His voice roughened by desire, he murmured, "We could go for a swim?"

He was too heavy to swim, but still, for a moment, Rebekah recalled how the afternoon sun had glittered on the surface of the lake. She imagined them as a normal couple, with his jet hair shot with sapphire highlights and his gray gaze alight with silver flecks.

His face in full sunlight was something she wished she could see, but since that would mean being alive in 1910, she was just grateful to have him here now, filling her heart and her soul until she could see nothing but him.

I can have that for eternity. I just have to be patient. She knew he would turn her, but only when he felt she was not losing out. Her coquettish smile hid the sadness as she said, "A swim sounds… perfect."

He dropped a kiss onto her mouth and then stayed. Drawn in by her soft tug on his firm lip, he lingered to taste her. "Minx," he said gruffly, as he finally drew back. Positioning the helmet on top of her head, he surrendered it into her hands.

If *he* pushed it on, a cricked neck would be certain, and a broken one did not bear thinking about. Rebekah took a firm grip on the nylon chin strap and yanked hard, for a human. She took her seat on the motorcycle and waited for Greg to do the same.

"I'll tidy up here, Greg. I'll catch up with you on the road." Connor collected the waders from the ground and, in a smooth flowing action, caught the new padlock and key Greg tossed at him.

"The other padlock is knackered," said Greg lightly at Connor's raised brow.

"Been showing off in front of the girls, again?" Connor quipped.

Greg scowled and kick started his motorcycle. He met Connor's amused stare but the throaty roar of the engine drowned out his words.

Connor grinned widely, easily working out the 'get lost, pretty boy' Greg uttered.

Giving a thumbs up to Rebekah, Greg moved out onto the road.

Her departure was more low-key as she pressed a button to start the engine and a well-oiled whine joined the chorus.

A dull flush crept over Greg's face as Connor shook his head, eyeing the gleaming chrome frame beneath the Marine's solid weight, acknowledging the grumbling purr emanating from the vintage Triumph motorcycle.

Greg's raised eyebrows said 'there has to be some perks to being out of hiding'.

With a final wave, Greg and Rebekah took off southwest.

Connor stood in the road watching until they were out of sight and then he vanished into the woods to sweep the fishing site and return everything to the shed.

Greg and Rebekah had traveled six miles and were well inside the exclusion zone, when Connor closed up behind them and shadowed their progress.

Familiar areas of woodland punctuated the endless rolling fields and as they crested a hill, their eco shelter came into view. The newly modified subterranean habitat made no bones about declaring its existence. New, easily detectable ventilation shafts emerged above ground level, renewing the air inside the eco-shelter more efficiently and making breathing underground easier. The subterranean generators also benefited from the better exhaust system.

The entrance tunnel to the eco-shelter retained its camouflage as a natural feature, still resembling a fissure carved into the hillside. The community inside still needed round the clock protection. The hive numbers ran into hundreds, and there would always be vampires whose curiosity was born of resentment.

Many vampires, having spent centuries as predators, resisted change, and were aggrieved the humans discovered in the eco-shelter were not now living on the 'farm'. Doctor Connor remained the only vampire to father a hybrid child. He was also about to begin trials of a blood substitute which could liberate both humans and vampires from their places on the food chain – a place in those trials hinged on staying in his good books. Getting on the wrong side of Connor could literally become a death sentence.

Where his family were concerned, he took no prisoners.

Drawing up side by side, Greg and Rebekah took a moment to appreciate the feeling of being home. Rebekah pulled off her helmet and examined Greg's hunched figure, his gloved hands flexing on the handlebar grips.

Many things in Rebekah's life made it worthwhile, but the changes were harder for Greg. His past life as a Royal Marine equipped him to deal with conflict and wars waged by mankind.

After the pandemic, he adjusted to fighting shoulder to shoulder for survival with his comrade in arms, Seth. He taught the eco-community how to stay below the vampire radar. They would surely have been rounded up during the vampires' grid search for 'food', were it not for him.

Abdicating control to vampire allies went against the grain, for Greg, although, as today proved, there were still challenges to face. He and Connor became a team when the pair faced death onboard the super tanker nomad vessel. Neither of them looked for danger, but Greg met anything thrown at him head on. When Connor needed him to risk his life, he did it without question.

Rebekah took a deep breath, enjoying the smell of damp grass and moisture in the air. A gusting breeze lifted her hair, the strands flapped around her face, and she knew Connor had arrived. She managed not to laugh when Connor materialized, as though from nowhere, laid a hand on Greg's shoulder and made the tough guy jump.

Greg scowled.

"You better get that carp home. Oscar will be sharpening his filleting knife." Connor smiled.

With a brisk nod and a grin, Greg wound open the throttle, the bike engine roared into life, and he raced away down the hill.

Rebekah dismounted and surrendered her motorcycle to Connor. The ease with which he lifted the 350lbs of metal and rubber from the floor still surprised her. She walked into the shade of the trees, following the well-trodden path which led down to the bank of 'the small lake'. It was a pool of clear water fed by a trickling fresh water stream. In summer, glints of sunlight dappled the surface, and in winter the bare trees let through enough natural light to lift the atmosphere to a hazy glow. It was a shaded idyll, and a perfect place to dally with a vampire.

We rarely have time alone. Rebekah smiled. *If breaking the rules got Connor out of the laboratory, then going fishing was worth the risk.*

Connor appeared on the path in front of her and held out a hand. "Now, where were we?" he asked, huskily.

Lifting her chin, her sweeping glance taking in his appearance, Rebekah swallowed loudly.

His dark pants were still damp and hugged his thighs. The open collar of his black shirt framed the strong column of his throat, and the tangled mane of black hair cast shadows over his face, accentuating the perfection of his bone structure.

"You know, you staying so incredibly young does nothing for my self-esteem," grumbled Rebekah, pushing strands of sweaty hair back from her face. A blush starting as heat in her stomach, rampaged up through her center as his narrowed gaze swept deliberately down her body.

His cool fingers closed over her hand, he pirouetted her slowly around, and backed her into the wide trunk of a nearby tree. His gray eyes gleamed as he looked down into her face. Placing his hands either side of her head, his clawed fingers gouged holes in the bark and a shower of debris whispered onto the ground.

"I still remember the first time I kissed you. When you begged me to... and I thought I was going insane." His youthful, forever-twenty-four-year-old complexion glowed in the dusk. A snarl tugged at his lip. "You intoxicated me, made my dead heart feel alive again, and every day since I have known you has been hell."

"Gee..." muttered Rebekah, her cheeks burning as Connor bared his teeth in a feral grin.

"Beg me." His nostrils flared as he stared into her eyes.

"I thought we were going for a swim," she said weakly.

Her heart thundered in her chest as Connor's fingertips drifted over her collarbone, peeled her shirt aside, and dipped into her damp cleavage. A sigh grated through his clenched teeth. "Beg me..."

Reaching up and pushing her fingers into his damp hair, Rebekah pressed her lips to his, enjoying the shudder that ran through his body as she whispered, "Please, Connor, make love to me."

His arms closed around her, and, winding her braid around his clenched fist, he tugged her head back. His other hand stroked down and pressed her hips into his, holding her clamoring body close as he hovered over her mouth. "You are more beautiful now than the day I first saw you... my Rebekah."

His firm mouth closed over hers, teasing her lip with his tongue until she yanked harder on his hair and whimpered. A growl of satisfaction rumbled through his chest as he finally deepened his kiss, igniting a hunger inside her.

There was a moment of vertigo for Rebekah as Connor swept her up into his arms and the undergrowth of the woodlands became a whisking curtain of green silk.

Before she could speak, she found herself lying on the soft grassy bank. Connor teased her as he pulled open her shirt and freed her breasts. With a sigh of pleasure, he ran his hands down over her hips, taking the fabric of her denim pants with them. The cool air made her shiver and she groaned. As his tongue drifted down her skin, he shrugged out of his shirt.

The hard wall of his chest grazed her burning skin as his hand lifted her knee, and he rested between her thighs. His fingers tormented the hard bud of her nipple, darting pleasure through her.

She delighted in the hard muscles of his torso rippling beneath her palms as hearing, seeing and feeling became a tangled web of sensation tingling through her body.

"Let me in, Rebekah," he growled.

As her thighs framed him, rolling her hips into his, he lost himself in her heat, feeling her softness close around him, and then he stopped moving. Rebekah sighed as the delight of his velvet strength took her breath away.

Her body trembled, and Connor groaned through gritted teeth. He dragged his hands from her body reluctantly, bracing his weight and clutching at the grass and earth as he fought for control.

"It's okay," she breathed, "Don't go. You won't hurt me."

He buried his face in her shoulder, a growl rumbling in his chest. "Don't move... please."

Wrapping her legs around him, Rebekah murmured, "Just stay still, hmm?"

Gripping his hair, she pulled his face up into the soft light. "I'll be gentle," she whispered. The white mask of tension tugged at her heart. He was her man, but he would always be scared, and the bruises he left in his wake told the tale. Taking him in deeper, she found a sensual rhythm that stirred the embers inside her into a tide of molten heat.

Connor's gray eyes locked onto hers, looking for reassurance and finding it in her pleasure glazed expression. As shudders racked her body, he kissed her, stealing her breathless sighs. Tentatively, he took up her rhythm, matching his movement to hers until he rode the flash flood of turbulent release that drained him, too.

As relaxation melted through Rebekah's limbs and her heart steadied, Connor eased his weight, rolling onto his back. He pulled her thigh over his stomach and tucked her in closely to his side, savoring the after-quakes of micro tremors fluttering through her that only his vampire senses could detect.

His silent chest heaved as he sighed, and welcomed the heat of Rebekah's cheek branding his skin as she collapsed against him.

Half an hour later, Connor roused himself from the hypnotic contemplation of Rebekah's deeply satisfied breathing, the slow slumberous thudding of her heart resonating through his own chest where she lay molded to his side. Drifting his cool fingertip along the thigh she draped across his hard abdomen, he said gently, "We need to get back."

The late afternoon had a firm grip on the day. The cloud covered sky he could see beyond the thin canopy of rustling leaves was tinted purple.

"Okay," she murmured sleepily and snuggled in closer.

With a wicked grin, Connor said, "I know what will wake you up..." He supplied the answer as she took in a breath to ask. "That dip in the lake."

Instantly recoiling, Rebekah muttered, "Oh no you don't-"

But, it was too late. She had the barest sensation of being swung up into his arms as he surged to his feet. She squealed and clung to his neck when he stepped from the bank, waded into the crystal clear water, and the cold tide splashed up over her body.

Her teeth clattered as he lowered himself down and sat on the stream bed, where the pebbles crumbled beneath his dense tissue.

Getting comfortable, he rested back against the bank of mud and wet grass.

"You pig." Her teeth chattered as the thick rope of her hair soaked up the water and an icy trail rose up her spine.

His smile stayed, but a hint of apology lit his eyes as he said, "It's colder than I thought, sorry, honey."

He released her as she fought to wriggle around and face him. Resting a knee either side of his hard thighs, she pressed her body to his from belly to shoulders and hugged his neck. "I'll forgive you."

"Mmm, this kind of forgiving I could certainly get used to," he said, his words muffled as he buried his face in her neck. Stroking his hands down her back, he pulled her hair free of its braid and locked his breath inside his chest as she dipped her head back into the water, exposing her throat. Slicking her hair back into a caramel curtain, she leveled a happy gaze at his satisfyingly tortured expression.

He swallowed loudly. "Osiris came to see me."

"Oh?" The gleam in her brown eyes teased him as she traced distracting circles over his chest, her smile blossoming when he trapped her hand beneath his and growled gently.

"He wants to marry Seren." Connor's gray regard was guarded.

"What did you say?" Rebekah frowned. "Yes, I hope."

"He's besotted by her, as I am by you. I took pity on him, of course I said yes." She didn't seem surprised and Connor looked crestfallen. "You knew?"

"Well, I guessed," she replied. A smile lit up her face.

"Ah." Connor shook his head. "The fishing trip. Oscar up to his armpits in flour. The marathon baking session in the kitchen cavern."

"A woman knows these things. Osiris has been quiet lately, even for him. Seren asked if Malachi had called him back to Egypt, you know, by their psychic connection, and he was appalled she would think that." Rebekah freed her hand and laid it on Connor's cheek. "He had to tell her something, though. He said he was hoping to have good news, and that Malachi is coming to London to share in it, but he had to talk to you first."

"So, two and two make four, especially when they have been inseparable for the last few months." Connor's composed features gave nothing away as his attention drifted out across the lake.

"Yes. But you are happy, surely?"

"It was always going to happen. And if I have to step aside for anyone, then Osiris is strong enough for the challenge of protecting my daughter." He looked at her worried expression and ran a thumb over the flush on her cheek. "Of course, I am happy."

"Good." Her hands ran up over his solid shoulders as she leaned in closer and landed a feather light kiss on his firm lips.

The water swirled enticingly between them, dusting goosebumps over her skin again and tightening her breasts. She trailed the hard peaks over Connor's chest. Wriggling into his lap and feeling him stir beneath her, she murmured, "They are the same, Connor. Against all the odds, our hybrid child has a hybrid mate. It is like the Gods smiled down upon them. They were made for each other."

Connor set his jaw and stared into her face, staying still as she tormented him further, rolling her hips until he was where he wanted to be, and just one move would engulf him in her fiery core. "But this… us," he groaned, "different can be good, too."

"You will turn me, when it is time. I know that." Concern sank like a stone in her stomach. "Just don't leave it too late," she said lightly.

They both knew Connor had saved her life more than once. But, he was stubborn, hanging onto the notion that until his blood substitute guaranteed that vampires could once again count on being eternal, and not starve when their human blood supply aged and died, he would give Rebekah the chance of living out a human life.

"I won't lose you. I promise I won't leave it too late." He buried his face in her neck and eased slowly up inside her. The breath rushing from her body was music to his ears. He grimaced as his mind sank deeper into the meditative state of revival sleep and every tendon in his body strained as he held himself in check. His sensation of wading through water, which tempered his strength, had nothing to do with the real thing stirring around them as Rebekah began to move.

He dropped his head back, the corded sinews in his neck a measure of his effort. He molded his hands gently to her waist and lost himself in her heat as Rebekah made love to him.

Chapter 3

Julian shut the oak door of his chambers and waited until the decisive click ringing in his ears died away. Finally, he let go of the door handle, satisfied that the corridor outside remained empty and Connor was not bearing down upon them.

His three companions stood in a row, hands clasped behind their backs. If Marius and Alexander were curious about the circumstances of the summons, they hid it well. Captain Gerrard's stony expression had bad news printed into every hard line.

It was not difficult to guess why they were here. Alexander hung grimly onto a feeling of 'living on borrowed time'.

Julian took up his preferred place before the empty fire grate and turned to face the gathering. "Captain Gerrard, if you will, an update for the jurors."

"It seems that Supervisor Matthew has not just disappeared from London, but from the entire south east of England, Principal Julian. The Elite Guard have left no stone unturned, and found no evidence that anyone else had a part in the abduction plot. But, I remain convinced he can't have worked alone."

The guards haven't dug deep enough, not eight feet or so beneath the stones in Matthew's garden, at any rate. Alexander had almost convinced himself that the slaughter of Matthew was a dream, but his hand still felt the pressure of the metal spike he drove into the base of Matthew's skull. He had heard a saying – 'bad men are capable of good things, and good men are capable of bad things'. *Nothing is black and white.* Now, Alexander just wanted to stay on the 'good men' side of life. *God willing.*

Julian stared at Gerrard as though it would somehow make the captain remember something new. Finally, the principal sighed. "It has been four months. I can't guess how he managed it, but it does look as though Matthew is smarter than we thought."

"Unless foul play is a likelihood?" Marius asked slowly. "After all, where would he go? Remaining hidden is not an option. He has no access to human blood."

"The only one who could know more than he is telling, is Serge." Julian frowned.

"Except, he wasn't in London." Alexander stroked his chin, trying to find something to do with his hands. "Principal Tavish didn't escort him down from the Loch Glascarnoch Hive until *after* Matthew went missing."

"True." Julian gazed into space and tapped his hard nails in a staccato of annoyance on the marble mantel shelf, then stopped abruptly and focused on Marius, as his second in command. "We shipped Serge back up there too soon."

"He's like a toxic boomerang," Marius muttered, deadpan.

"Something stinks and the councilor can't let things slip if he remains in solitary confinement in Scotland. It's time to bring him home. Let's see how tight-lipped he can be as a prisoner in his own house," said Julian.

"Matthew was not the mastermind behind Seren's abduction, that is certain, but he *has* committed a crime. If Serge knows where he is-" Marius' black gaze caught the lamplight and the grim smile he wore became carved into his still features.

None of those in the room enjoyed feeling impotent. Not capturing the vampire who almost cost Connor, Rebekah and Seren their lives was not something Julian could allow to stand. That scared the shit out of Alexander. *I'm in the firing line if Serge talks.* When his shoulders started to slump, he quickly smothered his feelings of despair.

Julian remained frozen in silent thought for a long time, and then said, "Captain Gerrard, dispatch a squad of the Elite Guard to Loch Glascarnoch and transport Councilor Serge to London, discretely. Have him escorted to his house and post sentries front and rear."

"I'm not sure Connor will agree. And he'll certainly want to tear a strip off Serge. He considers the councilor has had enough rope. He thinks it's time to end it. Him," said Marius quietly.

Serge had long been a thorn in Connor's flesh.

Julian raised an eyebrow. "And that is precisely why he is not here. I do not disagree, but before the councilor's skull is crushed, I want to know *everything* he does."

Marius made a noise suspiciously like a snort of disapproval, and Julian laughed quietly. Crossing the room, he laid a hand on Marius' solid shoulder. "I know Connor will find out, eventually."

Captain Gerrard grunted. "I will be relieved when he does. These have been the longest few months of my life."

"But the longer we keep him in the dark, the less of a distraction it will be from the lab work he's doing. We are on the verge of a breakthrough – these final few tests are crucial." Julian's glance took in all the conspirators standing side by side, until each vampire nodded.

"But it is not only Connor who will be distracted by Serge. A day or two will make no difference. We should delay his transportation, at least until after the party." Alexander was pleased with the steadiness of his voice. "We could do without worrying about Serge slipping the leash on such a special day. Let Connor be a father, just for today."

Alexander clenched his fists behind his back, his nails grinding into his palms. He had taken the route past the Serpentine in Hyde Park to get here – the favored place for vampire suicides. *If Serge is released, I don't think I can keep going.* He imagined how it must feel to wade into the ink colored waters until they closed over his head. Of course, the 'suicide' part was the act of allowing water into the chest and lungs and becoming waterlogged – a state that suppressed the appetite and felt like losing consciousness, or so he'd been told. *I was used by Serge. If it comes to it...* Trying to cross the ground back to being a 'good man' began to feel like sinking into a swamp.

"Alexander?"

He rocked back on his heels as though he'd been slapped. "I'm sorry. What did you say?"

Julian's probing stare latched onto the youngest juror. "I said, I'll send the Elite Guard, but we *will* wait one more day. *When* Serge arrives, we'll keep it between us."

Alexander nodded. The choking feeling of relief blocked his throat.

"Have you fed today?" Julian's tone sharpened and Alexander knew he was acting strangely.

"Not yet," he lied. "I will go to the dispensary now, before we set off for the party."

Julian's set features relaxed as he nodded.

"How are the preparations coming along?" asked Marius.

"Everything is in place. We just have to turn up and try not to eat the other guests."

Marius' face barely moved, but humor glinted in his eyes.

With a decisive nod, Julian walked to the door and opened it.

Like naughty children, each vampire put on an innocent expression, left the room and headed off in different directions. Julian closed the door and stood as if he'd been turned to stone. He could feel his sluggish blood throbbing inside his veins and knew it was caused by excitement.

Matthew's escape weighed heavily. As the hive principal, Julian's pride was not just dented, he had a gaping hole in his armor. *But, tonight, is for celebration, and seeing Leizle again.*

Chapter 4

Connor walked out of the main tunnel entrance of the eco-shelter and folded his arms. The moon was lost in a cloud cluttered sky, but, despite the pitch-black landscape, he easily picked out the figures of Julian and the pair of jurors emerging from between the trees and powering their way across the meadow.

"A night of firsts," said Julian, as the group arrived at Connor's side. "An engagement in the family."

"Indeed." Connor inclined his head. "Marius, Alexander, welcome." Lifting his chin and darting a glance into the woods behind his visitors, he asked, "Who is out there with Anthony?"

Julian laughed gently. "Believe it or not, Charles, Isaac, and your new lab assistant, Brynmor."

Connor's lips twitched. "Are there any staff left at the hospital?"

As though on cue, four vampires appeared at the tree line, at the top of the gentle incline. *They make an interesting lineup.*

Connor's surgical assistant, Anthony, raised a hand in greeting. His mild persona could not disguise the physique of a boxer, and he could snap vampire bones like dry twigs. At Anthony's left shoulder stood Charles, more akin to a small wiry haired terrier, but he kept order at the blood dispensary of the hospital with steely tenacious resolve. Isaac's towering height dwarfed Charles. His forte lie in his speed.

The fourth in the group, Brynmor, remained the only vampire Connor had ever met who wore glasses. He reminded Connor of Superman. A wing of black hair fell over his brow and his diffident crouched posture invited underestimation. But Connor had seen Brynmor in action.

A few weeks ago, a vampire flipped out in the blood dispensary. The mammoth-sized guy directed his charge at the soft target of Brynmor. *Big mistake.* Shoving a hand through the curtain of hair, Brynmor had turned to face the stampeding vampire. He grew three inches in height as his broad shoulders unfolded to present a solid wall of rock hard muscle. The swift back fist Brynmor delivered crunched into the vampire's face and knocked him off his feet.

Moving fast, Brynmor had pinned his attacker to the wall with one hand, and discharged a full barrel of muscle relaxant into his carotid artery with the other. When he stepped back, as the vampire slid down the wall, he tidied his coat and blinked as though the real savior had disappeared. And in some ways, as his cloak of reticence fell back into place, he had.

Yes, with these four as my wingmen, the night should be uneventful.

Connor waved a hand in acknowledgment, gave Anthony the thumbs up, and the four vampires instantly melted back into the trees.

"Isaac has to leave before dawn. The cadaver drawers in the mortuary are full. When the ones already locked in wake up from grave sleep, he has vampires coming in to take their place."

"Tell him, I'll be doing rounds in the morning, before I go to the laboratory. I'll drop by and we can decide on how to select the test group for the blood substitute trials." Connor grinned. "Isaac's life as the morgue attendant is about to become a lot more interesting."

"These are exciting times, Connor. I never thought I'd say this, but Sentinel Lars taking Rebekah and Seren to use as guinea pigs was the best thing that could have happened." Julian held his hands up as Connor glowered. "I was there, remember? I'm not saying I'd go through the battle again, just that it has united the hive."

"The blood substitute program certainly has a warmer reception in council," Connor conceded.

"Protecting the human eco-shelter has been easier, too. Captain Gerrard says the support of the Elite Guard is almost possessive," Marius added smoothly, the black pool of his eyes glittering like flint. "The London hive sees Seren as theirs to protect. Any outsiders setting foot in the south east of England had better have a damn good reason to be here."

"Did you reclaim the body from Darenth Water?" Connor frowned. "Who was *he*? He was certainly not there for Rebekah's protection."

"We'll never know. You didn't leave much for us to identify. Fractured bone doesn't have much personality," said Julian.

Connor remembered crushing the vampire's skull, but as for the rest... He shrugged. "I could tell he was in grave sleep as soon as I touched him. I wasn't taking any chances." Like a diabetic having a seizure, the electrical impulses in the vampire brain when the psychopath of grave sleep assumed control, ionized the air. "He'll be a warning, if nothing else."

Anyone who thought that perhaps Connor had relaxed his guard and gone soft would now know differently. *That can only be a good thing.*

"Forget about it for now, we have a party to attend," said Julian.

If there was a more preposterous statement to come out of a vampire's mouth, Connor could not think of it, and genuine amusement rippled through him.

"The woods are safe with Anthony in charge, and Captain Gerrard has a patrol concentrating on the outskirts of London," Julian added.

Ah, that's more like it. Turning to Marius, Connor said, "I'm glad you are finally going to pay us a visit."

"I will be interested to see the habitat at last." Marius serious expression did not move. "They will have a lot to teach us if our human farm is to become a settlement."

Connor's smile was grim. Nazi style 'concentration camp' was a much better description of the environment the hive subjected their humans to, but Marius knew Connor's views on that. Now was not the time, and Connor let it pass.

Juror Alexander's beaming smile appeared a little too readily when Connor caught his eye – like the flip of a light switch. "Are you looking forward to your first tour of the human eco-shelter?" The youngest juror had been very quiet since Connor's near death at Supervisor Matthew's hand, but Connor was not entirely surprised. *He blames himself for Councilor Serge's involvement.*

Alexander's first mission as a council representative required him to interrogate Serge in his prison cell in Scotland. He had clearly been hoodwinked, and Alexander took it hard.

Laying a hand on the young juror's shoulder, Connor said, "It turned out well in the end, Alexander. Once Serge is condemned to a century in Storage Facility Eight, we'll no longer have to worry about what scheme he might be hatching next. It's in the past, let's forget it, hmm?"

"You're right, Doctor Connor. But I learned a valuable lesson." Alexander's sober regard seemed sincere, and Connor felt satisfied. *It looks as though he's growing up, at last.*

Alexander's appearance belonged to a blond, blue-eyed youth in his middle twenties, but it was vampire years which counted, and *his* numbered barely a half century.

Of course, age is not everything. The transformation of vampirism froze the human form in the physical condition you possessed when turned. If you enjoyed an inactive self-indulgent human lifestyle, then, as a vampire, the formidable strength of an 'alpha' would be beyond your reach. Many vampires made that discovery only when they died in combat.

But, all rules could point to an exception, and in this case, it happened to be Malachi, Connor's maker. He was the oldest and scrawniest vampire Connor had ever seen. His sandblasted, desiccated skin came from centuries of hiding from the glaring sun by burying himself beneath the Egyptian deserts. However, Malachi's extraordinary strength had carried him through more than a thousand vampire years.

"Oh, by the way, Julian, Malachi is here."

Julian's smile was genuine. Sharing in the quest to save Seren had put their two-hundred-year-old gripe to rest. "It will be good to see the old buzzard. Is he looking well?"

Connor chuckled. "Malachi? He looks like Nosferatu, as always."

"And are we to finally meet Osiris' father?" asked Julian.

The Great One, leader of the Earth Walker tribe, Imhotep, remained an intriguing enigma to the London Hive. Malachi had offered no explanation for how the warrior and his brethren appeared to defy the passage of time. *They aren't undead, or vampires, but they are, for want of another word, enchanted.* "Not this time."

"Still, it will be good to see Malachi, again."

Swinging around into the mouth of the tunnel, Connor passed into the dark damp space which opened out into a circular cavern. An alcove excavated on one side housed the half dozen motorcycles the humans now used more freely – Greg's own machine stood in its own space and might as well have had a sign on it, saying, 'Do not touch'.

In a parody of a tour guide, Connor said, "And for our first time visitors, here, we have the entrance cavern."

Connor pulled a remote control handset from his pocket as he moved across the slick polished earthen floor. "Stay behind me. We've had motion sensors fitted since the abduction. We only plan to use them when the humans are here alone and in the panic room, but knowing we are all distracted by the ceremony, it seemed like a good idea to give it a trial run."

The defensive measure would not save the humans, who could only hide when faced with a vampire attack, but the alarm emitted two pulsing siren notes. One was outside the range of human ears, but would bring Connor, Julian, and Anthony, racing to the scene. Captain Gerrard and the Elite Guard would be hot on their heels.

Connor hesitated for the barest second before entering the descending tunnel. "Take in a lungful of air now. It will help your control when you enter the main caverns."

The vampires were well practiced at resisting their cravings, provided the humans did not bleed, but the human odors would be more concentrated below ground. Marius and Alexander, as first timers, had their form fitting plastic face masks tucked into their belts in case they were forced to make a hasty exit.

The group forged on at speed through the pitch-black tunnels. Connor indicated the shapes carved into the walls, which their preternatural sight picked out easily. "Feeling for these markers tells them how far along the passage they have gone. They cannot use a flashlight until they're behind the blackout curtain, and, of course, they cannot see."

Sweeping aside the flap of heavy sackcloth, Connor held it back as the others passed beneath it. Alexander stopped abruptly.

"Are you okay?" Connor casually took up a position beside Alexander, tensed and ready to restrain him.

"The sounds." Alexander's lip curled. "How many hearts?"

Connor had forgotten the lure of the descant of moist cantering heartbeats, each with its own rhythm, and each creating an enticing symphony. Even Connor's mouth flooded with saliva.

"And the smells." Marius, too, appeared transfixed.

"Do you need to go back, Alexander? Or use your mask… they have all seen one before."

Connor looked from one juror to the other. A solid shoulder brushed his as Julian, too, obstructed the path of the newcomers.

Marius gathered himself, the detached façade slipping easily back into place as he ran his hands through the sleek skull-cap of his hair and straightened his tie.

Connor lightened the mood, his attention still keen as he said, "I see you dressed for the occasion."

Marius' flawless complexion folded into a wistful expression. "A cause for celebration…" He fixed his gaze on a space in front of him, as though the dates he needed floated in midair. "My betrothal was something to rejoice in. She was beautiful, dark like your Seren. Of course, that was when George III was on the throne, and formal dress was an everyday event."

"Is that why you left England when you became a vampire?" Connor was intrigued. Glimpses into Marius' thoughts were rare.

"Yes." His features were rigid. "Who would wish to marry a monster? And back then, I could not risk ending her life." Marius shrugged. "So, my reputation lay in ruins as the man who did the unforgivable and reneged on a marriage proposal."

During Connor's mortal years, as a young man in 1910, a couple only saw each other in the company of a chaperone. Even stealing a kiss stirred heat in a young man's loins. *Anything more would wait 'til the marriage bed. I wonder if Rebekah yearns for marriage?*

The eco-shelter library housed thousands of books depicting periods throughout history. Inevitably, they featured families and couples, as society dictated they should be. They provided

Rebekah's only real notion of marriage. But when planning the engagement party, naturally, she and Seren browsed through pictures of wedding ceremonies.

Seeing Rebekah's eyes alight with happiness, her blonde head touching Seren's as they made modest plans, brought home to Connor how Rebekah had missed out on things other young women, before the rise of vampires, took for granted.

"What's that saying, sometimes you have to be cruel to be kind?" Connor did not have to add the rest. Marius sacrificed much more than a reputation, he hardened his heart to stone to save them both, him and his beloved. *We all have. Except now, I have a second chance.*

Taking in a brisk breath, Connor said, "Are you ready?"

Exchanging nods of reassurance, they set off through the community's inner access network. In the sconces fixed to the walls on either side of the eight feet wide tunnels, naked flames burned, and each one danced in agitation as the vampires whisked by.

"The lighting is crude," Marius observed. "You'd think after so many years..."

"Fuel economy," Connor threw back over his shoulder. "There's no reason to change things where there is enough oxygen for it to be safe. Farther underground the generators provide electricity for bulkhead lamps."

As the hum of the generator became detectable to vampire ears, another more compelling distraction rose to the fore.

The thrum of human activity grew louder, and Connor realized where Councilor Serge's label 'human nest' came from. This was not a typical 'only speak when you have to' day, and the noise was blaring to vampires as human spirits rode high.

The meeting cavern, with its domed ceiling, could hold fifty humans, at a push, and today, for the first time in twenty years, it would be put to the test.

Marius and Alexander could not know their limits in such a claustrophobic environment, and, as a safety measure, Connor knew Uncle Harry had issued modified beta blockers and pheromone suppressant spray to every human under their roof. But even so, the scent of human perspiration, adrenalin, and blood being pumped by accelerated heart rates, saturated the air. Connor took one final searching look at Alexander and Marius before they arrived at the arched doorway.

All tunnels converged in the meeting hall, like spider legs attached to a rotund body, and the first thing Connor did was point out the tunnel to the adjoining dining cavern. "Julian will stay with you, but the emergency exit is through there. There is an ascending shaft which comes out inside the woods, if you need it."

Connor smiled. But they all knew this was a test that *must* be passed, or...

Marius' response was emphatic. "If it gets too much, we will leave."

"Follow me, and move slowly," said Julian.

All four vampires entered the cavern and rested their backs against the wall.

Both Connor and Julian scanned the human faces and generated a reassuring air of calm.

Greg and Seth drifted over to join them, but Connor was not fooled. Greg wore his utility belt, with his blacksmith's hammer positioned within easy reach – his loose fingers hovered near the hilt. The bulge beneath Seth's combat jacket barely concealed his own weapon of choice; a mace, weighted with a metal ball.

Marius lifted an amused eyebrow, and Connor gave him an indulgent shrug which said 'they feel safer, what can I say?'. If there was any fighting to be done, Marius knew his opponent would be a very pissed off Connor, and he'd probably need Connor's surgical expertise to put him right afterwards.

"Greg, Seth, this is Marius and Alexander, the council jurors," said Connor, and watched the men sizing up the two vampires.

Marius' dark presence could have been the inspiration for Count Dracula, and like the count, the black abyss of his stare was soothing and hypnotic.

Greg jerked his chin, and Marius smiled.

Alexander raised a slim white hand, and some of the tension eased as Seth took a deep breath and muttered, "Welcome."

"I'll leave you guys to get better acquainted. Seren wants me," said Connor and he disappeared.

Julian patted Greg on the shoulder, and then withdrew quickly as he felt the solid muscle creak beneath the blow. "Sorry," he said, adding, "Good to see you."

Greg smirked. "I've been around. I just don't live inside Leizle's cavern."

At her name, Julian glanced across the room, and straight into her soft emerald gaze. Her chestnut hair shone like a fiery beacon in the glow of a bulkhead light. Her pale translucent skin, with the filigree of delicate pink lace where each thread-like capillary pulsed with the nectar of her fragrant blood, gave Julian cause to celebrate. Even with the throng already assembled in the room, he had singled out her alluring scent when he entered the meeting cavern and sampled the cocktail of odors.

The glimpses he caught of the graceful arc of her throat and the curve of her shoulders were free from bruising, and the marks left by his fingertips were merely smudges of dusky rose. He was winning his constant battle to be gentle.

She smiled, and he stopped breathing.

Veiling a coquettish glance, she turned back to Thomas. She tormented Julian with every gesture, and the murmur of her voice brought with it the overpowering need to be at her side.

It was not born of jealousy, but addiction of a kind. He had raged a war of his own against giving in to that. Julian scanned the room, and felt a little better at the reassurance that Leizle's pool of potential *human* suitors was filled with men at least twice her tender age of twenty. At twenty-three mortal years, if he discounted the two hundred which followed, Julian could persuade himself he fit the bill as an appropriate consort.

His attention drifted back to Thomas. True, he was closer to her age, at nineteen, but he and Leizle were raised as siblings in every way that counted. They had both come to the eco-shelter as toddlers, and both had been orphans.

Julian had been her only lover, and for him, it had been a torturous journey laced with guilt and delight. His character had been forged in the 19th century, so expressing emotions was hard. But now, she was his, and he could not give her up... *unless she begs me to.*

As though she felt the weight of his stare, Leizle's heart rate accelerated and a flush crept up her neck and stained her cheekbones red. She glanced across the room and mewed delicately. Detaching herself from Thomas, she threaded her way through the press of bodies towards him.

"So, is this Leizle?" Marius murmured. Darting a look at Julian's frozen profile, he added, "Of course it is."

Yes. Julian forgot to speak as she drew close. The satin gown she wore matched the alluring shade of her jade green eyes, and each step she took towards him dissolved his thoughts to nothing.

The fabric of his jacket creaked as he fought the urge to shrug out of it, throw it around her shoulders, and guard the glow of her bare skin and the curves moving beneath the clinging silk from other eyes. His expression tightened. "Leizle." Reverting to the social veneer which served as his protection, he took her hand and touched his lips to it. "You look beautiful tonight, as always."

Tearing his eyes from her flushed face, he said, "Juror Marius, Juror Alexander, this is Leizle."

Her hand slid over his arm, hanging onto his sleeve.

Julian planted himself firmly in the way of the introductions until he was sure her clamoring heartbeat and the pheromones on her skin would not be too much for the visitors.

"So, I am *Leizle* tonight, hmm?"

Her innocent expression melted his discomfort, his lips twisting ruefully as he murmured, "Hey, Red. A little touch of the green-eyed monster, I'm afraid." His smile chased the stiffness from his features as he dropped a kiss onto her upturned lips.

"Better," she said. "You are forgiven."

"Connor has gone to see Seren. What happens now?" asked Julian, tucking her hand into the crook of his arm and turning to survey the room.

"It is our first engagement party, ever, so we are making it up as we go along, but some of the people here have never met Osiris.

Seth's group have come in from the forest dwelling just to see the Egyptian warrior, as they are calling him, now."

"Where is Malachi?" asked Marius.

"He is Osiris' surrogate father, so he will be with him, dressing for the occasion." Leizle smiled widely. "Lord knows what will happen when there is actually a wedding."

"I think you will find, in some cases, the betrothal is thought to be the moment that changes lives." Marius' dark eyes twinkled. "The wedding is the formality, the betrothal is the heart."

"I hadn't thought of it like that," mused Leizle.

The murmur of human voices rose abruptly as a young man suddenly barreled into another, knocked him off his feet and pinned him to the ground.

Julian grabbed Alexander's arm as the young vampire instinctively jolted forward.

"Easy, Alexander, use revival sleep. Don't scare them."

Alexander's blue gaze dimmed as he locked his muscles down and animation drained away.

Julian released him slowly, satisfied he was back in control. "You know where the exit is. There is no shame in using it."

The scuffle dissolved into good natured laughter as the bigger of the two men pulled his victim back up to his feet and threw an arm around his shoulders.

Seth grinned widely and said, "That's Adam, my boy."

"Really? He *was* a boy, the last time I saw him," said Julian.

Adam was now well over six feet tall, and unlike his father's wiry build, he had a muscular physique. The scar cutting through his eyebrow added to his rugged good looks. His other badge of honor was the vampire bite on his leg inflicted by Connor at their first meeting, when the boy needed saving from the venom of a snakebite.

As luck would have it, their dramatic introduction smoothed the path of Connor's acceptance by Seth and his small group of refugees. Adam's story always captured the imagination when humans shared tales of their first encounters with vampires.

Once each of the communities knew of the other's existence, movement occurred between the two groups. Notably, Rebekah's Uncle Harry, chose to leave the eco-shelter and take on the challenge of improving the health of the tree dwellers and their living conditions. Evie now helped Oscar in the eco-shelter kitchen. She took a shine to the eco-shelter chef, left Seth's tree dwelling community, and became Oscar's constant companion.

The sense of unity added to the hum of excitement at coming together with a reason to celebrate, at last. What still felt surreal, was that this gathering of human survivors and their vampire protectors shared a common ground. Seren, as the best of both species, represented the beginning of something new and exciting.

At one time, Connor leaving the room would allow tension to build.

Julian inhaled, the salt-tainted atmosphere drifted over his palate, and he realized that this was no longer the case. Tucking Leizle close into his side once more, for the first time today, he relaxed.

Chapter 5

The murmur of human voices in the meeting cavern faded to a lullaby and Connor allowed his eagerness full rein. He whipped along the descending slope to the accommodation network, his speed turning the breeze of fresh air coming in through the ventilation shafts overhead into a gale that plastered his clothes to his body.

Papa!

Connor smirked. There was no hope of creeping up on his daughter. *Shhh, don't tell Mama I'm coming.*

Rebekah often felt frustration at being left out of the psychic loop Seren shared with her father, but Connor enjoyed surprising his beloved.

He slowed down, reducing the force of the gusting air his solid frame drove on ahead, and when he reached their small cavern, stopped outside the door and sank back into the shadows.

Rebekah drifted in and out of his view as she crossed the room to set her hair brush on a wooden dresser, and then began to sort clothes and drop them into the laundry hamper. Connor gathered glimpses of her delicate features, and each serious expression he noticed made him wonder what she was thinking. She thought she was alone, and the frown creasing her brow made him concerned, too.

Materializing beside her, Connor flipped the lid on the laundry hamper closed, catching Rebekah's fingers and making her jump. Her heart pounded in her chest, and he rode the tantalizing wave of the blood rushing through her body. Her features smoothed to a smile when, looking over her shoulder, she met his eyes.

"Ah, so *now* you turn up, when all the work is done."

He stroked a fingertip down the space between her eyebrows as though the frown line was still etched there, and asked, "What's wrong, honey?"

Her eyes misting with tears, Rebekah said, "You know the human saying, where did the years go?" A genuine smile broke through the sadness. "Our little girl is all grown up, and I didn't have *years*, it all happened *vampire* quick... it's a lot to take in."

Connor turned her to face him and wrapped his arms around her waist. He looked down and said gently, "And there will be no more children..."

"No. But hey, we have Seren, and she is more than we thought we'd ever have."

Connor did not need to say the rest; that a vampire fetus was the worst kind of parasite to have feeding inside her; that he nearly lost her and his own sanity in the same moment; that no force on earth would entice him to take the risk again.

"I'm happy. Even if I only had a baby for a short time." She glanced up through damp lashes. "I will have eternity to see her live life as a woman."

They both knew Connor would decide *when* to 'turn' her.

"Yes, you will." His gray eyes shone with determination, and she believed him. "Now, where is Seren? The guests are waiting for her and Osiris, to wish them well."

"She's next door, but you already know that."

"Hey, squirt, let's get going," Connor called out for Rebekah's benefit.

Emerging from her room, Seren ducked out from behind a thick curtain. Her movements were uncharacteristically careful as she protected the intricately entwined strands of her long hair, woven into a lustrous rope which lay over one shoulder. The diamond headed pins holding it all in place glistened like dewdrops on the coal black tresses. The shimmering silver shift dress she wore reflected the glitter of excitement in her gray eyes, and, as she walked towards him, Connor's chest tightened with pride.

He understood Rebekah's feelings, now. The child was no longer in evidence. A young woman stood before him, setting out on the adventure of life. *Well, half-life.*

"Papa." Seren smiled, rested a hand on his chest, and reached up to kiss his cheek.

"You look beautiful." His pride taking in Rebekah, too, he said, "You both do."

Connor tucked Seren into his side and squeezed her shoulders. At five feet eight inches tall she had a two inch advantage on Rebekah, but she still fit snugly beneath his arm. It had taken less than three years for Seren's hybrid hormones to rampage towards maturity. Connor believed the hostile environment she had been born into accelerated her development. *Survival of the fittest.*

The arrival of Osiris had allayed the uncertainty of her rapidly passing childhood. He, too, was a hybrid, and in him, the aging process had stopped once he reached maturity. It seemed as though Mother Nature recognized when every biological function had reached its peak, and then captured it for all eternity. Seren's future looked set to follow the same path, although Connor did not rest easy until it actually occurred. His vampire senses detected the moment the renewal cycle in her skin cells ceased, and he knew she had stopped aging.

Malachi had saved Osiris as a newborn infant, and witnessed the growth process first hand. Unlike vampires, who had their mortal years written into their DNA and then vampire years of frozen time, the young Egyptian had no such age markers. Although Osiris' real father was Imhotep, the leader of the Earth Walker tribe, the young warrior became Malachi's consort many decades ago. The two were inseparable... until Osiris met Seren.

Malachi? Connor waited for his mentor to respond.

I will escort my son to the meeting chamber. We will meet you there.

"It seems Malachi is making the most of his time with Osiris. We are to go on ahead."

Seren smiled. "It's okay Papa, Osiris and Malachi are sharing in an Earth Walker Wenuty ceremony for one last time."

Connor wondered if the young man would at last remove the bamboo catheter buried inside the brachial artery in his bicep. He still wore the serpent armlets, and Connor could smell the enticing aroma of blood whenever the young Egyptian came close. Perhaps the ceremony will bring Osiris' obligation to Malachi to an end.

Osiris' mother had died at the hands of feeding vampires at the moment of his birth.

When, as a premature infant, he fed from Malachi, their connection exceeded all others in Malachi's experience. The baby thrived, and the elder vampire felt something he had forgotten existed – happiness.

For many decades, as the guardian of the Earth Walker tribe, Malachi had protected the warriors against vampires who overran many Egyptian communities. After the centuries he had spent alone, he embraced the feeling of being needed. Imhotep, the 'Great One' of the tribe, decreed that Malachi be given human blood offerings in 'gifting ceremonies' as their undead deity.

But, Malachi never took the life of any tribe member. Naturally, when looking for somewhere safe to hide the child, he returned to the Earth Walker community – the place he considered his home.

In a twist of fate, Imhotep was searching for Malachi, too – his pregnant wife had been captured by a vampire patrol. The infant Osiris was Imhotep's son.

Osiris became the Wenuty Priest in his true father's Earth Walker tribe – the Hour Watcher, who made sure the planets were in alignment for each ceremony of worship where the tribe gave thanks to Imhotep, the 'Great One'.

That was the simple version, but Connor knew there was much more to the symbiotic relationship between him and the tribe that Malachi could not find the words to explain. *With Seren and Osiris betrothed, I must ask Malachi again about Imhotep.* Osiris owed his hybrid status to Malachi, Connor knew, but the near-immortal lifespans of other Earth Walkers? Connor felt sure Imhotep was the key to that.

"I know Malachi has missed Osiris, and I'm happy to have my two girls to myself, for now," said Connor.

Rebekah's gentle smile warmed his heart. "Not for much longer. Everyone will be waiting for us."

Connor nodded. "But first…" Reaching into his pocket, he withdrew a silver locket. Just as it glinted in the light, it magically appeared suspended around Seren's throat, resting against her pearl-tinted skin. The locket opened to reveal a photograph of Connor and Rebekah holding Seren as a baby.

"So you never forget who you are."

"Thank you, Papa," Seren smiled. "But how could I ever forget that?"

"As the centuries roll by, you may be glad of it, and it will serve to show others. You never know."

Connor took Rebekah's hand and walked with her towards the door. "Malachi says they are ready."

Rebekah frowned and Connor's cool fingertip lifted her chin. "Patience, my love. When I turn you, on your twenty-fourth birthday which is-" He looked at the ceiling pretending he had forgotten when, and she dug him in the ribs. "Okay." he laughed. "Three months from now, then you, too, will be able to hear Seren, Malachi, and Osiris' thoughts."

"Why wait." Rebekah's frustration was fleeting because she knew the score.

"The blood substitute passed the first trial, and another month should see us out of the woods. I want an eternity in your arms, my love, you know this."

Connor's mind was made up. When vampires could live without feeding on humans, the chain of dependency would be broken. Mankind need no longer suffer and vampire eternity would no longer hinge upon their dwindling food supply. Of course, they'd face another set of problems. Even if humans did not live on the vampire farms, there would always be vampires who preferred the real thing to a methadone like substitute. *Things could get very interesting, protecting free range humans.*

"Okay. Three months," Rebekah demurred.

Putting an arm around both of his girls, Connor guided them through the tunnels.

Even Rebekah could hear the hum of excitement in the meeting cavern before they rounded the final corner. When they arrived on the threshold, she gasped. The decoration within the room cast pinpoints of silver light over the walls and resembled a starburst of glitter. The arched arbor at the front of the cavernous space provided a focal point, and the main players in the group were gathered there. The huge smiles on the faces of Uncle Harry and

Oscar were outshone only by Leizle's. Julian stood beside her, his face reflecting his pleasure, although to a lesser, more reserved degree.

This would be an echo of the wedding ceremony to come, a few months down the line. The engagement of Seren and Osiris marked the birth of the age of a new species. They had achieved their state in very individual ways, but both were vampire/human hybrids.

Seren took her place at the center of the bower of glittering lights and turned to face the door. She held her breath as the soft brush of bare feet heralded the arrival of her soon to be betrothed. In the next moment, he appeared, framed by the arching stones of the meeting cavern doorway.

Osiris' heritage was unmistakable, and the months in London had left him unchanged. He rarely wore pants and a shirt, and when he did, watching his rippling muscles fighting against the confinement made Seren smile. He walked towards her, every inch an Egyptian warrior, his bearing proud and majestic, his white face framed by the fall of black hair. His black eyes fixed on Seren's face and the possessive gleam in them quickened her sluggish hybrid heartbeat. He smiled. He could hear it, too.

A golden cobra coiled around Osiris' head like a crown. The serpent's ruby eyes gleamed. Its hood flared as though ready to strike. A deep fan of gold rested at the base of Osiris' throat, molding to the contours of his strong shoulders. His bare chest glistened where Malachi had anointed him with oil. His white skirt flowed over solid thighs and a wide gold band hugged his waist.

Osiris' quiet confidence filtered through every line of his body and his aura of peace dispelled the illusion of arrogance.

Reaching for Seren's hand as he halted in front of her, Osiris leaned in and kissed her gently.

As the hour watcher, Osiris performed many ceremonies, but for once, time meant nothing as he gazed at Seren's face and the seconds ticked by unheeded.

Finally, a smile creased Malachi's thin cheeks and he cleared his throat. The dry rasp cackled around the room and several onlookers chuckled.

Osiris took his cue, dropping gracefully down onto one knee, he opened a palm to reveal a glittering diamond set in a platinum ring. In a clear, deeply resonating tone, he said, "Seren, will you be my wife and tie your heart to mine forever?"

Seren's eyes shone with her emotions. "I will. Yes, Osiris, I will."

Male grunts of approval rippled around the room. Greg's quiet salute of 'oorah' echoed in the air, earning him a jabbing elbow in the side from Seth as he began the round of applause more fitting to the occasion.

Oscar hugged Seren. Releasing her, he eyed Osiris' finery and settled for a thump on his broad shoulder before he disappeared to uncover the buffet tables.

The vampires retreated to one corner of the room, and when Oscar passed by, wheeling a trolley loaded with a spit roasted hog and his specialty, marinated rabbit, he cast an awkward glance at his preternatural guests.

Connor grinned. "Go and eat, Oscar. It's about time you overcame the British repression of feeling like a bad host unless your guests are drinking tea."

As Connor turned back, his mouth open to say something to Julian, all four vampires snapped to attention.

In a seamless flow of movement, Malachi and Osiris arrived instantly at their side.

"It's the siren at the London Docklands," said Julian, frowning. The humans remained oblivious to the oscillating alarm which only vampires could hear. Julian held his hand up and froze, focused on listening as the siren pulsed, delivering a message in Morse code. "An unknown ship passed through the Thames Barrier and is sailing up the estuary."

"Let's go." Connor shed his good coat and began to unbutton his dress shirt. He swung away, clearly set on changing into his usual clothes, when Julian called him back.

"Connor, you stay here." Julian covered his concern with laughter. "Father of the 'bride to be' can hardly go AWOL at the party."

Connor went with Julian to the doorway of the cavern. "You win, but sound the siren again if you need me. Protecting my family includes backing up my friends."

"Stay sober," Julian quipped. "Everything will be fine. It's probably Sergeant Hugh playing it safe, knowing we are all in the same place. All the vampire eggs in one basket, so to speak. I know Captain Gerrard stressed the better 'safe than sorry' approach. It'll be nothing."

Connor smiled grimly as Julian spun around and left, with the jurors on his heels. The gusting breeze of their wake whipped Connor's black hair forward to cover his worried frown. They both knew an unknown vessel arriving in the Thames estuary could not be good. Only vampires with power made use of boats. Fixing a stiff smile on his face, Connor pushed a hand through his hair and turned back into the room. *At least, here, I can protect them.*

Seren arrived at Connor's elbow. *It can't be Lars, Papa. That's a good thing.* Concern creased Seren's young ice-white features, and Connor watched with fascination as the capillaries beneath her skin laid pink lace over her cheekbones. Her hybrid physiology would always be a constant source of delight to Connor.

Say nothing to your Mama. Let her have this night without having to worry, hmm? He smiled down into eyes the same shade of gunmetal gray, and glittering with the same cocktail of fear and certainty. Being *born* strong was not Connor's experience, but his twenty-four human years were a dim memory when set against over a century of being a finely-honed, muscular predator. *You and Osiris stay close to your Mama. I'll make sure Greg and Seth are primed and ready.*

The sound of a harmonica swelled to fill the air, and the human community exuded a buzz of celebration. Connor sought out Rebekah and wasn't surprised to see her watching him from across the room. He went to her side and before the questions came, spun her out onto the dance floor.

"Later. For now, let's enjoy the party," he said.

Chapter 6

In the dark, the ship oozed silently up the river. Julian estimated the exposed hull to be around twenty-five feet in height. Taking into account the vessel's draft, he was looking at an ocean liner, although, not like any Julian had seen before. The hull gleamed with an oil-black finish. There were no portholes, but even in the pitch-black of night, his keen eye picked out the faint seams where they once had been.

"How is it propelled?" asked Captain Gerrard.

Julian shrugged. "Not by engine, that's for sure, which seems almost impossible, given her size."

"Do you recognize the flag?" Gerrard's eyes remained glued to the silently gliding mass.

Julian had a cold feeling in his dead bones as the emblem, if not the same, bore a striking similarity to that of Sentinel Lars. *Is this visitor associated with the Scandinavian Hive?* He hoped not. He would not tolerate seeing Connor fight *another* duel for Rebekah. If the intruders demanded Connor's head for killing Lars, then, for the first time, Julian would be forced to declare war.

Gerrard voiced similar thoughts. "If this is a vampire from the Scandinavian Hive, we better be ready to fight."

"Call the guardsmen to arms," said Julian, grimly.

The concrete quays of the London docklands were long enough to berth a vessel of such magnitude, and, thanks to vampire intervention, their excavation of the river bed meant the ship would not run aground.

"My men are on the hilltop," said Daniel, Gerrard's deputy, jerking a thumb towards the escarpment behind them.

"Armed?" Julian knew the answer, but it never hurt to be sure.

Daniel tapped his diamond hard nails on the curved steel of a longbow. "But, of course." He had used the weapon since the 1300s – although the bow he carried now was shorter than the traditional six foot.

With a gleam in his eye, Julian said, "Daniel, come with me. Gerrard, mobilize the Elite Guard."

Leaving Marius and Alexander to guard the quayside, Julian threaded a path through the clutter of loading machinery, coiled chains and grease-stained ropes to the nearest lookout tower.

With effortless skill, Daniel slung the longbow over his shoulder and accompanied Julian, taking the steel ladder welded to the metal frame three rungs at a time. Both vampires climbed aloft to the platform from where the dock-master would bark out the commands which kept loading and unloading moving efficiently.

From this vantage point, Julian watched the liner glide closer, the lapping ripples of a bow wave the only indication of the force driving her forward. Three hundred yards out, a row of vampire faces lining the deck came into focus.

"Who goes there? State your business." Julian's voice echoed across the divide.

Three times he hailed the ship and received no reply.

Down below, Captain Gerrard returned with only a thirty-strong squad of guardsmen.

Making eye contact through the gloom, Julian lifted a questioning brow, but waited while Gerrard scaled the tower, arrived beside him and said, "The rest of the platoon are out of sight. I estimate around a hundred vampires could be onboard, easily."

Julian jerked his chin in agreement. It wouldn't do to show their hand until they knew. Keeping the crew of the vessel guessing should give them an edge.

The squad of guardsmen fanned out along the concrete causeway, covering the full length of the dockside. The Elite Guard high on the bluff kept the upper levels of the vessel in their rifle sights.

Julian said slowly, "They aren't opening communications. I don't like it."

Silence descended and his unease grew. *I have to do something, or lose the advantage.* "Daniel, your longbow, please."

The vampire stepped forward, handed over his bow and balanced the shaft of an arrow, which resembled a sharpened steel needle, perfectly in his hand.

With expert ease, Julian notched the arrow into place, set his sights on a figure clearly visible on the vessel, and launched the metal spike in an unerring arc.

Surreal silence accompanied the lightning quick flight. Julian's target onboard tracked the incoming missile skyward, stepped aside and narrowly avoided being impaled by the metal tip which buried itself in the deck beside him. The twang of the steel shaft hummed through the still night air like a struck tuning fork.

Making eye contact with the distant vampire, Julian lifted his chin and called out again, "State your business and prepare to be boarded."

A taller fair-haired figure appeared on deck. "We weigh anchor and secure our vessel in dock. Da?"

"Identify yourself."

"Scandinavia; Vessel Ident Number SH463."

Julian looked at Marius down below, and the juror nodded.

"A Chief Admiral Vessel, registered in Stockholm." Vampires had limitless memory capacity, and it was Marius' responsibility to know the Ident Number of every vessel registered within the European Hives.

"And the reason for your unsanctioned visit?" asked Julian.

The vampire officer spread his hands in a placating gesture. He tapped the insignia on his shoulder and his clipped tone cut through the air.

"I'm sure you don't expect my commanding officer to shout across the water. We dock, and talk in a civilized fashion, da?"

"Very well." Julian returned the longbow to Daniel. "Remain here and stay alert. Gerrard, come with me." Julian vaulted the metal railing bordering the observation platform and landed silently at Marius' side. Captain Gerrard followed suit, and immediately set off to walk the line of his men.

Julian's gaze narrowed as a shuffling sound erupted, similar to the beating of wings.

Six vampires leapt overboard from the deck of the liner and landed on the concrete concourse, instantly spreading out along the length of their vessel.

Every vampire defending the quay side tensed. In the nanoseconds it would take for the vampire platoon to launch an attack, they bounced jittering looks at Julian, to Gerrard and then back again, looking for the order to engage the enemy.

With a clenched jaw, Julian resisted the knee jerk reaction of hostility.

A fusillade of loud thuds caused Gerrard to draw his handgun and shout, "Take aim."

The line of vampire guardsmen jerked into action, the shushing sound of hands brushing over metal preceding the resounding click of rifles being primed.

"Wait," said Julian, his entire body ramrod straight as he fixed his eyes on the vampire officer peering over the side of the vessel.

The guardsmen stood down, lowering their weapons.

Gerrard, too, relaxed when the cause of the reverberating thuds became clear – hatch doors swung open to expose holes in the smooth hull from where mooring chains fell out and clattered down over the near-vertical polished shell.

When the chains, as thick as a man's thigh, hit the concrete below, the waiting crew members burst into action. In a seamless concert of movement, they dragged the chains taut and used the tethers on the ends to tie them to the huge iron rings anchored to the quayside.

A dozen council guardsmen shadowed the movement of the visitors as they secured the vessel. The Scandinavian crew members appeared absorbed in the mooring process, until, the task complete, they leapt up and began to scale the featureless wall of the hull like spider monkeys.

"Halt," Julian barked, and the half dozen oil-black forms froze. "These crewmen will stay on the quayside under my guard, until I speak with your commander."

The mooring crew dropped back down and allowed the council guardsmen to corral them into a makeshift holding pen between the parallel walls of two huge storage containers. The detained vampires silently stood shoulder to shoulder. Two of Julian's snipers leapt up onto the roof of the metal boxes and trained large bore rifles, primed with armor piercing tungsten-steel rounds, on the gathering below.

A kill-shot on a vampire was hard to make if the soft spaces of eye sockets and mouths were out of the question, but there was always the crippling option of the softer tissue in the knee, elbow and wrist joints.

"There is no need, Principal…?" The officer's calm voice drifted on the night breeze.

"I am Principal Julian, and there is every need. I have received no papers allowing Vessel SH463 into London Hive waters, and none to request docking rights within the London Hive boundaries. You are not welcome."

"I understand. You wish to board?"

"Yes."

The vampire raised his hands in a sign of surrender. He disappeared and seconds later, ten feet above the waterline, a doorway opened in the apparent smooth shell of the massive hull. A ratchet squealed and a lowered metal gangplank extended out over the inky water to bridge the gap between the hull and dry land.

Scouring the darkened doorway for suspicious movement, Julian folded his arms and maintained a stony expression.

The walkway bounced on rubber buffers as it settled on the concrete, the metal clawed edges grinding as they dug into place.

The vampire officer appeared in the gloom at the threshold of the doorway. When he stepped forward, his fair hair gleamed in the moonlight. "If I may approach?"

At Julian's sharp nod, the tall lean visitor crossed the aluminum gangway and stopped ten feet from his host.

"My name is Bjorn, Captain Bjorn."

Julian frowned. He made an obvious show of peering past the captain at the darkened interior beyond the open hatch.

"No, you are correct, of course, I am not the *commander* of this vessel. But, if you will follow me, I beg your indulgence." The captain pulled a small drawstring bag made of cream leather from a breast pocket and tossed it into the air.

Julian caught the pouch and turned the signet ring it held out into his palm. "Scandinavia, but certainly not the hive principal?" *A hive principal would know he is breaking protocol.*

Bjorn solemnly inclined his head. "A high-ranking official; Chief Admiral."

Julian dropped the Scandinavian seal back into the pouch, stepped forward and gave it to Bjorn. "Juror Marius will accompany me aboard, and four guardsmen." He glared at the captain, planting his boots wide and inviting argument.

"Very well, but they leave their weapons."

Julian's gaze ranged along the side of the enormous ship. "I don't think so."

Bjorn smiled stiffly. "Very well."

Without turning around, Julian raised his voice and said, "Juror Alexander, I'll signal from the deck in ten minutes. If I don't appear, shoot the mooring crew and sound the alarm."

Julian took the lead and strode up the gangplank in the captain's wake, his expression remaining tight. He expected the complete silence of vampire occupation, but he had a sneaking suspicion the evening would be full of surprises. The corridor passing through the hull created an airlock, six feet deep. The outer door closed and the boarding party waited a second for the internal panel to move.

As the inner door slid open, a cacophony of cantering human heart rates bombarded Julian's ears, and the smell of human flesh filled his mouth with venom.

Julian shared a sharp look with Marius and said, "Captain, you have humans onboard?"

Bjorn's smile twisted with sarcasm. "But of course, my mistress demands it." The vampire's jaws snapped shut as he briskly swept away over the polished hardwood floor.

He said more than he meant to. Unease uncoiled inside Julian. *Mistress?* He was eager for answers but his escort appeared to have recovered his composure. Julian accelerated until he flanked the tall vampire's shoulder. His deliberate stride reverberated as, senses on alert, he used the echoes to gather information on the size of the vessel.

The evidence of human passengers originated below deck. *Not passengers, cargo.* Julian frowned. The group passed through a doorway. At Julian's nod, a pair of guardsmen took up sentry positions which commanded a view of the huge enclosed space, and a clear line of sight to the three other doorways exiting the room.

Julian caught Marius' eye, and the intensity he found in the juror's oil black gaze reassured him. Both vampires were on their mettle. In a casual move, Marius dipped a hand into his pocket, withdrew two heavily embossed rings, and slipped them onto his fingers. Julian grinned. Society had not softened Marius. His expertise in hand to hand combat could easily be overlooked because the dark vampire glided through most days, apparently unperturbed. But, Julian knew of the years Marius had spent in Burma. Ironically, the juror had joined protestors in skirmishes objecting to British colonial rule. The plague of 1904 caused a mass exodus of Burma, and, when one third of the inhabitants fled the city, Marius met an English officer. The respect Marius gained for the officer brought him to London.

Julian had never witnessed Marius in battle. *I have no idea if he's a battering ram or a strategist, but, Connor aside, I trust him to watch my back.*

As Bjorn strode on through a labyrinth of identical gangways, Julian's patience hit a wall.

"Halt," barked Julian.

The captain's cape flared as he whipped around. "My apologies, Principal."

He doesn't look apologetic. "Your ten minutes are running out." Julian grinned as the implication hit home.

"Your parlay will take longer than that," said Bjorn.

"Of course," said Julian. "But until Juror Marius or I appear in full view up on the deck, the clock is ticking."

Pointing down the dimly lit passage, Bjorn said, "The regent's reception room is through the gold door."

Without taking his eyes from the captain's face, Julian raised a brow. "Regent? Your vessel has no admiral?"

"A descendent." Bjorn silently met Julian's steady regard.

"Very well, present us to your *regent*." The ground kept shifting, and nothing he had learned so far made Julian feel easier. *Regent or admiral, this ship is bad news.*

When the gold door opened and Julian stepped over the threshold, for a moment, he stopped breathing and lost the power of speech.

The walls of the room were lined with panels of burnished bronze and gold. What should have appeared garish was softened by festoons of white silk bound with silver cord and each polished panel was transformed into a draped 'window'. Like a hall of enchanted mirrors, Julian was bombarded by many reflections of the regent's figure. He absorbed the glimmering images which dominated the room, digesting the feminine detail, and still, when he finally turned his attention to the woman herself and focused on her face, surprise jolted through him.

The quartz-like veins beneath her pale skin dressed her in a gossamer web of glittering thread. The hands she folded in front of her suggested nervousness, and the pleading light in her pale blue eyes was not what Julian expected.

"Forgive me," she said, in a voice that drifted as softly as the silk clinging to her body.

"The admiral?" Julian's voice sounded harsh in comparison.

"My father," she responded simply. "He is dead now."

"My name is Principal Julian." For some reason, he wanted to offer his human family name of Wouldham, but clamped his teeth shut before the word could escape.

Marius took his place on Julian's right side, remaining stoically silent.

In a low voice, Bjorn responded to the regent's inquiring glance. "And Juror Marius."

The ticking muscle in Marius' cheek demonstrated his resentment at Bjorn's interference, but he bore it, and inclined his head.

In a smooth maneuver, Bjorn obstructed the path of the accompanying guardsmen, preventing them from entering the room. "Principal, your men-"

"Wait outside the door," said Julian, conceding that a party of four vampires was a little excessive. Once the door closed behind them, he raised an imperious eyebrow.

"Regent Birgitta of Scandinavia is my bestowed title." Her blood red lips curved in a tentative smile.

"As a regent, you will know your arrival here is a breach of hive protocol." Julian inhaled deeply. "You have human cargo. And how many vampires in your retinue? Why are you here?"

Bjorn coughed discretely. "Principal?" He didn't quite tap his watch, but Julian caught the purposeful movement.

Without looking away from the ethereal beauty of Birgitta, Julian signaled to Marius. "Go and stand on deck, Marius. I will hear what Regent Birgitta has to say, at least."

"Thank you, Principal Julian."

His name on her lips enslaved his attention. He registered Marius leaving, but had no thoughts to spare other than the words which appeared like a script inside his head. "How can the London Hive be of service?"

Birgitta's hand moved in a hypnotic dance as she smoothed her brow in apparent distress. The pools of her eyes glistened as though with tears.

Julian knew this could not be so. But still, the weight of his heart jolted in his chest. *I feel sorry for her.* Julian frowned. *Of course you do, she's just a figurehead, but she needs something from you.*

Birgitta locked gazes with Julian. "I had a child, once."

Julian snatched a breath. "You had a child-?"

"No, no… not after I became a vampire. When I was human. My father, the admiral, he lost a battle when settling a dispute with a neighboring district." She waved a vague hand. "I don't remember the family's name, but when their army arrived in my father's house, they killed my son. As my father's heir, he could not be suffered to live."

The limpid blue gaze faltered. Birgitta turned her face away, presenting a vulnerable profile.

"Why do you tell me this?"

Without looking back at Julian, in a whisper which barely disturbed the air, she said, "I hear there is a vampire child."

Julian stiffened. His principal's cloak slipped firmly back into place as he said, "You are mistaken. There is no vampire child." His voice rung with conviction.

Birgitta's shoulders sagged. Her rigid metal breastplate seemed to be all that prevented her folding to her knees, and Bjorn dashed forward and gripped his mistress' arm.

A throne-like chair registered with Julian for the first time as the regent subsided into it. The wall of shimmering images, reflecting all the angles of despair in Birgitta's face, bored into his brain. One woman, he could withstand, but somehow, he felt as though her magnified emotions seeped into his soul.

Assessing the regent's hunched form, Julian took in the soft suede skirt hugging her thighs, and noticed she was barefoot. She appeared almost child-like, herself.

"There is no vampire child," Julian repeated slowly.

Birgitta turned towards him, her twisted blood-red lips taking nothing away from the beauty of a face framed by a braided coronet of white blonde hair. The anguish on her tight features hit Julian like a sledgehammer blow to the chest.

"But there is a child." The weight in his thorax crushed him as he recoiled from his own betrayal. The words were drawn from him. "The child is not a vampire, she is a hybrid."

Birgitta's expression flooded with joy. "The stories are true. How wonderful. How…?" In a silver-tinted flash of movement, she appeared before him.

Julian could easily reach out and touch her, and he clenched his fist to prevent the insult.

"I'm sorry, I am being ungracious. Please." Birgitta's glance commanded Bjorn to her side. "I have humans onboard. Please, feed, take my hospitality, and perhaps you will allow me to enter London. If I cannot see the child, may I speak to the father? He is a vampire? That's what the fable tells us."

Julian felt as though he could breathe again. *She doesn't want to see Seren.* Somehow, his weakness felt less damning.

"You cannot remain docked in London until I search your vessel." Julian felt the ground beneath him becoming firmer as he moved onto areas he understood. "My escort of guardsmen will accompany Captain Bjorn and myself, and an inventory of every human and vampire onboard will be taken."

"Of course, anything." Birgitta reached for Julian's hand, and the hum of static took him unawares. "Anything, if I can just come to court and meet the father." An innocent smile curved her ruby lips. "I have some humans on their last day, if you wish to attend a feeding ceremony onboard tonight."

"Last day?" Julian frowned. "You let them die?"

"They all have to die, surely?" Regret softened her features.

"No," Julian reclaimed his hand and stepped back. "They do not."

"The cattle onboard provide our sustenance. But sometimes, over-zealous crewmen take too much." Bjorn shrugged. "It's hard to curb their appetites. We have no way to tell how much we are taking."

"There are ways," barked Julian. "Show me your human stock."

"Captain Bjorn, extend every courtesy to the principal. I owe him a great debt." She smiled at Julian. "At dusk tomorrow, if arrangements can be made, may I enter your court?"

Julian inclined his head slowly. "After the inspection, I shall make my decision."

"Thank you," she murmured, and Julian wondered why it did not feel as though it was his decision to make.

Birgitta watched Julian leave. As the mirrored door closed, her own reflection slid into view. Her fingertips played with the chain around her neck and her features hardened to marble. *The principal is strong, but good manners are his enemy. I read two hundred years of firmness in his hand.* She tilted her head, mentally shuffling through her own seven hundred years to the era in which Julian would have been human. In the 18th Century, men were chivalrous and women protected. *He will do me very well.*

"He will lead us to Doctor Connor, Earth Mother," Birgitta whispered. "You were right. They care too much for their humans."

Chapter 7

Marius turned around when Julian joined him on the deck. Absorbing the implication of the principal's frown, he said, "Problem?"

"A complication. I'm taking three guards to sweep the ship." Julian's jaw clenched. "I'll be happier when I know the numbers."

Resting his hands on the guard rail, Julian scanned the dock. Everything remained in the freeze frame position in which he had left it and yet… it felt like a scene from a play, as if the plot was already determined, but he had not read the script.

The mooring crew were frozen in place – a set of statues accepting that the guns pointed at their chests, and down from the high-level flanking positions on top of the containers, would not waver. Thirty of the fifty Elite Guardsmen observing the liner from up on the bluff had lowered their weapons. But if the Scandinavian crew looking down from the ship thought it signified weakness, they were wrong. Every guardsman carried an icepick, and was poised to pull it from inside their belts in an instant. The honed weapon made scaling the hull simple. Guarding London from an invading fleet was not a new experience.

Daniel still occupied the vantage point of the dock-master's observation platform, with an arrow notched in his bow, charged and ready for flight. With the wind snatching at his black cloak, he resembled a demonic perversion of cupid. His focus never shifted from the doorway in the hull where the gangplank extended. It was not a matter of preserving Marius and Julian's escape, after all, both vampires could easily vault over the side to safety. His role centered on ensuring no one left the vessel without permission.

Gerrard, his hands clasped behind his back, stood on the quayside, with his eyes trained unerringly on Julian's face. It felt as though God was holding his breath.

There was no sign of the platoon of guardsmen waiting in the wings, but Julian knew a barked command from Gerrard would initiate a boiling cauldron of movement, and the ship would be flooded by his men in seconds.

With a mental shake, Julian rapped his fingernails on the hardwood rail, and barked his orders. "Hold formation, and no one leaves the vessel until we return from the search."

Captain Gerrard nodded.

Turning his back on the scene below, Julian scanned the hard set faces of his four guardsmen. "You two, with me, and Sergeant Hugh." Shifting his attention to the sergeant, he said, "I want numbers, both human and crew, understood?"

The sergeant's eyes gleamed as though his inner computing system had come online, and he smiled.

"Good man. Marius, Hugh will return within fifteen minutes, if he doesn't, you know what to do."

Julian, led by Captain Bjorn, disappeared below deck. The liner's eight decks had been streamlined into three usable levels. Down on the first level, cabins on either side of the passageways ranged the full length of the vessel, and each door hung open.

Bjorn smiled. "We have nothing to hide. Each crew member has their own space to feed and sleep. I ordered all crew to their quarters. It will make your job easier."

'We have nothing to hide' rarely proved to be true, in Julian's experience. *Even Connor and I have guilty secrets.* "Thank you, Captain."

Julian strode on ahead, leaving the sergeant to deploy the guards, one taking each side of the corridor.

"Principal," Hugh said quietly, and Julian swung around.

Joining him at an open doorway, Julian looked inside the cabin. The area was deserted. A glass beaker sat on a table, dregs of blood pooling in the bottom. Julian entered, picked it up and sniffed the residue, ignoring the saliva flooding his mouth. "Two parts bovine, one part human." He raised a brow. "Where is he?"

Hugh indicated a circular hatch buried in the wall. "All the others are open."

Bjorn cleared his throat. "I apologize for my oversight, Principal. Crewman 138 is logged in for grave sleep."

"In there?" Julian laid a hand on the metal door.

"Yes. Reclaimed torpedo tubes from a fleet of obsolete submarines serve the purpose well."

That answered another of Julian's niggling questions. Hungry vampires in grave sleep would cull the entire human herd without a second's thought. *So, this is how they restrain them until they regain control.*

"He's due for release in three hours."

"And how many other crew members are going to be 'missing' in grave sleep?" Julian snorted. "This is ridiculous. "Muster the crew for Hugh to take a proper inventory, and they will all stay there until the grave-sleep period is up and the others join the group."

Bjorn's jaw snapped shut when he realized Julian was playing hard ball.

Julian shoved his face in close and said, "Your Regent Birgitta expects my hospitality. While you are docked in London this vessel is a prison ship. *No one* leaves without my permission."

"Very well." Bjorn lifted his chin.

Not taking his eyes from the captain's stiff face, Julian said, "Sergeant Hugh, locate all shut down torpedo tubes and let Captain Gerrard know how many men we need to guard them, and make sure they are armed. Armor piercing rounds." Stepping back and releasing Bjorn from the blast of his anger, Julian added, "Continue the tour, Captain."

Only the sound of light footfalls on the metal stairways broke the silence as Bjorn led them down to the next level. Stepping through the bulkhead door, Julian stopped and scanned the huge windowless compartment.

"A muster point for all crew," Bjorn offered.

"The hull has a false skin. It should be wider than this."

Bjorn raised a subdued brow. "You are right, Principal. The oarsmen occupy the space between the two hulls."

Julian smiled. *Ah, so the vessel is propelled below the waterline by vampire oarsmen.* Glancing down at where the wooden floor was checkered with seawater boot prints, Julian said, "And where are they now?"

"They have a barracks area, they are not crew, as such."

"Bondsmen, then. Taken onboard against their will?"

"Oh no, they have no desire to leave." Something in Bjorn's face skittered icy unease through Julian. "Let me see them. Hugh, send a guardsman into each oaring channel, make sure they are empty."

"Access is via the upper deck. The hatchways are in the floor."

"I see. Sergeant, the rowing channels are flooded with seawater so make sure to tell the men to lock their throats down tight. A lung full of water won't kill them, but it'll stop them feeding for a while."

Sergeant Hugh disappeared and Julian said, "Barracks."

At the stern of the ship, the captain slid open three hefty ten-inch long bolts positioned equidistant between the top and bottom of a thick metal door. The rubber sealed edges sighed, and the greased hinges barely whispered as he pulled the door open.

Standing to one side, Bjorn invited Julian to take a look.

The large metal-lined box beyond resembled a bank vault, and the vampires crowded into the space appeared content to stand shoulder to shoulder, unmoving. Their dulled expressions were all the more unnerving as seawater dripped from their hair and clothes unheeded. The crust of dried salt deposits laid tracks down over their white faces where they had made no effort to wipe it away.

"What's the story?" Julian asked sharply.

The tightly packed bodies reminded him of bats in a cave. *If you turned the chamber upside down and they were hanging from the ceiling.*

"They are in revival sleep." Bjorn shrugged. They come from the same colony. I think they stay together for companionship."

The super tanker nomads came to mind. Those vampires fed from each other, forging a psychic connection so strong that they no longer needed speech. Julian stared into the nearest row of faces, and instinctively knew it was more than that. The mudslide of apathy in their gazes resembled a lobotomized mind, rather than a listless one. He made a mental note to talk to Connor about these vampires. *He had close contact with the super tanker nomads; he will know.*

Julian left Hugh behind to complete the headcount of the oarsmen, knowing he would catch up. Going down the metal treads of a stairwell to the lowest habitation level of the ship felt like descending into an invisible bank of fog.

The air looked clear, but it cloyed to Julian's mouth, lined his nasal passages and settled like water in his lungs. The odors of salt and sweet honey smelled familiar. *Humans.* But the intensity of it felt like a punch in the gut. He stopped moving and swallowed down the venom oozing into his mouth.

Bjorn's eyes glittered with spite. "Overpowering, isn't it. If you need to return above deck, I can assure you there are precisely one-hundred and eight humans, today."

Julian darted an annoyed glance at the captain. "I still wish to see." He signaled to the hive guardsmen, whose own discomfort showed plainly on their faces. "Return to the deck above and wait there. Tell Sergeant Hugh which way to come."

Finishing the descent, Julian noticed copper-brown discoloration around a series of circular drains set into the floor. At a glance, he recognized the metal-lined chamber for what it was. *A feeding room.*

Of the four doors in view, it was easy to detect which one led to the human quarter.

Crossing the slick floor, Julian laid a palm on the metal hatch, and said, "So this is where the humans enter. What's behind the other doors?"

"Private feeding rooms." Bjorn's laugh grated in his throat. "Some of the crew have... proclivities the rest of us prefer not to witness."

"And that's why your humans die. Your crew should be on siphoned rations only. Sick bastards."

"We prefer warm blood."

Julian darted across the space, rammed his face in close to Bjorn's, and pleasure rattled through him when the captain recoiled and alarm registered on his tight features.

"While you are docked in London, there will be no human deaths, understood?"

Bjorn nodded.

"Open up the three doors."

Hugh arrived in time to witness the inspection and determine that all three 'feeding' rooms were empty. Before pulling open the final door, both Hugh and Julian pulled masks from their pockets and pressed the thin transparent membrane over their faces. With his jaw clenched tight, Julian stepped over the threshold into the syrup-thick atmosphere beyond. Both vampires, with Bjorn trailing in their wake, passed briskly through the gangways between the holding cages. The human living conditions appeared to be clean and the 'stock' seemed healthy, even though their quarters were cramped. But there was nothing Julian could do about that right now.

After exiting the human quarters, the sweep through the rest of the ship turned up nothing of concern until they reached the lowest level. It took longer than Julian liked to pass through each hatchway in the succession of bulkhead walls which divided the vessel into compartments. At the end of the seemingly endless run of chambers, they came to a sealed doorway.

"Open this up."

Bjorn looked confused. "It's the old boiler room. Nothing remains inside."

"Open it up," Julian repeated, "or shall I?" He signaled the sergeant forward.

Hugh dragged an exploratory nail down, tracking the crumpled edge of the steel hatchway and scoring a bright silver line through the age-stained surface.

"The oxidation in the weld suggests it has been in place for years," the sergeant said thoughtfully.

Julian reluctantly backed down, deciding he had made Birgitta's captain jump through enough hoops. "Very well, Captain Bjorn. The vessel can remain in dock. At sunset tomorrow, a landing party of *twelve* vampires can come ashore."

Bjorn laughed gently.

Julian raised an eyebrow and waited for the captain to speak.

"My lady's retinue is never less than fifty crewmen."

"Well, your *lady* can slum it."

Bjorn's expression stiffened and ice glittered behind the blue eyes.

"Regent Birgitta will come ashore with a landing party of twelve. No more. The choice is hers."

With a grim smile, Captain Bjorn saluted. "Very well."

Julian and Hugh rounded up the hive guards as they returned up through the vessel, leaving behind only those on sentry duty outside 'grave-sleep torpedo hatches'. When Julian arrived back on deck and gave the signal to release the Regent's docking crew, the fast moving flow of vampires occurred in near silence. Like chess pieces, each vampire knew their role and attended to making sure each hefty chain remained secure before scaling the slick surface of the ship's side.

Marius and Julian walked down the gangplank and, when they set foot on the quayside, the structure smoothly retracted and the hatch door closed in the sleek black hull.

"Captain Gerrard, the Regent Birgitta will come ashore accompanied by a landing party of twelve at sunset tomorrow. Leave a contingent of the Elite Guard and make sure no one leaves the ship unseen. I have to warn Connor. They are here because of Seren." Julian laughed harshly. "A pilgrimage of sorts, it appears."

Chapter 8

Connor and Julian stood shoulder to shoulder on the top step outside the main entrance door to the council building. Above the London skyline, the navy blanket of stars crushed the sun until a fiery glow bled across the horizon. The soot-black buildings resembled a jagged row of rotten teeth.

"Funny how hours pass by much slower when you are waiting." Connor continued to stare outwards. "Everyone is in place?" The gusting breezes eddying around inside the shelter of the portico tugged at his greatcoat and for the tenth time he clawed his black hair back from his eyes.

In a reasonable tone, Julian replied, "The regent is en-route. The waiting is over."

Connor grinned tightly, asking again, "And everyone is in place?" *Julian cannot blame me for not liking this. We have been through enough.*

"Captain Gerrard briefed the council guardsmen. I saw them leave London this afternoon, in full battle dress. They are fully protected against the sun and were in place lining the route long before dusk, and they will stay out of sight." The words 'so don't worry' hung in the air, but a snort from Connor warned Julian not to say them.

"Was there *no* way to put her off?" Connor tried one more time.

"She would not have gone away. It is best to get it over with, I think."

The asphalt on the empty London streets glistened with the recent downpour of rain. Water dripped down the cloaks and pooled at the feet of the guards lined up along the curbstones of the final approach to the council building. The rain drenching their hair ran down over the impassive faces of the motionless sentinels.

The distant sounds of wheels turning and horses' hooves clattering invaded the silence, and Captain Gerrard's purple uniformed figure streaked into view. Seconds later, he skidded to an abrupt halt in front of Julian.

"Principal, the regent's carriage and her retinue are crossing the Thames at Vauxhall Bridge. I have covert platoons stationed in Hyde and Green parks. Guards remain in position on the quayside. If any vampire leaves the ship, we will know."

"And the size of the escort?" asked Julian.

The captain grinned. "Twelve."

"Good. This is it, then, Gerrard. Escort the regent to the council building, shut down the perimeter, and then, we get her out of London afterwards, as quickly as possible. The dispensary has blood crated up for transportation. After all, there's no need for bad manners." Julian smiled stiffly.

Connor remained silent. He almost wished the regent *had* flouted Julian's command. *We could have turned her back and ordered her to leave.* His attention became glued to the gap between the marble facades of the nearby tall buildings, through which the regent's out riders should appear. "I don't like it," he muttered.

Julian laid a heavy hand on his friend's shoulder. "Seren and Rebekah are both safe. Daniel and Isaac are in the entrance cavern of the eco-shelter, and we have sentries in the woods-" Connor shrugged, but Julian forged on. "Greg and Seth are hunkered down, rifles loaded with high velocity tungsten bullets. We have all the bases covered. Relax."

Connor laughed, the sound dry in his throat. He rubbed his forehead to ease the tension of his frown. "Sorry, Julian. I'm acting like a jerk. It's just that, in my experience, covering all the bases is impossible." He met Gerrard's steady stare and knew the captain agreed with him.

Julian did too, but being prepared and optimistic was the corner he had painted himself into.

He should have asked me first. The residue of Connor's anger at hearing the news still simmered, but Julian had pulled rank.

As if he could read his friend's mind, Julian said, "Connor, she would have come back. It is better this way."

The discordant tune of creaking saddles and clinking bridles became crystal clear and the three vampires turned, looking expectantly down along the wide street. Connor's teeth were on edge; each jangle of reins and stirrup was like nails dragging down a blackboard. The tightness in his gut ramped up a notch.

The jet-black carriage rolled into view. The solid, windowless construction clearly doubled as a refuge from the sun. Connor's lips twitched. *It's a mobile coffin.*

He folded his arms across his chest, ignoring the wing of black hair flapping in front of his face this time. He inspected each of the mounted vampires and the footmen running alongside, calculating their weight and potential to cause harm. The vampires in the retinue moved like a well-oiled machine, their movements determined and precise.

Connor resisted the impulse to rub the back of his neck, knowing Birgitta's escorts would be sizing him up, too. He wanted to *feel* the calm he projected. *The best security forces in the hive are out there. That really should be enough. It's one Scandinavian Regent, and a female at that.* But the voice inside his head said, 'a female who survived the battle for supremacy when vampires rose will be a fierce adversary'.

The polished carriage drew to a halt in the middle of the street.

A blonde vampire dismounted, looped his reins over the pommel of his saddle, and the horse's soft muzzle plucked at his rider's sleeve in a surreal moment of normalcy.

The blonde officer mounted the wide marble stairway with a confident stride and, inclining his head, acknowledged Julian. "Principal, your hospitality is appreciated-" His head snapped around as he honed in on Connor. "My name is Captain Bjorn. You must be Doctor Connor, yes?" He extended a hand and smiled.

Connor scanned the stark white features and the fixed attention of the cerulean blue eyes. He made the captain wait, asserting his own authority, before finally unfolding his arms and gripping the proffered hand.

The handshake lasted fractions of a second, but long enough for each vampire to take the measure of the other, calculating the opposition's strength and determination. Both men nodded.

The captain swung away and returned to the carriage.

The black lacquered shell of the vehicle reminded Connor of the obsidian gloss of a beetle. A footman stepped forward and opened the door. The carriage swayed as the regent shifted inside, her gray garb taking form as she emerged from the darkness. A delicate, pale white hand extended out into the moonlight and took that of the captain. Alighting in a flowing movement of white fabric, Birgitta stepped out onto the street.

Her silver breastplate accentuated her small waist and feminine proportions. The short leather skirt she had worn on the ship had been replaced by a longer version which flowed down over her body to her ankles.

Pushing back the white hood of her leather cape, Birgitta assessed her surroundings.

A braid of platinum hair framed large limpid blue eyes and accentuated finely-drawn full lips. Even from a distance, her bone structure appeared dramatic – the sum of the parts lived up to every definition of 'beautiful'.

But Connor saw a painted facade. His eyes narrowed as he read the sinuous body language and recognized a woman accustomed to adoration.

Julian shot a glance at Connor.

He nodded minutely, agreeing with the view Julian had shared after meeting her. The regent projected an air of confusing vulnerability, but was it real? His jaw clenched as he fixed a smile on his face. *I can play this game.* He learned, long ago, to keep his enemies close. *Little does she know, Brynmor has her in his rifle sight.* Neither did Julian, but Brynmor would only fire if the regent launched an attack. *If she comes in peace, then Julian will be none the wiser.* From what Julian had told him, it was a fair bet that Birgitta kept her skin covered, dressing for her role in life. It was a calculated guess that her skin, starved of air exposure, would be softer than usual. That was the hope, in any case. Brynmor's rifle was loaded with hollow tipped shells filled with muscle relaxant, designed to cut through vampire skin which had not yet hardened with age. *The regent will regret a show of aggression.*

Part of Connor hoped she *would* make a move. He preferred open warfare to smiles and deceit. It would solve his dilemma.

The large oak door behind Connor and Julian swung open. Marius stepped out into the chilly evening. "So, this is the regent," he mouthed for Julian's ears only.

Birgitta glided forward and mounted the steps.

Looking down from the higher vantage point, Connor watched the graceful sinuous sway in her stride and suppressed a tight smile. He recognized her use of feminine wiles, but still they fascinated him.

Her downcast gaze accentuated long black lashes and the delicate arc of her forehead where a coronet was molded to her hairline. Stopping one step below, Birgitta dipped into a deep curtsey. Rising again, she looked up into Julian's face. "Principal, I am eternally grateful for this chance to visit your hive." Her gaze moved smoothly to Connor. "And you must be Doctor Connor. The hybrid child's sire?"

Connor bristled at the detached breeding term, but showing it would play into her hands. He touched the fingers she offered in greeting, and disconcerting heat tingled through his palm and flowed like lava up his arm. He broke the connection quickly.

"Regent Birgitta," Connor said quietly, inclining his dark head. His granite gray gaze searched her perfect face and, as he expected, her smile did not reach her eyes. Even so, looking into them made him feel as though the ground beneath his feet shifted slightly. "My name is Doctor Connor. I am the father of the vampire/human hybrid child." He found it easier to hide behind a clinical façade. "I fear you will be disappointed if you have come here looking for answers."

"I have been told the child is out of bounds." Her face fell and sorrow filled her eyes. "But you have anecdotes, medical records, and theories, I'm sure."

"Principal Julian says you lost a child when you were human. I'm sorry. That must have been tough."

Birgitta surprised Connor. He expected crocodile tears not a joyous smile. "He was perfect, my Andrik. His life was cut short but I wouldn't change the moments I had with him."

Marius cleared his throat.

"Of course." Birgitta smiled. "If I can speak with Doctor Connor, and see the hospital where she was born? I shall leave you in peace."

"We can talk, yes, but here. The hospital visit is out of the question," Connor replied. He did not need to consult with Julian, they had already decided the regent would not be allowed to deviate from their own plan.

"Choose two vampires as your escort. The remainder will stay with your carriage." Julian's stern gaze discouraged argument. "And, Captain Bjorn will stay here."

Glancing over her shoulder, Birgitta pointed a red painted fingernail, picking out twin vampires standing at ease in worn riding boots, their cowled capes thick with mud. Their faces remained blank as both stepped forward – it was clearly what they expected.

"These are my personal outriders, Sascha and Valdar. Come."

Stepping aside, Connor ushered Birgitta ahead.

"Guard the entrance, Gerrard. Any… problems, you know what to do." Julian's stiff grin became a feral sneer. "Keep the upper hand, no matter what," he said, and followed the disappearing reception party.

Once inside the council building, Marius led the way along the corridor. Birgitta, flanked by her escorts, followed closely behind. Connor brought up the rear with Julian. The friends shared a sharp glance. Both knew the next hour would be dangerous.

The six vampires filed into the jurors' anteroom. Alexander stood up as they entered and Anthony turned into the room from where he had been looking out over the darkened city.

"I hoped Doctor Connor and I would be allowed to talk in private? I mean no harm…"

"Not alone, no. Anthony was there at the birth of the hybrid child. He and Doctor Connor can tell you everything you want to know."

Julian opened the door to the courtroom. Nodding towards the twins, he said, "Come this way. We will wait next door."

Marius, Alexander and Julian accompanied Sascha and Valdar. The door closed and, for a moment, there was silence. Anthony perched on the edge of the jury table and folded his arms, his aggression thinly veiled by a stiff smile.

Birgitta circled the room, running her fingertips over the carved oak panels until she reached the door once again. Turning around, she met Connor's eye.

He found himself feeling sorry for this proud blonde warrior, and without knowing why, felt compelled to speak. "The child was an accident. Not one we can repeat."

"What kind of accident?"

Connor weighed his options and against every instinct, he went with the truth. "The mother was dying of hypothermia. I raised my body temperature in a scalding bath and warmed her."

"You love her?" Birgitta cut in, her brows rising at Connor's soft tone.

Continuing briskly, he said, "There was a transient moment when we were both at the same core temperature that allowed conception to occur. At least, that's what we now believe."

"If you can't share the child's name, what is the mother called?"

Birgitta's words settled like stones in Connor's gut. "No. You don't need to know."

"Very well." Birgitta's chin dropped. "Does the child drink blood? Principal Julian says that your human cattle are well cared for. That you are in the process of establishing villages where humans volunteer to 'give blood'?"

"It is a slow process, but we are trialing enclosures which mimic villages. There are fence lines, but more to protect the humans from attack by vampires than to keep them in."

"Interesting. But the humans will die, in the end."

Connor grinned wryly. "We all will."

"Not if we can have hybrid children," said Birgitta. "Please, can I see the child?"

"No." He frowned. "No one sees my daughter. She is not a freak show."

"How old is she?"

"Human years do not matter," Anthony chipped in, and Connor glared.

"So, she is not a child any longer?"

"Enough." Connor walked to the door. "You have wasted your time. You will not see my child and you cannot replicate the process. She's not the answer to vampire survival."

"I'm sorry. I didn't mean to offend." Birgitta rushed across the room. She took three steps and stopped short. Her face froze and all expression drained away. Her arms dropped to her side and her shoulders jerked backwards, arching her spine at a hideous angle.

"Connor," barked Anthony as he rushed forward.

Already one step ahead of his surgical assistant, Connor darted across the floor and swept Birgitta up into his arms before her suddenly slack body collapsed. "Get me two vials of blood. Charles has stored them in Julian's chambers. Go." If he had let the regent fall, it would not have hurt her, but male chivalry was ingrained.

Her body felt firm, smooth, and heavy. For a moment, he was lost comparing Birgitta with the fragility of his Rebekah. Her warm, velvet soft skin, and feather-like human weight, was the only female form he had held in decades.

Hearing the soft thump of the door as Anthony left the room jerked Connor's attention back to the dilemma. Being alone with the regent could have serious consequences. "Julian," he shouted.

Julian appeared. Shock registered on his face as he shot a look over his shoulder and quickly pushed the door shut behind him. "What have you done? Jekyll and Hyde are jittery enough, do I need to disable them?"

"Don't be foolish. It's nothing I did. The regent is dehydrated." Connor bared his teeth in a smile of grim amusement. "I guess, in all the excitement of visiting London, she missed out on a meal."

Julian darted a glance at the closed door. "I'm not sure how the twins will take to seeing their regent being manhandled. Can't you lay her down on the table?"

For the first time, Connor noticed the exposed expanse of thigh and the swell of her bosoms, pushed up by her breastplate. "You're right."

Walking over to the large rectangular table, he laid Birgitta down. As he eased his arm out from beneath her shoulders, her body went into spasm and the bejeweled metal tips of her fingernails scraped across the back of his neck. Jerking back, Connor rubbed his hand over his nape. His fingers came away coated with grains of quartz dust – vampire skin cells – damp with pink plasma. *Damn, the woman is lethal.* She had drawn blood, at least, as much blood as thirsty vampire tissue could release when scratched.

As abruptly as it took hold, the tension drained from her body and her head dropped to one side.

"Where the hell is Anthony? If the Scandinavian Regent dies in London, we better get ready for war," grumbled Connor.

Julian quietly opened the door and peered along the hallway just as Anthony appeared clutching vials of human blood in one hand and a syringe in the other.

Connor plucked the first vial from Anthony's grasp and flipped the lid off with his thumb. Lifting her chin, he poured the contents into Birgitta's mouth. It pooled in her throat before slowly draining away. The blood would trickle down into her lungs and stomach and once it seeped through to the heart, the aortic network would take it up the carotid artery to the brain and, hopefully, she would wake up.

Chest compressions might speed it up, but I'm not going there. Connor satisfied himself with staring at Birgitta's face and looking for changes. Her lips were a shade of red more brilliant than fresh oxygenated blood. Connor speculated on how that could be. She had the perfect proportions of a porcelain doll, and he found himself wondering what she had looked like before becoming a vampire.

"Anything?" Anthony asked, offering Connor the next vial.

Grateful for the distraction, Connor looked up. "Not yet." Taking the open vial, he repeated the process, although the satin texture of Birgitta's skin registered more strongly this time, when he lifted her chin. He looked for the flicker of an eyelid. He didn't have to wait long. When the brilliant clear blue eyes opened and stared at the ceiling, Connor released a sigh of relief and took a step back. He felt rattled, and he didn't like it.

Birgitta quickly leapt to her feet. "I'm sorry. Foolish of me to neglect my feeding."

Julian visibly relaxed. "No harm done. Doctor Connor stepped up, as always."

Birgitta glanced through veiled lashes and said softly, "Thank you. I have taken up enough of your time. You are very kind, but now, I think I should leave."

Unease pulled the muscles across Connor's shoulders tight. Something felt off about the entire exchange but he couldn't put his finger on it.

"Please, no apologies are necessary," he said softly.

"Thank you." Birgitta stared at the courtroom door as though she could see through it, and within a second, the twins entered the room. "I enjoyed talking with you, Doctor Connor."

Before Connor could do anything more than draw in a breath to speak, Birgitta turned and walked out into the hallway, her escorts following on behind.

Marius and Julian accelerated to match their pace, but, Connor, hanging back, studied the regent and her henchmen. He arrived at the threshold to the council building in time to see Gerrard's rigid figure clearing out of the Regent's path when Julian gave the signal to stand down.

Without missing a beat, Birgitta glided down the steps, her leather cape flaring in her wake as she climbed into the black box carriage. With the wave of a pale hand, her jeweled nails glittered in the moonlight, and Connor rubbed the scratches scored in to his neck once again.

The entourage set off at a brisk pace, carrying on past the council building, it executed a U-turn in the street and reappeared like a parade of demons, the outriders' black cloaks flowing over the hind quarters of the horses and the footmen's attire flapping behind like bats in flight.

Captain Gerrard set off in pursuit, a squad of Elite Guards falling in behind him as he passed them along the route.

Julian mounted the steps three at a time and joined Connor's vigil as they tracked the coach until it disappeared from view.

"Well, that was weird," Connor said quietly.

"It was too easy," Julian agreed.

"Not only that. A regent with her own vessel, human cattle, and an army of vampires... and she allows herself to faint." Connor scowled. "I'm not buying it. We haven't seen the last of Regent Birgitta."

"You're right. We'll double the guard around the docks."

The uneasy silence was broken by Marius' approach. "I don't trust her."

Connor and Julian both laughed.

"You read our minds, Marius. Is life never simple?" Julian commented.

"That's what happens when you play with your food," Marius muttered. He staggered when Connor thumped him on the shoulder.

"Sense of humor, Marius? What is the world coming to?" said Connor.

The brooding juror straightened his jacket and tidied his cuffs. "Who said I was joking?"

"I think I'd better follow the carriage and make sure she boards her vessel safely," Julian said. "Anthony, you come with me. Connor, go home and tell Rebekah, Osiris and Seren to be on alert. Oh, and get Malachi to stand guard at the entrance until Anthony arrives back."

Connor lifted a brow. "I'm a step ahead of you, Principal. And Osiris is already guarding the entrance. He won't leave Malachi to do that alone. I'll wait here until you return."

"Marius, make a visit to the farm and put *everyone* on red alert until we've escorted the Scandinavian Regent out past the Thames Barrier. Anthony, let's go."

Watching until Julian and Anthony were specks in the distance, Connor ran through the encounter with Birgitta again.

"Do you think she'll be back?" Marius' question made the weight on Connor's shoulders feel heavier. He'd forgotten his stoic companion was still there.

"I don't know why she'd come back. We have nothing more to say." But Connor knew he was lying.

Chapter 9

In the dark interior of the carriage, Birgitta rested back in the seat and smiled. She knew the vampire council would not be fooled. *They are intelligent. They'd have to be complete imbeciles not to suspect they had been used. What they can't figure out is how, or why.* Her smile gave way to a drift of musical laughter. Enclosed alone in the plush black leather-clad interior, Birgitta relaxed for the first time since she had made her pledge to Lars. *I have set events in motion, my love. You will not go unavenged.*

The chassis rolled and Birgitta let the rushing sound of the wheels wash over her. Tuning out the clatter of horses' hooves, she closed her eyes. She could easily have made the journey quicker on foot, but making an entrance was more important. White silk and leather did not travel well through damp evening air, and she wanted to make an impression. It was not vanity, but powerful manipulation. *Men will always be vulnerable to the female form. Male vampires are not so different from their human counterparts.*

The sounds reverberating from the carriage walls changed as the tall buildings of the City of London gave way to the open embankment running alongside the River Thames. Gusting wind buffeted the cabin and the slapping noise of water grew louder. Birgitta sat up straight and smoothed her skirts as the carriage arrived at the docks and clattered over the concrete quayside.

Stepping out of the warm dark interior unaided, she felt the sets of hostile vampire eyes trained on her back as surely as if they were poisonous darts. *Principal Julian is wise to be on his guard. But it won't help him.*

The hatchway in the hull swung open and the gangplank extended with the whisper of a well-oiled mechanism. Bjorn went ahead to ensure all was in place for the regent's return, and Sascha and Valdar escorted her onboard. Birgitta barely registered the scurry of movement behind, as the loading bay door at the stern of the ship cranked open and the sound of horseshoes striking a metal gangplank, parallel to the first, rang out into the night. Two crew members dragged the carriage onboard, the walkway retracted, and the puzzle pieces in the smooth hull slotted back into place.

Back in her chamber, Birgitta took her place on her throne. "Bring the casket, Bjorn."

With a knowing smile, Bjorn pulled open one of the mirror-like panels and lifted an ivory box engraved with moons and star constellations from its resting place. He set it on a glass table at Birgitta's left hand. "The principal allowed you to speak with Doctor Connor?"

"Did you ever doubt it?"

Birgitta carefully prized the bejeweled nails from her fingers. Tapping gently, she deposited the granite-dust granules trapped beneath each one into a gold thimble-sized cup. *The skin fragments are barely stained pink.* Birgitta's expression reflected frustration. *A minor problem, nothing more.* Reaching into her cleavage, she extracted the three blue-black strands of the doctor's hair she had gathered when he carried her across the room. *He is pathetically predictable. Where is this fierce warrior who beat Lars in battle?* Birgitta acknowledged his strength. The muscles of his torso rippling as he moved were hard to ignore. Coiling the hairs around her finger, she tucked them inside the open box.

"The feeding ceremony for the inner circle will commence an hour before sunrise."

"Perfect, Bjorn. We are close to having this Doctor Connor just where we want him."

"Why not just kill him?" Bjorn's tone rose in apology.

Placing a cool hand over his, Birgitta said, "He has fathered a child. I believe we can learn more if we don't kill him."

Replacing the thimble inside the casket, Birgitta closed the lid.

Captain Bjorn waited silently while Birgitta rose, disappeared behind a screen, and returned, moments later, wearing a crimson gown. Her pale bosom swelled over the square cut neckline. The corset clung to her forever young form, accentuating the nipped in waist. The ruby satin skirt resembled a river of blood flowing over her thighs as she walked.

Cradling the ivory casket under one arm, Bjorn held out a hand and tucked her fingers into the crook of his elbow as the pair left the mirrored splendor of her suite, walked silently along the darkened corridors and descended through the levels of the ship.

Bjorn pushed open the hatchway to the meeting room and stepped back. The vampires of the inner circle – officers on the ship – lined the walls of the feeding chamber, each remaining silent and still. The master of the ceremony held an hourglass filled with black sand, taken from the excavation of Pompeii. Every vampire turned to face the door as their regent entered.

"Ulrik." Birgitta inclined her head. "Begin."

In a reverent tone, Ulrik began to chant, "Bless the flesh we once were. Bless the blood that spills so we can live. Bless the power of our Earth Mother, so we may live forever."

Taking her place at the epicenter of the circle, Birgitta jerked her chin.

A metal door slid open and a thin grimy woman shuffled in. Her hands clasped in front of her accentuated the hunch of her shoulders. With her head bowed, a swaying curtain of greasy hair obscured her face as she walked. The woman made her way to the round copper grate sunk into the floor and stopped, her body rocking gently on trembling legs. Gliding forward, Birgitta took hold of the thin human arm. Bjorn appeared at her side holding out a silver goblet. The woman whimpered as the blade of Birgitta's thumb nail cut into her wrist and the blood gushed into the goblet. She dropped to her knees when Birgitta released her, and one of the vampires stepped smoothly forward. Clamping his mouth over the wound as though biting into her arm, he ran his tongue over the torn skin until the bleeding stopped, the coagulant in his saliva accelerating the healing process.

Tugging on the chain around her neck, Birgitta pulled out the glass vial encased in a silver cage and eased off the lid.

Ulrik began his chant once more. When he again uttered the words, 'so we may live forever', Birgitta let four drops of the thick brown syrup contained inside her pendant plink into the cup of fresh warm blood.

Taking the goblet from Birgitta, Bjorn handed it to the first vampire in the circle. His long pale fingers cradled the silver bowl and he gazed down into the pool of blessed blood, murmuring his own prayer before taking a draft and passing it to his neighbor. Birgitta took a seat on an elaborately carved bronze chair and watched with satisfaction as, after drinking the sacrificial offering, each vampire's face reflected the same trancelike expression.

The door slid open once more, and sixteen humans shuffled into the room, one for each vampire in the circle. The humans were nudged along until each had a partner. This time, Ulrik took his place in the center and held the hourglass aloft. A growl rumbled in his throat as he steadily rotated the timepiece. The shuffling sand fell in a loud whisper to vampire ears, and each knew they were allowed to feed as long as the sand was flowing. *We may not siphon our humans, but we have a crude method of control. It prevents deaths, usually.*

The wet sound of vampire fangs sinking into human flesh always sent a buzz of excitement through Birgitta, but she would never feed in front of them. Her ice blue gaze scanned the room. Her blood red lips curved in a satisfied smile.

When the whisper of sand faded, each vampire jerked back. The punishment for not stopping was death. Their world was one of black and white.

When the vampire officers returned to their places against the wall, the weakened humans lay abandoned in the center of the room. The wounds in their flesh, either the carotid artery in the neck or the brachial artery in the arm, oozed as the lowered blood pressure allowed coagulation to occur without anything more than a soothing stroke of the feeding vampires tongue as they withdrew.

The only sounds were the exhausted groans of humans in pain. The crewmen stared into space as though blinded, the same entranced look remaining on their faces.

"The binding is complete, my lady," Bjorn said.

Taking the goblet containing the remnants of the blessed blood and the ivory casket from her captain, Birgitta slipped from her throne and glided sinuously towards a seemingly solid expanse of wall. Pressing on a rivet head initiated the snap of a lock, a panel clicked open, and a concealed fifth door disappeared inwards into the pitch-black aperture.

Without looking back, Birgitta walked into the shadows and the door swung shut behind her. The metal walls in the passageway dripped with condensation and the plinking noise was all that broke the silence as the regent skimmed along the floor, maintaining an eerily constant speed. She took the open rung stairway down into the bowels of the ship. The bulkhead lights cast a faint yellow glow but Birgitta would have found her way even in darkness. She could feel her Earth Mother's presence as though she shared her body. With every step, Morrigan's soothing voice grew stronger. *You have done well. First contact is made.*

Birgitta smiled when the warmth of approval drifted through her senses. At the end of the corridor, she pressed another hidden button which released an air-locked door with a hiss. It swung silently open. She stepped over the threshold into a square chamber. The door sealed behind her, but a sudden breeze shifted through the stagnant air and stroked over Birgitta's skin. The regent smiled at the greeting. A comforting musty smell emanated from the walls and floor, which were overlaid with thick oak boards. A large stone sarcophagus dominated the space. The gold statues on either side depicted two female warriors. Birgitta always took the time to study the most prominent one. The striking bone structure and delicate proportions were arresting.

Looking into the familiar face of the effigy, Birgitta said quietly, "Earth Mother, I bring you the hair and skin, the essence and vitality, of Doctor Connor. My soon to be beloved. Bring him to me."

A whisper rattled around the room making the wooden walls vibrate in a low hum. *He is yours, and through him, we will rule through the ages.*

Birgitta set the goblet down onto a stone altar.

"Mother, I bring the offering."

Opening the ivory casket, Birgitta removed the thimble holding the fine particles of Connor's skin and emptied the fragments into a beaten copper bowl. Extracting the black hairs, she dropped them into the bowl, too. "Earth Mother, bless these trophies."

Using her silver metal fingernail adornment, Birgitta sliced open her own wrist. Extending her arm over the dish, her blood splattered into it, soaking into the powder of skin cells to make a paste and coating the black hairs. Tendrils of smoke rose, swirling in lazy circles and thickening into a gossamer fine vortex.

Birgitta pulled the glass vial from where it rested between her breasts. "I take the blessing of your blood, My Mother." She eased it from its silver cage and pulled out the stopper secured to the chain around her neck. "In dreams, I come. In that Otherworld where dreams and reality dance together. In dreams, I come to you."

She poured the syrup-like blood in the crystal bottle onto the contents in the bowl and the cocktail burst into flames, the writhing black strands of Connor's hair glowing red hot before they melted. The wisps of smoke ignited into a flare which lit up the chamber. The thick paste bubbled, becoming thinner as currents stirred beneath the concoction.

When the blaze of light died away, Birgitta filled the crystal vial with the potion. Sliding it back inside the protective pendant, she pushed the stopper home, and tucked the vial into her cleavage once more.

Morrigan, I give praise for your power.

With an effortless nudge of her hand, she pushed the lid of the sarcophagus aside. The sound of grating stone could not drown out her Mother's voice. *We will be eternal.*

Turning away and picking up the silver cup of blood, Birgitta slipped her hand beneath the shrunken skull of the figure lying inside a golden coffin shell. She carefully poured the blood into the mouth of a desiccated wizened face.

Replacing the empty goblet on the altar, Birgitta laid a pale hand over the dull chalk-white parchment stretched over Morrigan's cheek. The blood drenched lips of the ancient corpse twitched as her stiffened eyelids scraped open. Birgitta watched the black pupils widen, punching a hole of clear vision in the shriveled film of cataracts covering the pitted eyeballs.

Gripping the edge of the stone coffin, Birgitta stared down into the deep well of Morrigan's gaze. Her body stiffened to a motionless statue. The air in the chamber dropped by thirty degrees and a film of ice crawled over the wooden floor and up the walls as the damp trapped inside it laid down a filigree of frost.

The cold mist plumed into the air and wreathed Birgitta's body in spiraling tendrils. The lace-like threads thickened into a curtain and then drifted upward, billowing and shifting until an apparition in her image floated overhead. "Blessed Earth Mother, guide to The Otherworld, I give thanks." The whispered words came from the ghostly lips of the ethereal image before it melted into the wall of the hold and silence fell.

The black pupils of her ancestor watched over Birgitta's rigid empty shell, the door creaking as though an invisible hand held it shut and defied anyone to dare enter.

Chapter 10

The wait for Julian inside his chamber became a form of torture for Connor. He circled the room until the friction of his agitated movement made the carpet feel warm underfoot. Finally dropping into a deep leather armchair, he sank into thought and resembled a corpse – even his skin took on a gray sheen.

Whipping the door open, Julian walked in and jolted to a halt when Connor shot up out of the wing backed chair like a spring-loaded puppet.

With a sharp glance, Julian said lightly, "You look like death."

Connor rubbed a hand down over his stiff face and grimaced. "You can say that again. How did it go?"

"The worst is over." Julian grinned. "The regent is back onboard her ship and no one will leave it without the alert being sounded."

"Is she leaving?"

Julian laid a hand on his friend's shoulder. "She will. I'll make sure she does."

On another day, Connor might have asked the how, why, and when of it, but he suddenly felt tired of chasing his own tail. He still felt uneasy. *The regent doesn't even know Rebekah's name. Why am I so worried?* The eco-shelter remained the best place to protect his family.

"Go home," Julian said firmly.

"I will."

Connor left the council building, but stress levels had taken their toll and he headed for the hospital.

The donated blood from the human settlement would have been delivered by now – as strange as it seemed, a large number of humans chose to remain on the human farm facility. *But they do have a choice.* They submitted to siphoning in return for medical care, food, and shelter. For some, not thinking had become a way of life – they had become institutionalized, and 'releasing them' to fend for themselves would be cruel. A middle ground existed where they *chose* when they wanted to donate blood.

The polished quartz facade of the hospital walls reflected Connor's worried frown back at him as he hurtled in and applied the brakes at the bottom of the steps. Smoothing his features to their usual reassuring expression was harder today. He pushed through the glass doors into the hospital reception and smiled widely.

Connor still had a lot to work out, not least, how to break the news to Rebekah.

He guessed he would face another assault on his will power. She was always keen to point out that as a *human* mother, she was a weak link. 'You won't have to protect me every moment if you turn me' was a familiar plea. Connor couldn't explain why, but he still held back from letting her pay that ultimate price, even though the hive now had a better relationship with the human survivors. Vampire future was looking up, and he was close to finding the precise blend of simian blood and perfluorocarbons which would unlock the vampire brainstem, but still, he held back.

"She'll wear me down eventually." Connor chuckled.

He powered through the long ice-white corridors and took comfort from being in familiar territory. Pulling open the heavy metal door at the top of a set of stone steps, he descended into the basement, swung left and stopped outside his laboratory. It took him seconds to jab the six-digit PIN into the keypad and go through the outer door. In the decontamination chamber, he subjected his naked body to the blast of scalding steam before pulling on sterile scrubs and hitting the button that made the inner door open with a swish. He pushed concerns about the vessel skulking out in the estuary to the back of his mind. *We just have to get through the next few days, and the immediate threat will have passed.*

"Is something wrong?" asked Brynmor. His laboratory assistant tilted his head.

Connor's laughter was genuine. "I'm that transparent?"

"To me, maybe." Brynmor pushed his horn-rimmed spectacles up the bridge of his nose, and Connor wondered for the hundredth time if they held only glass, or if Brynmor really needed correction to his vampire sight. It seemed absurd, somehow.

His assistant's innocent owl-like wink reminded Connor why, over the last four months, Brynmor had become his second man at the hospital. The tightness in Connor's shoulders eased as amusement seeped into the fibers of his being.

Since Rebekah and Seren's abduction, Anthony spent every spare minute that Connor didn't need him in surgery, guarding the perimeter of the eco-shelter. It felt good to have Brynmor as a wingman he could trust.

"I don't like this Scandinavian vampire being so close to my home, nothing more."

"I can understand that. Are you headed home, now?" Brynmor peered at Connor.

"Yes."

"Feed and take rap-sleep, first. You'll feel better."

Connor felt tendons grating as he moved. "You're right. I'll be no good to anybody dehydrated, but first, let's get the next set of samples into the centrifuge."

Brynmor rested his backside against the white marble countertop. "You know I can do that without you?"

Connor smiled. "I do, but it helps me unwind. Humor me."

Brynmor grunted and turned to face the glass fronted refrigeration unit. With expert ease, he pulled out trays of test-tubes – some filled with simian blood and others with the clear liquid of perfluorocarbon emulsion – and began combining the two components in predetermined, micro-measured quantities. He and Connor worked in silence for half an hour.

Flicking the switches on the bank of agitators and centrifuges, Brynmor stepped back and said, "You've wasted as much time as you need to, Doctor Connor. I'll record the results."

Connor set the dosing pipette down on an instrument tray and hovered, undecided. "Let Isaac know the samples can be trialed on the vampires who take grave sleep tomorrow."

"Okay. Now, go and take rap-sleep before you end up being a patient instead of the doctor."

Connor chuckled. "You win." With a wave of surrender, he left the laboratory and entered the airlock. Reversing the decontamination process, he pulled on his day-clothes and slung his greatcoat over one arm. He left the surgical wing and whipped along the corridor to the blood dispensary.

The vampires waiting in the dispensing area vibrated with subdued excitement – like addicts anticipating a fix. Connor wove a smooth path to the front of the queue, the row of bodies parting as though he had nudged them aside.

"Charles." Connor grinned with amusement. The small sandy-haired dispensary clerk exuded his usual quiet authority. He might be short and slight, but, like a terrier, he was fiercely protective of his department. His bark *was* as bad as his bite.

"Doctor. Glad to see things are returning to normal. Got a bit exciting there for a while. *Regent*, eh?"

Connor laughed at Charles' air of being 'underwhelmed'.

"All is well, now," he answered, injecting conviction into his words.

"Grave sleep?" asked Charles, automatically selecting glass vials from the nearest tray.

"Just rap-sleep, thankfully. I haven't got three hours to waste."

Charles frowned. "Just don't be an ass. You can't neglect your brain without crashing."

Connor should have been annoyed at the clerk's rudeness, but their friendship took the sting out of it.

"Yes, sir," Connor replied. With a solemn nod, he picked up the three vials of human blood Charles laid on the counter and headed back into his own territory. The surgical wing drew him like a beacon. 'Examination Room 2' was where he always ended up. He had first met Rebekah there, and felt closer to her the moment he stepped through the door.

Tossing the greatcoat over the back of a wooden chair, he unbuttoned the collar and cuffs of his charcoal-gray shirt and eased a hip up onto the examination couch. With one foot still on the floor, he popped the caps on the three vials, swallowed each one in quick succession, and dropped the empties into the recycling tray beside the bed. With a sigh, he rolled slowly back, drew up the trailing leg and hitched his body straight.

Closing his eyes, he surrendered to the weight pooling in his thorax and the exhilarating tingle as the blood permeated his arterial network and, feeling like a flame devouring a fuse wire, scorched its way up his carotid and jugular arteries. The three brain centers vied for attention, each crying out for a fix of red nectar to fill them, but today it was the turn of the volatile and explosive persona of rap-sleep – akin to becoming an intoxicated drunk, base urges rose and demanded satisfaction. As with human alcoholic inebriation, the pendulum could swing to aggressive violence or seeking sexual gratification. Rap-sleep fight parties were not for Connor. He chose to be a lover, not a fighter.

He expelled the air from his lungs, speckling his face in a fine spray of ruby droplets. He closed his eyes and played out the moment he had first met Rebekah in this room. Her honey blonde hair and warm brown gaze had barely registered back then, because his senses had been battling with the static charge touching her seemingly chilled vampire flesh jolted through his system. She had pulled off a great performance.

Connor smiled in his trancelike state of sleep.

As if he time traveled back, he relived the sensations of running a hand over Rebekah's stomach when he had examined her for broken bones. Connor's reclining body jerked as suddenly the flesh beneath his hand became so cold it burned. His eyes swept up the perfectly formed female body. Her breasts were naked. *No, this isn't how it happened.* His head rocked on the cushioned mattress and he screwed his eyes tightly shut. But still, the images thickened inside his head – the perfect female body beneath his hands felt firm and cold. He wanted to snatch his hands away, but they would not move. The vision of the rosebud tips of her breasts made him salivate. He swallowed noisily as the swathe of white blonde hair draped over her shoulder ignited a spark of fear. His own flesh tightened and, to his shame, his manhood stiffened as his hand drifted up and his fingers plucked the taut nipple.

The eyes looking up at him were clear crystal blue and triumph glittered in the deep pools.

"No." The sleeping Connor spoke aloud.

The weight pressing his body into the examination bed disconcerted him, his eyes snapped open and Birgitta's face filled his vision. The white gold coronet molded to her head gleamed in the light. Her thighs gripped Connor's hips. She straddled him and her nails slowly shredded his shirt as they stroked up over his chest.

Every muscle in his body jerked and yet he could not move.

Birgitta ran her fingers through the coal black strands of his hair. "You are asleep, my Connor. But this is what desires are made of, fantasy."

Her face drifted out of focus as her cold firm lips pressed to his. Confusion folded his brow. He was not used to registering anything as cold and it crossed his mind that this must be a dream. His mouth filled with her honeyed tasting venom and the room began to pulse. Red capillaries crawled over the pristine white walls as though he was inside a beating heart. The pressure in his head pulsed in time with the thrumming sound. *What's happening?* His body became heavier and he panicked silently that he was being locked inside a desiccating body. *She can't drink my blood, she isn't real.*

Skimming her hands up under his shirt, Birgitta pushed his arms up to either side of his head and he let her.

Becoming lightheaded, the room started to spin until he lost focus and surrendered to the feeling of floating. In the next moment, he was looking down from the ceiling at the shell of his own inert body lying far below – his chest heaved as if he was fighting for breath. The surreal entanglement of watching and yet still being inside his body defied reason. *This is a dream.* The ethereal glow of the regent's satin skin mesmerized him. Her waist flared into the enticing plump peach of her backside where her hips rode his. Her breasts grazed his chest as she kissed his skin. His body twitched as her tongue teased over his taut flat nipple and up over his collarbone. *She's going to bite me.* Even in his helpless state, he turned his head to protect his neck.

Her hair brushed his face as her mouth trailed along his bicep. He began to embrace a feeling of relief, when a sharp stabbing pain pierced the underside of his arm. He felt the intrusion of her sharp teeth and the dragging pull of his thick cold blood being drawn out from between the sinews and muscle layers.

Her blood-smeared lips came back into his view and he felt something scrape over the oozing wound.

"It is done, my lord. You will be mine." Her kiss tasted of his own blood as she leaned over him and ran her tongue along his lower lip.

The weightlessness he felt became a free-falling sensation and black clouds billowed in to obscure the vision of the naked Birgitta and his shameful compliance. The blackness felt coarse when it rushed into his lungs until he had nothing left to hold onto, his mind filled with coal dust and he tumbled to earth.

Connor's limbs jolted, his eyes opened, and he leapt from the examination couch as though a bolt of lightning threw him across the room. *What the hell? Fuck.* He pressed his back into the wall, but still looked over his shoulder when the flesh on his nape prickled. Pushing his hands through his hair, he dragged them down over his face and battled to separate the threads of his memories. He wanted to wipe away the blonde regent's ice blue gaze and lose himself in his Rebekah. *What the hell happened?*

Finally, he dared to look down the length of his body. The bulge in his pants washed a hot tide of shame through his cold flesh. *How could I? But no, I didn't do that.* He knew he had not found sexual release.

What does it all mean? His shirt was buttoned and the tails hung loose. Maybe it was just a dream. He crossed to a mirror mounted over a basin, but before he reached it, he could see his lips were too red. Leaning in, he touched them and his fingertips came away wet with blood. *Shit.* He twisted his shoulders, lifting his arms and straining to check his body and, sure enough, there was a blood stain under his arm. Whipping the shirt off, he contorted again, and in the mirror, he saw two indents in his tricep muscle. *She bit me? But-*

Shit, Connor, you're losing it. Opening the faucet, he splashed his face with cold water. Yanking half a dozen paper towels from the dispenser, he soaked them beneath the running water and rubbed at the wounds under his arm. They seemed to wipe away, leaving nothing to see. His fingers felt around the area and he wasn't sure if there were indents or not. He wasn't sure of anything anymore.

He scrubbed at his mouth with the dripping towels. The blood there was real. Hissing as his tooth caught on something, he pulled his lower lip down and found a deep tear. *I bit my lip when I was sleeping? That explains the blood.* He latched onto that hope.

Betraying Rebekah and Seren was something he could not face doing. *I would never do that.* Still telling himself it was a dream, Connor tucked in his shirt, collected his greatcoat from the back of the chair, and headed out into the clinical white corridors. He barged through the sets of double doors obstructing his path and, like a plane hurtling down the runway, his speed increased with each stride.

His dark gray-clad form whipped through the reception area leaving behind a comet tail blur for the vampires who had time to look his way. The aqua-tinted toughened glass door blasted open under a seemingly invisible force.

Connor hit the sidewalk at top vampire speed. The need to get home and tell Rebekah and Seren to stay on red-alert bit even deeper into his consciousness now. He fled across Vauxhall Bridge registering each blustering gale of icy needle-sharp rain. His skin felt strangely sensitive and for the first time in his vampire years, he felt vulnerable. The clouds obliterated the moon and the world looked sinister to Connor's eyes.

As the coal-black derelict buildings of suburban London gave way to the lush green pastures of the North Downs of Kent, the feeling of release he was used to, did not come.

Weaving a path through the woodlands, he heard a vampire approaching fast. Cupping his hands over his mouth, he gave the barn owl call sign which would identify him.

Anthony scattered earth into the air as he stopped short and locked eyes with Connor across the last twenty yards. Connor gave a thumbs up and continued on. *I'll fill Anthony in on my way back out.*

He made the final approach to the eco-shelter, and the slick wet grass of the meadow whipping by beneath his feet resembled a glacier of black ice. Skidding to a halt outside the fissure torn in the hillside, Connor wiped ice granules from his face and took a deep cleansing breath.

I'm home. The oily shadows swallowed his form as Connor swept along, hugging the curving wall of the tunnel and using the echo of his footfalls to map the terrain as he descended the slope. He could smell the sackcloth curtain before he got there and swiped it aside without breaking stride.

The torch flames danced as his fast-moving bulk whipped by and within seconds Connor had reached the main cavern. Greg and Seth were absorbed in completing an inventory of the weapons store. The high-powered rifles and boxes of tungsten 'hollow tipped' rounds were spread out on a tarpaulin laid on the ground.

"We'll need to ask Captain Gerrard to bring us more rounds," muttered Greg.

Seth nodded, easing the stiffness from his shoulders with a tight shrug, and Connor, assessing the gray pallor on their skin, guessed both Marines were running on empty.

They had yet to notice his arrival. It reminded Connor of how vulnerable the group would be without vampire patrols out in the woods.

"Greg." Connor laughed as both men grabbed weapons and swung around, explosive clicks resounding from the walls signifying the 'lock and load' action they both executed in a smooth practiced motion.

Connor grinned and lounged in the doorway. "You'd both be dead already, and you know it."

"Fuck, Connor. You should know by now, we win or die trying." Greg's scowl covered the nervous tick rattling through his frame.

Connor materialized beside the two Marines and said quietly, "Get some sleep. I've got your back here for now. When you're rested, we stay on red alert. The ship in the estuary is bad news."

"Who was it?" Greg asked.

"The regent from the Scandinavian Hive came to see Seren."

Seth's eyebrows rose.

"And I don't think we've seen the last of them." Connor frowned.

"You better tell Rebekah," said Greg.

"I'm on my way." Placing a hand on Greg's shoulder, Connor repeated, "Get some sleep."

"You got it," Seth replied.

As the guys started to repack the guns, Claymore mines and grenades, Connor left the meeting hall. The tunnels became narrower as the communal areas gave way to the individual quarters. He focused on tuning into Rebekah's scent and heartbeat. The slow deep breathing confirmed she was sleeping. *That's good.*

Papa?

Connor stopped suddenly. Seren's small figure appeared in front of him, the frown on her face was fierce and she still wore the dress from her betrothal ceremony. Osiris was not far behind.

What is wrong? I lost contact with you for a while.

Seren's connection was borne of their shared blood and DNA. While not the same as a vampire and his maker, it was always there in the background, like twins who know when the other is in trouble.

"I'm fine, squirt." Connor smiled, even though he knew he was lying.

Stepping closer, Seren kissed her father's cheek. "Mama has been worried."

"I know. Everyone is on edge. Where's Malachi?" Connor took Seren's hand and his steady gaze swept the shadows to include Osiris. "Anything out of the ordinary happen out there tonight, Osiris?"

The young Egyptian shook his head. "It was all quiet. Anthony returned and my master has retired to his chamber." Osiris' probing dark eyes glittered.

"Good. Oh, and Seren-" Connor looked down into her set expression. "Red alert until the ship leaves British waters. Our visitor came here to meet you. Julian and I agree that can't be allowed to happen."

Osiris straightened from his lounging position, his broad shoulders accentuating the solid wall of his muscular torso. "I'll keep her safe, sir."

Connor felt like a weight was lifted, and he squeezed Seren's fingers before letting them go. He knew Osiris was capable of that, provided Seren did what she was told. *And there's the problem. You're like your mother in that sense.*

Seren smiled, her chin lifting. *I will not do anything foolish, Papa. Don't worry about me. I promised Mama, too.*

Thinking of Rebekah filled Connor with a sense of urgency.

"Go," said Osiris.

Moments later, having shed his ice-crusted greatcoat as he ran, Connor entered his quarters where, as he expected, he found Rebekah sleeping fitfully. Her eyes opened and their bronze-tinted depths gleamed in the lamplight. Without speaking, Connor stripped off the rest of his clothes and slid into bed beside her. Pushing himself into revival sleep, he welcomed the heat of her hand stroking over his taut stomach.

"You're so cold," she grumbled, "more than usual."

Tucking her into his side, Connor dropped a kiss onto her hair. "Sorry. I should have taken a hot shower before coming here."

Rebekah hitched up onto an elbow and looked into his face. "What's wrong?"

Taking a deep breath, Connor asked himself the same question, but aloud, he said the same things he had told Greg, Seth, and Seren. What really bothered him was the feeling of being out of control.

Running her nose along his clenched jaw, Rebekah pressed her soft warm body closer and he felt her breasts burning against his hard flesh. His manhood stirred as her thigh slipped over his. When she kissed him, he lost himself in the incendiary burn of desire as her teeth tugged on his lip and she dipped her tongue inside his mouth. His hands ran carefully down to cover her backside and in a smooth movement he settled her over his hips. He caught every expression that chased across her face. The diamond dewdrops of perspiration on her skin entranced him as she sat up and took him inside her. The flush over her skin became delightful torture as her heartbeat thundered through Connor's head.

She rolled her hips, taking him in deeper, and the shudders rippling inside her took him close to the edge of the other primal hunger that was never far away when she touched him. He battled with the desperate urge to bite into her soft flesh and taste her. Rearing up to sitting, he pushed his hands into her silky honey-blonde hair, burying his face in her shoulder as he licked the salt from her skin. Resting his teeth enticingly against the thundering pulse in her neck, his lips tingled as the tide of blood rushed beneath his kiss. *So beautiful.* Slipping his arms around her and cradling her gently against his chest, he lifted his face and sought her eyes.

Rebekah smiled softly. He lost himself in her gaze, her brown eyes exuding the lazy warmth of sated desire, and suddenly, they became a frosted ice blue. The rich-gold silky strands of hair coiled around his fingers bleached to white blonde and the heat drained from his lover's flesh, becoming colder than his own. His body jerked, he gripped her shoulders and pushed her away as he recoiled.

"Ouch." Rebekah shifted in his lap, tears welling in her eyes as her hand covered a bruise burning on her upper arm.

Her pain brought him back to earth. "I'm sorry. I hurt you."

Sitting on the edge of the bed, she gingerly rubbed her arms. "It's okay. But what happened?"

Connor framed her chin in his trembling fingers. "I don't know."

"Is it this ship? The commander who wants to see Seren?"

Leaving the bed and pulling on underwear, Connor refused to meet Rebekah's gaze.

"What's that? Have you been in the wars?"

Her tone was wary as she padded barefoot over to where he stood frozen to the spot. He usually told her everything. "What-"

Connor knew what she had seen before her soft touch made contact with the back of his shoulder. "It's nothing. Just a scratch."

"It looks deeper than that." Like *he* would examine a patient, her fingertips probed over his tricep muscle. He stubbornly refused to lift his arm and give her a better view. His firm flesh remained unmovable beneath her human touch.

"Connor, what happened?"

His gray eyes were guarded as he shot a glance into her worried face. "It's nothing." He had a list of lies he could use: A fight in the woods. Vampire losing it in the hospital. But he couldn't bring himself to lie. "There's nothing to worry about."

Even though he knew he was driving a knife into her by shutting her out, he couldn't help himself. *Even I don't know what's happening.* Yanking his shirt back on, he quickly dressed.

"Where are you going?"

"I need to speak with Julian." Connor finally turned, faced Rebekah and took her hands gently in his. "You're right. I'm being an ass. I'm sorry." He brushed his lips over hers. "Just give me a day and I'll tell you everything. I just need to get it straight in my head first, okay?"

She pressed her lips harder into the firmness of his, and said, "Go. Just tell me everything when you come back. I don't want secrets between us. We've come a long way."

Connor threaded his fingers into the hair at Rebekah's nape, his thumb beneath her jaw tilting her chin up. "I promise. I'll tell you everything." His tongue tasted her lips as he kissed her slowly. Her pulse thumping beneath his thumb pad focused his mind. "I love you."

"I love you, too. Now, go."

Chapter 11

Julian stared into the large brass-framed mirror over the quartz mantelpiece. Seeing the reflected image made him smile wryly. Humans buying into the myths about the power of garlic, stakes through the heart, and vampires casting no reflection made it easy to debunk their suspicions. *What the hell am I thinking about that for?* But he knew.

Julian would give anything for a return to the simpler times of his human existence – 19th century London.

As little as twenty years ago, before the pandemic hit, there were enough humans to easily feed every vampire. Life became complicated when, as the principal of London, he had to enforce measures to protect the dwindling numbers of human survivors. The natural order no longer had free rein. Recent events raised the stakes even higher and he had made a mistake.

Bringing Serge back into the city was the wrong move. We are in crisis. I can't risk the councilor causing a distraction. It irritated him that Alexander had turned out to be right. He couldn't send Serge back to Scotland, but he *could* put a temporary solution into action.

He checked his watch, swung towards the door, and headed out into the deserted London streets.

It was a short flight into the heart of the city to Serge's residence. Long before he could see the graceful arc of the 18th century Georgian terraced houses on Eaton Place, he slowed to a walk. *Are the Elite Guard doing their job?* He had no reason to doubt it, but these were dark times. Enemies did not have horns or their allegiance tattooed into their faces, so nothing was certain.

Julian stopped on the sidewalk at the corner and cast a keen glance along the sweeping row of houses. The cream pillars supporting the portico which framed each imposing front entrance glowed in the ambient moonlight – the streetlights had long since been extinguished. Electricity was a commodity to use sparingly; only humans needed the reassurance of light. Set a long way back, a black door skulked in the embrace of each pair of majestic columns, and Julian sensed each portico was empty, until his inspection reached the councilor's dwelling. There, he noticed that two shrouds of darkness had texture. Julian frowned, wondering what had drawn his eye to the near invisible guards, and then he saw it, their faces appeared as paler orbs for a nanosecond when they shifted to survey the street. *Movement.* Julian smiled. *We are like cats, nothing passes unnoticed.*

Turning away, he retraced his steps up a side street. The front of Serge's home was in darkness, so the councilor must be skulking in his study. Tracking the brick wall which marked the boundary along one side, he turned left and followed the stout, aged fence-line around to the back of the property. The ancient oak trees had acquired a new role in recent years – they propped up the fence like the sturdy best friend of a drunken companion. Scaling the slope of a wooden panel tilted at a twenty degree angle until he could see over the top, Julian scoured the yards of waist high grass and tangled weeds between him and the house, and spied on the two guards at the rear.

The dilapidation and peeling paintwork could not obscure the beauty of the ivy strangled exterior.

This was once a 'smart' area of London. The families who used to live here had servants who toiled below stairs and they owned automobiles when others still rode in Hackney carriages. Julian wondered if Serge had been an affluent gentleman before the 'rise'. But, of course, now the servants were gone, so his existence had become a lonely one.

Resembling garden statues cemented in place by an incompetent landscape artist, one guardsman stood dead center of the servants' entrance, and the other blocked the coal bunker doors by resting one black boot on the padlock – the slightest vibration inside the cellar would galvanize him into action.

Satisfied that Serge was going nowhere, Julian eased back an inch. He heard a high pitched mechanical whisper, and froze. Above him and to the left, leaves shuffled and a gritty shower of bark dust skittered down the slope of wooden slats beside him.

Deciding that passive caution was the better option, Julian slowly shifted onto one elbow, twisted around, and looked up.

A black-caped figure crouched on a branch with a primed crossbow trained on Julian's chest.

Beneath a sleek cap of dark hair, jet black eyes in an impassive face stared back.

"Touché, sergeant," Julian said, his attention absorbed by the metal tip of the bolt which glinted like a demonic eye. He slid down the fence panel to the ground and raised both hands.

The air hummed with tension, but then Julian realized it was the hum of wood fibers creaking as the guardsman shifted position.

The figure recoiled into a crouch and settled back onto the crook of the branch. Resting against the solid trunk, he placed the lowered crossbow across his thighs. With efficient fluidity, the marksman released the mechanism and disengaged the bolt, which caused another faint metallic screech – like nails down a blackboard.

"Good evening, Principal Julian," a deep voice said, and the sergeant nodded. "The package is in the box."

"May I pass?" asked Julian, a smile twitching at the corner of his mouth.

In a flurry of dark fabric, the sergeant leapt from his vantage point and landed in the long grass on the other side of the sagging fence. The two figures near the house did not move, and Julian realized they had been watching the exchange, and he was the only one who was caught out.

Leaping over into the garden to join the squad leader, Julian extended a hand to the silent commander. "I'm sure we've not met, sergeant. It's good to know Serge is in experienced hands."

"I gather my squad passed inspection." The sergeant's lip curled.

"It was an ill-judged impulse. No reflection on you. I believe I was the one who got hung out to dry."

The sergeant nodded and smothered a grin.

Carving a swathe through the tangled grass, Julian and the squad leader headed towards the house. The guardsmen statues remained on point until their commanding officer spoke.

"Stand down."

His calm voice reverberated through the still air and both men fell back as though a force field repelled them.

Julian gripped the handle of the back door and it didn't move. The glossy black paint around the lock had been chipped away, and the new steel lock gleamed. *He leaves nothing to chance.* Julian quirked an amused brow when a bunch of keys rattled and one appeared before him. He used it and dropped it back into the waiting palm as his armed escort's bland expression made it clear that was how things worked.

Julian half expected to find Serge lurking in the hallway, but when he stopped to listen, the house was eerily silent. *Have they tied him up?* It occurred to him that his orders had been uncharacteristically non-specific. A cloud of dust plumed into the air when Julian raced down the hallway – the odor of dead human skin, house dust, and insect husks made Julian shudder. Thick strands of cobwebs hung down like those in a ghost ride at the fairground and Julian ducked beneath them as he opened a door and entered a room he had been in twice before and had hoped never to visit again – Serge's study.

His jaw clenched and he felt a moment of shocked annoyance when the room appeared empty, but then he heard a dry laugh.

"This is a rare honor, Principal. Is Doctor Connor at your heels, as usual?"

Julian's gaze narrowed and focused on the shapeless hunched figure which blended into a brown sagging armchair. Serge's reptilian yellow eyes had a zealous gleam.

"I see your stay in Scotland has not blunted your tongue."

Serge laughed and flapped his only remaining hand. "I'm a cripple. There is nothing you can do to me, Principal."

The sergeant stood poker straight in the doorway, his crossbow resting across his chest, as though prepared for Serge to rush him. It would take a suicidal fool to try it.

"Thank you, sergeant. Return to your post."

When the silence within the house settled once more, with just the occasional scuttle of insects, Julian said, "I'm sure, I can think of something, councilor." He heard dried-out skin crackle as the aged vampire grinned.

"Nice try, but I can smell your fear, Serge." Julian circled the room until the light cutting through a grimy window pane lit his features. He scratched a long fingernail idly down over the glass front of a photo frame. Suddenly curious, he picked it up. A smiling, ruddy-faced Serge had his arm around a smaller figure.

"Your wife?" Julian rubbed the glass until a clean patch unveiled the delicate pretty features of the woman.

Serge jerked forward in his seat, his clawed fingers reached for the photo and his empty jacket sleeve flapped with the sudden movement.

Julian felt frustration. *He is his own worst enemy.*

"It is- was my wife. Give it to me."

Holding out the photo until Serge snatched it from his grasp, Julian said tonelessly, "Are you going to tell me where Matthew is? Or what you know about Connor's ambush?" Julian tilted his head and stopped breathing. It was a vain hope that Serge would make life easier and he was not disappointed.

The answer, when it came, was an irritating riddle.

"You would be surprised who is willing to act against Doctor Connor. I don't know where Supervisor Matthew is. You are asking the wrong vampire. You should look closer to home."

Reaching down, Julian grabbed the front of Serge's threadbare jacket in a tight fist and yanked him to his feet. Pressing his face closer to the councilor's, Julian almost gagged on the cocktail of ancient body odor and mothballs. Huffing out a sharp breath, he growled, "You better take that photo with you. I don't have time for this now, but if you don't stop wriggling on the hook and give me some straight answers, you'll never see this room again."

Real terror glinted in Serge's darting look, before a slow blink smothered it.

"Give me a name, Serge, and then you can stay here." Julian's slow smile invited confidence.

Saliva speckled Julian's neck as Serge hissed, "A full pardon. Nothing less, *Principal.*"

Letting go of the councilor's jacket, Julian shook out a handkerchief from his pocket and wiped his hands. Locking eyes with Serge, he shouted, "Sergeant."

He heard the officer's cape rustling in the doorway behind, and keeping Serge pinned in a rigid stare, Julian jerked his head to call the squad leader forward.

"Take the councilor into custody. I don't want him in the morgue, others will know." Julian paused and studied the elaborate gold leaf ceiling rose overhead, and then, as if the answer floated down from above, he shot out commands. "Take him to the hospital chapel. We should still be able to revive the councilor, provided this other… business doesn't take too long."

"What other business?" asked Serge.

One of the Elite Guard gripped the councilor's arm and the other had the comedy moment of trying to secure a hold on the prisoner when faced with an empty jacket sleeve. They marched him towards the door.

"What other business?" Serge called out, straining his head to keep Julian in view as long as possible.

When they were alone, the sergeant asked, "Do you think he'll talk?" He crossed the room and peered around the cluttered study. A worn track in the carpet connected the chair to the desk and then to the door. Serge was a creature of habit.

"I'm sure of it." Julian picked up another photograph of two children. Past lives were a painful part of every vampire, packed away in neat boxes and stored inside their minds. Julian rarely thought of his wife, Eva, and he realized he knew nothing about Serge, the man, at all.

The sergeant left silently and Julian remained in the center of the empty room and grinned.

Hearing the faint exchange of Serge's high-pitched whine and the low calm tone of the sergeant, Julian whipped a sandstorm of dust into the atmosphere and joined the Elite squad of five on the portico outside the front door.

They were in formation and preparing to move out.

Accompanying Serge along the first part of the route, Julian then raised a hand and stopped. Within seconds the sergeant, still wielding the crossbow, stood alongside him.

"You know where you are going?"

"The hospital chapel, by the rear entrance." The tall vampire's face was ironed free of expression, but Julian caught the implied 'of course' tone in his voice.

Drawing to his full height and finding he was still two inches short of his companion, Julian grinned. "This is *not* babysitting duty. Treat Councilor Serge as a high priority prisoner. Once he is in the chapel, dispatch *one* guard to find Charles in the blood dispensary. He'll know what to do."

"Yes, sir," the guard said, his attitude alert and energized, this time.

"Good. Dismissed."

Julian watched the small party move away at the pace of its slowest member, Serge. The term 'hiding in plain sight' popped into his head. The poetry – or stupidity – of detaining Serge in Connor's domain and not telling him would make for an interesting conversation somewhere down the line.

When the street was deserted, Julian reeled around and headed towards the council building. It took him two bounds to clear the stairs. He shoved through the hefty wooden doors, and continued along three hallways until he reached the guardroom. Bowling straight through the outer office, he barged into Gerrard's inner sanctum.

The captain was already on his feet and reaching for a rifle. Everyone was on edge.

Julian held his hands up in mock surrender. "Stand down, Captain, don't shoot."

"Hardly a joking matter, Principal, if I'd shattered your face with a bullet."

"Fair point. I'm here to update you on Serge's location."

Gerrard froze. "I put my best man on duty. Has something happened?"

"No, not at all." Julian grinned. "I met your 'best man' and must congratulate you. He has brains and brawn. It's good to see Sergeant Hugh has a comrade he can count on."

Walking out from behind his desk, Gerrard gestured Julian into a seat. "What is the plan for the councilor?"

"I have put Serge where he can't cause trouble. Charles has been briefed. He'll use a steel coffin shell from the storage facility and work out the muscle relaxant dosage. Serge won't be talking to anyone until we bring him round. He'll have I.V. hydration and if it goes wrong and he dehydrates-" He shrugged. "He's no great loss."

Julian studied the serious, lined face of the sixty-human-year-old captain and put a hand on his shoulder. "We'll find out soon enough if Serge is bluffing, but first, we have a bigger problem out in the estuary. The regent's vessel is a clear and present danger."

"Understood."

Julian suddenly felt tired. "I'm going home. I need a change of clothes, these stink of Serge. See the councilor is settled in, check on the Scandinavian ship, and then report back to me there. I know Connor, Rebekah, Malachi, Osiris-" Julian suddenly laughed, realizing the list was too long to continue. "Hell, all of them, will want an update."

"Very good, sir."

The moment Gerrard disappeared, Julian took off at a speed which blurred his black garb to a shifting trail of smoke.

Within minutes he made the final approach to his Richmond home. He crossed the gravel driveway and stones sprayed up the brick façade as he stopped. Going inside, he washed and changed and, apart from damp hair, soon looked like his usual 'in command' self.

He sat at his Victorian partners' desk and waited. He had traced his fingers around the tooled edge of the leather writing surface a dozen times before the hum of stones rattling outside announced Gerrard's arrival.

He had left the front door open in clear invitation.

When footsteps approached his study, Julian said, "Come."

The captain tidied his windswept hair and stood to attention. "Councilor Serge is safely confined in the hospital chapel, sir. Charles has administered the muscle relaxant."

"Very good. And the regent?"

Captain Gerrard rattled off a brief report. "The regent stayed onboard the vessel. Once the sun is up, there is no shelter on the quayside, but it's only a sprint up the escarpment to the cover of the woods. Daniel and a platoon of Elite Guard are patrolling the trees with orders to kill on sight."

"You seem to have everything in hand. And Daniel will sound the siren if he sees anything suspicious?"

"Yes, sir."

Julian paced the floor, tossing a smooth pebble from one hand to the other. The copper colored stone formed a connection to Leizle. He recalled how beautiful she had looked at the engagement party in her green satin gown. The ache in his gut brought home how much he missed her.

"The ship will be escorted out of the estuary at sunset tomorrow," Julian stated firmly, "just as Regent Birgitta agreed." He circled the room and stopped in front of the captain. "You don't think it all seems a little too good to be true, Gerrard? The regent came all this way to see Seren, and yet she was fobbed off so easily. I don't like it."

The captain's silent frown said more than words.

Dragging a hand over his jaw, Julian said briskly, "Batten down the hatches until she leaves, and then the council will decide what action to take next. There will be other 'visitors' I'm sure."

With a sharp nod, Gerrard left and closed the door behind him.

Julian looked at his watch. *Marius and Alexander should return from checking on the farm settlement soon.* They willingly gave blood, and caring for their comfort was a fair trade. Protecting them from illness and injury remained a high priority.

The air pressure inside the room suddenly increased and Julian felt the fine bones in his inner ear rattle. A vampire approaching this fast was never good news. The study door hummed in its frame and Julian strode across and whipped it open.

Connor appeared in front of him. The glacial white pallor of his face accentuated the bleak look in his eyes. "Julian, something happened."

"What?" Julian fell back a step as Connor barged past. Tracking his friend's movement, Julian said, "What happened?"

Whipping round, his coat flaring and slapping his thighs, Connor dragged clawed hands through his hair and glowered. "I don't know. Maybe nothing. No, not nothing."

"Connor, focus. What the hell are you talking about?"

Unbuttoning his clothes, Connor shrugged out of his coat and shirt in one movement.

Julian's eyebrows climbed to comic proportions and he spluttered at his friend's half naked state.

"I had a dream. No, a damned nightmare." Connor rarely cursed and Julian felt his own worries settle like lead in his stomach.

"I think I've been bitten." Connor twisted around, lifted his arm and blindly tried to locate the marks he'd found.

"Bitten? By who? When?"

"Julian, just listen." Inhaling deeply, Connor began again, slowly. "I didn't go straight home, I stopped off at the hospital to feed and take rap-sleep. I had a dream." Connor rushed on when Julian waved a hand and went to talk. "No, not a dream about Rebekah, about *her*. The regent. I cheated on Rebekah." His voice grated as he forced the words out. "I think she bit me."

"Regent Birgitta bit you? She is onboard her *ship*," Julian insisted.

"Well, the bitch must have a damn twin, then." Connor ground his teeth.

Julian stepped forward and gripped Connor's elbow. Twisting his friend's arm into a contorted angle he peered at the small puncture wounds. They were healed, but dense vampire flesh compressed to fill puncture holes very quickly. Placing a finger over each indent, Julian pressed hard. "Well, there is something there, but whether it's a bite, I can't say. How can it be? She is under guard onboard her vessel."

Hope gleamed in Connor's eyes. "Are you sure? She couldn't have slipped out un-noticed."

Julian shook his head. "Not a chance."

Collecting his shirt, Connor dressed once more, concentrating on refastening the buttons. "Maybe it was a dream. Could I have done this?"

Julian shrugged. "In rap-sleep? Maybe. The bite is within reach, maybe."

They both knew it was a long shot, but it was something to hang onto. "What's that saying? 'Eliminate the impossible, and whatever you're left with is the answer, no matter how improbable'." Julian slapped Connor hard on the shoulder. "Whatever 'bit' you, it wasn't Regent Birgitta. Does that help?"

"It's a relief. It felt so real. She felt so real." Connor remembered his aroused state and rubbed his hand awkwardly over the back of his neck. "It does help, but I still have to tell Rebekah about the dream."

"Why? Nothing happened. Not in the real world."

"Then, why do I feel so damned guilty?"

Julian dropped his chin and shrugged. "Do what you have to, but she'll be hurt. And all for nothing."

"I'll think about it. Thank you, Julian."

"Hell, nearly a hundred years of friendship has to count for something. I just wish I could prove it's all in your head."

Pulling his coat on, Connor headed back out of the door. "Wish me luck. I left a very worried Rebekah back there. I have some serious groveling to do."

Chapter 12

The instant Connor left, Julian went in search of Marius and Alexander. He found them in the jurors' anteroom. Both vampires wore clean clothes and the high color across their cheekbones could be mistaken for the flush of exertion from the run back into the City, but no, they had fed.

Closing the door in silence, Julian drifted across the floor and took a seat in his throne chair. While shuffling his thoughts into priority order, he rapped his diamond hard nails on the surface of the table and added another clouded patch to the scratched varnish.

"What's on your mind?" Marius asked with a wry smile.

"I just had a very strange conversation with Connor, the regent is still in our waters and, I can't be sure, but I think we are looking at an attack. Apart from that, not a thing."

"What do you want to do? In my experience, taking action is always better than waiting." Marius' chin jerked up when the wailing sound of the docklands siren filled the air. "Someone from the ship must have come ashore."

Julian met Marius' coal black stare and felt a moment of relief. *We'll get to the bottom of this shit storm at last.* "You're right. Come with me, we're going to make sure Birgitta is on board her ship. Alexander, you too."

Alexander got up, joined his companions at the door and stopped abruptly.

"What about Councilor Serge?" the young juror asked, with a sudden frown at the extra complication.

"That is the only thing I *can* control, and I have. Serge is neutralized, for now," Julian said, whipping the door open.

Before Alexander could voice his curiosity, Julian added, "Serge's fate can wait, Alexander, *focus*."

If the juror felt the rebuke, he didn't let it show. He followed Julian and Marius, and the three moved along the corridor with less than an arm's length between each rushing figure.

They left the council building in full flight – their arrowhead formation allowing each juror to use the slipstream of their principal. Although their approach was deathly silent, the shrieking siren would have drowned out the noise of a herd of buffalos.

The trio swept around the final corner, emerged from behind a twelve feet tall metal container, and Gerrard and Daniel spun around. Julian stopped just short of the arrow head pointed at his eye socket.

At Gerrard's signal, the siren was shut off, but Julian's ears continued ringing for another thirty seconds.

Daniel grinned, lowering his bow. "You did say shoot first, sir."

"I did indeed, Daniel," said Julian with a wry twist of his mouth. It was the second close encounter in one day, and he was beginning to feel like he had a target on his back.

"The regent's ship has sailed," said Captain Gerrard.

Julian jerked in surprise. "She's left already?"

"Captain Bjorn delivered the news. 'The regent regrets the intrusion', was how he put it," said Gerrard

"Why sound the alarm now?" Julian frowned.

"It was the course they set. If the vessel is going home, they are taking the scenic route. The outpost on the coast reported a westerly heading."

"I see what you mean," Marius said, "something is not right."

Through a narrowed gaze, Julian scanned the rippling surface of the water, where blades of moonlight cut into black silk. Out in the estuary, was the hulking black shape of a super tanker. "Have the nomads come ashore?"

"Yes," said Daniel, "They came in after the Scandinavian vessel had departed."

"They unloaded supplies and most of the crew took off in the trucks. Captain Blake had his guide with him, and he'll be at the hospital collecting the tanker's blood allocation." Gerrard glanced at the position of the moon. "They should be back within the hour."

"That's too long," Julian said quietly. "They will have passed the Scandinavian vessel. I think a chat with Blake is in order. Marius, can you do the honors?"

"As you wish."

"I'll stay out of the way and watch. Blake might recognize me, and we don't want to remind him of past events." When Connor and he had hitched a ride, it ended in violence and Blake came off worst.

The pinball trajectories back and forth across the countryside were beginning to make Julian feel mentally exhausted. Physically though, he displayed the dynamic force of an automaton. The miles from the dockyard to the dispensary at the hospital were traveled by him and Marius in grim silence. Worries over Birgitta's visit felt like being gnawed at by rats.

Both vampires deliberately exuded calm as they pushed through the curtain of jellied-plastic strips hanging in the doorway at the rear of the dispensary hall.

Blake's broad back was unmistakable, even amid the throng of eighty or so queueing vampires, partly because of the empty space surrounding him and his retinue – super tanker nomads were treated like a contagion – and partly because of the unique color and texture of the nomad uniform, coated in a grimy crust of sea salt.

Exchanging a quick glance, Marius and Julian reversed back out and prepared to set their ambush in the quieter corridor which lead back out towards the main exit.

When Blake came into view, beneath the fluorescent strip lights the scarring on his face gleamed with the sliminess of a gray squid pulled from the water. The flare discharged by Connor into Blake's face had hardened his tongue to a coal like lump and the thin skin stretched over the bone of his empty eye sockets had a jaundiced glow. He made no effort to hide his disfigurement.

Julian hung back and Marius stepped out into the path of the troupe of marching nomads. "Captain Blake, if I may have a word?" he asked. "I am Juror Marius of the London Hive."

The captain's guide stayed close. Blake's hand gripped the young vampire's shoulder. As he turned his scalded features toward Marius, the shriveled lips twitched.

"Anything, Juror Marius." The young pale vampire said. He channeled Blake's words, using the psychic connection which, like a current of electricity, tied each member of the nomad tribe together.

"When you entered the Thames estuary, did you see any other ships? An ocean liner, perhaps?"

"Yes. We passed a ship headed west. She was pulling water at top speed. Seemed intent on covering a lot of miles before sunrise. Might even make the coast of Spain, the rate of knots she was going."

"Thank you. That's all I needed to know." Marius inclined his head.

The captain's hideous smile revealed the pool of mucus filling his lower palette. His nasal secretions had nothing left to stop them trickling down into his mouth. The gargling noise he made could have been laughter, Julian was not entirely sure.

The pallid nomad 'mouthpiece' grinned inanely, presumably at a telepathic comment Blake made and Julian found not speaking difficult. Curiosity was like an itch needing to be scratched. He jabbed Marius with an elbow.

"Was there something else you noticed?" Marius said diplomatically.

The nomad guide's grin slid away. "The captain just finds it amusing that you can't police your own waters."

Julian couldn't deny the truth of that.

"These are strange times, I'm sure Captain Blake has noticed the increase in traffic over the last few years. If he could keep us informed, there will be a reward in it for your crew."

Julian signaled to Marius. "You'll get double rations at the dispensary."

"That's very kind. Thank you, Juror."

There was a distinctly wet sound as Blake side-stepped around Marius and they bumped shoulders.

Julian could only imagine what the flesh beneath the sleeve of his coat looked like. As he turned to watch Blake's departure, he felt a thought which was not his own stroke over his brain. Scanning the nomad group filing past, instinctively, he focused on a small figure he had failed to notice. Despite the thick folds of the grimy coat and a cowled hood, Julian knew a female form lurked beneath. He could almost feel her smile deep inside the shadow. *How is Doctor Anthony? My name is Hera.*

Her name solidified inside his head, before Julian drew breath to speak. *Is she reading my thoughts?*

Her nod was barely perceptible. *Yes. It is new, but the captain makes me feed – he treats me like a nomad, now. I think he wants to 'feel' me inside his head because he can no longer see.*

Julian's narrowed eyes darted to the captain's back. He had stopped before the double exit doors as though he was asleep, but still standing. "He's listening." Julian's hard grin bared his teeth. "I'm sorry, this conversation is over."

Hera reached out and grabbed Julian's arm. The muscle twitched as though her hand was a Taser. *Please. He can't hear me unless I want him to.*

Julian frowned. Connor was the science and biology expert. He felt adrift. *Who is she?*

As though his curiosity was all she needed, Hera poured out her thoughts. A dip of her chin confirmed it. *I'm the hybrid onboard the super tanker. I look out for the humans. Anthony was very kind to us, and me. I'm sorry he's in trouble.*

Julian stiffened. "Anthony? You are mistaken."

Hera's grip became tight and she whispered aloud, "Tall, dark vampire with gray eyes. He disfigured Captain Blake."

The facts fitted, and Julian quickly reached the correct conclusion. *He gave a false name. To protect himself and Greg.*

Hera's eyes gleamed with the avalanche of questions, and pain shot through Julian's head as if a strobe light exploded inside it. Grimacing, he shook off her hand and fell back a step.

"Sorry," Hera breathed. "I forgot you are not a telepath." The anxiety in her probing look anchored him to the spot.

His name is Connor. You said 'you're sorry he's in trouble'. How do you know? What trouble do you mean? Julian's own questions were coming thick and fast, now. Even he could not be sure what Connor was going through. Taking a deep breath, he started again, slower.

"What trouble is he in?" Julian asked quietly.

All I know is, the air is alive with static, and I dreamt that Anth- I mean Connor, was dead – really dead. I don't know why I 'see' the doctor so well. Her hands flowed in an eloquent extension of her puzzlement. *But Blake is obsessed with his enemy and each time I feed from him, it feels as though Connor seeps into my brain.* Her shoulders dropped. *His hatred makes his blood taste like copper.*

"You feed from him?" Julian shook his head. "Never mind. Could it just be Blake's fantasy? To see Connor dead?"

Strands of black hair fell forward to frame her face when Hera tilted her head in thought. *That is why I hoped to see him here. To see if it was fantasy or real.*

Julian laughed gently. "We have come full circle." He took a leap of faith. *You're right, Connor is in trouble.*

Blake suddenly started walking and Hera's head jerked around. "He's calling. I must go." She grabbed Julian's arm again, and her lightning-fast stream of thoughts was like the burn of a Laser through his cerebral cortex. *The blonde angel will get inside his head.* She pushed her hood back a little, her copper-brown gaze locked with Julian's and she smiled stiffly. *Yes, much like I am inside yours, now. The gift is benign, it is the user who corrupts it.* She glanced over her shoulder. *I must go. Principal Julian, you are a good man, I think. I hope we will meet again one day.*

The nomads were on the move and Hera whipped along in pursuit. They poured out through the doors in a stream of hard flesh, and both Hera and Blake became lost in the throng.

The moment for answers slipped away, and Julian clamped down the urge to rush after the Spanish hybrid nomad.

The docklands siren began to wail again, a faster tempo indicating the urgency had shifted to 'Code Red', and Julian's options evaporated.

He hadn't needed Hera's warning. He found himself hoping he would one day meet her again, too. *Living with Blake must be a miserable existence.* No matter what, the tanker would be gone within the hour and Hera along with it. Difficulties facing the London hive were of no interest to the nomads – the eerie detachment of the floating community guaranteed their visits remained short and efficient.

Dammit. He swung away and left the hospital, wondering what havoc the regent could wreak. Getting closer to the source of the ear piercing siren, Julian felt as though the vibration would rattle his teeth loose. Only he, Marius, or Alexander had the authority to end the torture, and the expression of relief on Captain Gerrard's face when Julian arrived, at last, was almost comical.

With Julian at his side, a throat cutting gesture from Gerrard told a sergeant poised at the base of the alert tower to hit the button, and silence exploded to fill every space. For a stunned moment, Julian felt as though he had gone deaf.

Seeing Daniel standing to attention, Julian blurted, "Have you seen Connor? He should have responded to the siren."

"No. He hasn't arrived."

"What is the emergency?" Julian scanned the apparently peaceful dock.

"We send tugboats out past the Thames Barrier. They reported back. The Scandinavian liner is anchored off the south coast. She hasn't left British waters.

"Has a patrol gone out for a land based visual?"

"Yes, sir. Sergeant Hugh dispatched four men. They should return soon." As Daniel finished speaking, the avalanche of scree dancing down the steep embankment signaled the arrival of the four guardsmen.

"All clear, Principal. The vessel has gone out to sea"

With a report confirming Birgitta's departure, Julian should feel relieved, but he didn't. Hera's warning began to take on a solid form as penetrating as her presence had been. "Where the hell is Connor?" He turned to Marius.

"I thought he left for 'home' hours ago?"

"He did, but he returned to visit me earlier this evening. It's a Code Red. If he could be here, he would be. I don't like this. I'll have to go to the eco-shelter and make sure he got back."

Chapter 13

When the 'Code Red' siren in the docklands swelled to fill the night air, Connor stopped running as though he hit a glass wall. He swore under his breath. Guilt settled like a heavy cloak on his shoulders when he felt relief. *I will tell Rebekah.* But he greeted the gift of more time to find the right words as a blessing.

He executed a sharp turn and took a few strides along the heading towards the London docklands, but then swung back to go into the City, south of the river. Skimming the buildings, he treated the derelict streets of the London suburbs as a toboggan run, whipping along between the charcoal black façades and onwards towards the open space of the Embankment. The silver moon-washed waters of the River Thames boiled with froth as the wind tore at the surface. The suburbs receded into the distance and the gales whistling across the landscape dragged at Connor's clothes. Like the pull of the moon draws the ocean tides, Connor's path veered west, as though it was the most natural thing in the world.

Even as he asked himself 'where am I going?', a small voice whispered, *you know.*

The scream of the docklands siren was blocked out by a lilting melody. It grew louder inside his head, and what rattled him most was that he had never heard the tune before. *Where is it coming from?* Reluctance gripped at the flesh of his nape and his paced slowed. *I should go home. What am I doing here?*

Connor ignored the rushing scenery in which clusters of derelict buildings grew sparser until the towns became villages and then isolated farms and outbuildings. The landscape shifted from patchwork parcels of fields bordered by decaying fences or overgrown hedgerows, to thickets, scrublands and plains, none of which held his interest. The wide open space called to him, and without realizing it, he rushed up a sudden steep incline of a grass covered chalk-stone bank; the arc of its path to left and right barely registered because the acres inside the circumference of the circle was so huge. He stopped at the top. The climb of over twenty feet left him feeling exhilarated. Gazing out at the crest, his preternatural gaze picked out the opposite side of the sweeping bank, over a thousand feet away. A few lone standing stones reared up from the grass as though reaching to tear down the stars overhead, but they were impressive even in their solitude. He stood beside a twenty-foot sarsen giant and rested his hand on the still warm surface – where it had hungrily drank in the sun's warmth while it could.

Why am I here? Where do you want me to go?

"Look around and you will see," a voice whispered, its crystal tone like a feather stroke over his flesh.

He looked. Below him a deep ditch made the descent just as steep. On the scrubland to the south, beyond a clutch of crumbling buildings, five distant upright stones were scattered like lost children. Gray ribbons of asphalt cut across the rambling arena, but Connor found himself drawn to the raised ground to the north, where the sentinel of stones stood more erect and completed a circle like an open mouth of newly brushed teeth.

He moved slowly down the incline into the moat-like ditch, back up the shallower side, and began walking towards the northern circle. He passed an entrance cut into the bank on his left – it led to a chamber of some kind – but ignored it. Getting closer, and faced with the towering gray irregular form of the nearest standing stone in the circle, he stopped. The earth at its base was dark and freshly turned.

His fast run through the cold night had formed a mask of ice on his skin. When he frowned in confusion it cracked and brittle shards cascaded down his shirt front, and yet heat cramped his neck.

A warning? Fear? Connor pulled at the constriction of his collar, heedless of the buttons that tore off and scattered across the grass.

He kept walking, drawn into the embrace of the large clearing ahead, passing between two of the rough-hewn stones, most were twenty feet tall, and all but four of the twenty-seven giants ranging around him protruded from disturbed soil, as though they had recently erupted through the ground; teeth pushed up from the earth's core.

A wraithlike whisper filled his head, and the words, like a shower of crystal beads, once more took up the lilting song that he had been unable to think past since he had left Julian's house.

He flexed his shoulders, aware of the confinement of frost-stiffened cloth pulled tight across his broad frame. He shed his greatcoat, letting it fall at his heels, and walked blindly forward over a hundred and fifty feet of potholed and rock strewn ground, never deviating from his course, as if a tether pulled him toward the center point. When he stopped a dozen yards from a stone platform of mid-thigh height, covered in layers of fur that ranged from deep brown to silver gray, he was naked.

"I am cold." Surprise drew the words from him. Eddying currents wafting over his flesh set it tingling, and his human memories conjured a label for the feeling.

It's not cold. The answer drifted across his mind like script written in frost.

"But, I'm shivering." He ran his palms over skin which was slick with condensed moisture and his nerve endings prickled with the overwhelming sensation. His body began to shudder. He remembered feeling cold from when he was human. He frowned.

Just breathe.

So, he did, taking large inhalations in a strong movement that dragged gulps of air into his lungs.

Is your heart beating?

"No."

Her laughter trickled through him as a shiver.

But, have you ever felt more alive?

The pupils in his gray eyes dilated, his vampire senses sharpening until even the particles in the air danced around him like a curtain of fireflies. "What do you want from me?" His harsh whisper reverberated from the towering stones ranging around him.

There is no separation between you, your body and the air you breathe. Embrace it.

The cramped feeling at his nape trickled unease down his spine. In a stronger voice he demanded, "What do you want?"

As though he had not spoken, the voice continued on. *Feel. Embrace who you are. Remember the weak and pathetic human form you left behind?*

A blinding light exploded behind Connor's eyes, and when it faded, it was as though he was experiencing his vampire reincarnation anew. The dark night sky was deeper and the diamond dewdrops of the stars brighter. The air was purer. The light of the full moon cloaked the clearing in molten silver, bringing every blade of grass into needle sharp clarity.

Becoming engrossed in the crystallization of his sensations, Connor let his hands hang loosely at his sides, his feet at hip width apart activating the hard muscles that framed his pelvis. The shadows draping his body hinted at his manhood as the muscles of his abdomen rippled with the gentle sway of his shifting weight.

"Why am I here?"

The moonlight slanted across the grass, and the oozing ink black shadows of the standing stones facing him reached across the ground like clawed fingers clamoring to touch the stone altar table.

A movement caught his attention, and his gray eyes glittered with deep seated excitement. "You."

Her pale hair flowed like a river of platinum down over her shoulders, framing the alluring form of the naked high breasts which swayed gently with each graceful step she took. She glided towards him. Her long lithe limbs captured the ethereal glow of moonbeams and glistened with a pearly sheen. The curve of her belly and the whisper of the satin skin of her thighs as she walked drew Connor's gaze down to the swell of her hips and the glimpses of shadow that tantalized with each undulating step she took.

Her feet were bare and a silver pendant resting between her breasts was all that remained of her warrior queen adornments.

Connor stood still, swallowing down the heat that raged up through his chest when Birgitta undulated past, trailing her fingers over his powerful shoulders as she drifted around behind him.

His aroused body twitched. His muscles jerked tight.

Landing a kiss on his tense bicep when she stopped in front of him, her gleaming ice blue gaze lifted to hold his and she traced her finger along his clenched jaw.

Entranced, Connor stared down at her, and his manhood reared as, beyond her beautiful upturned face, the perfect orbs of her breasts filled his sight.

She smiled. "My lord, you can have your heart's desire. Surrender to my Earth Mother, and take your fill." Her palm smoothed over his cheek as she said, "Drink from the pool of your desire until your thirst is slaked. I am yours to take."

Running her fingers down over the trembling muscles of his chest, Birgitta took his hand and, turning away toward the stone plinth, she drew him forward.

The river of her hair mesmerized him as it rippled like silk, cascading down to graze the swell of her hips and the plump flesh of her backside.

When she stopped at the altar, she drew him in close behind and dropped her head back onto his solid chest. Her long lashes framed the pools of her crystal gaze as she lifted his hand and smoothed it over her breast. His male satisfaction was immediate as instinctively, he pulled her back and pressed his hips into the swell of her behind.

Her lips parted as she breathed, "You can't hurt me, my lord. Take me and make me yours."

A small whisper in Connor's head told him to resist and his fingers twitched as he withdrew, cool air filling the space between their bodies as he rocked back on his heels. But she closed the gap, pushing her hips back into his and groaning as she brushed over his velvet excitement. His control crumbled as his thumb played carefully over her nipple, and she arched into his hand.

"I won't break." Covering his hand with hers, she dug his fingertips into her firm breast.

He smoothed his hand down over the feminine swell of her belly, dipping between her thighs until she whimpered. When he stroked up and pressed his fingers into her ribcage, he froze, anticipating her recoil of pain. A growl rumbled in his throat when she reached behind, gripped his buttock and pulled him in hard against her.

His fingers closed over her nipple and Birgitta's sigh urged him on.

He gripped her throat, framing her jaw as he pressed her head back against his shoulder and kissed her, dragging his teeth over her lips. When, with a snarl, he broke the kiss and pushed her forward, she went with him, dropping her hands onto the fur cover of the altar, parting her thighs and urging him on.

Connor growled loudly as he gripped her hips and drove into her. Her body welcomed him, taking him deep inside. He threw his head back, hearing only her moans. The embers burning in his groin drove him on until an explosion of glittering sparks drifted behind his closed eyes and every muscle jerked tight as he took his pleasure.

Leaning forward and covering her, Connor gripped her hair. He lay his teeth on her shoulder as his hand cupped a swaying breast, and he relished the shudder rippling through her when he rolled the hard tip in his fingertips. The heat inside him cooled to ice cold satisfaction.

Her flesh was firm as he grazed his teeth over its surface and her body rippled with her delicate laughter. "Ah, I knew you would be strong, my love."

As, with a sated growl, he slipped from inside her and stood up, she turned to face him and, reaching up to bury her hands in his hair, she pulled him down and kissed his lips.

He frowned as experiencing a lover who gave him warmth, her pounding heart beating in a thundering tide beneath his body, tugged at his memory. Birgitta read the confusion in his clouded gray gaze.

"You have never let go, my lord. Never been all you can be. You have tasted my blood, we are one now."

He touched his lip and his fingers came away bloodied. His eyes ran down over her pure white neck and shoulders where a network of silver-tinted veins sprinkled glitter throughout her skin. "When?" He croaked.

Birgitta smiled. Her firm breasts brushed his tight chest as she turned her shoulder, moved aside her silken hair and revealed a deep bite. Her eyes glowed with pleasure. "As you filled me, you took my blood, the circle is complete."

A sense of betrayal, a feeling that he had reasons to feel bad, was washed away by the clear water abyss of her gaze and suddenly it was simple.

His voice grated over gravel as he gripped her shoulders and pressed Birgitta down onto the bed of furs. He felt her breasts firm beneath his chest as he crushed her beneath his weight. "You are my equal, my queen, but-" His lips hovered over her mouth. "Your body is mine." His kiss was harsh as he forced her to yield.

As she locked her thighs around him and guided his driving stroke, her hooded gaze glittered with calculation. Her nails dug into his hard impervious muscle and she thrilled in the ferocity he unleashed as his throat rumbled with menace. *This one will test me, his heart remembers her, but not for long.*

Chapter 14

For Julian, the journey out of London and across the South Downs of Kent represented a period of time when anything was possible. Similar to the Schrödinger's 'cat thought experiment', where a cat inside a box represented a paradox. Theoretically, the cat was simultaneously alive *and* dead, until the box was opened and you looked inside. That summed up Julian's feelings about Connor's whereabouts. Right now, Connor was both missing *and* at home, until Julian arrived at the eco-town and looked 'inside the box'.

The dimly lit underground tunnels of the human habitat felt narrower and more claustrophobic than he remembered. The walls closed in on him and as much as he tried to see the 'cat alive' outcome, the fear in his gut couldn't agree.

When, at last, Julian achieved a hard fought for air of calm and walked into the meeting hall, he found Rebekah pacing back and forth across the space.

She turned abruptly as he entered. "Have you seen Connor? We heard the siren. What's happening?"

Greg and Seth rushed into the room when they heard Rebekah speaking.

"The Scandinavian Regent has left the Thames estuary. The vessel was due to leave at sunset tomorrow, with an escort. It caused a bit of concern when they broke with protocol. However, it *is* better she has gone."

Rebekah's head jerked and she froze. "She?"

Julian swore inside his head. *Way to go, Connor. Leave me to explain.* "The regent is a female vampire. Yes." *Do I tell them about Hera? That she saw a blonde angel, although I wouldn't call her that. I'm not a complete idiot.* He studied Rebekah and wished Connor would burst in, covered in blood if need be – anything to end this feeling of dread. *Shit, I should have done more. I should have brought him back home myself.*

Rebekah's face stayed disturbingly neutral.

"It doesn't mean anything that she was female." Julian shrugged, but felt like he was falling into the hole he was digging.

"Then, why didn't Connor mention it?" Rebekah asked.

The hole got deeper. "I don't know. But it took us all by surprise."

"Julian, he left here to go and see you. Did he make it?"

He began to wish that someone would throw earth into the hole and bury him. "Connor dropped by, but he had already left to come home before the siren sounded. I guess he didn't make it back."

Greg grunted. "I didn't know he had gone back out."

"Where's Malachi and Seren. Maybe they know where he is?"

It was one of those moments where having a psychic connection was a Godsend. *Surely, they will know something.*

Before Julian had finished speaking, Malachi materialized in the doorway and moved slowly into the meeting hall. The expression on his face silenced the questions on everyone's lips. "Connor is with the warrior queen. Now I have seen her through his eyes-" Malachi blinked slowly, as if wiping away the pictures he spoke of. "I know who she is."

"What do you mean?" asked Julian.

"She is an ancient. Myths and legends have been written of the female ice queen, but she is more than that." The yellow stumps of Malachi's teeth gleamed in the dim light as he grinned. "What do you know of Druids?"

"They were thought to have magic powers. That's about all I know," said Rebekah.

Malachi nodded. "I believe this female, Birgitta, is descended from an Ovate Druid. They can leave their bodies and travel in The Otherworld. It is the path which leads to reincarnation. But she is a vampire, so has died already, but attained an immortal state. She is free now to travel through The Otherworld at will, and return to the shell of her empty body."

Osiris and Seren entered the cavern. "I saw Papa running through the woodlands and fields, and then he reached a henge. Standing stones. I heard singing, but then the vision faded. He is not alone but I can't reach him anymore," Seren blurted.

"Regent Birgitta's ship may have left, and her body may be on board it, but she is still here, or she was," said Malachi.

"Mama, don't worry. We will get Papa back."

"What does this regent look like?" Rebekah addressed the question to Seren. "I know you saw her. You are a terrible liar. Before Papa's vision faded, you saw her."

"I'm sorry. She is beautiful. I felt Papa's will crumbling. She is very strong."

Malachi stepped in and saved Seren from saying the worst. "Connor is under her spell. She has an alluring shell, this is true. But that would not sway him. She has an icy core and if he went with her, he did so against his will."

"What do we do, now, Malachi?" Julian darted an apologetic look at Rebekah. "He came to me because he thought he'd been bitten. And he thought it was Birgitta."

"But how?" Rebekah frowned.

"He took rap-sleep at the hospital. His guard would have been down. But he thought it was a dream." Julian carefully took Rebekah's hand in his. His guilt weighed heavier when he found her fingers stiff and unyielding. "Connor felt like shit. Don't blame *him*, this is her doing."

Julian sensed Leizle's light-footed approach before he saw her, and he felt even worse when happiness swelled unbidden inside him. Sensing the serious mood in the room, Leizle scanned the faces and sought the comfort of Julian's side. Automatically, his arm slipped around her waist. He couldn't resist a glance down into her serious face. Even dressed in combat pants and a thick sweater, she was entrancing.

Rebekah retrieved her hand and wrapped her arms around her middle. "Julian, we have to find him."

Leizle left Julian's side and put an arm around Rebekah's shoulders. "It will be okay," she whispered, "won't it Julian?" Her squeezing embrace tightened when his face remained bleak.

Malachi's pearly opaque gaze settled on Rebekah's face. "If Connor is enchanted, we must move fast. But more than that, we need to find a way to break the spell. My connection with him, and Seren's too, will help to track him, but it will take more than that to get him back. I wonder."

"You wonder what?" Rebekah's throat dried up. She blindly groped for Leizle's hand and gripped her fingers until the younger girl winced.

"He could be lost to us... but his connection to *you* is-" Malachi lifted a thin brow and looked perplexed. "Different. Unique."

"Unique, how?" Rebekah was unfazed, hope glittered in her eyes.

"His vampire detachment fractured when he met you. I can't explain it, but he has no will where you are concerned."

"But, *she* took him, anyway," Rebekah said flatly.

Julian responded, "No, she tricked him, drugged him, as near as damn it."

Malachi nodded. "None of us know. But I see inside him and his mind. Before the regent is a blank slate. She has enchanted him, wiped you from his memory."

"So, he won't just wake up with the good slap I want to give him?" Julian said ruefully.

"No. He has been brainwashed. Well, heart-washed is probably closer to the truth."

"Will time weaken her hold?"

"We don't know if her control is something she has to replenish. As Julian said, a drug. Or a potion. Or a ceremony? We don't know anything, yet." Malachi's inhaled breath crackled through saliva. "But I do believe that Rebekah is the best chance we have. If he sees her, he just might remember."

"If Seren and you can track Connor, Malachi, what are we waiting for? Let's get the survival gear and follow them," said Rebekah. She let go of Leizle's hand when the surge of energy made standing still impossible.

"You'll never get close to Birgitta. She will smell you." Julian frowned.

"Well, turn me, Julian." Rebekah gripped his arm. "Turn me and I can fight her. Perhaps that's why Connor never gave in and turned me. It's fate. You said yourself, new vampires are the strongest."

"And the most stupid," blurted Julian, anger glinting in his green glare. "She is an *ancient*. You don't stand a chance."

"Seren might be able to get close." Malachi was thoughtful. "I believe this is about revenge. For Sentinel Lars, but also against you, Rebekah."

"Me?"

"You stole her man."

"I didn't."

"Yes, Rebekah. You did," Julian said with quiet calm. "He was kinder to you than he needed to be. It seems obvious now, Regent Birgitta was connected to Lars. I agree with Malachi, this is about revenge. Like you did with Connor, you got under his skin, and she would know that."

Rebekah thought back to Lars' threatening advances, but then the undercurrent of kindness cut through the memories and she nodded slowly.

"She would welcome your child as another wound in your heart."

"I'm not letting Seren go anywhere near her. If it's me that is Connor's weakness, then leave Seren out of this."

"I can do this, Mama." She stepped forward from where she had settled beside Osiris in the shadows.

"No, Seren. Papa, if he could think for himself, would not want it." Rebekah shot a stern look at Seren.

"Rebekah, even if we *can* get you into Connor's presence, there is no guarantee of success," said Malachi.

"If Connor fights for Birgitta's army, we will never win him back. He does nothing by half measures, Rebekah. You know him, he would have died for you, and now-" Julian left the rest hanging.

"He will die for her," Rebekah's voice cracked. "If he doesn't recognize me, then I'd rather die."

"I'll think of something," The muscle in Julian's jaw twitched. "I just don't know what, yet."

"I'll try and keep Connor in my sights. He doesn't know I am there inside his head unless I show myself, so we will at least have an idea of where he is." Malachi's discomfort showed as he left the rest unsaid, that he would also know how besotted he was with the warrior queen.

The gathering broke up, like fractured pieces of an iceberg. Leizle left first, then Seren and Osiris drifted away. Greg marched from the room, clearly on his own mission of preparation. Julian realized he had no idea what any of them were thinking, and that rattled him.

When only Malachi, Julian and Rebekah remained, her fears found voice.

"Can Seren see everything that happens to Connor, too? Can you ask her not to?" begged Rebekah.

"Osiris will look after her. He knows how to fill her thoughts with other things," Malachi said on a smile. "Earth Walkers are masters of meditation, and Osiris is an elder of the tribe."

"An elder?" Rebekah was intrigued.

"Of course. He has no human years to measure because he was born a hybrid." Malachi shrugged. "He has been with me for many decades."

Rebekah dragged her hands through her hair and her vitality drained away. "I'm glad, Malachi, that he is here to look after her because I don't know what to do."

"Try and get some sleep." Julian propelled her gently toward the doorway. Leizle will bring you something to eat in an hour or so. You will need your strength for Seren, and for Connor. Don't give up on him just yet."

"Okay." Rebekah left the room and wandered towards the kitchen. *He does not know me as well as Connor, or he would know, I'll never give up.*

Walking into the kitchen cavern, disappointment settled inside her when she saw Oscar.

He wiped the flour from his hands onto his apron and greeted her with a hug.

"Now, lass, these are dark times." After crushing her ribcage, he looked down into her face. "You'll get through this. You and Connor are unbreakable. He will be back before you know it. You mark my words."

Tears filled her eyes as she hugged him back. "I know, Oscar."

"What you need is a nice hot bath. Releasing her, he gripped her shoulders and guided her to a stool at the table. "Sit there and I'll go fill the tub. Back in two ticks."

"A bath sounds good." She dropped obediently down onto the seat and smiled weakly.

Lying to Oscar was hard, and she wanted to blurt out 'sorry', as he disappeared. The curtain to the laundry bathing room obscured him from sight. As soon as she heard the water running, Rebekah leapt from the stool. Crossing to the bank of kitchen drawers, she pulled one silently open and weighed up the selection of knives. *I only need to cut myself, so small is better.*

She picked out a three-inch paring knife, lifted her shirt and pushed it carefully into the belt of her pants. Leaving the kitchen, at the dining cavern entrance she checked the tunnel in both directions. *What I don't need now, is to bump into Leizle... hell, or Greg, Seth.*

Pulling her coat tightly around her body, she made a break for it. Her running feet kept pace with her pounding heartbeat, and she hoped that Julian and Malachi were too occupied to hear it.

The familiar tunnel slipped by, the insect-like buzz of the bulbs in the bulkhead lamps urging her to turn back. *I have to do something, and if Julian won't help me, Anthony will.* Dancing shadows were cast by the naked flames of the torches in the final yards before, ducking out from behind the blackout curtain that marked the point of no return, she was plunged into the pitch-black of no mans' land.

Running her fingers over the grooves carved into the walls, she counted down the steps before a pool of moonlight relieved the strain on her sightless eyes. She still expected Julian's cold hand to grip her shoulder at any moment, even when she finally stood on the threshold of the entrance tunnel and looked out over the black sea of rippling moonlit grass.

She zipped up her black oilskin coat. Pulling on a dark woolen hat she carried in her pocket and crouching low, she darted across the meadow and into the woods. Her flashlight bulb cast barely a glimmer through the dark blue filter fitted over the lens, but it was enough for her to travel a well-trodden path. She still switched it off whenever the moon graced her with its favor.

Anthony was exactly where she hoped he would be, standing guard by the great oak. His face glowing blue in her flash light was a picture of surprise.

"Rebekah. What are you doing out here? Does Julian know?"

"Of course, he knows." Rebekah couldn't meet his gaze. Suddenly feeling warm, she pulled the knitted hat from her head and rammed it into her pocket. "Is it all quiet?"

Anthony frowned, shuffling his feet, clearly uncomfortable with this unusual turn of events. "What do you want, Rebekah? I'm not a fool."

"I'm sorry, of course you're not." She stepped closer and laid her hand on his sleeve. His solid frame shuddered. "I need to be a vampire if I'm going to get Connor back." Rebekah hung her head. "Julian won't turn me."

With a burst of acceleration, Anthony moved away. When Rebekah swiped the windswept hair back from her face, she found herself alone. Anthony's words drifted on the evening breeze. "And neither will I. If Julian doesn't think it's necessary, then listen to him."

"But only I can get through to Connor, Anthony. You know that. You know it has to be me, and how am I to get close to him as a weak human?" Rebekah spoke quietly, as if he was still standing beside her.

Anthony reappeared on the edge of a deep shadow to her left. "Julian and Malachi know what they are talking about. Trust them."

"Trust them? And if they discover they are wrong? Will sorry help, when Connor is lost to us all forever? When he leads the regent's army against us and is killed in battle. Will sorry help me, then?"

His silence was a hopeful sign.

"No, Anthony, I am doing this."

Anthony frowned as doubts gathered in his serious gaze. "If turning you becomes necessary, then Malachi will know when. Just hold off until they say."

Pulling the knife from her belt, Rebekah's eyes narrowed. "If you don't turn me, then I will bleed to death, Anthony. The choice is yours." Turning the knife in towards her body, using a double handed grip, Rebekah accelerated the blade towards her stomach.

The blade screeched as it hit stone hard flesh. Her fingers twisted and burned as the knife was plucked from her hands. "No," she cried out in frustration. Looking up, she saw Anthony was still twenty feet away, and he looked as shocked as she was – the hard surface of a male chest chilling her back registered at the same time as the cold blast of his words.

"Rebekah, please, Connor will kill me if he comes back and you are gone." Julian's voice blended annoyance with despair. He turned her around to face him and glared. "Promise me you won't try this again."

Tears blurred the image of his face as Rebekah swallowed hard and nodded.

"Anthony, have you seen Seren?"

"Seren?" Rebekah swiped the tears away and frowned. "Why?"

Julian's green eyes gleamed in the dim light. "It seems you aren't the only one who refuses to follow instructions. Seren has disappeared."

"Osiris will know where she is." Rebekah felt a surge of anger that she didn't share this connection. The enormity of what she could have done sunk in. *Would I be connected to Anthony forever... be able to read his thoughts as Malachi does Connor's?* The connections were complicated, Rebekah knew. Vampires didn't usually stay in colonies, so no one really knew how the death and connection thing worked. There were many variables.

Rebekah met Anthony's warm brown gaze and read relief. Her glance said it all but she said the words anyway. "I'm sorry."

"No problem, I'd die for Connor, too."

Julian's next words chilled her soul. "Osiris is also missing."

"Damn it, Julian, where are they?"

He shook his head. "All I know is, she is not gone for good."

"How can you be so sure?"

Julian pulled a hand from his pocket. Seren's engagement ring glinted in his palm and the locket Connor gave her dangled from his fingertips. "She wouldn't leave these if she wasn't coming back," he said firmly.

"I agree. But we need to find her."

Rebekah surrendered to Julian's embrace as the woodland became a brown silken tunnel of movement. They skimmed between the tree trunks on a sweeping run, and the walls of the underground tunnels were streaked with the light of torch flames whipping by. When they stopped, as she knew they would be, they were in Malachi's quarters.

On the table a map of Kent and the south coast was laid out. "We would naturally assume they have gone by land out past the Thames Barrier. We would expect them to be rejoining the ship."

Feeling lost, Rebekah said, "They? Which they? Connor and her? Or Seren and Osiris?"

As though Julian and Rebekah had been there all along, Malachi continued talking. "But, I think Connor is heading towards the north coast of Cornwall."

"The vampire safari park is down that way," Rebekah said. The whole peninsular was obstructed by the grid-work of big cat enclosures where vampires went to hunt 'big game'.

"And so is Stonehenge at Salisbury plain. Connor passed along that route."

"So, Seren has taken Connor's images, pinpointed his location, and set off towards Salisbury?" asked Anthony.

"That is my guess, yes," said Malachi. "The connection with Connor is not as clear as it was, and the more Birgitta's enchantment works, the less clear it will be. We must move fast, but I believe they are not yet onboard her ship. We have something to be thankful for."

"Will Connor go willingly? Leave England, I mean?" asked Rebekah.

Malachi's fish scale-sheened eyes blinked slowly. "He spends a lot of time looking at this woman. I'm sorry-" He threw the words in Rebekah's direction. "I believe he will do whatever she says."

"We'll set off for Cornwall, now." Rebekah turned to leave. "Get the horses. Greg can ride shotgun."

Julian caught her arm and bruising blossomed beneath his grip. Rebekah grimaced.

"We'll take a moment to plan. Going off half-cocked is not going to help anyone."

"What is the plan?" Rebekah focused on Malachi's pale shriveled face and waited.

The old vampire said quietly, "We need to track them. The ship had been located by Daniel and Brynmor, but it's left the English Channel. Why didn't they just head south to meet it? While Connor remains here, we need to follow them. What is Birgitta planning? Perhaps she wants the London hive, Seren, maybe Rebekah, too. They can't get that by leaving, so let's see where they go."

"What about Seren and Osiris?" asked Rebekah. "Can't you order her back?"

Malachi tapped his clawed nail on the tabletop. "I can try. But I am not Connor. Osiris may listen to me, we shall see." He closed his eyes and silence descended, broken only by Rebekah's quiet breathing.

Keeping his eyes closed, Malachi began speaking. "They are moving fast. I think Seren has a fix on Connor and she is not giving in."

Osiris, we need to plan, bring her back. Malachi saw his protégé shake his head and his dry lips compressed.

"What's happening?" Rebekah gripped Julian's arm.

"Wait," he said gently.

"Osiris is on her side. He must think they are on the right track. He says, by moving fast, they have a chance of stopping the regent taking Connor onboard the ship."

"They can't risk being seen," said Julian.

Malachi fell silent again and Julian pressed his finger to his lips when Rebekah took a breath to speak.

Rebekah couldn't contain herself. "Can they see him... the *real* him?"

"No," said Malachi. "Just what he is seeing."

"But how do they know where he is?" Rebekah asked.

"Osiris. He recognized standing stones," said Malachi, "but it's not Stonehenge. He explored Wiltshire when I was hunting on Dartmoor. I didn't think much of it at the time."

"Connor's not at Stonehenge?" asked Julian, irritated by his own confusion.

"No." Malachi was impressed despite himself. "There is a lesser known but more spectacular henge north of Stonehenge, Avebury. There were three circles of more than one-hundred and fifty-four standing stones. Something like thirty-six remain. Underground chambers at each of the four cardinal compass points beneath the outer circle would be a perfect hiding place from sunlight. I think Birgitta has resurrected Avebury Henge, either the north or south ring of sarsen stones. While we were focused on her visit to London, her guards were busy on another mission. She planned ahead."

"She might have Connor, but she can't have my daughter, Malachi. You tell Seren to get herself back here, right now." Tears of anger welled in Rebekah's eyes. "If I hadn't distracted Anthony... stupid."

"I'll try and speak to her." The silence as Malachi connected with Seren was torturous.

Rebekah stared at Malachi's blank face and only Julian's cold hand on her arm stopped her from pushing the old vampire again.

"Wait." Julian's low whisper kept her silent.

Malachi's eyes snapped open and resignation clouded his gaze. "They won't come back."

Rebekah ground the heels of her hands into her eye sockets and bellowed with anger. "Seren loves me, I know she does. And she can't do this without me. I'm going after them." Wiping her damp palms over her denim thighs, on a low vehement note she added, "That bitch is not going to have him. He's mine, and I'll die first." Turning to Malachi, she said, "Tell me where they are, and what I have to do to break this spell."

Julian's voice grated with exasperation. "We've been through this. You are human. You can't get near to the regent without being seen and heard." He held up a finger to silence her. "And I don't want any more stunts, okay. You becoming a vampire is not a solution."

Malachi reached out a bony hand and lifted Rebekah's chin. "Julian is right, you becoming a vampire would be a mistake, but not for the reason he says."

A deep frown carved into Julian's forehead.

"Your blood is in Connor's system?"

Rebekah blushed. "He has bitten me, yes."

"No, not bitten." Malachi looked for Julian's confirmation. "The blood transfusion that rehydrated Connor when he was sentenced to death was directly into his vein. He must have been near desiccation, his tissues locking up. It was Rebekah's blood?"

"Yes." Enlightenment dawned for Julian.

"What, Julian, tell me." Rebekah tugged impatiently on his arm.

"Your DNA, residues of it, are locked inside his tissue." Julian looked to Malachi for confirmation.

"I believe the key is to get him to bite you," Malachi said. "Your blood flowing into his brain may act as its own brand of drug. His body will recognize you as himself, like an alcoholic taking a drink. I think you can break through Birgitta's wall... but only if you are still human."

"It may work." Rebekah's eyes shone. "Let's do it." She turned to rush out of the door... and walked into the wall of Julian's chest. His hands closed down on her arms and he held her still until she looked up at him.

"I'm going too," said Julian.

"No. She knows you."

"If Seren goes to her, she'll be expecting *me*. She'll know I will come."

"Exactly, and she'll kill you."

Rebekah's eyes glistened. "What have I got to lose, Julian?"

"Nothing. But I can't lose Connor and you. Leizle would never forgive me."

"Very well. Pack a bag and get your ass into gear. I'm moving out in an hour."

Julian laughed. "I think I'd be the one waiting. But, us being together is not the best plan. You're right, the regent knows me and she'll expect me to do something. We need to try and keep her off balance."

"It's not what we wanted," said Malachi, "but perhaps Seren *is* the best person to follow Connor. She can feed information back to me. Osiris will keep her safe. You know he will die before he lets anything bad happen to her."

Rebekah frowned, reluctant to let hope grow too much. "I guess you're right. But I'm not sitting around and waiting. I'll set off with Greg and head towards Cornwall."

Julian's jaw twitched. "It makes sense."

The glance Malachi and Julian shared was loaded with communication. Rebekah didn't need to be Einstein to know they were humoring her. *I don't really care.* What she did know was that sitting here doing nothing was not an option.

"Although, you and Greg can't go out alone, but I think there is a way to increase your chances," Julian said cryptically.

Chapter 15

Connor lay on his back, his legs entangled in the thick bed of animal furs and his bare chest gleaming with an illusion of sweat. His glazed stare reflected the navy sky. In his peripheral vision, he could see the jagged silhouette of the towering granite stones which shielded them both from the biting wind.

Birgitta smiled. He would lie there with his head empty of thoughts, like a man-shaped side of dead prime-steak, until she stirred. Her draped body fit perfectly into his, with her thigh thrown over his hips. The early morning dew condensed on their cold vampire skin. *It is time to enjoy my conquest.*

She sighed, and ran her fingertips down over the ridged muscles of Connor's torso. They hardened beneath her touch, and she pressed a kiss to his cold skin.

He turned his head to watch streaks of pink bleeding across the heavens, so pale that humans would not yet see them. Diamond chip clusters of stars continued to twinkle, as if they rejoiced in the coming of the sun.

"Dawn comes, my queen." Connor stirred, gripping the animal pelt lying across his thighs and pulling it aside. Rolling towards Birgitta, his hand covered her bare backside and stroked down the smooth firm length of her thigh. Out of habit, he looked for bruises on her perfect white skin.

Her soft laughter fanned an icy breath over his chest. "I told you my lord. We are equals. You can be the warrior you were born to be, with me."

He kissed her shoulder, his tongue tracing a path along the cold glaze of her skin, up her throat, and finally, his kiss found her lips.

She buried her fingers into the coal black strands of his hair and as her tongue plunged into his mouth, she felt his erection stir and press into her belly. Winding her leg around his hip, she ran her nails across his braced shoulders. "Make me yours, Connor."

When he tried to roll back and take her with him, Birgitta would not let him. Parting her thighs, she pulled his solid weigh down on top of her. Wrapping her legs over his bare backside, she lifted her hips and took him inside her in a slow deep stroke.

Connor's lip curled as the sensations burned fire into his groin. Her body undulating beneath his ignited a white hot flame of need. The hard tips of her breasts grazed his chest as he took up her rhythm.

As his hips thrust harder and faster, he muttered, "Sorry, sorry."

Birgitta gripped his hair and pulled hard until his eyes snapped open and he stared down at her. "No regrets." A smile lit up her face and Connor kissed her. Losing control, his pumping movement crushed her beneath him.

There, my lord, rut like the stallion you are. Birgitta knew he had never had this freedom before. She could tell by looking into his face. She also knew, instinctively, that out of necessity he must suffer the passive role with his human woman. Her gasps whispered tantalizingly into his ear as she clung to him. Feeling him tense, she tightened her own body and faked the ultimate moment of pleasure.

When Connor rolled away, spent, his hands staying on her skin and pulling her into his body once more, Birgitta went along with it. Tracing circles over his chest with her diamond hard nails, she calculatingly displayed the signs of a woman in love. *Men are so gullible.*

Lifting her head from his shoulder, she kissed his hard jaw. "We must gather ourselves. Dawn is coming." Birgitta smiled prettily.

He leapt effortlessly to his feet, and his toned muscles flexed in an enticing array of masculinity as he gathered his scattered clothes from the grass. He shook them out and, with a frown of concentration, pulled on black pants, tucked in the shirt, and shoved his arms into his greatcoat, shrugging to settle it over his shoulders.

Birgitta flowed gracefully to her feet, standing as naked as the moment when he first saw her.

"My queen, your charms are for my eyes only."

Striding back to the altar table, Connor picked up a large animal pelt and tore holes into the tanned hide. He held it out until Birgitta slipped her arms in through the holes, and then he draped the fur over her shoulders, wrapping it around to cover her breasts. He passed his own belt around her waist, cinched it tight, and dropped a kiss onto her lips. "There, your modesty is protected."

Her long slender thighs remained bare, but the gesture made her smile.

Mewing softly, she said, "Thank you." Her gaze swept down his body, her lowered lashes casting dark crescents on the perfect white skin of her cheekbones. "We must leave here, but where does my lord want to go?"

Taking her hand, Connor turned northwest. "The beach. It's been such a long time since I've sat on a beach."

Birgitta let him draw her along behind with contrived girlish enthusiasm. Her laughter floated on the breeze as she matched Connor's pace and they covered the miles to the coast in a matter of minutes. *New experiences are good – they take him further from the life he knew. Further from her.*

Standing on the beach, looking out to sea, Birgitta leaned back into Connor's body. She knew by the hum of Morrigan's presence that her ship was just out of sight, across the water. "So, where does my lord want to go?"

Connor chuckled, turning her to face him and slipping an arm around her waist. Dipping his face, he dragged his teeth over her lips. "Anywhere? Let's set sail and just see where it takes us." He dropped his head back and closed his eyes. His fingers trailing up and down her spine let Birgitta know he was thinking.

"I have never visited England. I'm sure there are many things you could show me." Her tone was idle.

"You want to stay in England?" Connor's gray gaze sought her face, but his expression was one of mere idle curiosity.

Birgitta shrugged. "We can go anywhere. It is the beauty of having an army of vampires at my command. I can build us a castle on an island, if you wish it." *Will he take the bait?*

"Castle on an island?" Connor's head jerked around and he spoke faster. "If you like castles, I know where there is one going begging."

Birgitta enjoyed his sudden enthusiasm.

"Well, my love." Her smile was indulgent, the mask slipping for a moment as calculation swept across her face. She reached up and ran her nails down his chest from his shoulders, shredding his shirt and greatcoat against the hard surface of his body.

Connor jerked back, fighting a moment of anger as she stepped closer, crushing his lips with hers, and gripping his hair until the anger flared into passion.

He shrugged out of his tattered greatcoat. The newly fashioned fur dress of Birgitta's joined it on the ground and he lifted her up into his arms. Striding into the surf, he carried her out to where the waves lapped against a landslide of rocks and laid her back onto the shelf of fractured stone. With Birgitta urging him on, rearing up to press her breasts against his chest and kiss him, he made love to her. Bracing his hands over her prone body, his clawed fingers tore lumps from the rocks, grinding them to gravel in his moment of release.

Back on dry land, Connor rested against a tree trunk, safely concealed in the shadows as the sun rose over the hazy line of the horizon and set fire to the sea, as if its surface was burning oil. The fiery glow slowly became an orb as the sun rose. The distant ship floating like a black berg on the glittering orange sea interrupted the perfect symmetry of the sunrise.

Birgitta sat beside him, her hand resting on the soaked fabric of his drenched pants.

"You know." Connor's grin was feral. "I always fancied living in a castle like Count Dracula."

Birgitta played along for a moment. "Transylvania?" Her sarcasm drifted just below the surface.

"The next best thing, Saint Michael's Mount. And, better yet, three hundred square miles of lions and tigers stand in our way. We'll wait until sunset, and hunt in the Exmoor safari park region on the way." Connor gave a dismissive wave to the vessel out at sea. "You will see far more of England travelling with me, on foot."

Birgitta's laughter tinkled like splintered glass. "You are not as I imagined an English gentleman would be."

He gripped her hand, pulled her to her feet and, threading his fingers into the tangled mass of her long blonde hair, he yanked her chin up. "I'm no gentlemen. You are my warrior queen, but not here, in my arms. Here, I am the warrior."

Birgitta's crystal gaze glittered. "Come, show me this land you call England. I am falling under its spell."

"As I am falling under yours," Connor said as he kissed her.

Her narrowed eyes delved into the flint depths of his and, as he turned away, dragging her along behind him, a triumphant smile emerged. *He has no notion that I have all the control.* Her fingertips stroked the pendant suspended around her neck. It was her insurance, in case his will became strong enough to fight her. *I shall enjoy this one more than the others.*

Chapter 16

Marius and Julian walked through the moonlit woodlands at a deceptively casual pace. The humans in the eco shelter were all asleep, even Rebekah, for which Julian was thankful. *The only time I know she'll stay out of trouble is when she's asleep.* Oscar was on guard duty, and if Rebekah woke up, then he would stick to her like glue.

The pair of vampires reached an isolated glade. Julian crossed to a felled tree trunk and planted his boot on the rough bark. Marius stood silently and waited.

"We have a problem, Marius."

The juror's black gaze gleamed with humor. "When have we not had a problem? Since Connor met Rebekah life has been eventful." The flat tone could have been insulting, but Julian knew Marius enjoyed the relief from centuries of boredom.

Julian chuckled. "The bad news is, Seren is her mother's daughter. She and Osiris have left on their own quest to find Connor."

"Malachi can order them back, surely."

"We tried that. But in the end, they have forced our hand and perhaps that is for the best. What we needed was information, and now we have it." Julian straightened and turned to look at Marius. "Connor has not left England. That is good news. The signs are that Birgitta is in no hurry to set sail with Connor as her consort. We need to get Rebekah and him together before Birgitta changes her mind."

Marius' brows rose. "Why is that important?" He knew Julian would have an answer.

"Malachi is sure that Rebekah is the key. If we get her near enough, she can break this hold Birgitta has over him. The regent will be expecting some reaction from the council. To do nothing will look suspicious." Julian shrugged. "We need a show of force."

"You want to launch an attack?" Marius' body language told Julian he was ready.

"As soon as we know where they have gone to ground, I need to make a show of going to Regent Birgitta, all flags flying, demand to talk terms and negotiate Connor's release, or at least pretend to," said Julian. "I am the principal, no one else can do that."

"What do you need of me?" asked Marius.

"I need you to get your hands dirty. Keep Rebekah under the radar, but get her close to Connor somehow, anyway you can."

"Let me play Devil's advocate, for a moment. If Regent Birgitta has what she came for, is it wise to make such a powerful enemy?" Marius' black eyes turned ash gray as he answered his own question. "Of course, she has taken the only vampire who can provide the answers to the survival of our hive."

Julian quirked a brow. "And for love... perhaps. Friendship. Standing shoulder to shoulder against evil."

He gave Julian a sour look. "I have avoided the 'touchy feely' stuff for hundreds of years. It gets you nowhere, in my experience."

Julian's interest was piqued. "In your experience? Do tell."

Marius retreated behind the black curtain of his stare. "Let's keep this simple. Our hive cannot afford to lose Doctor Connor, correct?"

"Correct," replied Julian, formally backing up a step.

"But there is more. You don't think Connor will be enough. You think she wants the hive."

"Connor was selected for a personal reason, and this is about revenge."

"Why would you think that?"

Julian's white teeth glinted in the dim light. "She is Scandinavian. Sentinel Lars was her betrothed. Malachi discovered the link when he 'made contact' with Connor."

Marius looked as though Julian had slapped him. "Why didn't Connor think of that when he met her?"

Julian thought back to his first encounter with the regent, and the sensation of surrendering his thoughts as though they were being drawn from his mind. *She mesmerized me, like an Indian snake charmer.* "And you could ask 'why didn't I think of it?'."

"You are both too close to the problem, perhaps," said Marius.

"It is of little consequence now. Will you look after Rebekah when the time comes?"

Marius nodded. "Of course."

"Let's get back to the council building. Once we have a bearing on where they plan to meet up with her ship," – It was inconceivable that the final aim would be anything else – "I'll use Lars' vessel in the confrontation. Perhaps it will rattle Birgitta and make her do something rash."

Chapter 17

Connor gazed out over the rough meadows where lumps of weather-stained rock broke through the dark soil like decaying teeth. The perimeter fence of the vampire safari park ranged across the land as far as the eye could see, from one coast to the other.

"We transformed the heathland of Exmoor, Dartmoor, and the land in-between when we chose this location." Connor pointed out the craggy outcrops of granite which broke through the forested areas like pale gray tips of icebergs. Taller trees reached for the sky, some dotted around and others grouped together, standing to attention like soldiers on parade. Scrubland plains filled in all the spaces. "We varied the terrain to challenge and occupy the big cats. It keeps them sharp, and-" Connor bared his teeth as he grinned. "It guarantees us more satisfying sport."

A dead rabbit dangled from Connor's right hand, the still warm body brushing his thigh as he spoke. "They 'mark us' when we are hunting. I always chose the 'Red Zone' where the biggest lions are kept. This-" He lifted the rabbit up to where Birgitta could appreciate it. "-is our ticket to blending in once we are inside."

They planned to avoid hunting near other vampires, who would all be wearing the supple loincloth and bare chest of the hunting park uniform, but they didn't want to stand out like sore thumbs.

Dropping the carcass into the grass, Connor stripped the torn remains of his shirt from his shoulders. Frowning, he looked around. "Where is my coat?" His gray eyes reflected confusion. A faraway look drifted across his face as he chased a feeling, a memory. His fists curled as his frustration grew.

"How is a dead rabbit our ticket?" Birgitta called him back.

He visibly shrugged away the search for his coat, becoming absorbed in holding out and inspecting the tattered cotton shirt.

Connor set to work, tearing the fabric into wide ribbons. Stepping closer, he said, "Come here. Raise your arms." He wrapped the widest of the torn strips around Birgitta, and wound it twice around her ribcage to cover her breasts before knotting the ends over one shoulder, and leaving the other uncovered. Dropping to his knee, he tied a strip of material around Birgitta's waist and the fur pelt, torn in half, became her short skirt.

Regaining his feet, he towered over her, wearing nothing above the waist.

The regent and consort had scaled trees, rested in each other's arms, and made love in the bracken and on grit covered damp ground. His chest was streaked with dirt; the evidence of the bursts of activity that had filled their night in the woods would add to the hunting illusion, if he was seen from a distance.

"I don't want you baring your chest," he growled, a playful feral sneer on his face. As lust swelled his groin, his growl became frustration and his laughter was harsh. "How could I confuse the neediness of Rebekah with this? His arm encircled Birgitta's waist as he yanked her in hard against the stone wall of his torso. Her smile held conceit as she watched the cloud of doubt rush across his eyes. "You can't break me, Connor. Do your worst."

His grin was maniacal in its pleasure as he crushed her lips beneath his. "Let's hunt, but first."

Bending to scoop up the dead rabbit, he tore open the pelt like a child eagerly stripping paper from a present. With a sharp thumbnail, he sliced the small body open. Dipping his hand into the cavity, he scooped out the swelling pool of blood, and smeared it over Birgitta's naked shoulder blade. "The wardens use paint, but red is red, hmm?"

Reaching over his shoulder, he wiped his hand over his own flesh. "We'll pass muster, from a distance."

They set off at a crouched run across the scrubland, keeping low. Connor scanned the ground up ahead as he ran, until, finding what he needed he dropped to his knees. Digging out the earth from around a boulder of granite, he loosened the rock, lifted it into his chest as if it was a rugby ball, and kept on running.

The twenty foot tall fence was still only a smear across the landscape when Connor gave Birgitta the signal to veer right. With a sharp turn, she peeled away and headed towards where the earth fell away in a sheer rock-face and the surf crashed against the base of the cliffs.

Connor executed a less acute angle, and launched the boulder diagonally to his left. It rose high in the night-sky, whistling as it whipped through the air. Like a shot putter, Connor froze, tracking his missile as it picked up speed and soared. It hit the top of a natural arc and then hurtled downward in a rapidly decaying curve.

The harsh screech of tearing metal as the stone clipped the boundary and tore a bite from the razor straight top edge, was the sign he was looking for. It was never the plan to punch a hole in the metal fabric and risk the animal stock escaping, but the shockwave of the direct hit rippled along the surface of the tightly-knitted wire mesh.

Connor heard the rustling swish of vampires hurtling away along the fence line before he picked out their flapping black silhouettes.

Making a sharp angled turn, he caught up with and overtook Birgitta. Signaling that she should follow, and fast. Leaping from the ground, he gripped the metal fence and scaled it in a powerful pumping crawl. The vibrations from his boulder strike were still twitching along the tightly strung wire as he straddled the top and reached down to pull Birgitta up behind him. He caught her hand as she jumped, swung her up and over his shoulder, and she landed lightly in the lush grass inside the perimeter.

Sparks lit up the night sky as the vampire game wardens welded a new section of wire mesh over the jagged tear the granite missile had punched through it.

Connor knew the next step would be to run along the fence line and look for intruders.

The fortified boundary was primarily for keeping the big jungle cats inside. It was rare, but every now and then a vampire in rap-sleep would burst through it. It was common knowledge to London hive members that the guards were armed with muscle relaxant in both darts and bovine syringes.

It was a compelling deterrent, usually.

Connor speculated, for a nanosecond, on why Birgitta made him feel exhilarated, reckless. He shook his head as he swung a leg over and dismounted the fence.

Rushing forward in a crouched run, while the white-hot sparks spat out by the welder were still darting into the sky two miles away, Birgitta and Connor made it to the inner perimeter.

"This one is electrocuted," he muttered. Cradling his hands and bracing them on his thigh, he nodded. Birgitta planted her foot on his interlocked fingers and he boosted her up as she launched herself into the air.

She bounced gracefully on landing, like a gymnast, and then peered back through the fence, clearly wondering what Connor would do. He grinned. Disappearing into the darkness, he returned moments later with a sturdy sapling. Stripped of its branches it became a flexible pole.

With a short burst of acceleration, he rammed the end of the pole into a pothole. His hefty weight bent the wooden fibers into a bow before he swung, feet first, up into the air. The sapling sprang back, uncoiling and propelling him higher. The sound of splintering wood crackled through the night as he twisted overhead, pushed the sapling away and cleared the fence.

Landing on his shoulder and rolling to his feet, he grabbed Birgitta's hand and sprinted for the thick canopy of cultivated woodland.

Stopping inside the cover of deep shadow, Connor listened to the activity of wardens shuffling along the outer fence. "They won't waste too much time looking. The damage could be a failed attempt. It wasn't a man-sized hole punched through it. They have the animals secured, and that is all that matters."

Turning away, he tugged on Birgitta's hand and gestured for her to choose her own path. The small wooded areas gave way to scrubland with long grass and waist high shrubs. Outcrops of rock rose to thirty feet in places. In daylight, big cats often used them to bask in the sun, but at night, for vampires, they became lookout posts, used to identify the strongest most challenging prey.

Standing still for a moment, Connor honed in on a cluster of heartbeats. Two were beating faster. Connor put up two fingers and mouthed the word 'cubs'. The jabbed thumbs down signal told Birgitta they were not fair game.

The pair of stalking vampires made their way over the moonlit pasture, and the rumbling breathing of a pair of lionesses grew louder. The stench of rotting flesh filled the air and Connor froze. He watched with fascination when the nearest animal swung its head from left to right and the twin glow of reflective cat's eyes swept by like passing searchlights. Its mouth hung open, testing the air for danger. Another tawny mass beside her also radiated the hum of nervous energy.

Saliva pooled in Connor's throat.

Both feline thudding heartbeats were amplified by ribcages which bellowed with agitation. Sensing danger, their rumbling breath huffed through velvet nostrils and both sets of reflective eyes winked in the dark. The undergrowth rustled as they moved restlessly.

Choosing his prey, Connor tuned into the creaking sound of tendons tightening as the animal prepared to flee. Timing was everything. He crouched, ready to unleash a deadly burst of movement. The cat's vocal chords vibrated as it inhaled, the primed muscles in its haunches uncoiled and the huge front paws left the ground.

Connor appreciated the balletic grace of the cat even as he launched himself forward. The two collided in midair. Connor clamped his arms around his prey's extended, exposed ribcage and, turning his head, he shoved his face into the lion's neck. Burrowing in deep, he bit through the fur, into the skin, and a rush of hot blood spurted into the back of his throat as he tore into sinews and tendons. Closing his jaws and anchoring his teeth into the flesh, he enjoyed the thick warm tide pouring down inside his thorax, and filling his lungs and stomach.

He hit the ground on his side, holding the limp cat tightly against his chest. The weight of the animal pressed down on top of him as he savored the dying heartbeat and the gush of blood slowed to a trickle. Lying beneath the carcass, Connor relished the intoxicating buzz of being fully hydrated, feeling it fizz like a lit fuse racing along each capillary. Finally, rolling the dead feline away, he leapt to his feet.

He listened, and then looked around for Birgitta. She walked into the moonlight. The exposed porcelain skin of her shoulders and stomach gleamed, and despite the glitter of exhilaration in her gaze, it was clear she had not fed. But, nonetheless, she was enjoying herself.

She headed towards Connor, easing into a loping walk that accentuated her lithe limbs.

Suddenly, a cougar broke cover. Its heartbeat accelerated fast, the cat's jaw hung open as it leapt effortlessly to shoulder height. The feline barreled past, heading for the safety of the forest and, in a knee jerk reaction, Connor broke into a powerful run.

Birgitta caught Connor's gaze and said quietly, "No."

He dug in his heels, stopping like a train hitting the buffers. He froze and the tension dissolved as if his muscles were wax melting in the sun. His slack hands hung at his sides and for a moment, staring at the shuffling undergrowth where the cougar had made its escape, he appeared lost.

Birgitta running her fingertips across his shoulder blades reanimated him. "Come." Climbing with ease up the steep slope to the top of a granite tor, she looked down and beckoned.

He scaled the glacier smooth rock face closest to him, hunkered down beside her, and gazed out across the terrain.

"You should feed, my love," said Connor.

"Oh, I will. But I'll choose which animal. All in good time. Wait."

Obediently, Connor embodied the stillness of an alabaster statue. His gray eyes stared into the mid-distance as if he fell asleep without closing them. The minutes slipped past and neither vampire moved until Birgitta lifted her head and scented the air.

The trees beyond shuffled as a large cat passed through the undergrowth with stealth and cunning. It stalked a smaller prey. A badger, a rabbit, or a fox, it didn't matter which. The lure of movement and warm blood were all that registered.

Rising to her bare feet in a fluid movement, Birgitta watched the graceful animal. Its haunches tensed as the cat dropped closer to the ground. The odor of crushed grass and broken leaf stems clung to the thick tawny coat as its belly grazed the gritty earth and its head became still. The shoulders rocked as it prepared to pounce.

Connor stood up, too, sensing that this was the moment Birgitta waited for.

As the cougar's leap closed the distance between the majestic cat and the large russet-red fox which darted between bushes, Birgitta stepped off the edge of the plateau of rock. She landed silently and held out a hand, palm facing forward, as if demanding that the cougar 'halt'. The feline's gaze glittered as it registered the female figure with a white face and fierce expression. Unleashing an anguished growl, as if a lightning bolt impaled it through the chest, the cat fell to the ground.

Mimicking Birgitta's descent, Connor landed on the dry earth at the base of the granite tor. "That, my love, is cheating." He smothered his disappointment. "The fun is in the chase."

Birgitta smiled, artfully biting her ruby lip with ice white teeth. "But, if I want to feed, why waste my energy grappling with prey, when I have other things that excite me more."

Tendrils of confusion clouded his thinking, and Connor felt as though a deeper meaning slipped through his fingers, somehow. Just as the hard glitter in her eyes registered, they melted to hypnotic limpid pools.

"A useful strategy," Connor said. "When fighting a *vampire* enemy."

His blank expression rippled amusement through Birgitta. "It stops a beating heart, dead. But vampires are impervious. You are safe, my lord." She stroked her nails down over his hard jaw, looking up into his dull gray stare. "I cannot harm you."

Birgitta dropped to her knees beside the warm carcass, and stabbed the sharp edge of a thimble she had slipped over her thumb into the animal's neck – the metal blade glinted before it punctured the cat's flesh. A ruby stain oozed into the fur before she lifted the dead cat in an embrace like a long lost lover. The heavy feline head flopped back, exposing the oozing cut in its throat, and Birgitta drank her fill.

Rising once more, she stopped in front of her new consort and, as if he was cattle she owned, her sharpened gaze ran over his virile frame.

"What a pair we make, my lord. No one can stand in our way."

A ripple of unease rattled through Connor, but then she kissed him.

"Come, we have the rest of this safari park to travel across, and when we reach the other side? What then?"

Connor's planned adventure focused his thoughts once more and obscured the feeling of doubt. "Yes, I have a castle to show you."

Chapter 18

Side by side, Osiris and Seren entered the circle of granite standing stones. The pearly glaze of early dawn transformed the weather worn rock into shields of dull metal. Although the enclosure created a wide open arena, the atmosphere within their silent embrace felt eerie.

Seren knelt down and delved into the band of black soil around the base of the nearest stone sentinel. Punching into the earth easily made a hole that swallowed her hand up past her wrist. Pent up energy radiated from her slight form, and Osiris waited, wishing he could ease her fears.

Resting back on her haunches and brushing the soil from her hand, Seren said quietly, "Most of the stones are new. This is the site she lured him to. Malachi was right. The regent made it into a shrine." Seren inhaled deeply, her vocal chords grating. "She sees this as a triumph. I think she came here for Papa. It was never about me."

Osiris studied her stiff profile as she rose to her feet.

"We'll know for sure when we find him," he said.

Scanning the rambling meadow of the grassland enclosure inevitably brought their attention to the distant stone altar, and the tumbled mass of furs covering it were hard to ignore.

Seren spared the spot a cursory glance as she strode past. Osiris reached out and encircled her wrist, pulling her gently back towards him. He held her trapped in his embrace until she finally looked up into his beautiful face and met his probing gaze, framed by long lashes.

The black silk of his hair fell forward in a curtain as he ran a fingertip down over her cheek. "Seren-"

She reached up and hooked a silky strand of hair behind his ear. The moonlight cast shadows and carved his features in the palest marble-toned flesh. "It's okay, Osiris. I'm okay, really. Papa is not himself. I do understand that." Standing on tip toes, Seren kissed him.

He smiled, but troubled thoughts gleamed in the deep black pools of his gaze. He released her, took her hand in his, and said, "Just remember, nothing we find is real."

In silence, they finished their inspection of the site. Walking the perimeter outside the stones brought the next clue.

With a sudden frown, Osiris dropped to a crouch and played the moonlight over the dew soaked meadow. "The grass heading northwest is flattened. What is the last vision you have from Connor?"

"The sea. A beach. I think it's real and not a stored memory, but things are more muddled now."

Breaking into an easy jog and towing Seren along with him, Osiris said, "We'll head to the coast. Perhaps you'll recognize a milestone when you see it."

The meadows gave way to weather eroded bedrock, with moss cowering from the wind on the sheltered surfaces. The boulders embedded into the earth acted as perfect stepping stones for Osiris and Seren to bounce lightly from one to another until they transitioned into smaller rocks. The ocean glittered in the rising sun and both Osiris and Seren pulled their supple leather cloaks closer, throwing a flap over one shoulder. They were hybrids – not so vulnerable to dehydration as a vampire, but not human either. Respect for the sun was a safer course to take. They stopped when the rough ground ended in a landslide of rocks which became pebbles and, finally, at the bottom, silt.

With the sure step of mountain goats, the pair wound a rapid path down the cliff face.

The sea wind tore at their clothes and transformed Seren's black hair into a nest of writhing snakes until she covered it beneath a hood.

Shallow craters dug into the sand made it obvious that Connor and Birgitta had spent time lying out on the beach.

Her pinched features told Osiris that Seren refused to think any further than that.

Surveying the scene, Osiris noticed the trail of disturbed sand between the scooped out area marking the place Connor and the regent had rested and the distant crashing waves trying to claw their way up the shoreline. Tension knotted his gut. *Did they board a ship, or just go walking in the surf?*

Deep pitted holes which could only be the heavy tread of vampires also led along the beach. The tracks disappeared into the sea at the base of a landslide of jagged boulders which blocked the path when the tide was in.

Leaping up onto the fractured rocks, Osiris crossed the craggy platform and felt relief when he saw the same heavily planted footprints left the water. The tracks of two vampires meandered further up the beach until, at the escarpment of the cliff face, they disappeared. Craters dug into the wall of rock suggested Connor and Birgitta had scaled the cliff to the landscape above.

Returning over the boulders, Osiris faced Seren's curious, hopeful expression.

"We know they were both here. And even better, we know they were alone and did not board a ship," he said gently. "Their tracks lead back inland."

Seren smiled. "You are right. That is good news."

Osiris looked at the rocks, preparing to drop down onto the sand again, when he noticed a piece of clothing sunken into a crevice. He pulled at the sand encrusted fabric stuck between two boulders and lifted it up. The sodden garment hung shapeless from his hand, but Seren recognized it immediately.

"Papa's greatcoat. He would never leave it behind. It meant too much to him. Do you think he left it deliberately? A sign that he's playing along?" Seren's eyes lit up at the prospect.

Osiris waited until the fervor on her face faded. "I'm sorry Seren. He would have left it in plain sight, if that were the case."

"No. That would be too obvious." Seren lifted her chin to a determined angle, the wind snatched her hood away and, before her hair covered her face, Osiris saw tears glittering in her eyes.

He tilted his head and considered the idea. "We are closer than we were. Can you hear him? See what he is thinking?"

Seren turned into the wind and her hair streamed in black wings back over her shoulders as she gazed out at the rolling sea.

Moments later, her shoulders slumped, desolation written in every line of her body. Finally, her voice cracked when she replied, "He is fading from my mind, Osiris. I can feel him, but his vision is clouded with... her."

"I know." Osiris landed softly on the sand beside Seren and took her hand. "But it is not real. It is just his empty shell. He loves your mother. You know this."

"But why doesn't he know it? How can he forget us?"

"He hasn't forgotten."

"This coat-" Seren dragged it from his grasp and hugged it, squeezing until the salt water streamed down over her combat pants. "He would never part with this. Not if he was in his right mind. I know that."

Seren walked back up the beach, clambered nimbly up the rocks to sit down on a ledge near the top of the cliff, and looked out to sea.

Osiris settled beside her, put his strong arm around her and pulled her close until she rested her head on his shoulder. "He went west."

Seren nodded. "Yes. And he is exhilarated. I think he has been hunting."

"The safari park." Easing the coat from her fingers, Osiris flared it out on the rocks beside him to dry out. "We can't follow, yet. There is no point until we know he is not just going to hunt and return here. Why don't you sleep, my love?"

Human sleep was calling, like a black cloud rumbling in from the horizon, and Seren would have no choice. She had not slept for nine days – the longest period she had ever endured.

Osiris sensed the wave of relaxation arrive when her body slackened beside him. He scooped her up, carried her over the last few feet to the cliff top, and lowered himself into the embrace of a meandering tree root. It creaked as his solid frame forced it to mold to his shape as he rested back against the tree trunk.

Settling the sleeping Seren into his chest, he listened to the whisper of her breathing, which was disconcertingly slow. He was a hybrid, too, but, he had escaped the need for human sleep. The

Wenuty Priest made sure the ceremonies of his tribe were carried out at their precise times, but it had taken him a while to realize that, of all those around him, only he and Malachi did not sleep. When he asked his father, Imhotep, why, he received the enigmatic suggestion that he should talk to Malachi. The elderly mentor had always been part of his life – he thought of Malachi as a father, too. And so it was, that as a broad chested man-child of seventeen, he learned of Malachi's true role in his life.

When Osiris' mother died at the hands of vampires, only Malachi's quick thinking in delivering him from her dead body had saved his human life from the preternatural feeding frenzy in the sacrificial chamber. Malachi believed that when he cut the umbilical cord, the vampire transformation of the infant was interrupted, and becoming a hybrid was the end result – Osiris was unique, or so Malachi believed, until he met Seren.

Seren snuggled into his chest with her hand resting on his thigh, and his mind turned to love. *We are engaged, and soon she will be mine to cherish. I hope her father will be there to see her happy.* He looked up at the sky, his keen eye drawn instantly to the last remaining visible star and, before dawn chased it away, he made a wish. *Keep her safe, and let her come through this with her heart whole.*

Malachi's voice drifted through his mind and he resolutely shut him out. His plea to return home was not one he could obey, and part of him felt guilty. He did, however, send him a message in return. *Connor has gone west, and we will follow the coastline in pursuit when Seren wakes up.*

Malachi's response was immediate. *Do not be hasty, Osiris. Rebekah and Greg will be leaving soon. Wait for them... please.*

Resolutely, Osiris sank into meditation and tuned Malachi out. He would not make a promise that he could not keep, and Seren's wishes would be his guide.

The feline heartbeats on the distant safari park were like listening to the swells of the ocean in a seashell. The rhythmic thrumming marked the passing of the hours as Osiris realized his hope that Connor would hunt and return was an empty one. *Doctor Connor is not coming back. When Seren wakes, we go on.*

She slept until the bright blue sky was tinged with the lemon-tones of a mellow late afternoon, but waking her any earlier would have been impossible. Osiris smiled. Sleeping like the dead was literal, in Seren's case.

Her eyes snapped open to full alertness and she said, "Is it still morning? I'm sorry, I didn't mean to sleep so long."

"As though you have any control." Osiris laughed softly. "It is late afternoon, and Connor did not come back."

Seren untangled her long limbs from his and stood up, stretching the remnants of sleep from her body.

Drawn by the enticing arch of her feline stretch, Osiris rose behind her, slipped his hands around her waist and kissed her neck.

"Mmmm. Good morning, anyway, Osiris," she husked, letting her head drop back onto his shoulder and her hands drift down to caress his hard thighs.

His fingertips found their way beneath her shirt and brushed over her bare midriff, his voice rough as he said, "We have to find your Papa. The wedding must be soon." Desire tightened his face as she turned in his embrace and he captured her lips, the black silk curtain of his hair brushing over her skin.

She took his face in her hands and kissed him. "Waiting is hell for me, too."

A lopsided grin melted the ferocity from his face, although his obsidian gaze still glittered and his chest pounded with the quickening of his usually slow steady heartbeat. "I know. It is what keeps you safe from me."

Seren laid her hand on his chest, feeling the vibration that matched the slumberous hybrid rhythm of her own heart and shook her head ruefully. "Papa suffers so much. To be with Mama and not hurt her. At least, we are the same. It will be wonderful, my love."

Osiris growled gently. "Which brings me back to where we were. Let's find your Papa." He stepped back reluctantly and eased the gold armlet from his bulging bicep, pushing it downward and exposing the bamboo feeding tube buried in his main artery.

Renewing the wax plug, he ripped a strip of cotton from the hem of his linen skirt, exposing an expanse of hard thigh, wrapped it around his arm and pressed the deep metal cuff back into place. "Cats have a great sense of smell. I don't want to cause a stir and have the game wardens investigating."

He hung Connor's dried out greatcoat over a branch, sheltered by the thick foliage. He'll need this when he gets back," Osiris said resolutely.

"Wait," Seren's gray eyes faded to ice as she tuned into Connor's sudden exhilaration. She gripped Osiris' arm. Puzzled, she said, "Is there a castle near here? They are still going west, to a castle, on a rock."

Tearing a rough square foot of thin leather from his cape, Osiris hunkered down. Building a pile of kindling in the dip of a fractured boulder, he pulled a fireboard and short spindle from the pouch at his waist, and used friction to start a fire. He charred the end of a thin twig in the burgeoning flames and when the tip stopped glowing, he handed it to Seren. "Draw it."

She sketched with firm sure strokes the picture which had solidified inside her head.

"Okay." Osiris took the charcoal taper and wrote on the thin hide. 'Head west past the safari park', rolled up the leather map and tucked it into the greatcoat pocket.

Osiris added fuel to the crackling kindling and created a flickering blaze which he hoped would burn long enough to act as a beacon.

"Let's go. If Connor can see this castle, it has to be west, in Cornwall. You would know if he had crossed the channel. Your link is too strong for him to be that far away." With a sure finger, Osiris tilted up Seren's chin and frowned down at her. "Don't let him see you. He can only see what you put in there. So, tread carefully, he mustn't know we are coming."

Tears glazed the faded gray of her eyes. "He is far too preoccupied. And the window into his mind is shrinking. I feel like he is slipping away, Osiris."

"All the more reason. He would never forgive himself if he hurt you, once we have him back. Let's not give him more guilt to carry."

Pulling the supple leather cape forward to cover his chest, he settled the hood into place and took her hand. It was still light, and the gray clouds promised a shower of needle sharp rain, but a ray of determined sunshine was always a possibility.

They walked to the cliff edge and dropped the twenty feet down onto the moss covered boulders. Osiris' bare feet fared better than Seren's boots, so she took them off and slung them around her shoulders by the tied shoelaces.

They ran along the coastline, clambering over rocks the sea had torn from the grasp of the land.

The yowling of pumas and tigers punctuated the journey. It was not only the sun they were hiding from.

The tall wire mesh fence running along the cliff tops created the outer perimeter of the safari park and vampire wardens patrolled it. Seren hugged the base of the cliffs. Osiris kept one eye on the overhanging ledge above, suddenly diving in and pressing Seren into the bare rock face when a warden peered over the edge.

"They seem to be patrolling outside the perimeter fence. I wonder if Connor caused a stir when he went through the park," Osiris said.

"Maybe, we should ask?"

"No, I don't think Julian would agree. The fewer vampires know where we are, the better."

Twenty or so miles of coastline was covered without any further incident, and finally, Osiris leapt up, hung from an exposed tree root by one hand, and shepherded Seren's climb up from the pebbled beach onto the coarse green grassland of the moors.

A heavy downpour began as they got to their feet at the top of the rise. "Once we have this castle in sight, if we see anything to confirm Connor is there, then we'll keep watch and feed the information back to Malachi." Osiris frowned. "And no, before you ask, we are staying put until we know what Julian has planned."

Chapter 19

Marius stood high on the steep bank, within the deep shadow cast by one of the ancient monoliths. He could see for miles out to where silver gray ribbons of disused roads cut across the flat landscape. The abandoned village dwellings at Avebury were already crumbled shells, their construction submitting to the elements and neglect with pitiful enthusiasm. He waited patiently while three distant dark specks gradually approached. He felt more comfortable putting distance between himself and the circle of standing stones Birgitta's henchmen had erected. When he assessed the level of endeavor and forward planning the recreated henge implied, Marius' mood had darkened. *I hope Julian realizes what he is up against.*

As the last known location of Connor, like bloodhounds collecting the scent, Avebury Henge quickly became the starting point of the human/vampire combined search.

Marius made the journey on foot in a fraction of the time the others would take, and getting there first allowed him to scout out the 'scene' without worrying about Rebekah's feelings. Combing the site, he found the pile of furs, took note of the tears in the fabric and inspected the scuffed footprints in the ground at one end of the altar, and drew his own conclusion. Blood speckled the furs and was smeared onto the stone, and the ritual Connor had been drawn into took on more significance. *If she took his blood, and, as Malachi says, is of Druid ancestry, then it will be hard to get him back.* For the first time, it occurred to Marius that they might have lost him for good.

In a sudden decisive movement, he gathered the crumpled furs from the altar table and buried them to spare Rebekah the details of the 'crime scene'. He knew Anthony would arrive first, and his jaw muscle ticked as he worked out how much Rebekah needed to know.

Dirt clung to his traveling clothes and, enjoying a moment of peace, he pushed back his cowled hood and pulled off the thin leather gloves the sun forced him to wear. Vampires may not be the

'Dracula' of myth, but a healthy regard for their Achilles heel was prudent. Holy water, crucifixes and stakes in the heart were merely useful distractions used by the real vampire race. *After all, our heart is not beating, so why would hammering a piece of wood through it kill us?*

Resting back against the tower of granite, Marius tracked the final approach of the pair of geldings carrying Rebekah and Greg at a hurtling gallop through the late afternoon sunshine. The overgrown asphalt road deadened the drumming hooves to a low thudding note. Marius grinned. Despite the adrenalin rushing through their system, the humans' heart rates were barely detectable until they drew closer – the use of modified beta blockers by Rebekah's community was a stroke of genius.

Anthony ran across the scrubland on a parallel trajectory, literally trying not to scare the horses. With a final spurt, he was the first to arrive beside Marius. Both vampires exchanged arched looks, and, with preternatural speed and brevity, Marius shared his findings before Rebekah and Greg arrived in a plume of equine sweat. Both horses breathed heavily and snickered as they drew to a halt.

Slipping quickly from her saddle, Rebekah rushed up the slope, grabbing thick tufts of grass to aid her climb. She arrived breathlessly at the spot where Marius hid in the purple-tinted shadows. Bracing her hands on her knees, she gasped, "Did you find anything helpful?"

It crossed Marius' mind to tell her about the blood, but even *he* recognized that tact and diplomacy was a desirable strategy. "Just confirmation that Connor was here. If Seren is right, they headed down the north coast of the Cornish peninsula."

Greg joined them and handed Rebekah a canteen of water. "So, we set off now?"

"In a moment," Anthony replied.

The vampires adjusted their thin leather tunics. It was force of habit to prepare for the worst, even though, in spring they had less cause for concern. They pulled the long sleeves down to cover their hands, made sure the cowled hoods protected their faces and disappeared, heading out across the plain to another set of stones. Squinting, Rebekah realized the distant outcrops formed an entire circle. She exchanged a frustrated glance with Greg. It was like a false ending to their trek – the place holding the clues they needed was another ten minute run, for them.

When Rebekah, flushed and sweating from her sprint, stepped into the peaceful setting beyond the circle, she found Marius and Anthony crouched down on the grass, side by side, like golfers lining up a tricky putt.

Rebekah watched with a curious frown.

Greg shrugged. "Search me," he muttered.

Even though dusk was falling, the two vampires could pick out the swathe of flattened grass, just as Seren and Osiris had before them. They were not solving the puzzle, just following in Seren's footsteps, identifying which route to the Cornish peninsular the regent and her new consort had taken. An additional clue was the wisps of gray cloud that only vampire sight could see, to the northwest, spiraling up from the fire Osiris had set on the cliff top.

Marius and Anthony turned around and, at Rebekah's raised brow, shared their findings.

"What are we waiting for, then?" Greg yanked the woven straps of his backpack tight over his shoulders and strapped a sheath to his thigh and slid a blade into it.

Rebekah screwed the lid back on the water skin and tossed it into Greg's waiting hands. Returning over the rough ground, negotiating the mulched bog in the bottom of the deep ditch, and going up over the mound to where the horses waited wasted more time than Greg and Rebekah liked, but it had to be done. In concert, they removed the bridles and placed them inside the saddle bags, and released the horses to graze the pasture until they were collected by Seth and Adam.

"Okay, let's go," said Rebekah.

Anthony brought up the rear as the group made their way across country to the coast. Running into the brisk wind coming in off the cold sea made Greg and Rebekah's faces glow like beacons. When they reached the cliff top, puffing hard from the forced run, the humans doubled over and concentrated on catching their breath.

Flowing over the edge and onto the beach, Marius searched for their next clue, but any tracks left behind were indistinguishable. The sea wind had sifted the grains of sand and kept her secrets.

The line of copper veined boulders reaching out into the waves rang a bell with Marius. *That looks like the feature on the beach Malachi described from Seren's vision.*

Going on ahead, Anthony combed the area and when he studied the nearby tree line, his body jolted. The tall dark shape draped over a thick branch took a moment to resolve into an empty coat rather than a vampire ready to attack. He loped over to the tree and picked up Connor's greatcoat. Returning to the others, he said, "Here is the next clue in the treasure hunt." Searching the pockets, he grunted when he found a piece of leather and unrolled it.

"Seren has left a message. A picture of a castle. It must be Connor's vision. I don't know what it means, though."

Marius took the hide from Anthony and peered at the roughly drawn picture. "This is St Michael's mount and the castle on its peak. There is no mystery."

Anthony laughed. "Trust Connor to choose a castle used in a Dracula movie."

"Trust Connor to choose a castle on the south coast. He pushes the concept of 'taking the scenic route' to the limit," said Marius.

Rocks tumbled down from above, one bouncing from Marius' shoulder, as the pair of humans scrambled down and finally made it onto the beach.

"How do we let Julian know?" asked Rebekah, inspecting the drawing and handing it back.

"He will know already. Malachi has the same link to Connor as Seren. We are the ones working in the dark," Anthony explained.

"Well, that's reassuring," said Marius on a wry smile.

"Humor, Marius?" Anthony grinned.

"Sarcasm," he quipped back.

They followed the coastline. The vampire safari park extended across the West Country and there was no way around it. To go inland and find a route across to the south coast was better left until further down, where the peninsular became narrower.

The group jogged along at the steady pace set by the humans. Marius scouted the terrain ahead in bursts of movement and reported back on the easiest path to take. Rebekah kept up with Greg, although she had no load to carry and the Marine had his usual pack filled with survival gear. The low thrumming growls they heard coming from the cliff tops grew steadily louder until both vampires had to concede the safari park could become a problem.

Hunkering down at the base of the escarpment, they spoke in quiet tones.

"The big cats can smell you." Marius said, his probing gaze picking out Greg and Rebekah's tense white faces. "Take more beta blockers. I don't know if it will be enough, but we have to go on."

Both humans popped the pills, Greg re-secured the webbing straps over his shoulders and they got to their feet once more.

"Stay close to the foot of the cliff. At least that way if a vampire gamekeeper is drawn by the commotion, they won't spot you," said Marius.

He grunted with annoyance when a tumbled pile of boulders blocking the beach up ahead came into view. "A bit of good luck would be helpful," he muttered.

Leaping up to the top of the uneven slabs, Marius scanned the downward slope. Greg also began to climb, and Rebekah followed in his wake. "Anthony, it's easier if we carry them until the beach is clearer.

Greg reared back. Even his close association with vampires had not eroded his fierce independence. "Get stuffed. I can look after myself," he muttered, glaring up at Marius until his boot slipped a few inches and he righted himself in an arm waving dance.

"That was close," grinned Marius, reaching out a hand and hauling Greg up beside him.

"Funny, ha, ha," grumbled Greg.

Rebekah climbed up onto another flat shelf. "When you girls have finished, we have a castle to find." Swinging around, she started down the other side. The slab she stepped onto shifted and her foot skidded over the rough surface. Her boot disappeared into a deep crevice between two boulders and Rebekah bit back a yelp. Sitting down suddenly, she screwed her face up in pain.

The stone was hard beneath her backside, but she rocked back and forth anyway. Her scrunched face held back the expletives she couldn't say out loud. Finally, staring up at Greg, her brown eyes clouded with pain.

He dropped down beside her, braced his hands around her knee and ran them down either side of her calf, his fingers probing her limb as he went. Rebekah hissed, and when Greg withdrew one hand, his fingertips were smeared with blood.

"Shit, Rebekah."

Tears filled her eyes and she thumped the rock beside her. "Fuck, fuck, fuck."

Greg jumped with surprise. "Steady on. Connor won't let me play with you anymore if you've got a potty mouth when he gets back."

Tears spilled down her cheeks as her groaning laughter dissolved into sobs.

Greg put his arm around her shoulders and glanced up at Marius. The dark vampire's ramrod straight attitude as he focused intently on something behind Greg, made the Marine's hackles rise. "What?"

Before Greg could twist around to look, the black cloak Marius wore flared as he leapt into the air and over the crouched humans like the man-sized bat of myth and legend. The flapping leather dragged across Greg's hair and both humans cowered, shielding their heads with their arms.

"Get Rebekah out of there," blurted Marius.

Blocking out everything else, Greg framed Rebekah's leg with his hands, clamping them together to protect her shin and calf. "Three, two, one," he said, locking eyes with her and gritting his teeth. In a smooth movement, he eased her foot up. Her boot scraped against stone and it took a wiggle to free it. Rebekah dug her fingers into Greg's shoulder as she pulled too. The boot came out, and Greg scooped her up and leapt back down the way they had come.

The sickening thump of vampire bodies colliding made Greg wince. He glanced up in time to see Anthony, saliva bubbling from his lips, hit the vertical cliff face with a crunch. The crater he made clattered gravel onto the ground as he slid down to the sand and took a step forward. His blood crazed gaze tracked Rebekah, and Greg understood.

"Get Rebekah into the water. Anthony has gone feral," Marius said urgently.

Wading into the surf, Greg lowered Rebekah's feet into the water. His arm supporting her around the waist, he looked over his shoulder to see if that was enough.

Marius obscured his view of Anthony, but the noise of grinding teeth was unmistakable. Greg dropped to his haunches, plunging his hand beneath the water and grappling through the rocks at his feet. He picked up the largest stone he could lift with one hand. Water streamed from his clothes as he stood up and gripped Rebekah on the shoulder to urge her down until she was sitting at his feet, waist deep in the sea. "Stay there, and stay still."

Marius, like a bullfighter, made himself as large as possible, holding his thin leather cape away from his body to obscure Anthony's view. Suddenly, with a sickening thud, Marius was thrown back, landing in the water and sending a deluge of spray up over Greg's chest. The Marine had his sights set on locating the second combatant.

When Anthony surged up, water cascading down over his face, Greg pelted the rock. It only caught his quarry on the arm and Greg plunged back into the sea looking for another missile, but Anthony was already closing in.

Appearing from nowhere, Marius rammed a shoulder into Anthony's chest, which launched him fifteen feet into the air.

The crazed vampire landed on his backside on the beach, a shrapnel shower of sand fanning up around him. His lips drew back in a snarl. Springing to his feet, he whipped around on the spot and leapt up the cliff face. His fingers excavated deep holes as he hung there, glancing back over his shoulder, his white face a stiff mask of despair. Lunging upward, he scaled the rocks, showering debris behind him. He swung up over the overhanging clumped grass and disappeared.

The sound of water slapping against the rocks was the only noise breaking the stunned silence. Marius' head tilted, as he strained to hear what was going on beyond their view.

Greg's wet combats creaked when he finally reached down and helped Rebekah to stand, her water-logged clothes making her stagger and almost fall. He clamped an arm around her waist. "Okay?" he whispered.

Rebekah grinned. "Icy water is a great anesthetic."

"Well, let's see what you've actually done."

Wading gingerly out of the surf, Rebekah tested her leg. "I can walk on it, so it can't be broken. That's not so bad." She smiled.

Marius remained frozen, like a hunting dog on point, listening, until he heaved an irritated sigh. "Damn it, they have caught him."

"What? The tigers have Anthony?" Greg said absently as he helped Rebekah to sit on a flat dry rock further up the beach and dropped to his knees before her.

Marius' raised eyebrows said 'really?', but aloud, he said, "No, the wardens. He didn't check in through the gates for a hunting session, so he's under arrest. Damn it." Marius looked at Greg. "Can we do without him?"

"That's for you to say, Marius." Greg's frowning look said otherwise. "But he and I, well, we are used to each other."

Marius drew to his full height and jerked his chin at Rebekah. "Get the wound dressed. I'll be right back." He scaled the cliff in a charcoal blur and disappeared.

Rebekah pulled up the leg of her combats. Greg worked quickly, opening the field kit and tearing open a package which held antiseptic and a sterile dressing. With deft sure moves, he dried the graze which ran vertically up her shin, pressing gently on the bone to check it was not broken. Rebekah hissed through firmly clamped lips.

"Sorry," muttered Greg, as he continued the examination. "The good news is, you're right. Nothing's broken."

Removing a small aerosol can, he sprayed the graze with 'liquid skin' which dried into a transparent film over the wound, sealing it. He added dressing and bound her leg in Saran-wrap, taping it top and bottom. "That's as good as it gets."

"Thank you, Greg. It's only a graze," said Rebekah, "not such a big deal under other circumstances." She looked sheepish. "Stupid."

The yowl of restless felines still stalking the perimeter was unnerving.

"Great," muttered Greg, holding out his hand and helping Rebekah to stand. "I never thought I'd say this, but where the hell is a vampire when you need one? They better get back here soon."

Chapter 20

Within minutes of leaving the beach, Marius hit top vampire speed and retraced their path, but back along the cliff top. He overran his destination and executed a U-turn under the cover of trees. Taking a cleansing breath, he clawed his sleek cap of black hair into place, conjured an air of relaxation and, using the main road, he approached the safari park and waited at the security gate. Marius remained stock still. To look impatient would give too much away.

Walking through the gate when it swung open, Marius' brows rose over an ingenuous smile as he fixed his attention on the chief warden. "There is a commotion out there in the park. What's happening?" he asked casually.

Side by side, they crossed the no-man's land between the outer and inner perimeter fences and entered the registration lodge. The slick path worn into the polished quartz floor marked the route vampires took through the facility. Each vampire checked in at the counter, collected hunting clothes and went through to the 'dressing shed'.

Faced with the warden's wall of silence, Marius continued the charade. "Identification number LH3456743."

"Good evening, Juror Marius." The vampire behind the counter immediately turned away. Seconds later, he placed a wooden crate on the bench, with a suede hunting loincloth folded in the bottom. It was Marius' personal hunting attire, made to fit his never changing physique to the millimeter.

Marius' coal black eyes swept the counter and his chin jerked in thanks.

When Marius made no move to pick up the crate, the warden said, "Juror Marius. You are here to hunt?"

"That was my intention, yes. Unless-?"

The warden fidgeted beneath Marius' probing look. "We had an eventful night, and now... But things are under control."

"What, precisely, does an 'eventful night' mean?" Marius let the silence hang to the point of awkwardness.

The warden assessed Marius, as though deciding what to say. "We had a perimeter breach."

Marius remained silent, forcing the warden to continue.

"Then a cougar died... a heart attack, the vet thinks, although we can't be certain."

"And-" *Shit, Anthony, what have you gotten into?* "Have you caught the vampire responsible?"

"We think so, yes. He was circling the granite platforms in area 'A', but he didn't come in through the gates."

"Where is he now?"

"In a holding cave. We are preparing to administer muscle relaxant and then he can be transported back to London."

"You need to follow protocol, but Principal Julian has his hands full right now. Bring the syringe. I'll administer it and take him back."

The warden coughed. "It's Surgical Assistant Anthony," he stated.

Marius tight smile bared teeth. "And are you suggesting there will be some favoritism."

The warden rocked his weight from one foot to the other. "No, of course not."

"He may be Doctor Connor's assistant, but breaching the perimeter is a serious offense." Marius held out a hand. "I'll administer the muscle relaxant and remove him. My hunting session can wait."

"Very well," the warden replied stiffly. Turning on his heel, he passed through a door marked 'Wardens Only', and Marius followed him without hesitation.

Barely registering the hanging rails of park uniforms, Marius breezed along the space between the rows and out through the exit door beyond. He expected to emerge outside, so finding himself in a rock-lined tunnel which descended quickly below ground level was a surprise. A clicking noise echoed from the walls, sounding like a metronome and it took Marius a moment to realize the warden had collected a set of iron keys which swung in time with his powerful stride.

The grind of fingernails scraping over rock vibrated through Marius' head, punctuated by feral rumbling growls which made Marius clench his teeth. *Anthony better pull himself together.* The row of cave like cells emerged out of the gloom, the only illumination being a shaft of moonlight slicing down from an iron grill overhead.

"Third cavern on the left," the warden said, and placed the barrel of a bovine syringe into Marius' hand.

As if I needed to be told. Dust plumed into the air, escaping in a haze through the bars of the third cave – evidence of a recent scuffle. Marius peered through bars as thick as a man's forearm. His speculation on how vampires could be 'imprisoned' inside the caves disappeared when he looked into Anthony's clouded brown gaze. A thin garrote of tempered steel cut a groove into the firm flesh of Anthony's neck. The ends disappeared inside the wall, and Marius had no doubt they were secured to a ratchet mechanism. If a vampire was so far gone into grave sleep that he separated head from shoulders, then that was one less problem for the wardens to concern themselves with.

Anthony's arms flailed but when he looked up, a flash of clarity lit his eyes. It almost made Marius smile. *He's faking it to avoid being questioned. Quick thinking.*

Adjusting his grip on the syringe, Marius nodded to the warden, who unlocked the iron gate. The metal hinges creaked as it swung open, and Marius stepped in. Pausing just beyond the reach of the supposedly enraged Anthony, he dodged in under his guard. Jabbing the needle up into the space beneath Anthony's jaw with a vicious shove, Marius pushed the plunger home.

Anthony's face froze in a shocked expression, and Marius pushed his friend back against the wall to release the tension of the garrote.

"Release him," barked Marius, and as if he uttered a spell, a clicking sound heralded the unwinding of the hidden ratchet, the loop of metal loosened, and the stiff wire levitated eerily. Easing the garrote up over Anthony's head, Marius guided the medicated vampire down to the floor.

The warden's expression showed a measure of relief. *What did he think, that I wouldn't follow through?* Marius bristled. "Let's get him out of here," he said, tossing the syringe to the warden.

Grabbing Anthony's wrist, Marius ducked his head and hefted Anthony's floppy body up over his shoulders. "It's quicker if I just get him back to London, now. Principal Julian will deal with him. Problem solved."

Before the warden could protest, Marius strode back the way they had come, and in a gliding maneuver, he swept back through the staff quarters and passed through the reception lodge without breaking stride.

"Open up, now," he called out, when he faced a closed gate in the perimeter fence. Another warden leapt into action, unlocking and opening the gate. Marius broke into an easy jog and headed towards London. Once he had covered enough ground to be out of sight, he veered left and when the land ran out, he jumped down onto the beach. The combined weight of both vampires drove Marius' boots two feet down into the coarse gravel-like sand. Wading out of the pit, he set off along the coast to where he had left Greg and Rebekah. *I hope they kept out of sight.*

He spotted them huddled at the foot of the escarpment. Marius frowned, something struck him as odd, but he couldn't make it out, not until he was a lot closer. Both humans had dug holes and buried the lower half of their bodies. Greg's blanket of sand erupted as Marius arrived, his upheld hand urging Rebekah to stay put.

Greg rushed forward when Marius stopped and bent to offload Anthony onto the ground. Marius chuckled when the weight of Anthony's falling arm almost knocked the Marine off his feet.

"Bit more than you bargained for?" Marius joked as he hefted Anthony upright and sat him back against a boulder.

Greg grunted and brushed damp sand from his combat pants. "What the hell has happened to him, anyhow?"

"A dose of muscle relaxant. He'll be back with us in about half an hour."

Dropping down in front of Anthony, knowing his friend could still hear, despite his slack features, Marius murmured, "It was just the dregs. I managed to discharge most of the dose along the corridor."

Greg opened his mouth, and then snapped it shut again.

Marius confirmed his thoughts. "It's a long story, Greg. I'll tell you later, for now, get ready to move out." As he spoke, Marius pulled a plastic vial of blood from the pocket of Greg's pack, lifted Anthony's chin, and poured it into his mouth. It gurgled as it seeped down his throat.

"Will he be okay?" Greg raised a skeptical brow.

"He'll be fine. Load up." Marius walked over to Rebekah as she stood up amidst a cascade of sand. "I'm going to carry you-" He lifted up a finger as she spluttered. "No argument. You're injured. Exertion will make the wound throb. Throbbing means it will be pumping blood. I'm carrying you."

Rebekah held her hands up. "You win. I just want to catch up to Seren and get to Connor. I'll go along with anything you say, at this point."

"Thank goodness for that," said Marius.

A low rumble, almost a purr, filled the air and stones scattered down the escarpment.

"The big cats are still restless. I think we should get going," said Marius. Action suiting words, he scooped Rebekah up into the archetypal damsel in distress lift and began nimbly stepping from one stone to another. "We'll keep walking along the rocks. "Greg, you and Anthony catch us up as soon as you can."

Greg glanced over to where Anthony had begun rolling over onto the ground like a man who had forgotten he had arms, trying to get up. Greg raised an eyebrow, but all he said was, "Once Anthony knows which way is up, we'll set off."

Marius focused on the path ahead. It felt odd, but he had complete faith in Greg.

Chapter 21

The blustering winds picked up to a gale, tore at Seren and Osiris' racing forms and tried to throw them to the ground. A fanciful mind could imagine that Birgitta had enslaved the elements, but Seren was too focused on hanging onto the gossamer-fine threads of Connor's thoughts to give that corrosive notion space inside her head.

Even though the physical trail had ended at the vampire safari park, Connor's visions had broken through in splintered fragments, as though fractured by signal interference. Osiris and Seren continued south west across country, travelling as if they rode a zip wire, deviating only when it was faster to go around a landscape feature than power on over it.

Stopping at the top of a steep incline, the pair scoured the vista ahead, to where the sea wore a skin of glittering diamonds, even in the golden muted light of a dull afternoon.

"What if they are headed to the south coast to pick up the regent's ship?" Seren asked. With a worried frown, she gripped Osiris' arm.

"We'll wait and see."

"But, I *can't* see... my connection to Papa is breaking down. No, not breaking down, it's her, Birgitta, her power is getting stronger."

In silent agreement that there was only one way to be sure Connor was still in England, they set off over a rock strewn field, dodging around granite tors which broke through the earth like a giant's teeth. They slowed when they reached the coastline, dropping down and crawling forward to where the ground fell away in a vertical cliff. Below them sat the coastal settlement of Marazion, with colorful paint peeling from the empty shells of the gift shops, restaurants, and guest houses, and out in the bay beyond, St Michael's Mount, with its own spread of derelict dwellings.

The island of rock emerged from the sea like a mottled green iceberg. The seawall framed the harbor where small boats would once have been dotted along the concrete quay, curving inward like the pincers of a crab and forming a protective embrace which faced the mainland and shielded the vessels in stormy weather. To the left on the island, emerald lawns swept down from the deep angular stone terraces of cultivated gardens.

Behind the cluster of dwellings which lined the harbor, rose the steep craggy slopes which earned the island its name of 'mount' – a small mountain. The crowning glory broke through the thick dark embrace of an evergreen forest – the clustered turrets of the castle stabbed skyward like the sharpened stakes that vampires laughed at. Its blackened windows glistened in dark gray walls; the Cornish stone had become the color of ash in the recent downpour.

The darkening sky was iron gray with thick bruised clouds and at least the sun was not a concern.

Finding a deep crevasse in the fractured bedrock, Osiris and Seren hung onto the rough straw-like grass and swung their legs over the edge. They slid down inside, and used it to cover their descent to the gentler slopes. Hugging the gritty walls of the buildings which lined the streets of the town, they dived in through one where a broken faded sign on the wall said 'Godolphin'. Weaving a path through the dust laden interior and out onto the terrace, they crouched low and scuttled along behind the seawall to where a stairway of giant stone slabs led down to the beach. Side by side, they peered out across the water.

The cobblestone causeway which linked the mount to the shore was submerged at high tide. At a fork in the path, sat a huge rock. It towered over the flat concrete platform built onto it, where motorboats could offload passengers when shuttling humans to and from the island if the tide was coming in and parts of the causeway became impassable. The now evacuated human community would have used the steps that cut across the outcrop and walked across the beach to the mainland. But at high tide, passengers had to disembark at the harbor at Marazion.

The salty tang of seaweed saturated the air, and a skirt of the reddish brown plant crawled over the rocks lying at the base of the seawall. Tractors hadn't cleared the tidal deposits from the sand since humans were rounded up and seaweed now covered most of the beach.

Edging closer to the start of the causeway which tethered the island to the mainland, like an infant to a stubborn parent, Seren fully absorbed the dramatic impact of the castle.

She said, "I know he is in there, but I'm getting nothing now. It's as though he has been swallowed up in a dead zone."

Osiris stared out over the bay. "Her magic is strong. Malachi says she is descended from the Druids. We'll have to get inside the castle to find your father."

Ducking down behind cover, they sat with their backs pressed into the wall. Osiris took Seren's hand. "They will have lookouts posted. The trees are very thick, perfect for hiding from both the sun and your enemies. The slopes could be crawling with them, and we wouldn't know it. Our best option is a flanking maneuver. Following the headland to the left will take us *around* the mount and away from the harbor. When the tide is in, we'll walk along the seabed and swing around to the sea-facing side of the island." Osiris frowned. "How long can you hold your breath?" Hybrid existence was a juggling act.

Seren searched Osiris' majestic profile. "It doesn't matter. I don't need to hold my breath."

"What?" Osiris assessed the rippling stone-gray sea, his attention fixed on calculating the distance and triangulating the angles of their approach.

"I'm going in through the front door."

His head jerked around. "What? Don't be ridiculous."

"Think about it. I am what she came for. The regent. Or at least, the reason she gave. She has my father. What would be more natural than for a young hybrid rebel to choose her father's side?" Seren squeezed his hand. "Why would I want to stay with a weak human mother?" The words broke in Seren's throat and her face reflected her sadness.

Putting a fingertip beneath her chin, he waited until her black lashes swept up and she met his gaze. "You'll have to do better than that if you're going to fool an ancient."

"I can do this. It gets me inside the castle."

"Or killed."

"No, I am unique. If nothing else, they'll keep me alive as an experiment."

Osiris' jaw muscle twitched. "I'm a hybrid too. And I can read Connor's thoughts. I should go."

Seren reached up and cupped his face. "They know about me. They don't know about you. You can feed information back to Uncle Julian. We are not going to let this bitch win."

Osiris' brows shot up and he smiled. "Hang onto that determination." He assessed the darkening sky. "We have two hours before the tide goes out far enough for you to make your dramatic entrance. The sun will set not long after, but you can pull up the hood on your cape if there is a break in the cloud."

His hand crushed Seren's fingers as he growled in frustration. "I won't let you go in there alone. I can't. You're right, they won't kill you before they get you inside, so I'm going to be hiding in the castle when you get there. If things go wrong, I'll be there to save you."

They settled down to wait, and Osiris wrapped Seren in her cloak, put an arm around her and held her close. He appeared relaxed despite the wind dragging over his face and tearing at his clothes. The dull afternoon light faded into dusk before they stirred.

Hugging Seren by the shoulders and using his free hand to hold back the strands of flapping hair which obscured her face, Osiris said, "If the causeway is passable, walk very slowly. Call out early. Get their attention before you continue."

Seren's gray eyes glittered with exhilaration. "They won't be expecting me. This is our best way to get in under their guard."

Drawing her closer, Osiris kissed her. "Stay safe. No matter what happens, I will come for you."

In silent agreement, behind cover, they both shifted into a crouch.

Osiris darted a look over the wall, gave Seren's fingers a final squeeze and moved back. Kneeling, he shed his cloak and shirt. The bronze skin of his naked chest gleamed in the moonlight. Tying a supple leather strap around his head tamed the sleek curtain of his hair. He tied another around his bare thigh as a makeshift utility belt, pushed two sheathed knives into it, and hid them beneath the flap of his thick linen skirt. A vial of blood remained in the leather pouch he slung around his narrow waist. He was Seren's Egyptian warrior.

Vaulting the seawall, he landed in the mounds of slimy seaweed below and darted a few feet along, to where masonry had collapsed onto the beach. Dropping to his haunches, from between two rocks, he scooped out dark muddy sand and spread the sludge over his body.

"Won't it wash off in the water?" whispered Seren.

Osiris smiled. "Yes. But getting into the sea unseen is where the danger lies. They won't notice me when I scale the castle walls. They aren't expecting an attack."

Looking into his earnest face, Seren almost changed her mind and went into the water with him.

Doctor Heinrik, when she was held by the sentinel, had made her skin crawl. She had felt powerless when he probed and took blood, and subjected her to his clinical fascination. She had read up on 'natural poisons' – had even gathered Belladonna berries and planned to make a suicide pill. *I never wanted to feel that kind of fear again.* Connor had gone ballistic when he found out the reason she was researching toxins and made her swear to abandon her idea of 'giving herself an out'. He promised she would never become a guinea-pig again. *But what good is that promise now?* Although, it was easier to give up on her 'last resort' plan because she had Osiris. *It would cause him pain.*

Resolutely tidying her clothing, she made sure her boots were laced tight, yanked on her belt and tucked the trailing end inside. When she could put the moment off no longer, she squared her shoulders and checked her pockets to make sure she, too, had a vial of blood – and quashed the regret that she didn't have her suicide pill.

Pushing back the hood, Seren straightened her leather cape, left the shelter of the seawall, and descended the wide moss covered stairway. She walked along to where the broad path of cobblestones emerged from beneath the packed sand. Now the tide was out, it meandered in a sweeping arc out to the mount. Discounting the right fork, which led to the outcrop used as a waypoint by motorboats, she chose the much longer path which crossed to the island and ended to the left of the harbor. Seren's eyes remained fixed on the castle on the peak and she willed a door to open, a window, anything.

Even at low tide, salt water pooled in dips and crevices between the uneven cobbles. Seren did as Osiris said, and walked at the slowest pace her vampire senses could manage.

The carpet of boulders on either side of the causeway rose higher than the path in places, seaweed covering each one like thick blades of greasy blackish-brown hair – the sea of slimy heads ranged twelve to twenty yards out. Seren knew, just by looking at them, that the rocks would be slick as a glacier and treacherous underfoot.

Up ahead, the dense green canopy of the trees on the steep slopes of the mound shuffled with agitated movement. *They have seen me.* Osiris' guess that there were vampires on watch turned out to be correct. The shivering foliage whispered through the still night and suddenly, candlelight appeared in one of the oily black windows of the castle.

A smile tugged at Seren's lips. *Here goes nothing.* "Papa," Seren called out. She continued walking. "Papa, I know you are there." Despite herself, her sluggish heartbeat kicked up a notch.

The trees twitched violently and black figures oozed out from between the rows of terraced cottages onto the concrete quayside. They stood shoulder to shoulder as though a spear passed through each body and kept them perfectly aligned. The pale gray circles of each of the faces were in sharp focus to Seren, even from fifty yards away.

Their vacant expressions created the feeling of staring into empty vessels, as though they were wind up dolls that had run down. The door of the castle remained closed. *Well, let's see how much fuss I can cause.* Taking deep breaths, Seren gradually increased the timing of her respiration, and her heart rate peaked along with it. Stopping her heart at will was simple, but this required more effort. Her heartbeats scampered through her chest, the palpitations feeling like a kick drum thudding inside her ribcage.

The line of vampires oscillated as if some were fighting to step forward, but the others held them in check. A low grinding noise hummed along the row, smothered behind clenched teeth, at first, but building into a bark, like hyenas unleashing explosive cackling bursts.

"Papa, I know you are there. How can you leave me with weak humans?" Seren spat.

Almost at the end of the causeway and still seeing no sign of Connor, she stopped and stamped her foot, cracking the cobblestones beneath her boot. Clenching her fists, Seren let out a piercing shriek. The noise scraped over the eardrums of the waiting vampires. A flush stained Seren's cheeks as she raged against her father and exuded frustration.

The smell of blood plumed in the air as she deliberately bit down on her tongue. The watery red saliva ran down her chin. *Papa, where are you?* A black-clad figure broke ranks and lunged forward, covering dozens of feet in a mere second. For the first time, when she focused on the blood-lust twisted features, Seren hoped Osiris was still watching her back.

Seren lifted her chin, baring her throat as the vampire's clawed grip closed around her neck. Osiris' calming presence flooded into her mind and she relaxed. *You are here.*

The bright orb inside her head reflected Osiris, his black hair wet, the thick strands of it winding around his neck like a nest of eels. *Just hang on, fight them, I'm coming.*

Her heart filled with despair as she shared her sorrow with Osiris. *If he would see me die like this, Papa is gone.*

A dark figure appeared on the battlements high above and stared down, his hands resting on the stone wall. In a blur of movement, he vaulted over the top and a vibration set every tree shaking as he hurtled down the slope.

The grip of the vampire dug into Seren's flesh and grated over her hard skin. When she twisted away, his chest collided with her shoulder. Suddenly, the hefty weight of the vampire flew backward, his body arching as though an electric current pulled every tendon tight.

From an elevated position, framed by the arch of a lynch gate, a male voice bellowed, "Take your dirty hands off her."

The vampire sagged, dropping to his knees like a puppet with severed strings. He immediately jerked upright again, and his dark form receded like a shadowy ghost.

Seren peered at the charcoal silhouette framed in the stone arch with iron gates at his back, and picked out a fierce white face she knew as well as her own. "Papa." Her whisper was a warning to Osiris. "He's here." She blinked as the silver glow of moonlight bathed his figure and it separated into two forms. *Birgitta.* Seren felt certain it was *her* powers that had saved her. *For Papa's sake? For hers?* The stone arch became an empty space. The crack of snapping wood and the shuffling of leaves marked Connor's progress through the overgrown hanging branches of thick evergreen trees.

Seren pinned her gaze on the spot where he would emerge. *Osiris, go now... go.*

Connor stepped out into the gathering dusk, brushing broken twigs and tree spines from his broad shoulders as he walked. The white clad figure of the regent remained in the shelter of the canopy. A pale gray specter with a smile on her face.

Seren could see the woman was beautiful, but the brittleness in the blue eyes felt like the blast of an arctic breeze. Focusing on Connor as he strode forward, the ice cold chill gripped Seren harder. His gray gaze held nothing but thunderclouds.

"What do you want?" The words were spat from between stiff lips.

Seren inhaled and prepared to deliver the performance of a lifetime. In a low quiet voice, she said, "You are my father. You can't leave me to look after *her*."

Connor's penetrating glare wavered. "She is your mother."

He reached a hand behind and Birgitta drifted forward to join him. The moment his fingers closed around hers, his eyes lit up. The ice hard façade reflected the man now inside. His only concern was Birgitta's pleasure. *This regent is a sorceress.* Seren tried to reach out to him. His thoughts solidified inside Seren's mind as though she had crossed to the other side of a force field. The last words he had said merely circled inside his head like caged birds. Seren smiled. *He is an empty vessel. A puppet with the regent pulling the strings.* Seren hoped Malachi could hear her, but she felt alone, except for Connor.

Shifting her attention to Birgitta's frozen features, Seren spoke. "I am stronger than a human. I won't be cut out like a cancer and left behind. I want to stay with my Papa."

Connor's irritation was clear. Shifting his position, he blocked Seren's view of the regent. "You will go where I tell you." His narrowed gaze glittered in the moonlight and he lifted a hand to touch Seren's cheek.

Staring into her father's eyes, she looked for a glimmer of hope and saw only an empty cavern. Her fist clenched as she suppressed the urge to slap his face, just to get a genuine reaction. *He must be in there somewhere.*

"Let's not be hasty, my lord." Birgitta's voice was a sigh on the breeze, enchanting. "Let me see the child. She is unique, no? It would be a shame to leave her without your guidance."

"She has a mate."

"He doesn't know I'm here." Seren sneered as she smiled. "He is tied to Malachi. If I have to choose, I choose my father."

Birgitta appeared beside Connor once again, and her radiant face wore a reassuring smile. "Let me speak to the child." Birgitta extended a delicate hand – her sharpened nails gleamed with a pearl-like finish – and Seren reached out to take it, even though she didn't want to.

Sinking into revival sleep, Seren let her distaste for the cold satin feel of Birgitta's touch slip away. The drugged feeling of well-being which invaded her mind brought relief. As she became acclimatized to Birgitta's saccharine scent, the razor edge of the regent's nails dug into Seren's flesh. Her palm grew warm, and tendrils of heat seeped up her arm and filled her chest. Seren stopped breathing. She felt herself drowning in the icy waters of Birgitta's will.

"Tell me about your mother."

Seren could not speak. Her tongue clung to the roof of her mouth and the regent's triumphant face filled her mind. *You want to see my mother.* A picture of Rebekah solidified inside Seren's head. Her blonde hair soaked with sweat, the conjured image was hunched over. Dull brown eyes dominated a pinched face which looked spiteful and waspish. Seren suppressed her guilt as she said, "My mother is a pathetic weak whining woman."

Birgitta smiled. "Nice try, my dear, but I have seen a more vibrant woman in your father's mind."

Seren's chin shot up, resentment tightening her face. "I think Papa sees her differently."

Birgitta laughed. "She has spirit, this child of yours," she said, without taking her eyes from Seren.

Continuing on as if the regent had not spoken, Seren said smugly, "Papa loves her, after all."

The hand holding hers jerked and Seren's smile was sharp with satisfaction, knowing the barb had hit home.

Birgitta's features hardened. "He pitied her. Nothing more." Her laughter scraped down Seren's spine. "He knows that now."

"Good," said Seren. "I hated seeing him fooling himself. My mother could never satisfy him." An awakened awareness of the needs of the flesh colored Seren's coquettish glance. "He sacrificed too much to pander to her feebleness."

Birgitta joined in Seren's gloating appreciation. "He does not have to hold back with me, Seren."

Nausea roiled in her stomach when Seren heard her name on this blonde ice warrior's lips. She swallowed hard, drawing Birgitta's attention to her throat. Fascinated, as every vampire before her had been, Birgitta reached out and pressed a crushing ice cold thumb to the carotid pulse in Seren's neck.

Seren stood as still as a statue. Giving away nothing of her feelings would keep Birgitta's interest. Like a recoiling snake, Birgitta slowly withdrew.

Connor gazed out over the bay, apparently entranced by the view of the coastline.

Seren frowned. Unsure of where Osiris might be, she blurted, "Papa, say I can stay."

Birgitta turned to Connor and ran her palm down over his hard chest.

His awareness snapped back and his steely gaze focused on Seren's face. "If you stay with me you will never see your mother again." By his tone, Connor might as well be talking about throwing away an old garment.

"She's mortal, she'll die sooner or later." Seren shrugged. "Why would I choose a weak relationship over what I have with you?"

"She is as beautiful as you said, my lord." Birgitta tilted her head.

The birdlike gesture brought to mind a vulture inspecting a carcass which Seren promptly banished incase the regent sensed it.

"It will be interesting to see how different she is from the rest of us," said Birgitta.

"Very well. Stay." Connor turned back towards the swathe of trees.

Birgitta mewed delicately. "Don't make the child go through the forest. The castle is so much better when viewed from the path."

Connor immediately changed direction. Trudging steadily over the rock strewn grass, he made his way to the bottom of the wide flight of uneven stairs fashioned from flint gray slabs. A black metal handrail gleamed in the moonlight in some sections, but he didn't touch it. Seren followed suit. She could almost feel Birgitta's gaze boring into her back from where she walked close behind. As Seren turned the first bend, a flash of movement caught her eye and she glanced over her shoulder.

The group of vampire guards had scattered like marbles, each darting back under the cover of the trees. Seren guessed that each one had a designated area to patrol. *I hope Osiris is already inside.* Passing by the fairytale magic of the giant's well with its towering boulder perched at an impossible angle, Seren wanted to investigate, but she showed no sign of her curiosity. Where it narrowed, the towering moss-covered walls flanking the path bounced each footfall back through the eerie night.

Seren focused on her father and the gliding regent, but still found time to wonder at the imaginative mind which created the castle.

Ceremonial cannons aimed out to sea between the castellations of the outer wall on the final approach to the west facing entrance of the fortress. The twelve foot tall door to the castle hung open, a carpet of golden light bleeding down over the steps. It looked beautiful. Inside the reception hall, where the dark flagstoned floor was worn smooth with age, Seren was distracted by the motes of dust dancing in the air. Her vampire sight transformed the floating particles into swirling fireflies and the child inside her rejoiced.

Without pausing, Connor strode along a wide winding corridor, and Seren hurried on behind. Moonlight poured in through deep window recesses and she fought to keep her bearings in the twists and turns. Beyond a book lined room, the door hung open and four steps led down into an enchanting banquet hall – the black beamed vaulted ceiling made the room expand in a Tardis-like illusion. It exuded grandeur. Alabaster friezes of hunting scenes ran the entire length of the space and a grand white marble mantel framed a black iron fireplace. A rough-hewn stairway spiraled down in one corner, but she could not see to where it led.

The moment she had crossed over the threshold of the west entrance, she had felt the effect of the force field, like a dome covering the castle. Inside the banquet hall, her thoughts became sluggish. She knew she had entered a prison. Reading Connor seemed easier, but the sense of being entombed made her doubt that she could project anything she saw outside the castle walls.

Seren immediately registered the low thrum of distant heartbeats. Turning to Connor, disappointed, she assessed his unresponsive profile. Reluctantly seeking out Birgitta instead, Seren asked, "There are humans here?"

The regent smiled. "Of course. You drink human blood?"

Seren shook her head. "No. I'm a hybrid. I can survive on animal blood. I'm not sure I could..."

"If you are thirsty, you will drink anything."

"I can hunt. When the tide is out, I'll hunt for rabbits, badgers, foxes, anything really."

Birgitta laid a hand on Seren's shoulder. "You will not leave the castle unless your father says so."

As if the regent willed it, the heavy front door closed with a distant thump and oppressive silence descended. Seren nodded, showing she understood, and then Birgitta removed her hand.

"Welcome to your new home." Inspecting Seren's small frame, Birgitta said, "I'll have a bondsman bring you clean clothes. You've had a long journey."

"Thank you, Regent Birgitta. I left London in a hurry. I didn't want Principal Julian or Juror Marius to stop me."

"You'll need to bathe too." Birgitta waved a hand and a vampire appeared at her shoulder. "Ulrik, take Seren to her room, and make sure she has everything she needs to clean up."

The tall blonde vampire dipped his chin and set off at a slow pace, waiting until he was certain Seren was following. The stone staircase they ascended was beyond the reach of the candlelight, and the darkness felt like a relief. Seren could relax her face and, for a short while, not guard her expression.

Is Osiris in here already? Seren listened, convinced that if he was inside the walls, she would feel him, but the distraction of human smells made it hard to concentrate. It was not hunger that bothered her, it was the thought of the miserable conditions they must be enduring. The air in the stairwell was ice-cold. Even with her slow hybrid circulation, she felt the capillaries contracting and stiffen with the sudden chill.

The drafty castle did not seem a likely place for humans to be comfortable and well cared for. Seren guessed the regent was only concerned with their survival. Looking out of the window over a wide terrace surrounded by battlements, she made out the distant view of Marazion. The causeway was a glistening ribbon strewn across the beach, and Osiris was nowhere to be seen.

Chapter 22

Osiris experienced a whiplash moment when he sensed Seren was in trouble. He'd watched her measured walk along the causeway. His gut churned. *I don't like it.* But he knew she was right. Both of them trying to sneak into the castle was a long shot. And having Seren in their company would divide the enemy's attention. Anything that did that would be good. Even Malachi's news that Julian was setting sail with the Elite Guard could not sway Seren from her decision.

She had said, 'The longer Papa is in there alone with the regent, the less chance we have to get him back. I'm not waiting.' Osiris couldn't argue with that.

When he saw her standing there shouting Connor's name, she looked beautiful and wild. Osiris loved her spirit. He drifted slowly along the beach, using the three-foot-high dune of seaweed as a shield. It stank of salt and percolating decay, but he burrowed into the slimy heap anyway, dipping his chin to keep his face in shadow as he peered over the top to where the confrontation unfolded. He felt helpless. When Seren's position on the causeway was far to his right, he forced his way through the tangled fingers of weed and commando crawled smoothly to the water's edge. Advancing into the lapping surf, his black hair becoming a sleek seal-like wet cap, he risked a peep above the surface and tuned into where the scene played out.

The moment the vampire flew at Seren, he told her he was coming. He rose out of the sea, the water streaking his bronzed chest with dirt as it ran down over the tight girdle of his muscles. The surf splashed around his abdomen as he strode forward, but then, like sensing the pulse of air when an aircraft breaks the sound barrier, he felt, rather than heard, a boom. The attacking vampire was thrown backwards, and Osiris sank quickly beneath the waves.

The lower half of his face remained underwater as his narrowed gaze watched Connor and the regent, Birgitta. *The burst of energy came from her. She has power beyond a vampire. Malachi, this is a forceful adversary.* Reluctantly, he sank below the surface and walked along the sea bed. Despite the slick moss and slime-covered boulders littering his path, he powered through the dark murky water.

He arrived at a steep slope of jagged barnacle-covered rock and climbed to where the manmade seawall rose in a cliff-like ascent. Placing his hands flat on the walls, he listened to the dozens of heartbeats thrumming in the lower regions of the fortress. The water amplified the noise. Swiftly scaling the sleek wet façade, when his head broke the surface, he twisted around to scan the sea. The black hull of Birgitta's ship loomed on the horizon. *So, the regent has already transferred her human cattle.*

Osiris smiled.

The castle reared up into the sky, but the ascending stairway approach was obscured by thick woodlands and cultivated gardens. Further around to the left though, the fortress sat much closer to the cliff edge. Osiris perched on a wide shelf in front of the seawall and waited for the regent, Connor, and Seren to draw the vampire bondsmen away and back towards the castle. Moving swiftly around to the left and leaping up through the once immaculate but now overgrown terraced gardens, he followed a stony pathway which led to the base of a broad cylindrical turret. The wide tower extended the full height of the castle, to the battlements, where it flared out with buttresses and was flanked by a pair of taller columns. The sea salt encrusted door at its base was seized up with rust. Wiping his wet hand over the lower pane in a nearby tall narrow window, Osiris peered inside. A wide spiral staircase took up the full width of the stone column. Pressing his chest close in to the wet gray façade, he climbed slowly up to the third level.

A yellow glow illuminated a window in the turret above the battlements. The scuffing sound of footsteps made him flatten his body into the space beneath the stone rampart overhead, and Osiris knew he had no choice but to break in. Inspecting the windows on the third floor of the castle wing beside the turret, he searched for one with rusted hinges and grime encrusted glass, hoping it meant the room was rarely used. Vampires were not house proud, but looking out into the world was essential to survival, even for those at the top of the food chain.

Crouching on the stone ledge, he pulled out a knife and prized the soft lead from around a small pane. Re-sheathing the blade, he tapped until he could remove the loosened glass and listen for telltale noises coming from inside. Satisfied the room was empty, he reached in through the hole, unfastened the latch, pushed the window open, and swung in over the ledge. As his body crossed the threshold, his hard flesh tingled. He felt an oscillating hum in the air. The sounds outside the castle became muffled. *Malachi...* Osiris' mind reached out to his master but discovered, as he suspected, that the 'power' emanating from inside blocked communication.

Dust plumed into the atmosphere and clung to his damp skin as he dropped down onto the bare oak floorboards. Silently turning the wrought iron handle, he re-secured the latch and replaced the glass, using his fingers to press the soft lead back into place. Untying the belt of wet leather which had tightened across his forehead, Osiris ran his fingers through blue-black hair which the salt water had turned into a tangled mass. *I can't pass as a Scandinavian guard, even if I kill one and take his uniform.*

Inspecting the room, he scanned the wooden chests ranged across the floor. Passing along the row, he pulled a wooden plank from the top of the nearest one and found silverware and crockery. *Vampires don't need plates and forks.* He grinned. The human cattle would not be indulging in fine dining. The next set of crates revealed drapes and bed sheets. Osiris moved purposefully on, lifting and re-stacking crates automatically, examining the contents of each.

Digging in with his nails, he lifted another lid, easing it up until the inch long staples came out. He moved aside a layer of soft leather cloths, and the refracted gleam of copper and silver danced colored jewels of light over the smooth stone walls. He smiled broadly. *Ah, perfect.* Near the top, Osiris found a candelabra and domed serving bowls, but digging further down, he found what he hoped for.

Selecting two large serving salvers, Osiris crimped their edges together, rested them on top of a closed crate and pressed the folded seam flat. Lifting up the sheet of metal, he held it against his bare chest and molded it to fit the ridges of his abdomen. Happy with the result, he repeated the process, buckling another salver to cover his back. This was more difficult, but by pressing his fingertips along his spine, he got a close enough fit.

Osiris' muscled form flowed in an effortless dance as his mind ran ahead of each task. Without pausing, he tore a linen tablecloth into wide strips and bound the makeshift armor into place around his torso. Taking a knife from its sheath, he shook out one of the larger pieces of tanned leather, cut a hole in the center, and pulled it over his head. Using strips cut from another hide, he secured the makeshift tunic in place and covered his vest of metal. As a final touch, he rubbed a piece of white linen into the dust and grit on the floor, shook off the loose debris, wrapped the cloth around his head and knotted it at the base of his skull. It covered his black hair which was his biggest barrier to blending in.

Closing the wooden lids, Osiris returned the crates to precisely where he had found them. He patted the leather pouch on his hip containing the vial of blood, checked his knives were secure, and crossed to the door. He rested his head against the thick panel to listen and felt the vibrations of footfalls beyond the room.

His focus wandered further, hoping to locate Seren by tuning his thoughts into hers, but the same force field he felt when he climbed in from outside bounced his thoughts back into his mind. Frowning, Osiris recoiled. *The regent can't know I'm here.*

The human heartbeats came from down below, and he could almost feel them through the soles of his feet, or so it seemed. Osiris relaxed, knowing his own heartbeat and smell would be disguised for a while. Like Seren, he could slow his circulation when he needed to, but for now, he felt safe.

The humans were certainly on a lower level, but Osiris' instincts told him there was another presence inside. The force field shrouding the castle felt too powerful for the source to be one vampire alone. *If another exists, they are hidden down there somewhere.*

When the footsteps he listened to faded, he cracked open the door and peered through the gap. The castle was illuminated by large candles in copper holders set into alcoves in the wall. Carbon stains trailed up the stonework from where the flames danced.

The other doors which ranged along the hallway were closed. A wide strip of burgundy and gold patterned carpet ran down the center of the flagstoned floor. The heavy oak door in the turret hung open, and the wide spiral stairs appeared from above and continued downwards.

Osiris stepped out into the hallway and swung swiftly down into the darkness of a stairwell, keeping his eyes and ears open. He descended three levels before the cold damp air cloying to his skin made him feel certain he was in the bowels of the castle. *Dungeons.* Sure enough, a deep stone ledge created a doorstep and interrupted the spiraling descent and, cautiously pushing open a dark oak door and peering round it, he saw a passageway lined by a row of iron barred cells. The walls gleamed in the dim light, like freshly hewn stone. *Could the regent have created these cells? And if so, why?* The static hum in the air was stronger here too, but no heartbeats. He doubted he'd find anything inside the dungeons. Easing back through the oak door and swinging around, the Egyptian barreled straight into a tall uniformed bondsman. The vampire's meaty hands closed around Osiris' throat and, feeling the sluggish pulse beneath his fingers and thumb, he froze.

"What the-?" Tightening his hold, the vampire's gaze clouded with distraction as the blood in the carotid artery pumped harder beneath his palm.

Sagging against the wall, Osiris let his head fall to one side.

The vampire's breath rattled in his throat. "How did you escape?"

From inside the pouch on his hip, Osiris withdrew the vial of blood. He reached out and dug his fingers in a viselike grip, deep into the hard sinews of the vampire's extended forearm, and smiled.

As confusion registered on the guard's face, Osiris dropped the vial and stamped on it with his bare foot. The smell of blood wafted in the air and the guard's lips drew back. The rattling breath became a loud growl as the vampire darted a look downwards. His grip slid from Osiris' neck, and he jerked down towards the pooling blood.

Osiris grabbed the vampire by the hair on the back of his head, drove his own knee up, and rammed the guard's face down fast.

He felt the shudder of the vampire's cheekbones shattering and the crack as his victim's nose broke. The vampire surged mindlessly back up. Osiris gripped his foe's head in both hands, twisted it around fast and heard the crackle as the discs in the vampire's neck exploded and the spinal column fractured. When he let him go, the guard collapsed at Osiris' feet.

Without pausing, he grabbed the vampire by the boots. Dragging him quickly through the door, along the passageway and through slimy pools of water, Osiris headed past the dungeons, honing in on a pale patch of light thirty yards away. When the light through a window bathed his face in a silver moonlit glow, Osiris smiled. *Perfect.*

Whipping the dead weight of the felled vampire around into the window bay, Osiris dropped the guard's legs and grabbed both his arms – pulling him up from the ground made the head fall back and the guard's shattered face stared up at the ceiling. Stooping and hefting the slack weight up over one shoulder, Osiris turned and opened the window. He sat the vampire on the stone window ledge and, with a push, tumbled the body out into the overgrown gardens below. He spared a moment to witness the vampire's fate and wish he had crushed the guard's skull and given him the final release. A crack rang out as the rockery walls of the garden terraces broke the vampire's fall, and broke a few more bones in the process. In a black blur, the heavy body rolled with increasing speed – like the runaway tire of a car, it bounced and disappeared into the gorse and brambles which fought to reclaim the eroding soil from the hands of human gardeners who were no longer there to win the fight. As things were, the felled vampire would lie motionless, his dense corpse sinking deeper into the undergrowth until his brain dehydrated.

Retracing his steps, Osiris heard voices and melted into the wall, staying out of sight inside the six-foot deep window alcove. *The castle guards are on the move.* Each one marched by without glancing around. *They're in a trance of some kind.* He heard the whispering of female voices. Osiris frowned as he tried to make out the words but found they were like butterflies. Each time he focused on one, it danced away. An ionized thrum buzzed through his inner ear and he realized Regent Birgitta was communicating with another vampire, or entity. *Is this sorcery? Witchcraft?* Osiris knew Malachi's theory about Birgitta being of Druid descent, and being able to inhabit 'The Otherworld'. *Is another entity sharing Regent Birgitta's mind?*

Osiris remained still, gathering what scraps of information he could.

He knew Malachi would not be reading any of this, because he had lost contact when he entered the castle. *I'll have to get outside to report back. I need to know when Rebekah will get here.*

The weight of the responsibility of looking out for Seren was one thing, but Rebekah, a mere human, would be an even bigger challenge. Osiris returned to the window where he had disposed of his unfortunate opponent and, reaching up to anchor his hand into the seams in the bricks, he swung out of the window and clung to the wall like a spider. Moving quickly up, he reached a parapet which marked the separation between the servants' quarters, and the upper floors where the grander reception rooms were.

Facing out to sea, Osiris clung to the ledge. The metal plate on his back prevented real contact with the stone façade and he didn't feel as secure as he would like. *Malachi...*

He waited, tuning into the sounds swirling on the wind that gusted around him, snatching at the hem of his thin leather tunic. Closing his eyes, he used deep breathing to bring calm and emptied his mind. He smiled in reflex as he saw an apparition of Malachi's wizened features solidify inside his head and the ghostly image spoke.

"Osiris, Rebekah is close now. As principal, Julian will demand parlay to negotiate terms for Connor's return, and Marius will smuggle Rebekah into the castle."

Seren is already inside. Osiris frowned. *Is it wise to let Rebekah come too close?*

"Connor and Rebekah need to be face to face. If you can find out where he takes his sleep that would help."

The regent keeps him by her side. Malachi, there is a force inside the castle. I believe Birgitta has a mentor, sister, guide, someone who she communes with. I doubt Connor is present when that occurs.

"Good. Look for a pattern. And locate the flesh of this guide." Malachi's fish-scale regard shimmered.

The flesh? Osiris opened his eyes and gazed out over the rolling gray sea in the bay. The night sky was smudged with clouds which hid the stars. *There is a body?*

Malachi's laughter disturbed his image. "Birgitta is a Druid. They leave their body to travel through the realm of The Otherworld, but I believe there is a body. The one she communes with will be real, not a ghost."

Osiris digested this information, only stirring when he realized the spray from the sea had soaked through the leather of his tunic and water dripped from his hair and down his neck.

I'll keep an eye out for Marius and Rebekah. In the meantime, anything I discover about this 'entity' and Connor's routine, I'll let you know. About to adjust his grip and start moving, Osiris froze again. *Do we need Seren to stay in there, what good is that?*

"Seren knows she is a distraction. It will help when Julian arrives."

Osiris was not entirely convinced. *If things get desperate, I'll cause a diversion and get Seren out of here. Understood?*

"Trust me, Osiris, no one wants to hurt Seren, not even the regent."

But Malachi hadn't seen the cold expression on Birgitta's ice white features. Osiris felt sure Seren would be executed if she became a problem. The young warrior's anger thrummed, even through the medium of thought. *Understood? I'm not losing her.*

Osiris slipped a fingertip beneath the soft gold armlet wrapped around his bicep, touching the bamboo catheter still inserted into his brachial artery. Even though Malachi no longer expected to drink Osiris' blood, the Egyptian kept his intravenous feeding tube in place. Times were uncertain, and Osiris was never one to close off escape routes.

Aloud, he repeated, as if swearing an oath to himself, "If things become desperate, I'll cause a diversion and get Seren out of here."

Chapter 23

Greg hunkered down between two boulders. Using his backpack as a cushion offered small comfort, but he couldn't have slept anyway. He had watched Anthony's writhing attempts to regain his feet fade away to the stillness of a corpse washed-up on the beach. Just when he began to think Marius had made a serious error and 'killed' Anthony with the injected relaxant, his companion's boxer-like bulk abruptly sat upright and levitated to standing.

A cold chill crept beneath Greg's skin as he hunched forward, every muscle tensed and ready to fight. *Shit, I don't know if Anthony still has all his marbles.*

Anthony's towering form whipped over, held out a hand to pull Greg up, and grinned. "Hop to, Marine. We have got some ground to make up."

Greg's irritation drowned out any feeling of relief. He struggled from his wedged position and onto his feet without help, and grunted. "Fuck off, vampire. You're the weak link in this team, mate."

Anthony's look of shock-horror earned him a right hook from Greg which he easily dodged. "Did Marius say where we'd find them?"

"All he said was 'Botallack'. Does that mean anything to you?"

"Of course. When you've been alive as long as we have, there are few places we haven't explored. Botallack is a Cornish mine from the 1800's. Interesting choice." Anthony became still and, to Greg's irritation, appeared to wander down memory lane.

"And, how do we get there?" Greg planted a boot on a rock and tapped his foot.

"Head west," said Anthony, with raised eyebrows which said, obviously.

Greg loaded up his backpack, hitched it higher, and replied, "Let's go."

"The going gets tough down the coast – less beaches and a craggier coastline. Just say if you want a lift."

Greg settled his night-vision goggles into place, ignored Anthony's enquiring look, and set off at a forced run. As he expected, the vampire breezed past him two seconds later.

The pair made good time through the darkest part of the night. Viewing the landscape through the green hue of night vision goggles, the swooping, reeling figure of Anthony resembled a dark specter, which Greg found unnerving – the sinking sensation in his gut that he was a burden got worse each time Anthony stopped and had to wait for him. The third time Anthony returned, he blocked Greg's path and cocked an eyebrow.

"Damn it," muttered Greg, but gave in. Using a rock to boost himself up, he climbed onto Anthony's back, and anchored a thick forearm around the vampire's throat.

That feeling of being a burden became a hundred times worse when they rounded the headland, and like Spider-Man, Anthony climbed a rock face and sidestepped along it as though he was glued to the vertical uneven surface. Greg looked down, once. He swallowed loudly and Anthony laughed.

"Hang tight, Marine, we're almost there."

Descending to where the sea threw up a Claymore spray of heavy droplets over them both, Anthony negotiated a swinging turn into a tempestuous inlet.

Greg's arm ached as all his weight shifted and his legs swung out over the abyss. Anthony reached back, anchored his fingers into Greg's utility belt and pulled him back in.

The wind dropped and an eerie calm surrounded the pair. They still heard it shrieking, but they were in the eye of the storm where it couldn't touch them. When Greg peered over his right shoulder, down below, where the sea boiled with fingers of froth trying to claw upwards, were two square towers. The walls of the inlet were high. One stone structure sat on a platform, lower than the other. An apron of grass, almost like a cultivated lawn covered the ground from its base to where the tumbled rocks met the boiling surf. The other, higher up and to its left, sat on the cliff edge. Steep treacherous pathways of flat rock connected the two.

"Botallack," said Anthony.

A narrow path clung to the side of the inlet wall and Anthony lowered Greg onto it. It was far from a safe place to be, but at least his boots were on solid ground.

"Carry on towards the mine, I'll scope out the area." Anthony vanished.

Greg took a deep breath, and focusing on sidling along the crumbling path took all his concentration. Eventually, it widened, but dipped down towards the fork between the towers. Greg chose the easier and, in his eyes, the sane option – he climbed up to the higher tower and away from the sea.

The black rectangles of doorways and windows were clear to make out and a warm tide of relief made him sweat when he heard Rebekah's voice.

A movement glimmered in the aperture and he saw Marius standing in the doorway watching his progress.

When Greg got close enough to hear, Marius said, "Watch your step, there are no floors and it's a long drop to the bottom in places."

Anthony appeared beside Marius, and Greg knew he had been left to fend for himself those last twenty yards. Greg grinned. His pride had not taken a slam dunk, at least.

Once Greg got inside the shell, he removed the night vision goggles and waited for his eyes to adjust. Stars shone from overhead – it was not only floors the tower was missing – and he could make out Rebekah sitting on a wide six feet deep ledge, resting back against a stone wall.

"You made it." She smiled, and her white teeth in a grimy face made him smile too.

"'oorah," he muttered quietly.

Shifting his shoulders to ease the discomfort of the field jacket stuck to his sweaty skin, Greg hunkered down and became absorbed in re-packing the medical kit which sat on the rock beside her.

"You okay?" he asked.

"Do you know why pirates wear eye patches?" Rebekah mused aloud.

"Because they only have one eye?" Greg frowned. *She's delirious.*

Her cheeks were pink from the rushing wind of riding with Marius, but Greg touched his hand to her forehead to check for fever.

"I'm okay. The dressing is holding. I'm annoyed at all the trouble I caused, more than anything. Pirates," she said again quietly.

"Okay, why do they wear eye-patches?"

"To see in the dark." Rebekah laughed at Greg's surprise. "Your eyes take half an hour to adjust when it suddenly gets dark." She looked at Marius who nodded. "They wore a patch so when they went below deck, or into a cave, they could switch the patch to the other side and have perfect night vision in one eye immediately. Clever, huh?"

"Very clever, and I can't wait to see how you shoe-horn that into after dinner conversation."

Greg pretended to rock sideways when Rebekah punched him, but his grin faded when Marius' crow black form drew closer.

"What now?" asked Greg.

"We head across the peninsular to the south coast and St Michael's Mount."

Anthony had settled on a block of flint-like stone on the opposite side of a cavernous hole in the floor. He was easing out his stiff fingers. He gave Marius a nod of assurance before he rested his head back and closed his eyes.

Greg shot assessing looks at Anthony every few seconds and then checked out the visible square of sky overhead. "Why don't you just leave me behind?" he asked. "I know where we are going. You can carry Rebekah-" He ignored her snort. "And I'll do a forced march across the peninsular. I'll catch up with you during the daylight hours."

Marius grinned. "Except daylight is barely eight of the twenty-four hours, and sunlight even rarer than that. And then there's the gorse on the heathland – it will rip you to shreds if you run into it."

Greg's hair was still soaked from the spray thrown up by the sea, his clothes were damp and even a waxed jacket couldn't keep the chilled night breeze out of his bones. He couldn't remember the last sunny day and feeling comfortable was a million miles away, but he was made of stern stuff.

Regaining his feet and slinging the backpack over his shoulder, he jutted out a stubborn chin and said, "I know how to navigate enemy territory. I'll set off now."

"I'm carrying Rebekah, and Anthony will carry you," said Marius, frowning at Greg's scowl.

"Been there and done that, so I think I'll pass."

In a streak of black shadow, Marius' white face appeared six inches from Greg's and made him jump. "Don't push me, Greg. I'm doing this for Julian. I don't need additional problems."

Greg stared into Marius fathom deep black gaze and breathed out a dry-throated chuckle. He slapped Marius on the chest and muttered. "Good one. You had me going there for a moment."

"Bloody humans," Marius growled, but a smile tugged at his lips.

Greg made one last stand. "If Anthony carries all the equipment, I can run faster."

"The direct route to the castle is across boggy ground, and lumps of granite are hidden everywhere. Knowing our luck, you'll break an ankle. I already have one injured human. We can do this much faster if Anthony carries you."

Anthony opened his eyes and they glittered in the dim light, the black shadows pooling in his eye sockets and hollows of his cheeks made his expression appear anguished. With a sigh, he said heavily, "I'm sorry about my lack of control back there at the safari park, Rebekah."

She grinned. "I'm fine, but Marius was pissed."

"How much time did I waste?" he asked.

"A couple of hours," Marius said wryly. "We should get going, now. We're out of the communication link here, and Julian might already be nearing the castle. We need to get Rebekah there. After all, she is quite important to the plan."

"I don't know why we couldn't have gone in the ship," said Greg.

"Two reasons. Getting Rebekah into the castle is hard enough, without having to smuggle her off a ship which the regent would be watching long before it reaches St Michael's Mount. And the other, heartbeats. We don't want to raise suspicion, not even for a second," said Anthony. "Connor may be under the regent's influence, but he might recognize Rebekah's scent."

Anthony shot to his feet and the block upon which he sat cracked beneath the explosive force. Flexing his thick set arms, he said, "Let's get this done. Marius is right, we have wasted enough time. Greg, I'll carry you."

Greg's brows shot up at the swift topic change, but he got to his feet when Rebekah did and all four left the damp shade of the tower and walked out into the starlit night. A steep slope of rocky steps meandered up to their right.

Turning his back, Anthony glanced over his shoulder. "Hop up."

Greg scowled, wiping his hands down over his damp thighs, as though steeling himself to touch something dubious.

Anthony grinned. "I'll be gentle." Circling abruptly out of sight, Anthony reappeared behind him, ducked under the Marine's arm, gripped the utility belt around his middle and lifted his feet from the floor. Anthony propelled them forward, side by side. "I get it. Piggy backs are for children, and you're not a fireman's lift kind of guy. Now, let's get moving."

The acceleration up the rough-hewn stairway felt like a terrifying fairground ride, but before Greg betrayed himself and yelled out, the sheltered terrain of the mining plant surrounded him and he inspected the series of arched tunnel entrances and the nearby stone chimney stack with interest. He was surprised to realize he had been here before. As a young teen, he had holidayed in Cornwall and done the tourist thing but, frustratingly, he couldn't remember much about it. *I must ask Anthony.*

Groups of stone cottages bordered the coastal road which connected all the Cornish villages. Rushing on they passed through half a dozen until wind beaten meadows came into sight. What were at one time farmed fields – some planted with crops, others filled with herds of cows or sheep – were now a tattered overgrown patchwork quilt. Just as Marius said, large scrubland areas with stone beacons, huge tors, and large expanses of gorse and heather blocked their path.

Anthony waded through gorse spines and thorns that shredded the bottom four inches of his pants legs without breaking stride and Greg cautiously lifted his feet clear.

As their navigator, Marius and Rebekah raced on up ahead.

Greg held tightly onto Anthony's sleeve with one hand and the collar of his coat with the other. His stomach muscles burned with the effort of lifting his knees, his feet felt more like they wore lumps of lead rather than leather boots, and the accelerating wind froze his face, but he still felt a rush of exhilaration.

The last few miles across the Cornish peninsular could have been accomplished faster but then icy rain fell from the early morning sky in driving sheets. Rebekah's teeth chattered loudly, and despite burying her face in Marius' broad shoulder, her lips turned blue. In silent agreement, Marius and Anthony detoured through a village. As the wind whistled along the street, the funneling effect made it colder than before and Rebekah shuddered in Marius' arms.

"Five more minutes," he muttered.

Diving down a narrow lane, Marius walked quickly up to the front door of a small cottage in the middle of a row. He kicked the door until the lock snapped, turned and barged backwards into the room. A thick layer of dust covered every surface. Lowering Rebekah gently to her feet, Marius said, "Wait here."

He left and returned seconds later with a large quilt wrapped in plastic. Tearing the package open, he laid it out over the floor and produced pillows which had been stored under the beds in vacuum packed containers.

"How did you know about this place?"

Marius shrugged and went to move away.

"Marius...?"

"Before the pandemic. I knew the family who lived here."

"Knew?" Marius was two centuries old, so he could not know them from when he was human.

"It was one of those freak events. The parents were in a car crash. Although, I didn't find that out until afterwards."

"So, how did you find out?" The wafting breeze from the hallway heralded the arrival of Anthony and Greg. Rebekah whispered urgently, "How did you find out?"

Marius smiled. "I came here to feed. I followed a drunk guy. We were still a secret back then." He jerked his chin towards a wall in the room. "He lived next door." He pushed his hands through his hair, restoring it to the sleek cap Rebekah was accustomed to. "When I heard a baby crying it saved the man's life. Children's heart rates are faster than adults. I detected four children and no adults."

"They were orphans?" Rebekah whispered, her hands clenched tight.

"Not quite, but the parents had braved a storm to get food. The car ended up in a ditch. I recognized them from a picture on the mantelpiece. I took them to the hospital and they all lived happily ever after."

"Thank you, Marius. You did a good thing." The tension drained from Rebekah, and with a sigh, she sank down onto the padded quilt and made herself comfortable, using a pillow to lean against the wall.

"I checked in on them every few years or so. I saw their children grow up, get married, and give them grandchildren and, in the end, their deaths."

Anthony and Greg swept into the room, both dripping wet.

Without speaking, Greg lowered the backpack to the floor, and dug out two energy bars and glucose drinks. Settling down beside Rebekah, he bumped shoulders. "If you're a good girl, I'll let you have some dry clothes after this."

The room was eerily silent apart from the two humans chewing. Rain pelted against the windows and ran down the walls in places where the frames leaked. Marius stood staring out into the rear garden. "The rain should ease off soon. Change into dry clothes, now. You'll both catch your death in that wet gear."

"Humor, Marius?" Rebekah quipped in a familiar exchange.

He smiled. "I think, that for the first time, it is."

With a low chuckle Rebekah rummaged inside the backpack and pulled out dry combats and thin thermal shirts. The dimly lit room made changing clothes feel safely discreet while both vampires kept their backs turned.

Greg and Rebekah settled down and listened to the lullaby of the falling rain.

"Hey, Anthony," Greg said. "Botallack. Why would vampires know about a Cornish mine?"

His vampire companion frowned and his silence stretched until Greg shifted uncomfortably. "Sorry-"

"I don't know about Marius, but I know Botallack because I fed there once. Tin miners – or copper, I can't remember which – were a hardy close knit clan. I was passing through and, sad to say, I most likely deprived a woman of her husband, without giving it a second's thought. Not my finest moment."

"We all make mistakes, Anthony. It's hard to keep a clean sheet when you live for hundreds of years. Here, in the 1800's, they used women and children in the 'mining processes'. One night, by chance, the victim I chose was a female arsenic worker." Marius' voice was low.

Greg and Rebekah waited, knowing the older vampire would continue when he was ready.

"Her blood burned. That is to say, there were granules in it that tasted hot. I was confused and curious, so I went to the mine at Botallack, from where I'd seen the woman leave. Those chambers we passed earlier were built in 1906. During the tin production process, arsenic and sulphur fumes from the furnace were drawn through those tunnels into the arsenic labyrinth, and then exhausted out of the tall chimney stack nearby."

"Arsenic was a byproduct?" Greg's whisper was sharp.

Marius nodded. "Remember, back then, they thought arsenic was medicinal. It was even given to babies. The mine workers sent children into the labyrinth once it was cool, to scrape the arsenic powder from the walls and collect it. I remember watching the arsenic workers getting ready – they used cotton wool nose plugs, handkerchiefs over their faces and smeared their arms with clay."

"But why children?" Rebekah asked. "Were the tunnels that small?"

"No," Marius replied. "For the same reasons that women sifted the dirt from the arsenic and then, in Penzance, African slaves prepared it for shipment – they were considered dispensable. Especially children, who could be replaced if they died."

"That's disgusting." Rebekah snorted.

"It is life. You can have another child." Marius held up a hand to ward off Rebekah's anger. "I'm not saying I agree. But it's how they thought, back then."

"So, the hot taste was arsenic?" Greg asked.

"Yes." Marius grinned. "It gave me a heady feeling, a type of high. Of course, nature has a way of coping with these things. It turned out that the arsenic workers gained some immunity from poisoning. It also gave them resistance to cholera and dysentery, so in a twist of fate, many outlived the tin miners. Poetic justice, some might say."

"I do remember learning about arsenic at school." Greg lowered his voice at a signal from Anthony. As if reciting a passage from a textbook, he murmured, "It was used in wallpapers and fabrics as a green dye. 'Paris Green' was a favorite color of the ladies, but if the dress they wore got wet, the fumes combining with oxygen were deadly and could kill a 'lady' in three months."

Rebekah looked shocked – she had been only six when the world changed, so survival training replaced the schoolroom.

Marius chuckled. "That's why the British loved going to the seaside for fresh air. Had they but known it, it was not the fresh air making them feel healthier, it was the arsenic in the wallpaper in their homes making them ill."

"So, that is why Botallack made a big impression on you, Marius," said Rebekah.

"Indeed. Arsenic workers carried a pouch of arsenic powder with them to put on their tongue when they felt fatigued. It gave them a 'hit', so they were addicts of a sort, but in this case, the addiction had an upside. And I enjoyed the sense of the miners having their 'just deserts'."

"Amen, to that," Greg whispered.

"Living forever is quite a ride, eh?" Rebekah murmured.

Marius blinked slowly, and his stillness exuded sadness. "It is also a heavy load to carry. You make the most of now, Rebekah… don't wish your human life away."

A comfortable silence fell and, in time, both humans dozed while they could.

The rain pounding on the roof eased off, then stopped as suddenly as it had started and Anthony woke Rebekah with a careful shake. She rubbed the sleep from her eyes and stretched out the kinks in her muscles.

A few minutes later, the group left the cottage, and mounted up in their travelling pairs.

The dull cloud of afternoon had brought with it an early dusk by the time the mottled green island out in the sweeping embrace of the bay came into sight. They had to get a lot closer before Rebekah and Greg could pick out the castle turrets breaking through the deep green canopy of the evergreen trees.

The four friends dropped to their hands and knees and edged forward. Finally, they commando crawled to where they could see out over the oily surface of the dark sea, and look down to where the streets of Marazion occupied the slope to the water's edge.

As they laid on their bellies in the coarse grass overlooking the rocky outcrop of St Michael's Mount, the moonlight transformed the ripples on the sea into a glittering field of broken glass.

"Julian is not here, yet," said Marius, scanning the horizon. "We'll move into position and lie low."

Retreating from the edge, at a crouched run, they headed round to the west side where they had a better view of the castle. It was on the seaward side of the mount, on the highest point.

Settling in for the wait, Rebekah tucked the binoculars she slung around her neck inside her combat jacket. They kept their heads down in the clumps of grass. They had to assume there would be vampire lookouts on the mound, and maybe on the mainland, too.

Marius and Anthony embodied felled statues. Greg and Rebekah only moved when their muscles burned with tension, and the minutes ticked by to an hour. Rebekah lost the feeling in her fingers and pulled a thermal pack out of her hip pocket. Popping the activator inside the bag of gel generated warmth and she almost sighed with relief.

The wind rustled clumps of long grass and other rustling sounds made Rebekah break out in a cold sweat.

Marius leaned over and, close to her ear, said, "It's only a rabbit."

Rebekah smiled. Of course, Marius knew she was scared. *He smells fear.*

She tapped his arm in thanks. Human voices carried for miles to vampire ears and made talking in the silent lull of approaching sunset risky. *Why does sound carry more at night?*

Marius' boot nudged hers, and Rebekah squinted out over the bay. She released a sigh when she saw the outline of the vessel oozing over the water like an iceberg carved in coal. *Julian.* For the hundredth time, she wished she was part of the psychic loop Malachi, Seren, Connor, and Osiris shared.

The arrowhead of rippling waves racing away from the hull indicated the ship was under the power of vampire oarsmen. *I wonder who's onboard. Julian and Malachi, of course, and most likely Captain Gerrard and Sergeant Hugh.*

The moon broke from behind a cloud and illuminated the ship as it drew closer to the mount. Sentinel Lars' vessel, with its faux-Viking embellishments, was an impressive sight, but it gave Rebekah a jolt. Her imprisonment by Lars had left its mark.

Julian and Malachi stood in full view at the prow of the ship and council guardsmen lined the deck.

Greg turned and gave Rebekah an encouraging thumbs up. *This is it. Once Julian has their attention, then Marius and I will get inside the castle.* She didn't even want to consider how. Just the thought of being submerged in the icy water was enough to make her flesh cold.

Until Julian made his play to cause the distraction, they had to assume the castle lookouts were scanning the coastline. Reaching the cliff might have been a stroke of luck, but the rest was down to them to *make* it work.

"Let's see what reception Julian gets. Be ready to make a move," said Marius.

The ship passed behind the mount, off to its west side, and decelerated suddenly. Rebekah imagined the vampire rowers applying reverse thrust to their oar strokes. The waves scudding away from the hull faded as it drifted to a stop.

Pulling out binoculars, Rebekah scanned the scene. Onboard the vessel, Julian's moon-bleached face wore a stern expression. Swinging her attention to the castle, she noticed a dim glow in one window high in a turret. It was the only sign that the place wasn't derelict. *Why would they put a light in a window?* The obvious answer was that it was a signal. A beacon to let others know they were there. *But who?* As though Greg read her thoughts, he leaned in and muttered, "See that light? I'm guessing it's a signal to the regent's vessel out in the Channel."

"Connor must know Julian is there." The remainder of the castle remained dark and motionless. Greg shrugged, his attention and Rebekah's turning back out towards the water again when Julian rang a brass bell. The mournful clanging noise cut through the darkness.

Julian put both hands on the rail and called out across the divide. "Regent Birgitta, I'm here to parley. I am coming ashore."

An orange glow poured out through an aperture in the glistening gray stone wall as the arched entrance door on the west side whipped open. Connor stepped from the black shadow of the castle and out into the moonlight, a hostile expression fixed on his handsome face.

Rebekah covered her mouth as her stomach churned and she smothered a gasp.

The hard lines of his body radiated anger as he bounded down the flight of flat stone ledges to the fortified wall, where open black mouths of cannons sat in each crenellation. His movement jerked as he raised a fist. "There is nothing to say."

"I am coming ashore, Doctor Connor. To talk, or to fight. That is your choice."

"I have nothing to say to you," he replied, on a low rumbling breath.

Julian's silence betrayed his surprise. Rebekah felt sure he had not expected Connor to radiate such aggression.

"Where is Seren?" asked Julian.

"My child is not your concern," he replied.

"She is not just *your* child."

"She is here to be free of her whining mother."

Greg patted Rebekah's shoulder as her eyes filled with tears. She sunk low on her elbows, her cheeks blotching beneath the bruising grip she kept clamped over her mouth.

With a penetrating glance, Marius cleared his throat, and murmured, "You know it's not really him talking."

Rebekah nodded and grinned stiffly. "Getting a grip." She wiped her nose with the back of her hand and her expression hardened.

The group focused again on the scene unfolding down below.

"We are not leaving until we see the child." Julian's cold tone rang through the night.

Yanking his cape around him, Connor turned away and leapt back up the stairs to the castle doorway. He threw his words back over his shoulder. "Come. Talk, and then you will leave."

Without hesitation, Julian gave a signal and the crew lowered a rowing boat over the side of the ship. He abseiled nimbly down after it and plunged into the water, setting the small boat dancing. Still tethered, it knocked gently against the hull. Captain Gerrard and Sergeant Hugh followed behind, their olive-green guardsmens' garb giving them a beetle-like appearance as they scuttled down the slick surface of the hull. They, too, disappeared beneath the surface.

"Why the boat?"

"It has spare clothes and blood supplies from the dispensary. Julian doesn't know how long they'll be there or if they'll be fed," Marius said.

The small rowing boat skimmed across the divide as though jet propelled and disappeared into the embrace of the harbor.

Apart from a glimpse of movement behind the wall at the quayside, even with binoculars, the humans could not make out anything helpful. She scanned the silhouette rising above the trees. The chapel, founded by Edward the Confessor, dominated the skyline. The chimneys rising like sharp spines added to the stark beauty. The castle was forbidding and fascinating in equal parts.

Rebekah could not see any sign of Julian anywhere along the hundred meter climb up the mound. She huffed with annoyance and elbowed Marius.

"Julian has just gone into the west entrance," Marius replied. Ignoring Rebekah's scowl – knowing that being human was like seeing in black and white in a world of blazing color – he added, "We should get going. The causeway is only there at low tide, but they'd see us anyway. We'll go back around the bay and approach from the east side."

"Another swim coming up, then?" said Greg.

"I don't like it. Connor is in there, Seren, and now Julian." Rebekah stared out at the castle with narrowed eyes.

"There is nothing we can do about that. We still have to get you inside. If Malachi is right, only you can do this, so let's get moving." Marius shuffled backwards over the grass, tapping Rebekah's boot when she did not immediately follow. On the other side of Greg, Anthony jerked his head.

Rebekah wriggled her hips and struggled to get her limbs moving. Greg and Anthony lagged behind, putting their heads together for a moment, and Rebekah wondered what they were talking about. The rough grass made backing up slow going until she could squirm around and move forward.

Using the cover of shrubs and lumps of granite, they were finally able to regain their feet and run along in a low crouch, tracking a course parallel to the coastline. Looking out, the turret where the light shone was now on the far side, obscured by the other features of the castle. Dropping onto their stomachs again, they crawled to the cliff edge and looked down to where pebbles glimmered beneath the shallow water sloshing around large boulders.

"Let's go," muttered Marius. Swinging his legs over the edge, he dropped over the cliff, landing in the sea with the splash. Scraping his wet hair back, he leapt up onto a large flat rock and held his arms out to Rebekah.

Lying on his belly beside her, Greg said, "You gotta be kidding me."

"We don't joke," said Anthony, with a grin which made that a lie.

Suddenly the wind picked up and Anthony said, "Go, go, go."

Rebekah surged up to her feet and launched herself over the cliff. Marius, like a fielder in baseball, tracked her hurtling body, stepping back off the rocks and into the water. At the very second he hit the mark where she would pass over his head, he leapt twenty feet and caught her in his arms. Instinctively, Rebekah grabbed his shoulders as they both fell. He cushioned their landing, although Rebekah's teeth snapped shut with a sharp crack.

"Okay?" he whispered.

Rebekah nodded. Her jaw clenched in determination.

Marius registered the gushing blast of air coming from the cliff top and shot a glance up. Swinging around, with Rebekah still in his arms, he waded quickly into the surf.

"Greg." Rebekah strained to look over Marius' shoulder.

"They'll follow on. We have to get going."

Something in Marius' tone made her shudder. The debris scattering down over the cliff face confirmed her fears. *They are under attack.*

◇◇◇

The compressed airwave flattened the grass of the meadows. The vampires came in fast.

"We have to stop them following Rebekah." Anthony leapt to his feet and turned to face the landscape. A black figure solidified

222

out of the darkness. Anthony hurtled headlong towards the speeding vampire. Punching him hard in the stomach, he ruptured the vampire's abdomen, gripped a handful of the firm flesh, yanked and twisted. Anthony withdrew his hand and dropped the lump of dry vampire tissue onto the ground at his feet. The vampire jerked back, his hands cradling the hole in his torso, and then ran on. He staggered as his legs weakened. Greg barreled in, rugby tackled him to the ground, and, lifting the heaviest stone he could find, he dropped it into the open chest cavity. The vampire rolled over, and digging holes in the earth with each clawed grip, he crawled towards the cliff.

"It's no good. I'm picking up another three coming in," Anthony's tone was heavy. "Birgitta's power makes then more zombies than vampires."

"Plan 'B' it is then."

"You don't have to do this, Greg."

"Sure I do. It's okay, Anthony."

Pulling a knife from the pocket of his combats, Greg flipped it around and jabbed the blade into his thigh. Blood gushed, soaking his pants leg instantly.

Anthony growled as blood lust rose inside him. The sweet scent of the red nectar flooded his brain with a firework display of hunger.

Greg pulled a short length of nylon webbing from his utility belt and, swaying on his good leg, used it as a tourniquet and pulled it snug, but not as tight as he needed to stop the blood flow. Answering the question he knew was burning a hole in Anthony's mind, he said, "I don't want to bleed out too fast. I need to keep a clear head as long as I can."

Fighting with his own feeding instincts, Anthony put thirty yards or so between himself and Greg, and targeted the fastest moving incoming threat and drove a shoulder into the body of a blood-crazed vampire, flipping him up and over. The vampire's spine snapped as he landed on a granite boulder rising from the ground.

Anthony knelt on his victim's chest, gripped him by the hair and slammed his head back, cracking open the skull.

Turning back towards the cliff edge, Anthony saw two of Birgitta's bondsmen mere yards from where the bleeding Greg backed up, swinging his mallet in arcs which dropped lower as his strength drained away.

"God damn it." Anthony clenched his jaw and flew forward. Hitting one vampire squarely in the back, he shoved him onwards and past Greg. The vampire's heels dug in and he pushed back. His boots excavating troughs in the grass as Anthony rammed all his hefty weight into a final shoulder shove. Both vampires tumbled over the edge and the sharp crack of granite hard bodies slamming onto the pebbled beach below rang out.

A gusting downdraft, like the passing of an express train, plastered his thin waxed jacket to his body. Self-preservation kicked in and Greg dropped to his stomach, held his breath, and peered through the clumps of grass. The sharp yank on his backpack dragged him along on his belly and his hands scrabbled at the ground beside him, grabbing at handfuls of tangled weeds and grass. He felt the greasy stalks snapping in his grasp and, for a moment, he thought he would be dragged over the cliff. The rushing wind died abruptly as the vampire overshot his prey and veered away.

His upper body hanging precariously over the edge of the sheer drop, Greg dug his toe caps into the soft ground and gasped for breath. In the darkness below, he caught a sharp burst of movement on the shore.

Stones erupted into the air, scattering as Anthony rolled over and jack-knifed to his feet in an explosive maneuver. He yanked his opponent up by the back of his coat and rammed his face into the cliff.

Anthony survived the fall, thank God for that. Greg's skewered thigh burned and the muscle began to scream. He felt his boots slipping as his legs shuddered with the strain of stopping him from sliding. Blocking out the pounding blows continuing on down below, he tried to wriggled backward, and his face glistened with sweat as fear gripped him. Retreating back onto solid ground, he rolled over, and his breath rasped in his throat as he stared at the night sky.

The sounds of combat faded. Greg grinned. *If Anthony loses, I'll soon know.* His head swam with a woozy feeling, ink blots filling his vision. Smothering a cough, Greg staggered to his feet and, dragging his foot, headed for the trees. The last vampire hit him squarely in the back. His stomach turned over and nausea rose up to choke him as his feet left the floor. He hit the ground hard and, winded by the impact, he groaned. Pushing up, he braced his arms and scrabbled forward, scanning the darkness. *The bastard is playing with me.*

Scrabbling up again, tilting his weight onto his good leg, Greg stared blindly into the deep shadowed night. He lifted his chin, spread his arms wide, and said, "C'mon you fucker." Greg knew Anthony would stay at the bottom of the cliff in case any vampires resisted his blood red charms and followed Rebekah. *Shit.* The bat like creature flew across the slick wet grass. Adrenalin flowed fast and Greg felt a curious detachment. *He really does look like a bat. I can see where horror stories got that image.* Another vampire darted into view and Greg squeezed his eyes shut.

He felt the first thud break a few ribs. He flew backwards through the air, his arms flung out from his body, and he felt teeth piercing his neck. The hard tug on his leg reminded him of a shark attack he'd once experienced. He'd lashed out and kicked the shark on the nose in a burst of aggression that saved him. But, not today. A second set of teeth sliced through his combats and tore into his thigh muscle. The inkblots of unconsciousness swimming inside his head grew larger. The crash landing into the boggy ground knocked what little breath he had left from his body and the starlit sky filled his vision, each one exploding like a shower of firework sparks. The wet sound of flesh being torn – no, not torn, sucked, because of course, they never ate the flesh – filled his head. The stars flared, becoming bigger as they blurred out of focus. Greg welcomed the cold numbness invading his body. *We did it Anthony.*

Chapter 24

The tide in the bay was still coming in, but the water was already deep. The three vampires trudged across the seabed in single file, their open eyes staring straight ahead despite the gritty silt swirling in the currents.

Glancing up, Julian could easily track the bottom of the rowing boat Sergeant Hugh dragged along. The harbor wall wore a green coat of moss and the group set a course that cut through the bobbing clusters of other boat shells, avoiding anchor ropes and rudders.

The water became darker when the concrete of the quay loomed overhead, and Hugh stopped to wait for Julian, near where boats were moored at the quayside.

At Julian's signal, the three vampires surged from the water, hoisting themselves effortlessly up onto the concrete walkway. Julian and Gerrard stood in ever-growing puddles of seawater while Hugh moored the rowing boat between two badly weathered, decaying speedboats, collected a canvas wrapped bundle from the bottom, and then joined them.

Moments later, the three marched along behind the waist-high harbor wall, past a row of ramshackle dwellings.

At a break in the row, a cobbled lane ascended and Julian surveyed the path beyond. A lynch gate crypt at the corner of a grassed garden marked a fork in the path.

Beckoning to his companions, Julian rushed on and chose the fastest route to the bottom of the wide stone stairway. The uneven angles and pitches made it challenging for humans to negotiate. In places, a black metal handrail on one side of the ascent gave encouragement to feeble souls who wished they had not started out on the climb to the castle, but Gerrard and Julian took the direct route up the hillside, clearing the handrails in effortless vaulting leaps. Sergeant Hugh shouldered the linen sack and followed on behind.

Halfway up the northern slope, they passed the infamous heavily-shuttered well. Legend had it that the fortress perched on top of the great granite crag was built by the giant, Cormoran. At night, the giant was said to wade across to the mainland and eat the cows and sheep in the fields, until 'Jack the Giant Killer' dug a deep pit – now called a well – and woke the giant from his daytime nap by blowing his horn. When the enraged Cormoran burst out through the castle door, blinded by the glare of the sun, he fell into the pit, and was imprisoned there.

Further along the cobblestoned route was a representation of the giant's heart – disappointing to many, the cluster of huge boulders merely marked the spot of a small heart-shaped pebble set in the pathway.

Built in the Iron Age, the basic construction of the castle was boxlike with castellations and soaring chimneys transforming it. Julian and his party paused at the row of black cannons and took stock. They were small bore and fitting to ceremonial use rather than the battlefield.

Peering at his companions, Julian said, "Here goes. Stay close and keep your eyes open."

Both vampires nodded sharply.

The imposing black walnut door Connor had retreated through remained ajar and a blade of yellow light spilled out over the uneven ragstone step. When Julian cautiously pushed it open, dozens of sharp rivets winked in the candlelight and the huge iron ring in the center, there to summon attention, creaked gently. Julian crossed the threshold first, peering inside. The steep flight of steps in front of him made him pause. *Am I walking into an ambush?* He felt vulnerable down in the well of the entrance space. The iron portcullis suspended overhead did not improve matters. He held up a hand to Hugh and Gerrard. Pointing ahead and nodding. They would wait there until he reached the upper level of the entranceway. He slid his hand along the metal balustrade and mounted the stairs. The flagstoned area above had doors on the left and right, and one on the right side stood open. He beckoned and the others followed, and from the doorway they could see Connor standing like a sentry in front of a fireplace, below a coat of arms. The small reception hall, in years past, would have been filled with the paraphernalia of the castle's ancestors – shields, helmets, guns and swords. But, the fortress had been gutted of furniture, artifacts, and items of interest before the vampire barter system could be enforced. Like the victors in any war, vampires moved in fast and feathered their nests, stealing treasures they coveted.

"Doctor Connor," said Julian, and frowned when his friend's rigid stance did not change.

Seconds passed and Connor did not even blink – his glassy stare showed no recognition.

Gerrard raised his brows in a 'what now' look.

Julian shrugged, clasped his hands behind his back and mirrored Connor's attitude. "We wait," he muttered.

After endless moments, Connor spun around and darted from the room.

Julian rushed after him.

Connor's hurtling path passed through a cozy chamber that took Julian's breath away. In the center sat an antique Victorian partners' desk – very much like his own, but much older – its well-used five foot square tooled-leather surface was beneath glass to protect it from further deterioration. Moonlight spilled in through a huge bay window, picking out the rich embossed pattern on the cream carpet. The floor length claret drapes were certainly not in keeping with the historic use of the castle as a monastery.

A compact chandelier descended from the high vaulted roof, centered perfectly above the desk. Julian wanted to stay, sit in the seat and savor the history, but he raced onwards.

Feeling like Alice trying to keep the white rabbit in her sights, he whipped along taking right and left turns in a wide hallway. He swore softly when he took the wrong direction. The short detour ended at a worn leather bench-seat inside a deep glazed alcove. Rushing back, he almost bowled into Connor who had stopped on the threshold of a book-lined chamber.

Inside the room, Birgitta reclined on a chaise, dressed in a supple white leather skirt so thin it flowed over her curves like poured cream. Her silver breastplate accentuated a tiny waist, and her complexion had a pearlescent glow – the pose drew the eye of every vampire and the smile on her red lips exuded triumphant conceit.

In contrast, Connor's attire could be best described as the color of ash. He wore a ring with a jet stone which Julian had not seen before.

With a silent sigh, Julian gave thanks that it was not on his friend's wedding finger, but before he could take heart from that, the regent rose and left by the doorway opposite and Connor, like a dog on a lead, fell into step behind her.

Julian waited a mere second, for Gerrard to arrive beside him and then followed. Four stone steps took them down into a banquet hall. Even stripped of its furniture, the space was breathtaking. The vaulted ceiling with dark brown beams crowned the plaster hunting frieze which circled the room. The stained-glassed windows threw a harlequin of fragmented shapes over the white walls in an explosion of color – wooden shutters were a recent addition.

Emerging from a spiral stone stairwell in the corner, in a fast moving stream, Birgitta's guards poured in and surrounded the visitors with soundless efficiency.

There was a shuffle of movement as Hugh brought up the rear and was quickly swallowed up by the circle of silent vampires.

Seawater dripping from the hem of Julian's cape pooled on the oak floor. With Gerrard and the sergeant flanking him, Julian stood equally still – all three visitors were in the same soaked state and only the percussive sound of water droplets falling broke the silence.

Shifting his weight onto one foot, Julian could see between the heavy-set shoulders of two bondsmen and gain an uninterrupted view of Connor and Birgitta, who stood before a tall marble fireplace at the far end of the room.

A uniformed guardsman stood beside Birgitta.

Another vampire Julian didn't know appeared to be acting as Connor's personal aide. *Or he keeps tabs on Connor.* Julian feared that getting Connor and Rebekah alone in a room together would be impossible, but then, where Rebekah was concerned, he'd been wrong before.

His patience wearing thin, Julian tapped his boot.

His attention slid past Connor to a female vampire. He tuned into a sluggish heart rate and jerked to attention. *Seren?* He barely recognized the girl. An intricately woven braid swept the swathe of black hair away from her face. The emerald silk gown she wore burnished in a halo of light.

The myriad of colors cast by the tall arched stained-glass windows accented the three finely dressed figures as though their presence drew the slanting beams of moonlight from the sky.

"You came to talk, so talk." Connor's eyes gleamed with silver-tinted anger. His black hair, glistening with oil, made his face appear chalk white and dull, the usual quartz-like glow had drained away. Julian registered the differences in his friend and frowned.

Birgitta reached out and caught Connor's fingers in hers. "My lord, we are not heathens. Let us talk in comfort. Offer Principal Julian our hospitality, after all, he has come a long way."

As though a switch flicked inside him, the anger melted from Connor's features and a convivial smile replaced it. "Come, Principal Julian, you are soaked through. Ulrik will escort you to where you can change and we will set a fire for when you return."

The uniformed vampire beside Birgitta stiffened to attention at the sound of his name.

The circle of bondsmen nearest Connor parted, offering the visitors only one direction to go in. Julian knew he, Gerrard and Hugh were being managed, but for now, they would play along. *If I have Birgitta's attention, then Marius will have a chance.*

"That is very kind. Sergeant Hugh has our dry clothes."

As though Connor might think it was a lie, Hugh silently swung the linen sack of clothing into view.

Birgitta's focus remained on Julian. She released Connor's hand and glided to within touching distance. When Julian met her gaze, the glacial ice melted to limpid pools, vulnerability stirred in their depths, and Julian found he could not swallow.

"Principal, you mustn't think badly of us. We fell in love." Birgitta laid a cool hand on his wet sleeve.

A rivulet of water ran down from his hair and gathered in pearl drops on his lashes, and yet, wiping them away did not occur to him. *They fell in love.* Julian sneered, fighting the drowning feeling inside him. "Doctor Connor has a family."

"No, he has a *child*. And she has chosen him. The mother will be dead a few years down the line-" Her perfectly drawn scarlet lips pursed as she mewed with regret. "Perhaps sooner. Surely Connor is entitled to an eternity of love?"

Julian opened his mouth to argue. The blue pools became ocean deep and he felt as though he was being dragged under. Suddenly, a memory of his Eva, his love, back when he was human, solidified in his mind and his jaw snapped shut.

He remembered writing a love letter to Eva two weeks before their wedding. He lifted his hands and could almost feel the rich vellum sheet between his fingertips.

7 August, 1806

My Eva,

The hardest thing in the world is to be in love and to yet attend to business. As for me, all who converse with me find me out, and I must lock myself away, or others will do it for me.

A gentleman asked me this morning, 'What news from London?' and I answered, 'She is exquisite'.

All the language on earth could not say how much I am ever yours,

Julian.

Birgitta took a deep breath, the letter faded, and Julian saw only her face, once again.

"You see? Love. There is nothing greater."

"I will talk to Doctor Connor, alone," he said.

"But, of course." Birgitta stroked her fingers along Julian's sleeve, running her metal jeweled nail tips over the back of his hand. "Come, let us be comfortable, no? You must change into dry clothes."

Feeling as though trying to think used all his concentration, Julian turned to Sergeant Hugh and took the linen sack. He dug through the three packages inside and pulled out his own garb. He passed the cloth sack to Gerrard and in a flat tone, said, "Sergeant Hugh, take the rowing boat and return to the ship."

His sergeant's mouth dropped open before he smothered his surprise.

"But, Principal-" Captain Gerrard stopped talking at Julian's upraised hand. He obediently took out his own parcel and returned the bag to the sergeant.

With a final confused glance at Julian, Hugh swung around and left the room, accompanied by a pair of Birgitta's guards. Their footsteps echoed in the hallway, the closing of the distant front door made a muffled thump, but everyone remained frozen in place.

Captain Gerrard clutched his folded clothes to his chest and fixed his attention on Julian.

The principal stared into space, absently rubbing the back of his hand as though trying to remove a stain.

Connor moved first. Approaching Julian, he halted within arm's reach. "This way, Principal," he said.

"Call me Julian, please. We have known each other a long time."

Connor's brows rose, his gray eyes examining Julian's face, and something shifted in their depths.

Does he remember? Julian smiled.

But, the grin Connor reflected back was hollow. "Friends, of course. Julian."

The strange vampire hovered near Connor's shoulder.

"What should I call your aide?" Julian asked.

"His name does not matter. He is of no concern to you." Connor's gray cloak swung in an arc as he spun on his heel. "Follow me."

Julian obeyed, but faltered when Connor gave no sign of noticing the closed door blocking his path – iron hinges reached across at the top and bottom and splayed into a clawed grip over the solid planks. But then, a nanosecond before Connor collided with the hefty wood, it whipped silently open.

Rushing forward, Julian stepped through it into a small rectangular space. Connor had vanished and only Ulrik remained.

Inside the small room, on one side was a leaded window in a deep pew-like alcove with a bench on either side, the seats covered in worn cracked leather. On the opposite wall was another door. Gray light slipped in underneath it. *It leads outside. Connor must have gone that way.* As Julian turned towards it, his feet became too heavy to lift and the bundle of clothes fell from his slack grasp.

Ulrik scooped it up before it hit the floor, broke open the wrapper, and set it on one of the leather bench seats.

Julian rotated slowly on his heel and began shedding his clothes. As he stripped off his coat, shirt, and pants, his brain absorbed several things at once: The sudden breeze as the outside door – now behind him – opened and then closed again; the rich smell of tobacco emanating from the wooden panels inside the room; and the white blur of Birgitta disappearing back into the hall and that door swinging shut.

Ulrik stood to attention and stared out of the small square panes of leaded glass as if he was alone.

Once Julian had buttoned up his collar and used his fingers to comb his hair as best he could, Ulrik ushered him back the way they had come. Glancing around the hall, Julian noticed that Seren had left. Birgitta commanded the center of the room with Connor at her side. The sweeping archway of the cavernous elaborately carved ceiling framed the couple, and Julian felt uncomfortable. *Something is wrong.*

Gerrard had disappeared, too. *Did he go through the outside door?* The words 'divide and conquer' came unbidden to his mind. He darted a sharp look at Birgitta and saw only a gentle smile. *Something is wrong.*

"Good," said Birgitta, "and now, we talk." Turning, her hips undulated in a mesmerizing rhythm as she led the way.

Moving slowly, Julian fell into step behind Connor. He walked through a door and past Birgitta, and steeled himself not to look back.

Julian was not surprised they had returned to the 'book room' – a hybrid between a library and a parlor.

Both Birgitta and Connor looked out of place in the cozy space. Intricately carved plaster panels framed bookcases. Pictures of past inhabitants covered every wall. Lamps still sat on side tables and the pieces on a chessboard implied that a pair of apparitions were deep in battle.

Birgitta's polished silver armor and white draped silhouette put Julian in mind of a ghost. And Connor's dark glowering presence was better suited to a dungeon.

"Nice place you have here," said Julian.

The musical chime of Birgitta's laughter echoed in the room. Connor didn't twitch.

Arching her brows delicately, Birgitta said, "I'll leave you for a moment. Now, you are dry, you can sit, no? Be civilized." She gestured to armchairs arranged in front of the grate where, as promised, a fire now burned.

Birgitta withdrew and for a moment Connor's aide held his ground. Julian glared at him until, with an accepting nod, the vampire left them alone.

Connor crossed to the bookcase at the far end and picked out a volume which he seemed to find fascinating.

Like a castaway who needed to get his bearings and find solid ground, Julian walked over to the chaise covered in golden and burgundy striped fabric and sat down. He tidied his cuffs and eased his shoulders inside his jacket.

"Connor?"

As though a button had been pressed, Connor turned around and began talking. "I am a member of the London hive, but you don't own me, Julian. I can leave England if I wish to, anytime I choose. I choose now."

"But what about Rebekah? And Seren?"

As though saying her name made her appear, the door opened and Seren came in, and just behind her, Captain Gerrard. He strode across the room as if he'd been there before, silently pulled out a seat at the chess game, and sat down.

Birgitta closed the door and her eyes traveled from Julian to Gerrard, and back again. "So much better." She inclined her head.

"Seren has made her choice." Connor spoke as though the interruption had not occurred. "As for Rebekah, the woman is a feeble human. I confused pity for a dumb animal with something more. I was bored."

Julian tried hard not to look at Seren. He tuned into her rock steady heart rate and for a moment considered the idea that Birgitta had enchanted her too.

He rubbed the back of his hand absently, and his gaze was drawn to Birgitta and the silver salver she was holding, set with four crystal goblets. His attention became torn between the scent of warm human blood, and facing the idea that Seren might be lost to the 'other side'.

"She is my biological mother, Principal Julian. But you can't expect me to care about her." Seren's voice held no emotion.

Searching her closed expression, Julian said, "Rebekah is far from feeble." With Birgitta in the room, he found his enthusiasm for the task draining away.

Birgitta smiled as she held out the tray of glasses. "Please, feed. It has been a long journey. I won't send you away without extending hospitality."

As Julian reached for the nearest goblet and Birgitta leaned forward, the silver filigree pendant around her throat swung forward, catching the light. A dried brown smudge on her skin showed where it usually rested.

Julian recognized the gleam of dark ruby inside the intricate silver cage. *Why would she carry blood?*

The room was filled with the distracting shuffle of movement as Connor took a seat and Seren settled beside him. Gerrard's profound silence penetrated Julian's preoccupation and he turned to make sure the captain was still there.

Gerrard, too, held a glass of warm blood, but he had lost interest in the chess pieces and his eyes tracked Birgitta's flowing form.

Julian frowned. *The sooner we leave, the better. Connor is beyond our help, it's down to Rebekah, now.* He drained his glass and got to his feet. "Thank you for your hospitality, but Seren has made her choice, as has Doctor Connor. There is little point us remaining." Julian's arched glance took in Captain Gerrard. "We shall take our leave."

The captain appeared not to hear. He still stared at the alluring regent. Irritation reared inside Julian and he turned to face Birgitta. Her limpid gaze defused his anger and without knowing why, he sank back into his seat.

Chapter 25

Anthony could not remember feeling nauseous, not since he was human and was punched so hard in the gut during a street fight that he vomited on the floor. Leaving Greg to die made him feel sick. He peered up the sheer rock face from the boulder strewn seafront and listened.

No one is following. The sickening thumps which had set an avalanche of debris tumbling down from overhead had moved further away. Gritting his teeth and tearing his thoughts from the pact he and Greg had sworn, he turned his back on the cliff. The seawater parted in a trough as Anthony plunged into the surf, trying to block out the distant guttural noises of the feeding frenzy up on the clifftop until the seawater closing over his head did it for him.

Once fully submerged, he knew he was undetectable. Hiding would not be so easy for Marius, with Rebekah to look out for.

Striding along the seabed with renewed determination, when Anthony reached the underwater ledge of the granite crag where the mount erupted upwards from the bedrock, he tracked a path around the island. He searched the murky green-black depths for Marius, who should be watching out for him, too. He wasn't sure how things would go, but Rebekah needed air, that much he did know. *I'll feel better when we know what the hell is going on.*

The currents dragged silt, detritus of seaweed and discarded garbage across his vision and over his skin. Nature's cycle was unrelenting and messy. Anthony's narrowed gaze chased the flitting shadows of darting fish. His heart, if he had one, would have leapt in his chest when a mass dived from above in a fluid glide – insanely, he thought it was Rebekah swimming. Air bubbles streamed up over his face as he snorted. *It's a seal.*

He began running, the algae covered rocks cracking underfoot as he leaned forward to increase his speed. When, a few minutes later, he saw a dark pillar of billowing shadow, he knew, even before the orb of a glowing pale face nodded, he had found Marius. *But, where is Rebekah?*

He swerved right and set a course that would converge with Marius up ahead. As he drew close, he saw Rebekah hanging onto Marius by the shoulder, one hand gripping the lapel of his coat. She was looking down and turning her head into Marius' chest as he powered onward, using his hand to shield her face from the fast moving flotsam.

Anthony frowned. *How the hell?*

In a sudden surge of movement, Rebekah let go of Marius and kicked for the surface. He immediately cut his speed and Anthony overshot them. Skewing around in an arc, he watched Marius reach up, grab hold of Rebekah's boot and slow her down.

Anthony accelerated. *What the bloody hell. He's trying to drown her.*

Marius felt the rushing current as Anthony's hefty bulk hurtled in like a torpedo. He held up a hand, signaling above. Anthony applied the brakes as he looked up and saw Rebekah's head break the surface, and then Marius tugged on her combat pants and pulled her beneath the water again.

He realized Marius was just trying to keep Rebekah's visits to the surface to gulp air as invisible as possible. *No splashing.* Veering to one side, Anthony avoided a head on collision, but his shoulder thumped into Marius and jerked him around. Like a silent movie with a soundtrack of rushing water, Anthony watched Rebekah jolt as Marius lost this footing and tore a patch from the leg of her pants. Her body whipped like a spinning top, a stream of bubbles erupted from her nose, and panic filled her eyes.

Her hands flailed as she tried to see which way was up in water which a night sky had turned into an abyss of darkness in all directions.

Anthony dared not grab her. *I'll snap a bone.* But then he remembered how Connor, when he entered the eco-shelter, sank into revival sleep, unlocking the center in the vampire brain which released the chilled-out mellow persona. *I can do this.*

Using precious seconds, Anthony closed his eyes, tensed every muscle until he could feel the grains of dried blood grating through his veins, and then relaxed. Opening his eyes again, the scene unfolded in slow motion. Marius churned up the seabed around his feet as he dug his heels in and tried to stop his rotation. Rebekah, like a doomed astronaut with a sheared umbilical cord hung limply, suspended in the water. Taking her up would cause a splash and give away their position. Anthony crouched, judged the distance, and pushed his solid weight upwards to the glimmering glass-like surface. Hanging his head back, his face barely emerged into cold night air, and he sucked in a deep breath.

Dropping like a stone back to the seabed, he caught Rebekah's billowing shirt as he swept past and took her with him. Turning her onto her back under the water, he rested her head on his shoulder and applied gentle pressure to her chest. Finally, the bubbles of air still deep inside her lungs gathered on her lips and nose. Her eyes focused on his face, and Anthony prayed. *Let me be in time.*

Holding her nose, Anthony kissed her. Closing his open mouth over hers, he breathed out gently, filling Rebekah's lungs with his unused air. First aid worked on the basis that humans use only a small part of the oxygen in the air when they breathe. In Anthony's case, he hadn't used any.

After an initial jolt of panic, Rebekah relaxed and breathed in Anthony's kiss as the world came back into focus. When he drew back and looked down into her eyes, Rebekah gave him the thumbs up and pointed to the surface.

He carefully guided her, letting her body slip through his grasp until her boot settled on his shoulders. Skulling her hands, Rebekah drifted up, resting her head back until only her face broke the water and she could breathe until her chest no longer wanted to burst. She gazed up at the night sky, her spiked lashes framing the picture. She let go of her panic, took a deep breath, and sank below the surface. She felt Anthony tug on her clothes and, with the whiplash decision making she associated with vampires, Marius and Anthony appeared to have agreed a plan, and, as before, guarding her face against the churned up sand and shell fragments which hurtled towards them, the group rushed forward.

The granite ledges at the base of the mound made the terrain rough, but being swept along between two vampires, Rebekah tucked up her knees and watched the dark gray slabs of rock covered in green splotches of moss whip by. When they reached where St Michael's Mount reared up from the sea, the group settled on a ledge in the shadow of the fortress with their heads and shoulders above the water, pressed back against the rocks and gathered their thoughts.

Rebekah was wedged between Marius and Anthony, her breathing coming in fast puffs through her nose, covering her mouth with her hands to stay as silent as possible.

"I'm sorry," Anthony muttered, shooting a glance which took in both his companions.

"What the hell was that?" Marius said evenly, his dark eyes glittering in the dim light.

Anthony shrugged.

Rebekah took her hands away from her face, and her grin made the pressure marks on her cheeks blanch white. She nudged Marius with her shoulder and shook her head. 'I'm alive, move on,' was the message in her probing look.

Twisting onto one hip, Rebekah struggled to dig her hand into the cloying wet fabric of her combat pants pocket. She squinted with the effort and Marius shared a quizzical raised eyebrow with Anthony.

Her hand reappeared holding a small container sealed with wax which she gave to Marius, who easily broke the seal and flipped the lid. She took the two modified beta blockers he tipped out onto her palm, washed them down with a sip of salt water and screwed up her face. Once they kicked in, her lowered heart rate would help when she entered the castle.

Anthony noticed the blue marks of early cyanosis on her lips and fingernails. *At least her body heat won't be a problem, her flesh is as cold as ours.*

Without Rebekah seeing, Marius put up two fingers.

Anthony knew he was asking about Greg and minutely shook his head.

The dark juror's clenched jaw twitched, showing he understood. He jabbed a thumb towards the castle behind and mouthed, 'stay here'.

Getting up, he turned and scaled the steep overgrown terraces of the sea-facing garden until he reached the vertical face of the castle. Pressing his chest close to the brickwork, he picked up the vibrations of movement inside the walls. Like Osiris had before him, he found the drumming heartbeats of the gathering of humans unexpected and distracting.

As he climbed, his clothes rained water down onto the undergrowth below until the wind whipped up and the moisture became a mist of spray.

Working his way along each row of windows, he found the one Osiris had tampered with. He pushed gently on the frame and it opened. Marius smiled. All Malachi had been able to tell him before he and Rebekah left, was that Osiris had plans to enter the castle from the seaward side. Marius took it as a good sign that the plan had gone ahead. *It must mean Seren is inside, too. I have to find Osiris.*

Cautiously, Marius swung in through the window and pushed it shut. Rebekah would be freezing, so he had to be quick. Marius took three steps, and then sensed someone approaching the closed door. Darting sideways, he took cover behind a stack of crates.

The door opened, and the whisper of furtive footfalls entered. He closed his eyes and concentrated on gathering the scent and using the sounds to estimate the size of his opponent. He frowned when he detected the odor of blood and heard a very faint heartbeat. *Osiris? They are sneaking about, whoever it is.*

It seemed too good to be true. Marius shifted position until the shadow of the mystery visitor came into sight. The irregular bulky outline told him very little. *But, it's not a vampire.*

Marius surged to his feet and stepped out into view. He smiled as Osiris, his arms folded across his chest, appeared to be waiting.

"How did you know I was here?" asked Marius.

"I didn't, not for sure. I come here to get outside and 'talk' with Malachi. He said your mission is to get Rebekah inside the castle. Osiris' lips twitched. I came for an update."

Marius noticed the damp trail he had left across the floor in his hurry to find a hiding place, and grimaced. "Just as well it was you."

"So, what happens now? Where is Rebekah?"

"Now, I know how to get in, I'll bring her up. Where is Connor? Can we get her close to him?" Marius asked.

"Connor is never far from the regent, or the vampire aide who guards him. There is a feeding ceremony before dawn, but I'm not sure when."

A spark gleamed in the abyss of Marius' obsidian gaze. "I'll bring Rebekah up, and we'll have to trust the rest to calculated luck."

Marius and Osiris shared a grim glance before the juror crossed to the window, opened it and dropped like a stone to the ground below.

When Marius skimmed down the slopes and sat beside Rebekah again, her purple lips were a concern. He smiled. "I found Osiris. Rebekah, we're going in. Anthony, get back to the ship and tell Malachi how far we've got. They cannot communicate when Osiris is inside." Taking hold of Rebekah's cold wet hand, Marius swung her up onto his back.

She locked her arms around his neck and clung on.

He turned his face to hers and muttered, "Hold tight. We are nearly there." He scaled the walls, as before, but this time he knew precisely where he was going and the ascent was taken as fast as Rebekah's comfort would allow. Letting her fall did not bear thinking about. Every twitch of her ice cold fingers caused him a tinge of alarm.

They were nearing the window ledge when Osiris reached out, took her hand and helped Rebekah to climb up, plant a knee on Marius' shoulder and lunge into the room. Marius leapt in behind her.

Rebekah clamped her chattering teeth closed, automatically stripping off the heavy waterlogged outer layers. In survival mode, she pulled the heat packs from her combat pockets, clicked the activators inside and hugged the gel-filled pouches to her chest. Osiris opened a crate, sorted through it to find a large linen tablecloth and held it out as a privacy shield. "Take the rest off, then I'll find you some dry clothes."

She didn't hesitate. Behind Osiris' makeshift screen, she pulled off her cotton T-shirt, shucked out of her pants, but kept her underwear on, and then wrapped the sheet tightly around her body. Briskly rubbing her arms, she scanned the room and whispered, "Where is Connor?"

From the open window, where he was busy wringing out his coat, Marius shot a look at Osiris.

Rebekah's eyes darted from one to the other, but she waited.

"We will have to bide our time," said Osiris slowly.

Rebekah's raised eyebrows said it all – we have time?

"All the humans are on the lower levels. We'll hide you down there," said Osiris.

Marius joined in. "Once you are in position, I'll wait outside and keep watch. I'll know if things change out there."

"And us?"

"We just have to stay out of the way until I find Connor," said Osiris.

"I can do that."

Marius stern look silenced her. "*Everything* depends on it, Rebekah."

Osiris slipped out of the room and returned moments later with a grubby tunic and loose pants. They were crumpled and stank of stale sweat. It wasn't a huge leap to guess they came from a laundry pile.

Osiris shrugged.

Rebekah barely hesitated as she took them from him and pulled the tunic on first. When she stepped into the baggy pants, Osiris was one step ahead of her. He tore a strip from the linen sheet to make a belt to hold them up. Tucking in the tunic, Rebekah pulled the belt tight and lifted her chin at the defiant angle that Marius had come to recognize and dread.

"I'll go out and see if the coast is clear. Where do they keep the humans?" asked Marius.

"Lower level. There are stairs in the turrets, and one in this part of the castle," Osiris replied.

Marius lifted a finger that said 'wait here', crossed to the door and listened. He was the only one without a heartbeat and a pulse, so he stepped out into the hallway. Whipping along the corridor, he heard distant voices, but quickly decided that if the group moved fast, they could make it to the stairway without being seen.

Heading back, he ducked inside the door and beckoned.

Osiris and Rebekah followed cautiously, hugging the shadowed alcoves in which statues stood, while Marius strode forward as though he belonged.

A vampire swung around the corner at the end of the hall, his vacant gaze staring straight ahead. Marius didn't flinch. He continued walking, closing the gap quickly. The vampire's eyes flickered over the approaching tall black clad figure, and sudden shock registered on his features. By this time Marius was within arms' reach. *They don't expect intruders to already be inside.*

As the vampire opened his mouth to challenge him, Marius shot out a clenched fist. The sickening crunch rattled through the air as the vampire's teeth crumbled. The tendons tore as his lower jaw dislocated. Marius withdrew his fist in a shower of shattered tooth enamel and the vampire wore a comical surprised expression, unable to close his mouth. Hooking his fingers into the gaping hole, Marius sneered as he yanked hard and the mandible came away in his hand.

Osiris darted forward in support, delivering an upper cut that penetrated their victim's stomach. His hand came away smeared with the thick paste of decaying blood. Lifting the crippled vampire by the throat, Marius rammed him into the space behind a statue. He shrugged out of his black coat and used it to cover the giveaway glimpse of the guard's white face.

Stepping back, happy that the body would go unnoticed in the dark crevice, Marius gestured with an urgent wave and swung around to continue on towards the dungeons. Rebekah and Osiris hugged the wall and tried to keep up. Darting down into the stairwell, Marius reappeared a second later and, with a jerk of his head, beckoned them forward. At the bottom of the stairs, the carpeted hallway gave way to flag stones and the air felt heavy and stagnant.

To vampire senses, the atmosphere vibrated with a chorus of human heartbeats.

Speaking too low for Rebekah to hear, Osiris said, "We can't get her any closer until we know where Connor is. The guards will assemble here. If the feeding ceremony is before dawn, I'm not sure that it's a great idea to bring her so close. We need time to watch Connor."

Marius gave him a penetrating look. "What do you suggest? We need her close enough to use the other humans as camouflage."

Crossing to a closed door, Osiris pressed an ear to the wooden panel, tried the handle and found it locked. Taking a chance that a locked room is usually empty, he pulled a knife from the sheath strapped to his thigh and forced it into the space between the door and the frame. Pressing the tip of the blade into the metal tongue, he used his hand as a hammer until the lock fractured.

Pushing open the door, when the buckled nugget fell out of the hole, Osiris caught it. He checked the coast was clear and gave a nod.

Once all three were inside with the door shut, Marius said quietly, "Rebekah, you need to stay here and keep quiet."

"What's the plan?" Her words were less than a whisper.

"I'll locate Connor. Marius will keep watch outside." Osiris was already at the door when he spoke.

Rebekah nodded, but clenched and unclenched her hands as if standing still was impossible. Left alone, she retreated to the farthest corner of the room, slid down the wall and sat on the floor. The hard stone blocks bit into her shoulder blades, but that was good. *It will keep me alert.*

She didn't have a watch, so she spent the time counting to six hundred, knowing that was ten minutes, or thereabouts. Once she had reached six hundred three times, the wall digging into her back urged her to move. *Half an hour?* In vampire terms, that was a lifetime.

Getting back to her feet, Rebekah crept towards the door, wishing she had X-Ray vision. *Right now I'd settle for any vampire senses, but superhuman hearing would be good. Marius is out there somewhere.*

She backed away, shaking out both arms, hoping to get rid of the urge to open the door at the same time. She started counting inside her head again. She had never enjoyed the game of hide and seek, even as a child, and knowing she was this close to Connor was torture. *What's the worst that can happen? I get caught. But then I'll be taken before this Scandinavian Regent. And Connor will be there.* Her heart talked her head into a win/win scenario.

Moving purposefully towards the door this time, Rebekah took hold of the cold metal handle. *Connor is going to kill me...* The thought hit a wall. *No, he won't. He doesn't care about me anymore.* She gripped the metal tighter and pulled the door open a crack. The hallway appeared deserted. Her defiant streak rose to the fore. *The best way to get to Connor, is the direct route. So, here goes.*

Easing the door open, she scanned the hallway. Straining to see in the dim light almost made her eyeballs ache. Taking four strides along the corridor, she ran into a solid chest that hadn't been there a moment before. Scrunching her eyes closed, she prayed it was Marius, but she knew she couldn't be that lucky.

Not sparing the time to look, she swung back around and ran. Reaching out a hand and trailing it over the wall, she swallowed the yelp of pain when her knuckles smacked into the protruding angle of one of the alabaster statues. Still running, her legs pumped until the muscles burned and her lungs felt raw.

Her tunic suddenly yanked tight around her neck, her body swung forward and, for a moment, her feet left the ground. The cotton fabric cut into her throat like a garrote until she was jerked back into the same hard body she ran away from, and then the choking pressure eased. The hallway tapestries blurred as she was whipped around, and this time, in the flickering glow of candle light, she stared up into an unfamiliar sneering face. *Shit.*

In his firm grip, the bone in her arms creaked and her bruising flesh felt like a Chinese burn. Rebekah gritted her teeth and smothered a grunt of pain.

"How did you escape?"

The question caught her off guard and she laughed.

The blonde vampire frowned, icy annoyance gleaming in his blue eyes. "Come."

He shifted his grip to the back of her tunic, twisting the fabric until the neckline pulled tight, and then marched her back along the hallway.

Rebekah kept quiet. *I'm no good to Connor if I die here.* She hung onto the hope that the plan could still play out.

He turned sharply and took her down another flight in the curving stairwell, and a row of cells behind iron bars came into view. From the other end of the passageway, an older looking vampire approached, stopping in front of Rebekah and her escort. His weather-beaten face crumpled into a puzzled expression. "How-?"

"Did she escape?" Her captor shrugged, and lost interest in the conversation. The door of the nearest cell groaned when he pulled it open. His companion moved aside as Rebekah was pushed past him and into the cool damp interior.

"She didn't escape," the older vampire said heavily.

They both peered in through the bars, two sets of eyes boring into her like Lasers.

"What do you mean?" her escort said, a frown etching lines into his smooth skin. His bone-white fingers folded around the bars.

"She's an outsider, she stinks of seawater. Didn't you notice?"

"I'll tell the regent we found a stray," said the tall blonde guard.

"If you want to die." The old weather-beaten vampire jerked a thumb towards Rebekah as he turned away. "If she got into the castle without being seen, someone will have to pay."

"What would you do?"

Nervous amusement bubbled inside Rebekah as she listened to the exchange.

"Keep her here until we send a sentry to check outside the castle. Say nothing yet."

"They want five humans for the ceremony. She's wearing slave clothes. I could just include her in the head count. The regent has guests."

The vampire with weathered skin smiled with grudging respect. "That would work. But only four will die, tonight. The girl does not drink."

Rebekah's dismay was tinged with hope. *The regent has guests. The girl must be Seren. Will the others include Julian? I hope so.*

"It solves the problem, although-" His teeth gleamed as he stroked his tongue over them.

Rebekah's stomach cramped. The sharp glint in his eye unveiled hunger.

His hand ran up and down the bar, dislodging a shower of rust, and polishing the iron rod to a burnished finish. "If she is a stray, no one knows she is here."

The older vampire shuffled from one foot to the other. "I want nothing to do with that."

"Then take a walk."

Rebekah suddenly felt cold. As goosebumps tightened her skin, she backed up into deep shadow. She knew he could still see her and lifted her chin in a look of defiant aggression. She glared as the key grated in the lock and the hinges creaked when the gate moved.

"Don't touch me," she spat.

The vampire's silhouette eclipsed the pale light glowing in the corridor. His burst of harsh laughter smelled of rotten flesh and bile burned in the back of her throat.

"Don't fucking touch me. Your regent will have you gutted and your head on a fucking stake."

The black shape swayed in hesitation. "No one knows you're here."

"Oh, someone knows." Rebekah grinned even though her heart thumping in her chest betrayed her.

The vampire retreated one step.

Relief that she had found the right words hit hard. As the gate swung closed and he disappeared, she sank to the floor, the skin on her back burning as it grazed down the roughhewn wall.

Voices floated down the hallway. "She will die in the feeding ceremony."

Rebekah knew she was meant to hear the words. *Connor will be there... and maybe Julian, too.* She hung onto that hope.

Marius watched Rebekah running full tilt towards him, and just when he made a move to grab her, the vampire guard appeared. Even if he could have intervened, it would be one more to add to the body count and being noticed was never the plan. *Not yet, anyway.* He faded back into the shadows at the end of the corridor. He was looking for the upside of not breaking cover and saving Rebekah from the guard. *It is what we wanted, to get Rebekah and Connor in the same room.* He shrugged. *Not a perfect plan, but Julian will be there. Things are as good as they can be.*

When all was quiet, Marius returned to where Rebekah should have stayed hidden. He entered the room and found Osiris standing with his thick arms folded across his chest. His dark glare said 'what the hell is going on?'.

Marius shook his head. "Women."

Osiris grunted. "I don't know how Connor stands it. Where is Rebekah?"

"She was captured by a guard-" Marius held up a hand as Osiris inhaled sharply. "I know it's not ideal, but it puts her in Connor's orbit. She's a fast thinker. It's our best shot."

"Things better play out fast. The force inside the castle is stronger here, near the dungeons." Osiris leaned out into the corridor and peered towards where the staircase dropped down into darkness. Darting back inside, he said, "I think the other source of psychic power is beneath our feet."

"You think there is a level below the dungeons?"

Osiris nodded. "There is a shroud of white noise over the castle. I believe it keeps the bondsmen and the regent's court powerless to resist her will. It was confined to the ship before, and now it is within the boundary of the castle."

"Someone here is stronger than the regent?"

"Not stronger." Osiris frowned. "Connected. Combined."

"We better see what we can find. Anything we uncover could be ammunition for Julian."

Chapter 26

After Rebekah was dragged in through the open window of the castle, Anthony sat and paused on the flat rocks below and looked out across the bay at the distant cliff top. *I'm sorry Greg.* Even though they had a pact, Anthony never expected that the Marine would have to make that final sacrifice. *Shit.* His part of the deal was to bury Greg's remains and say the prayer the Marine insisted he memorize.

Reluctantly getting up, Anthony walked back into the sea, taking the most direct route from the castle to the beach.

The precise spot from where he and Marius had launched themselves from the precipice was impossible to find. *I'm looking for a mass of torn flesh.* Anthony scaled the vertical face with explosive force, gouging lumps out of the rocks. He swung himself up over the overhanging ledge and rose to his feet. Lifting his chin, he scented the air and detected the faint aroma of blood.

He concentrated on searching the uneven landscape where outcrops of granite and clumps in the meadow created shadows that looked like deep black holes in the ground. He spent far too long double checking patches of tangled undergrowth – he could easily distinguish blades of grass from weeds, even in darkness, and found it hard to admit that he didn't want to find Greg.

Wisps of a familiar odor thickened into fumes until they filled him and settled in Anthony's gut. He couldn't put the moment off any longer. The dewdrops on the grass sparkled like diamonds. The clusters were denser on Greg's still face. The sweat on his skin resembled a layer of frost, and the dark blood stains that soaked his clothes covered most of his body.

"I'm sorry, Greg."

Saying the words out loud made it seem more real. Dropping to his knees beside the sprawled figure, Anthony arranged the body into the erect posture of a soldier, and straightened Greg's clothes. Assessing the injuries from head to toe, he found the feeding sites of two vampires. He pulled the fabric of the combat pants closed over the torn flesh of Greg's thigh. The wound in his neck was not as bad as Anthony expected. The trail of scratches dragging down over Greg's muscular throat suggested a fight broke out between the hunters. Anthony snorted. *They couldn't even finish him cleanly.* That was what happened when vampires were killing for sport. They weren't hungry, and were easily distracted by rivals for their meal.

Rocking back up onto his feet, Anthony turned away and became absorbed in locating a burial site. He chose one at the base of an unevenly shaped granite tor. Crouching down, he pulled out clumps of weed choked grass by the roots. Shoving his hands into the growing crater, he scooped out the stony earth until he could no longer reach the bottom without dropping down inside it. Most physical tasks vampires made short work of, but Anthony took more care, making sure to collect the largest of the stones which had broken away from the main tor to build a cairn.

Returning to where Greg lay, Anthony took hold of his arm and hefted the body up and over his shoulders. Gripping Greg's leg behind the thigh, he anchored the weight in place and started walking, not fazed by the huff of breath he heard. He knew the stomach and chest were being compressed by his solid frame. *Lungs are like bellows, you squeeze them and air comes out.*

As his stride ate away the distance, he suddenly froze in mid-step. A faint throbbing sensation beneath his hand where he gripped Greg's arm ignited a flare of hope inside him. *He can't be.* Dropping to his knees, he lowered Greg to the ground. He wiped the glaze of moisture from his friend's face and put an ear to Greg's mouth. Anthony jerked back when he felt the merest whisper of a breath. *He's hanging on. Tough bastard.* Pressing a hand over Greg's forehead, Anthony closed his eyes for a moment and absorbed the firework display of electrical impulses he detected beneath his palm. His lips compressed into a thin line. *What do I do now? The kindest thing is to kill him myself.*

Without letting that thought escape, Anthony lifted Greg and sprinted along the cliff top. Tracking Julian's ship out in the bay, at the closest point, Anthony launched himself over the edge and down onto the beach. He prowled up and down the water's edge like a caged tiger. He daren't call out to Malachi. *I wish I had some weird damn mumbo jumbo kind of connection.* What he really wanted to do was yell, 'Greg's dying, get a tender over here now.'.

"Damn it," he growled. He stopped pacing. "Fuck, here goes nothing." Holding Greg tight to his chest, he strode into the surf. The water was icy cold. The underwater sprint in the freezing temperature would either finish Greg off, or, by keeping his core temperature low, it might just save him. *He's already close to hyperthermia, anyhow.*

When the dark torpedo shape of the ship loomed overhead, Anthony continued on to where the funnel of its shadow cut down through the water. Moving to the stern, he released his hold on Greg's legs and grabbed a link in the thick chain of the anchor. Tugging on it like a bell ringer, he started an oscillating, rocking motion which rattled all the way up into the hull above and the anchor winch groaned under the strain.

Just as he knew they would, the crew reacted. Daniel dropped down into the water and a comet trail of bubbles rushed to the surface. Sinking like a jet-propelled stone, a cloud of silt erupted where he landed with his lips clamped shut, his eyes open, and a flare gun in his hand.

Anthony nodded, appreciating Daniel's quick thinking.

Reacting in a nanosecond, Daniel shoved the flare gun into his belt and reached for Greg's free arm. They each took a turn in scaling the anchor chain and towing the dying Marine with them.

When their heads broke the surface, Daniel looked at Anthony. "What are we doing?"

The choppy water slapped against the ship's hull. Rivulets of water streamed down Anthony's tense face. "Maybe nothing. Greg's dying, or dead, I'm not sure which." He shrugged. "It just didn't feel right to finish him off."

The pale oval faces of other crew members appeared above, looking down into the slate gray rolling sea.

Anthony glared up at them. "Daniel, get up there and tell them to drop the ladder." Shouting this close to the castle would be suicide.

Almost before he'd finished speaking, Daniel scurried up to where the anchor chain disappeared into the hull, braced his foot on the last section of joined links and boosted himself up. A guardsman reached down, grabbed Daniel by the hand and swung him up over the rail and onto the deck.

The rope ladder appeared moments later.

Anthony slung Greg over his shoulder and raced to the top, dropping Greg over the handrail into the waiting hands of Daniel. Without speaking, they bore the slack body down the gangway and disappeared below.

They headed straight to the heart of the vessel – the campaign room.

As Anthony shouldered his way into the cabin, he said, "Malachi, have we got adrenalin onboard?"

Malachi's skin crinkled audibly as he frowned. "That's Greg."

Anthony swept the nautical maps and historic blueprints of St Michael's Mount from the table and laid Greg down on it. He grabbed a coat from the back of the door and covered Greg's wet body, using the sleeve to wipe seawater from his friend's face.

With a flick of a wrist, Malachi dispatched a guardsman to get medical supplies with a low voiced command. "He's going to die. You do know that?"

Anthony didn't look away from Greg's blue-tinted face. "Yes. I know he'll die. But adrenalin will open up the capillaries and maybe, just maybe, with a donor." At that point, Anthony's brown eyes met Malachi's transparent mother-of-pearl gaze.

The elder vampire bared white gums and a row of pointed teeth.

When the guard arrived back in the room with an assortment of vials and a tray of syringes, Anthony chose the one with the longest needle.

Stabbing it through the seal on an adrenalin vial, he pulled on the plunger to fill the barrel, pointed the needle towards the ceiling and flicked it with a fingernail. He pushed the plunger until a pearl drop of liquid formed on the needle tip and then, holding the primed syringe ready, looked at Malachi.

Baring his scrawny forearm, Malachi buried his teeth into his own flesh and pumped his fist until the slow flow of his vampire blood oozed out of the gash. Pressing a thumb on Greg's slack chin, he opened his jaw and let the blood flow into the dying man's mouth.

At the moment the level reached the corner of Greg's lips and began a slug like trail down over his cheek, Anthony located the space between the ribs with two fingers, and centered the needle over the unconscious human's chest. With a smooth firm action, he pushed the needle into Greg's heart and discharged the dose of adrenalin.

Greg's throat gargled, the blood in his mouth slopped over his chin as the level rose and then dropped suddenly. His slack body twitched and then became still.

"It's not working."

Malachi smiled. "Of course it is, listen."

Frowning, Anthony muttered, "What do you mean?"

The noise, like splintered glass being ground under a boot, was barely audible, but at last, Anthony tuned into it. "Is that a good thing?"

Realizing Anthony had never turned a human, Malachi humored him. "Yes. The pain is excruciating. The noise you hear is vampire DNA rampaging through Greg's system. It will transform the fluid inside the human circulation, and the moisture in the skin cells, into crystals. There are two grades of crystalized cells, one absorbs the blood we drink and lubricates the others, the ones that are hard. That is what makes our flesh dense."

"He doesn't look like he's in pain."

"It will be many hours before he wakes, and when he does, he will be exhausted. He didn't ask for this. Be ready for his heightened senses to make him question his sanity." Malachi adjusted the coat-blanket over Greg's body. "Daniel and Sergeant Hugh will take him to a cabin and restrain him. Anthony, you saved his life."

Anthony smiled grimly. "I hope he'll thank me in the morning."

"He still has the final choice." Malachi laid a hand on Anthony's shoulder. "But at least he has the chance to make it."

Anthony frowned as Malachi left the room, but for now, he just wanted rest.

Chapter 27

Seren lay out on her thick mattress, her body making an indent that strained the springs to their limit. *What is happening out there?* Since she left Osiris out on the causeway, she had literally been in the dark about the events unfolding around her. *Where is he?* Even though she could still see some of what was going on inside Connor's head, for the most part, his mind remained empty. Seren rubbed her hands down over her face in an unconscious gesture she had seen her Papa do a thousand times. He seemed to be an animated shell.

Half an hour had passed since the vampire escorted her to this room to 'human sleep'. They didn't really know anything about her, and the differences between vampires and hybrids made it easy to fabricate lies.

Seren was sure the time would come when this besotted version of Connor would hand her over for experimentation. *I need to warn Osiris and Malachi. Papa might not recognize Mama, at all. This plan is too dangerous.*

She had searched every shadow for Osiris, but the regent and Connor were never far away. *He wouldn't risk being that close.* She reluctantly faced the fact that she could be here alone.

The vampire guard waited outside her door. The regent called him her 'aide', there to smooth her way as she settled in at the castle, but Seren knew Sascha reported back to Birgitta. *She doesn't trust me anymore than I trust her.*

Rolling smoothly up out of the body shaped crater in the bed, Seren dropped her bare feet soundlessly to the warm wooden floor. She slipped out of the fine emerald silk dress and laid it over a chair. Stooping, she rolled up the tapestry rug beside the bed, deposited it into the trough in the foam mattress, and arranged her silk dress over it. From the doorway, the thick brocade drapes which decorated the four poster frame hid her pillow from view. It would pass a fleeting inspection. She hoped that a check from the door was all Sascha would do. *A young girl is entitled to privacy.*

Scrabbling around under the bed on hands and knees, she pulled out the travel clothes she had kicked underneath it when she was first brought to this room. She shook off the dust and put on the stained combats. From the hem of the shirt, which was stiff with salt spray and dirt, she tore a strip of cotton and used it to pull her hair back into a ponytail.

She ran lightly to the window and pushed it open. Hitching up onto the window sill, she stared down at the mesmerizing flow of the white frothy lace crowning each wave. When the gossamer strands reached the granite cliff, they shattered into a snow storm of fractured pieces. It would be so easy to drop off the ledge and disappear beneath the waves.

Bracing a hand on the side of the window frame, she leaned out and looked up towards the battlements. She tried to 'feel' for Malachi, Osiris, anyone. The sense of loneliness unsettled her. Having a head filled with silence when she went looking for others was something she had never before experienced.

To escape the dragging weight of impotence, she swung her legs out through window, dug her fingertips into the mortar between two granite stones, shifted sideways and pushed the window shut. She preferred to climb in bare feet and made use of the detail carved into the façade to boost her small frame upwards.

A few minutes later, perched on the parapet wall, a crenellation as her throne, Seren felt like she could breathe again. Although, the buffeting gusts tore at her clothes, they could not shake her solid weight. Even with the cold wind shrieking in her ears, she could at last sense Malachi's presence. Throwing her thoughts out there, she reasoned, if I can't 'hear' inside, then Birgitta won't be able to listen to me out here. *Malachi?*

Malachi's rush of relief filled Seren with a warm tide.

As if the elderly Egyptian stood beside her, Seren whispered, "The regent has Papa brainwashed. He does not think for himself, at all. Don't let Mama come. It is too dangerous."

The warm tide cooled and this time his words appeared inside her head. *It is too late for that, Seren. Your mother is inside the castle with Marius.*

Seren frowned. *Where are they?*

I do not know, child. Osiris hasn't reported back yet. He knows they are coming.

Seren's languid pulse rate moved up a notch. "Osiris made it inside?" She wanted to feel relief, but she feared for his safety, too.

Malachi clearly read the anxiety she felt. *He knows what to do. Do not worry about him. Just keep a look out for your mother. It is only her that needs to come close to Connor, the others will remain hidden.*

The sea spray riding in the wind laid a crust of salt over her skin as Seren stared across at the oil black silhouette of Julian's vessel. *Very well, I'll stay at Papa's side, and help if I can.* There was no going back and, with communication cut between those outside and inside the castle, Seren knew it was down to her.

Swinging over the parapet, she picked her way back down the side of the castle. She paused on the ledge and peered into the room through the clouded glass of the window, expecting to find it empty. Her hand was already pushing the handle down when she jerked back as if the metal burned. The door moved. Pressing back into the stone wall, the subliminal flash of detail she had seen made her freeze.

The visitor was not blonde. The darker skin felt familiar, but, judging by the gleam of silver, they wore armor. The image did not fit any guards, or bondsmen, as Birgitta called them. *So who?*

Clamping her jaw closed and suspending her breathing, Seren risked another darting glimpse. The visitor had his back to her now, and even with a metal plate molded to his broad frame, she recognized the tapering physique and muscular thighs. She smiled and the jolt of fear dissolved into relief. *Osiris.*

Pulling open the window, Seren swung in through it, barely touching the floor as she launched herself across the room. Osiris whipped around. A grin broke out on his face and he opened his arms to catch her. He took a step back to absorb the impact of her flight. His lips found hers, a growl rumbling in his throat. One hand swept firmly down her spine and covered her backside. With his other hand, he pulled the ponytail loose and pushed his fingers into her hair, molding his grip to her skull.

For a moment, nothing else mattered as she tasted him. The metal plate between them went unnoticed until he slowly released her. His hands framed her face. "Are you okay?"

"I'm better now, knowing you are safe. Where's Mama?"

Absorbed in assessing her delicate features, Osiris didn't reply. "Osiris?"

"She has been taken by the guards." When Seren jerked in his arms, he said, "It sounds bad, I know, but Rebekah is strong, and this is our best chance at getting her close to Connor."

"Who's looking out for her now, Marius?"

"Yes."

"I promised Malachi I'd stay at Papa's side, help out if I can."

Osiris' brows rose in surprise. "You can hear Malachi?"

"Not in here, no." She gestured towards the open window with a jerk of her chin. "Out there. On the roof."

"Ah, I see." Osiris frowned. "Seren, does Birgitta have another vampire with her, an ancient. One that boosts her powers inside the castle. Have you noticed anything?"

Happy to stay in the circle of his arms, Seren leaned against his armor covered chest. "Not that I have noticed."

Running a thumb along her cheekbone and hooking a lose strand of hair behind her ear, Osiris said, "If you sense things are going bad, get out of there… here. Promise me. Let Julian and Gerrard handle it. They are full vampires."

Seren reached up and landed a kiss on his nose. "I promise. I'd better get changed again."

Osiris settled his hands on Seren's hips. "That will be more distraction than I can stand. I had better go, but even if you can't see me, I'm watching over you." With a brief kiss on her lips, Osiris headed for the door.

"Wait. Where is Sascha?"

"Your guard? He had urgent duties elsewhere it seems. The regent must have called him."

With a final wave, Osiris slipped quietly from the room.

Seren shed her combats, feeling her confidence draining away as she did so. They were only clothes, but they were *her* armor. She donned the green silk which made her feel vulnerable. Somehow, wearing a cumbersome floor length skirt with three layers of lace petticoats felt like being hobbled.

She buttoned up the bodice and pulled her skirts straight. *The feeding ceremony must be starting soon and they'll come for me.* She began to pace the room. *I'll wait. I'll wait.*

Minutes ticked by and Seren sunk down on to the side of the bed and sat, swinging her feet. The atmosphere inside the castle seemed to make breathing harder, and a sick feeling of foreboding dragged her mood down.

Chapter 28

Sitting on the floor of her prison, Rebekah rested her head back against the hard stone and closed her eyes. The cold numbed the cheeks of her backside. The pitted surface had become embedded in her shoulder blades, but if she didn't move, she didn't feel the pain.

The worst things were the throbbing bruises left on her upper arms by the vampire guard when he grabbed her. But, she refused to pull up her sleeve to inspect the injuries in case the movement drew attention. The guards were still out in the tunnel.

Weak shouts of protest penetrated her meditative state. As the ragged gasping crying of human voices drew nearer, she took a deep breath and got to her feet. After all, this was what she'd been waiting for – the chance to get close to Connor. Walking forward, she gripped the cell bars and rested her forehead against the rusted iron rods. The weak yellow glow of light bathed her face. She could see the prisoners from that position.

Three humans. A silent, tall thin man, and two shorter women – or girls, it was hard to tell. Through the grime ingrained on their puffy faces, tears had made pale tram-lines down over their cheeks. The two women could not have been more different in stature. One had a boyish, flat chest, the other woman's breasts overflowed the confines of an ill-fitting bra which might, once upon a time, have been up to the job. The big breasted woman with dull dark hair, put her arm around the smaller one.

"Be strong," was all she said, squeezing the bony shoulders so tightly that Rebekah listened for the crack of breaking bones. "It's nearly over."

They were dressed in the same stained tunics and shapeless pants that she wore.

The sudden eclipse of her view made her jump back. "It is time." The key grated in the lock and the door creaked open. The three humans framed in the aperture looked in Rebekah's direction with dead eyes, showing no interest at all. The thin girl's attention returned to her feet, greasy strands of fairish hair falling in a string curtain across her face. The man was bald beneath his cotton cap. The bones of his skull showed through the tight skin. It looked as though the razor edges of his cheekbones would slice his face open if he smiled. He didn't smile.

The vampire guard moved them forward with a sharp jerk of his head. They shuffled as they walked, and instinctively, Rebekah's eyes dropped to their ankles. Leather straps performed the same task chains and shackles would have. They had tied the three together so, like children in a three-legged race, cooperation was the only way to cover any distance. But, it also meant they could lean on each other.

"Get in line," the tall blonde vampire said, and Rebekah could see by the way his uniform pulled tight across his chest that he expected her to resist. *Little does he know, I want to see this regent... and my Connor.* Tears blurred her vision and she swiped them away. *He is mine. I won't let the bitch have him.*

Casting her eyes down and slumping her shoulders, Rebekah fell in line with her fellow sacrifices. *Will Seren be there?* The idea of her daughter witnessing what was to come made her stomach churn.

The vampire with the weather-beaten face, who walked beside her, shot a glance at her profile. "It will be quick," was all he said.

Rebekah guessed he mistook the sweat on her skin and the raised heart rate as fear for herself. The thought almost made her smile but she clenched her jaw and hid behind the tangled fall of her feathered hair.

The corridor seemed never-ending. At the foot of a staircase, the blonde vampire pulled a knife from his belt. The thinner of the two women whimpered when he dropped down beside her, but he merely sliced through the leather straps. *It is too late for them to run, now.*

The dark stone stairwell was hard for them to climb when their legs were shaking so badly, and the vampire's motive became clear. *He cut them lose so they won't fall. How irritating would that have been for 'blondie'?*

When they emerged in the upper hallway, 'blondie' – who Rebekah decided might be younger in human years than his friend, but was the one in charge – whisked on ahead and disappeared from view. The weather beaten older one ushered each stumbling human past him. Last in line, Rebekah could almost feel his impatience as he fell in and brought up the rear. The air in this plushly carpeted hallway seemed warmer, so Rebekah felt certain they were above sea level now. The slanting silver glow of light cutting across the floor up ahead confirmed it.

The lead vampire slipped inside a large oak door, Rebekah heard a murmur of voices, and then the door swept open and 'blondie' waved them forward.

Inside the room, rows of candles danced shadows over bare walls. The chamber was essentially a stone box. The window alcoves along one wall were eight feet deep. The ledges were steps which narrowed as they cut into the wall, but boards wedged into the apertures sealed them. Rebekah couldn't decide if it was to shield the vampires from daylight, or to block the escape routes of humans. *Eliminate all hope.*

"You will wait here." Their jailers, having handed over their charges, closed the door as they left. The four vampires who had replaced them lined the walls and became eerily still.

Rebekah felt shudders rattling through the thin girl beside her and took her hand.

Whispering shuffling sound overhead made every human in the room look at the ceiling. Rebekah couldn't say what the signal was, but at precisely the same moment the four guards in the chamber 'woke up', for want of a better word. They closed in on the group of humans and herded them into a corner, where a much narrower stone spiral staircase rose to the room above. Darting a look down, as it also descended, Rebekah saw a metal grid locked into place. *Up, it is then.*

Taking the second position in the row, this time, she followed the thin man's awkward jerking ascent.

The upper chamber had a fireplace and the vaulted ceiling gave it a spacious feeling. The stained-glass windows were dull – the cloudy night sky reflected the darkness felt by the humans who feared this was their last night on Earth.

Her eyes grew accustomed to the gloom, and Rebekah scanned an elevated dais upon which sat four occupied thrones, the fifth seat, although ornate, did not match the others and was clearly an addition, from a nearby parlor, perhaps.

As she hoped, she instantly recognized the burnished bronze tone of Julian's hair. Her heart leapt. *I have someone on my side, at least.* On his left, sat Captain Gerrard. The imposing central figure of the Scandinavian Regent registered as an oppressive force, even though Rebekah refused to look at her. Resting an elbow on the armrest of his chair beside Birgitta, Connor leaned toward her slightly, with his face presented in profile.

The empty additional seat was a relief. *No Seren, then.*

When she was shoved from behind, Rebekah walked into the middle of the room. Julian did not move, and neither did Captain Gerrard. When Rebekah dared to take a closer look at the principal, she noticed his green eyes were dull. His face remained a blank slate of boredom. Connor's bowed head was so close to the regent, that the dark wing of his hair touched the white gold of Birgitta's.

Anger boiled inside Rebekah and, as though she had fired her rage like a dart, Birgitta's crystal clear eyes latched onto Rebekah.

"You. Come." Birgitta rose gracefully from her throne and her companions froze in mid action. As she glared down from her vantage point, a vampire escort prodded Rebekah in the back and she jerked forward another step.

Rebekah stood ramrod straight, her eyes fastened on Connor's vacant stare. The regent approached and completed a circuit around her, as if inspecting an antique she might buy. *No, not an antique, a dog.* When she re-appeared in Rebekah's vision, judging by the sneer on her delicate face, she had found Rebekah wanting.

"I know you."

Rebekah finally met the regent's glittering blue gaze. "I don't think so."

A feminine breathy laugh made Rebekah's skin crawl. She clenched her fists.

Birgitta leaned closer, her beautiful composed features melting out of focus. She stopped barely an inch from Rebekah's nose. "No, you're right. But I *have* seen you. Through my lord's eyes, and your half breed, of course."

"You have me at a disadvantage," Rebekah spat. "I expected a rival, not an ice cold bitch."

Birgitta's hand shot out and framed Rebekah's throat. "You have lost. And now, you die."

Glaring into Birgitta's porcelain smooth features, Rebekah ground her words through gritted teeth. "Let me hear it from Connor. If I die at his hand, then I will believe you."

"I have nothing to prove. He would walk on hot coals if I told him to." The regent sneered.

Laughter caught in Rebekah's throat. "Told him to? You have nothing more than a shell." She cast a jeering look at where Connor sat motionless. Panic clutched at her for a moment as she wondered why Julian and the captain showed no reaction.

Without shifting her glare from Rebekah's flushed face, the regent said quietly, "Leave us."

The three terrified humans were led from the room, and a keening wail of relief echoed in the stairwell. *I did something good.*

Connor, Julian and Gerrard rose and left by the wooden door at the top of a short flight of stone steps.

Once the room was empty, desolation poured into Birgitta's gaze. "You took what was mine. Now, I have my revenge and you are powerless."

Malachi was right. This began with Lars. Rebekah thumped her own chest hard, her eyes glazing over as the pain rattled through to her spine. "I... I have Connor's heart. His soul. He would walk on hot coals without my asking. He is *mine*."

"Not anymore." Birgitta dragged a metal nail tip down Rebekah's cheek, and ruby beads oozed from the scratch. "He is a vampire. He has no heart. I thought I would need a binding spell." Her crystal blue eyes bored into Rebekah's. "But I needed none. He took me. Rape, you pathetic human's would call it. He saw me and took what he wanted."

Rebekah could not hide the pain and doubt – the color drained from her face.

Birgitta leaned closer. "You still think he is yours. He was happy to find a mate who could match him. He is very... powerful when he makes love. But you could not know that."

"Let him tell me that himself. I want to die, if that is so... but let *him* do it. Or are you scared?"

Her chilled breath blasted Rebekah's hair back from her face as Birgitta yelled, "Guard."

A vampire pushed through the door. His eyes darted around the room and his fists were primed for danger before the tension drained away and he stood to attention.

"Tell your lord, I have need of him, now."

The guard disappeared instantly.

With a fixed smile, the regent recoiled like a serpent, deliberately stroking her fingers down over Rebekah's jaw.

A moment later, Connor strode in, irritation thrumming from him in waves. "Your guard summoned me like a servant. I won't-"

The fresco of his queen, her blue eyes flashing when she glanced at him, and the gray pallor on the face of a human girl stole the thoughts from his head.

"What is going on here?"

"Connor."

But it was the human girl who uttered his name. He drew closer, her smell lit a fire which scorched a path through his gut and venom filled his mouth as the frantic pulse in her neck pounded inside his own head. "You!" he spat on a laugh.

He stood beside Birgitta, his fingers absently playing with the white gold braid which lay over her shoulder.

The intimate gesture gutted Rebekah. "I've come to take you home."

A snarl curled Connor's lip. "Principal Julian tried that tack. I'm a free man." Turning to face Birgitta, he filled his lungs with her fragrance. "I am already home."

"You love me." Rebekah's chin lifted to a defiant angle.

Connor let the silk rope of flaxen hair slip through his fingers and stepped away from his queen. He pushed his face in close to

Rebekah's. His scent was sour lemon, not the cleansing aroma she was used to, and the depths of his eyes were cold granite.

"I pitied you," he said.

As if Connor was not there, Rebekah slid her gaze over the glittering translucence of Birgitta's features, recognizing triumph in the half smile on her face. "He is the father of my child, and you can't have him."

Connor's hand closed around Rebekah's throat. "You don't speak for me. Don't insult my queen with your filth. Even Seren is disgusted by you."

Rebekah's vision blurred with tears as she choked out, "You will have to kill me before I believe that." She reached up and tore the neckline of her grimy tunic, exposing her collarbone. "Sebastian could not finish me. Do it if you have the guts... and let her watch."

Connor's features tightened with rage. "You don't tell me what to do."

His head snapped around at the weight of Birgitta's hand on his shoulder. "Perhaps the feeding ceremony should continue. You don't need to dirty your hands... you can watch her die."

"You coward," snarled Rebekah. "Do what your mistress says, cuckold, lackey. And I thought you were a man." Hawking as much moisture as she could gather in her dirt-dry mouth, she splattered Connor's face with speckles of saliva.

Without taking his flint hard gaze from Rebekah, Connor said, "Leave her to me. Go."

Birgitta stroked her hand down his rock hard cheek. "Have fun, my lord."

Time stood still until she had left the room.

As the heavy door thumped shut behind the regent, Connor's cold glare narrowed and his fingers tightened around Rebekah's throat. Focusing on her reddening face, grinning viciously, he ground out, "I think the time for talking has passed."

His hand moved up to grip her hair, and tears burned in her wide open stare as Connor wound his fist into the stiff, tangled strands and inexorably dragged her head back. Her thumping heartbeat drew his scathing assessment to her chest. Adding to her tear, he ripped her tunic open, baring her breast. Despite herself, she whimpered when his cold hard face pressed into her neck, his chiseled features ramming up beneath her jaw.

On a rumbling growl his tongue flicked over her skin, and then his lips settled almost in a kiss. His growl suddenly swelled to vibrate the air in the room, becoming louder as he opened his jaws and, with a jerking movement, buried his teeth into her flesh. With a grunt of satisfaction, he tore into her artery. The frantic storm of electric impulses inside her brain, as terror shot through her, exploded in a glittering array of sparks which filled his head.

The compulsion to drain every drop of her sweet nectar consumed him. As feral satisfaction grated down his throat, he jerked and his jaws locked half open as a seizure gripped his body. Like Napalm burning in his veins, a trail blazed up into his brain. Flash backs of Rebekah, Seren's birth, and his devastation at almost losing her to Sebastian thundered through him as raw undiluted grief.

Tearing his mouth away, a spasm arched him back, every muscle locked tight, and he clutched Rebekah to his heaving chest. As the memories filtered into every corner in his mind, he snapped his gaze down, desperately searching her face.

She hung in his arms, her features slack and the thought processes inside her head registered as the cascading embers of a dying firework. Clasping her tighter, he froze, aching to feel her heart thud against his skin, but he felt nothing. Her eyes drifted half open and the flush in her cheeks faded.

Connor bellowed, "Nooooooo." Scooping her up into his arms, he shouldered his way through the closed wooden doors. Spotting a guard at the end of the hallway, he switched direction. Tempering his grief with commonsense. He wanted to smash through anything and anyone obstructing his path, but explaining his actions rose as a specter in the sanest corner of his mind. Dashing back through the banquet hall and into the anteroom where Julian had changed his clothes, he shoved his way through the door on the left and stepped out on to the courtyard within the battlements. Ignoring the turret and the stairwell inside it, the rushing wind tore at his clothes and tried to tear Rebekah from his grasp as he stepped up onto the wall on the seaward side of the mount.

He leapt from the parapet. Holding her close to his chest, he plunged feet first into the icy water. The shock jerked through her body and feeling the jolt clench her heart, he dared to hope.

Landing heavily, before the ledge of rock beneath his boots crumbled away, he waded into the shallows to where the upward slope became a ribbon of gravel, and dropped to his knees at the water's edge.

Resting her down onto the gritty bank, he tried not to look too closely at her pinched white face. Ignoring the network of blue fibers creeping beneath her skin, he ripped his arm open with his teeth and slipped his other hand under her neck. When he lifted her up, her head flopped back.

"C'mon, honey, don't leave me. Please, please..."

He stroked back the wet hair plastered to her forehead and obscuring her face. As her slack jaw dropped open, he lifted his arm, pumped his fist and watched the corded sinews of his forearm pulsing. His thick blood seeped out and he suppressed his impatience as the oozing flow slowly filled Rebekah's mouth.

His eyes remained fixed on her immobile features, their expression eerily content, as if death brought relief. *What happens now? Damn it Rebekah, fight!*

He wanted a dramatic awakening, something positive to hang on to, but he had never done this before. Connor's desperation locked his body tight. He continued to drip feed his blood into her mouth, waiting patiently for it to drain away before refilling the reservoir of her throat once again.

"C'mon, honey, c'mon," he muttered. *Do I stop and wait?*

Resting his hand on her chest, he willed her heart to flutter, desperate to feel it quicken to a kicking drum beat. What he really wanted, was to turn back time and have her alive again, but it was too late for that.

So, he listened for the crackling sound of grinding glass instead.

He looked for evidence that, although her body lay slack in his arms, his venom was infecting her collapsed veins. His vampire

DNA should be devouring the last remnants of her blood until it captured her human state, like a freeze frame photo. Please, don't let it be too late.

He laid his hand on her cold gray forehead.

Malachi always said the brainstem was the last barrier to be breached. It would be the last organ to succumb to the assault of his blood forcing its way up into the medulla.

Rebekah thought she had entered hell. Her open eyes saw Connor through an ice-white cloud, her eyelids unable to blink. Her eyeballs stung with salt water and then her throat filled with thick paste that suffocated her.

Inside, her body burned, and the excruciating pain, as though a lit match was being dragged through her veins, just kept building. The scream tightening her throat was smothered by the weight of his congealing blood trickling down into her stomach and lungs. She tried to swallow, but could not.

Connor's cold hand resting on her chest froze her heart, and then, as if it was a magnet, a ball of fire gathered beneath it, and the incendiary fury of the blaze cut a path through her center and desiccated her windpipe.

"Honey... Rebekah..."

His touch on her forehead was a pool of alluring ice in the inferno of her body.

"You have to drink." Connor knew the reflex of drinking and swallowing would help to unlock her brainstem and let his blood flood into her brain – accelerate the process.

Her fingers twitched and fear clutched his chest. Could he kill her again if he had resurrected an empty shell incapable of thought? Rebekah's slack body erupted into sudden movement. She clawed at the wet fabric of her tunic and ripped it aside. Her nails, like feral rats, tore at the flesh of her stomach until his iron grip closed over her hands and held them still.

Shifting until her head rested on his thighs, he freed both his hands, ready to ease her through the next stage. "I know it hurts," he said persuasively, "but drink."

Keeping both her hands trapped inside one of his, he held the torn wound in his forearm closer to her lips, laying it gently across her mouth. "Drink, honey."

The smell of his blood exploded like a firework inside her sinuses. The heat in her throat surged until a cry finally erupted, spraying thick blood out of her windpipe and over his face. Then, she latched onto his arm and bit in hard.

She focused on his intent gaze, looking for reassurance and finding it. A sneer rippled over his blood-soaked features, satisfaction raging in his eyes.

Fear for him filtered into her surreally alert mind, and she shouted his name silently inside as the burning thirst ached for more of his blood. Her eyes relayed her panic. *What if I can't stop? Connor, please...*

"Easy, easy," he murmured, grimacing in response to the dragging pressure of her teeth.

The sensation of the surf breaking over her thighs drained the heat from her body, and she was suddenly too cold to shiver.

Feeling the viselike grip of Rebekah's jaws fading, Connor eased his arm away, sucking at his hard dry flesh and using his teeth to drag the edges of the wound together. His eyes remained glued to her intoxicated features.

Her blood red lips smiled as, in her mind, the night sky became the flaming red glow of a brazier.

Resting on an elbow, Connor leaned over her.

His face filled her vision and the gray eyes staring down were crystal clear... and loving. *I did it, I saved him, for Seren, Julian. Even if it's too late for me.*

When the red tint drained from her vision, the colors seemed unbearably bright and she closed her eyes.

"Rebekah, honey."

Connor's voice was like sunshine on her skin, and she forced her eyelids open once more. His concern made her heart rock in her chest, but her body felt heavy, still, numbed, and not her own.

"Rebekah." The tender expression on his face was surprising. *He doesn't look sad.*

Connor scooped her up from the gravel and carried her out of the lapping surf. The hard bed of rocks beneath her backside barely registered as he rested beside her. His smile, clouded with fear and uncertainty was confusing.

"What?" she said, and her jaw snapped shut. Her own voice rattled through her head in a chorus of echoes. The numb feeling in her chest became a nerve tingling burn of pins and needles, and her body arched in searing agony.

Pulling her into his arms, Connor cradled her body as her muscles jerked into spasm. Burying his head in the crook of her neck, he muttered, "I'm so sorry, forgive me, honey."

Burning tinder fizzed along every nerve ending and a crackling sensation surged in its wake until suddenly, when everything went quiet, she opened her eyes and the particles in the air glittered like fireflies.

"What happened?" The words left her mouth before she registered them as thought.

When Connor's face appeared in her vision, he took her breath away. His skin glowed with silver dust floating in pearl-tinted emulsion. Eyes she thought were gray, had a metallic sheen with glitter swirling in their depths, and every strand of his hair was a different shade of sapphire through to ebony.

"You are beautiful." Her words outraced her thoughts again as she pushed her hand into the silky strands, and cobalt highlights flickered beneath her questing fingertips.

He smiled. The luminescence of his teeth, and the fine quartz veins moving beneath his skin entranced her.

"It was not how I wanted it to be, but..." He leaned in and fire of a different kind ignited in her chest as his kiss devoured her lips. Her response surged up and she pressed into him, welcoming the avalanche of sensations. He dragged his mouth away and finished hoarsely, "...you are a vampire."

She knew, but didn't know. The feeling of being dead, but impossibly alive confused her senses. Laying a hand over her own chest, she felt the flutter of a dying bird beneath her ribs and, unquestioningly, she smiled. "I have you back. That's all I wanted."

Realization darkened the glittering gray of his eyes to mercury. "But Seren is still inside, and Birgitta thinks I am... disposing of you. I have to go back."

"Then I will, too," said Rebekah. Feeling the world tumble like a gyroscope racing to catch up, she darted to her feet.

Connor fell back, giving her room, and grinned. "This is going to take some getting used to, for both of us."

Rebekah merely thought about standing, and then she was. "It's as though there is no delay..." Her voice rang with fascination. "I think, and it is done."

Connor rose to stand beside her. "Mmm, now you see why I have had such… difficulty when touching you." He reached out to graze a fingertip down over her skin. "You were always beautiful, but now, everything is so much more."

He staggered backward as she barreled into his chest, her hands buried again in his hair as she kissed him. He laughed against her lips as he collided with the rock face and slid down it, carving a groove with his body that tore his shirt from his back.

As Rebekah straddled his lap, and her smooth hands explored his hard chest, pulling open his shirt, his laughter faded.

"I've missed you," she breathed with husky intent.

His loud gulp stuck in his gullet as she kissed the base of his throat. Desire trickled through him, flooding his groin, and thickening his body beneath her seat. "Oh God," he murmured as pulling her close, his hand closed over her cool breast, teasing the tight flesh. "Not now, not like this," he said harshly, but his hands could not leave her skin.

He needed to wipe the contaminant of Birgitta from his heart, his soul, and untying the strip of linen holding up Rebekah's pants and tearing away the fabric of her underwear, he entered her hard and fast. He flirted with revival sleep, and, as her body clamped around him, he realized he did not need to, and he lost himself in her driving rhythm. His lips closed over her breast as she arched into him, and he was hers.

Her soft sighs were intoxicating. Her fingers dug into his shoulders. Surrendering to the need to brand her as his, he gripped her by the waist, held her still and drove into her as he had always wanted. He kissed her mouth, swallowing her groans of release as the burning tide flowed through him, too.

As the ripples inside her died away, tugging at him, he buried his fingers in her hair and pulled her head back. His gaze blazing down into hers, he said, "You're mine..."

The answering copper-toned glint in her eyes told him everything he needed, and he kissed her again, in a gentle worship of the woman he loved.

Suddenly, he groaned. "Damn, I have to go back and pretend."

"You can't pretend." Framing his tense face in her hands, she looked into his eyes and said, "I can tell, you can't pretend."

"I have no choice. Just until Seren gets out." Her heart was crumbling before his eyes and he kissed her. "I won't..." The enormity of what he had already done cut him open. "I promise... I won't touch her. I promise."

Diamond tinted tears, the last Rebekah could ever shed, turned to ice on her lashes. "You will... you will have too." Kissing him hard, and feeling her lips throb despite their new found firmness, she growled, "Just come back to me. Promise me that."

Holding her close into his chest, he pushed up easily to his feet, and as the warmth of their lovemaking still burned where his body clung to hers, he said, "Don't get heroic on me, Rebekah. You promise me *that*. I can't be worrying about you. I will find Seren and..."

They both realized they had no clue how Birgitta would react, only that she would not give up quietly.

Gathering the torn fabric of Rebekah's pants, Connor knotted it around her waist and said absently, "Do you know why? Why me?"

Rebekah quirked an eyebrow. "Have you looked in the mirror lately?"

He grimaced. "Seriously."

"Seriously? She said it was revenge. For Lars."

"Damn it. Of course. Scandinavia." Connor grunted. "It's no surprise she has a connection to Lars."

Rebekah's intent gaze gathered every detail of Connor's face, and she understood. "Not just a connection. I think she loved him. As much as she can love anyone. This has as much to do with taking her revenge on me. She thinks I got under his skin."

Connor tilted her chin up with a finger, and said, "I know you did. And thank God. It made him careless when I needed it most."

"So, we know why she came here."

Connor looked thoughtful. "Well, maybe now I am able to think, I'll find out the rest."

"The rest?" Rebekah looked puzzled.

"The how. If we're going to rid ourselves of her, we need to know where she gets her power from, or at least, what we need to do to defeat it. I don't think she will just walk away."

The agitation vibrating through Connor was entrancing, and Rebekah knew her human self would not have been able to feel it. She smiled. "Go. I promise to be good." Glancing out at the cliff face across the water on the mainland, she added, "I'll wait for you up there."

"Good girl." He grinned, but his mind was already back inside the castle. "I'll get Julian to help find Seren. Just lay low for now."

With a final fleeting kiss, Connor turned away.

Rebekah appreciated the true grace of his flowing movement for the first time. She could see every muscle rippling beneath his shredded shirt as he sprang up over the rocks and scaled the rocky outcrops of the castle's foundations. He carried on up the vertical edifice and disappeared over the battlements at the top.

Vampire night vision was so much more than she believed possible when, pausing to look over the wall, Connor mouthed 'I love you', and she saw it as clearly as though he was still standing beside her.

Reluctantly turning away, she scanned the rippling expanse of water and walked forward. It felt warmer than a bath, was her first thought, and then she became lost in the rainbow colors slicing through the depths as every tiny organism caught her eye.

"Okay, get a grip." With her next step her foot twisted as it fractured a rock. Taking a deep breath, the grains of salt floating in the air felt like grit dragging over her tongue, and she smiled. *This is going to take some getting used to.*

Ignoring the crunching of her boots, the strange feeling of the water being as easy to move through as air, and the hypnotizing colors the moonlight cast over the sea, she forged forward. She suddenly realized that she had not released the deep breath she took in five minutes ago, and she felt fine. The water rose to her shoulders.

Connor does this. It would be nice if I had someone to hold my hand, but here goes.

As the sea closed over her head and still nothing terrible happened, she released a sigh of relief, and the burst of bubbles boiling through the water made her panic. She clamped her mouth closed, waiting for her lungs to burn with oxygen deprivation. But nothing happened. She did not need to breathe in again. Instinctively knowing the direction to take, she crossed the deepest part of the channel and quickly found the submerged causeway. She chose a path in the deep water parallel to the band of slippery seaweed covered boulders which flanked the cobblestoned path. She stayed beneath the surface for as long as possible. When it was too shallow to remain hidden, she broke into a sprint. The unexpected force drove her across the sand and into the face of the cliff. Turning her head at the moment of impact, she avoided a mouthful of gravel but felt a sharp blow on her cheekbone.

Sidling quickly into the purple shadow of a crevice, she gingerly touched her cheek. The skin felt smooth. *Okay, I got away with that one. I must be more careful.* Turning back, she concentrated on climbing the cliff and found she was rolling over the top onto the thick coarse scrubland before she realized it.

Okay, lie low. Lying on her stomach on the ground, she rested her chin on her hands and gazed out over the rippling water.

Chapter 29

Back inside the fortress, Connor concentrated on not thinking about Rebekah as he made his way to his private chamber where, he now realized, he spent most of his time. He felt drawn to this space – it drew him like a moth to a flame. Now that he could think clearly, realization dawned. *She has secrets to keep, and this is where Birgitta wants me to stay.* He had been trained – conditioned. She came to him in this room, but this was his 'prison', of sorts. He had become a pet, taught to obey its master's command. The sick feeling in his stomach was psychosomatic, but the disgust made him feel just as nauseous. *How could I have let her do that?* With the benefit of clear thinking, as he washed the salt and dirt from his body, he sifted back to find his last real memory. *It was the night I took rap-sleep at the hospital. Somehow, she bit me... it wasn't a dream.* Everything pointed towards powers beyond that of a normal vampire. In his hundred undead years, he had come to realize that the raw material was the key to what you became. Birgitta must have been a shaman or 'cunning woman', as witches were originally known. They were not magical in the myth and legend sense, but could harness nature.

After drying his broad chest with a cotton towel, but leaving the blood streaks on his neck untouched, he pulled his stained shirt back on. He left the room, took a circuitous route back to the heart of the castle.

The book-lined parlor was empty. When he opened the door and glided down the short flight of steps into the banquet hall, he glanced at the narrow stone stairway descending in the corner and tuned into the hum of heartbeats which radiated from somewhere below his feet. The elusive smell of human blood and sweat hit him for the first time, but as he expected, the hall was empty. The only evidence of the feeding ceremony was the odor of fear tainted sweat and speckles of blood on the floor. It was precious stuff. Vampires tried not to waste a drop.

He frowned as, being 'aware' for the first time, he noticed he was alone inside his head, even though, if he knew Malachi at all, his maker would be keeping tabs on what was going on. *Birgitta has the power to block out others' psychic connection.* His cold flesh tightened as Rebekah's words came back to haunt him. 'You can't pretend'. *Shit, what if she's right?* He shoved the thought aside and eased into a robotic stride. *Surely, Birgitta will expect my behavior to be odd. I've just killed the mother of my child.* He wouldn't have to 'act' there. He really had done that, but thank God, Rebekah survived. *I don't need to pretend I am high on exhilaration.*

He decided that none of the heartbeats emanating from below had the resonance of Seren, or Osiris, for that matter. Connor was not fool enough to believe that Seren would be here alone and unprotected. As he strode the length of the hall, he caught a scent of Birgitta. *She's behind me.* Fixing a harsh smile on his face, he turned around. Letting his eyes roam over her curves without really seeing them, he bared bloodstained teeth in a bitter smile.

"Ah, my queen." He stepped closer, and smelling human blood on her breath, he said, "I see you have fed, too."

The light from a nearby lamp stroked over her fine bone structure as she mewed prettily. "You were gone too long." Birgitta ran her hands up his body and over his shoulders. Pressing her breastplate into his chest, she played with the blood splattered fabric of his collar. "Tell me, how did it feel?"

Snaking his arm around her waist, Connor pulled her up hard against him and suppressed the revulsion as he kissed her. Letting her go, he assessed the blank beauty of her white face, looking for clues as he said, "What did I do to deserve such good fortune, hmmm?"

Placing a cool hand on his cheek, her blue eyes probed his, the expression in them unreadable. "Now, you are free of her."

"Remind me, what did I see in her? Pathetic wrench. She begged. It was laughable." His brow creased. "She didn't taste as good as I expected."

Her hand drifted down his cheek and stroked over his chest.

"You're right, I am free. I have nothing left to tie me to London, or even England." His stiff smile was convincing. "We should make our home where we can make our own memories. I've not seen much of the world."

"Ah, I can show you all the wonders of the world, my lord."

"Where do you call home? You don't live onboard the ship, surely?"

"We have plenty of time to learn about each other. For now, the feeding ceremony is over but we have guests to entertain."

Connor was pleased of a reason to be in Julian's company. *With his help, we can solve this puzzle.* "Of course, you're right. We have all the time in the world."

Birgitta pursed her lips. "Your Seren..."

The venom tainting her tone was not lost on Connor.

"Forget about her," he growled, impatience pulling his lip tight. "She's not a proper vampire. She is a runt, an experiment." He laughed. "A failed one at that."

Birgitta's glance was sharp as she fingered the silver pendant around her neck.

Connor plucked it from her grasp. "That is pretty. Very old."

She tidied the fall of her skirt and pulled her metal bodice into place, fidgeting until the pendant slipped from between his fingers. "It belonged to my grandmother, Morrigan."

"Unusual name," he said, veiling the intensity of his gaze. "A Druid name?"

The distant clang of iron beneath their feet signaled movement in the castle dungeons, and Birgitta took his hand. "Come. We will talk when we are alone."

Connor studied the nervousness skittering in her eyes, squeezed her fingertips and dropped a kiss on her lips. "You go, we mustn't keep the principal waiting. The sooner we escort him back to his ship, the better. I just want to change my clothes. Her blood disgusts me."

"I shall see you in a moment. We are in the Wedgwood suite." Birgitta turned and walked away, her hips swaying in an enticing rhythm. With clear headed detachment, Connor could see why men fell at her feet. Losing Lars must have been a dagger to her ego.

Making certain no one saw him, he set off at a fast run in the opposite direction to his room. Taking the stairway to the east turret three steps at a time, on the first level he passed swiftly along a sweeping balcony and arrived outside Seren's door. *Is she in there?* He slipped inside the room and found it empty. "Damn it, Seren," he groaned.

Connor whipped around as the heavy drapes covering the lead-framed window twitched. Lunging forward, he gripped the brocade fabric and shoved the sturdy figure hidden behind it backwards. He heard glass crack and a voice hissed, "Connor, it's me."

Stepping back as though stung, almost silently, Connor said, "Marius?"

The curtain billowed as the dark juror swept it aside. Splintered glass fell from his shoulders on to the floor as he raked his hair back into place. "Doctor Connor, glad to have you back with us."

"Marius, what are you doing here? You took a chance. What if I was still..." Connor struggled for a word to describe his betrayal.

"Besotted?" Marius grinned at Connor's fierce expression. "If you were, you wouldn't be here. You have not been thinking straight." Marius took pity on Connor, recognizing a man berating himself when he saw it. "In answer to your question, I've been here a while, keeping an eye out and hoping Rebekah doesn't get herself killed."

Connor's expression froze.

"Tell me you've seen her? This awakening... it was her doing, correct?" Marius asked, suddenly feeling uncertain.

"It was, yes," Connor said shortly, "But she *did* get herself killed."

Marius' jaw clenched as Connor dragged his hands down over his face.

"What did you do?" Marius asked slowly.

"I turned her. I had no choice."

"Thank God."

Connor dodged past Marius and yanked open the drapes. "She's out there, on the clifftop waiting. Can you go to her?"

Marius nodded. "I can. Osiris is somewhere inside. I've not seen Anthony since I entered the castle."

"And Greg?" Connor smiled grimly. "I know he wouldn't have missed out on this."

Marius' black eyes lost their luster. "I'm sorry. He didn't make it."

"What?"

"I'm sorry."

Connor crossed to the bed and sat down heavily. "Jesus, Marius. What have I done?"

"Not you... her," he said flatly. "How do we stop her?"

Connor laughed harshly. "All I've got so far is a name. Morrigan."

"Well, keep looking. I'll talk to Malachi. It might mean something to him."

Marius stared through the window at the oil black expanse of water. Julian's vessel was still anchored out in the bay. "Malachi is on board. He and Seren have been tip-toeing through your head since you disappeared."

Shame stung Connor as he wondered what they had seen.

"Although, not since you entered the castle, the psychic shield is too strong."

Connor hated the feeling of relief that the true depth of his betrayal would stay between him and Rebekah.

Marius crossed the room and laid a hand on his shoulder. "Stop feeling bad, find Seren and tell her to get out. Then, we find a way to stop Regent Birgitta taking over the hive. Man up, Doctor Connor, and get on it."

Connor chuckled as Marius' familiarity echoed something Greg might have said. Marius had unbent a lot from the staid 19th century vampire he *had* been, until humans had muscled their way into their existence.

"I'll find Rebekah and make sure she's safe... and she's a vampire, after all this time." Marius shook his head as though he couldn't quite get his mind around it.

Marius pushed open the window, and the curtain billowed wildly when a stiff breeze gusted round the room. The cracked pane of glass slipped from the frame and dropped out of sight, and, with a final nod, Marius followed it.

The dull splash reassured Connor that Rebekah would not be alone for much longer. "Well that's one good thing." It eased his worry that she would blindside him by doing something impetuous.

Fixing a convincing sneer of loathing on his face, Connor strode through the corridors to his chamber. Stripping off the blood soaked shirt, he buried his nose in it. Like a human enjoyed perfume, as awful as the thought was, the fact that the blood smelled of Rebekah calmed him. *She didn't die, I have to hang onto that.* Recalling how her face glowed with its vampire reincarnation stirred excitement in his gut. She was his first and only creation, and they could spend centuries discovering how that special bond felt. The grating noise deep in the bowels of the castle jolted him back to the present. *First, I have to finish Birgitta.* Connor knew the ending would be violent. Negotiation was not an option.

Changing quickly, buttoning up coal-black pants as he walked, he retraced his steps. He chose the route which took him out onto the courtyard within the battlements. He resisted the urge to search the distant cliff top, knowing he needed to force Rebekah from his mind. Stepping in out of the blustering wind, he tidied his hair, straightened his collar and, resting a hand on the door knob, he paused outside the blue suite – an entrancing set of rooms decorated with intricate white plaster carvings bordering Wedgwood blue walls. Blue was an expensive dye in years gone by, and, just as having many chimneys was a declaration of wealth, so was the extravagance of using blue in interior design.

Connor pushed the door open and stepped inside the spacious room. A shadow moved fast over the wall beside him, and Connor spun around in time to grip the blade of a sword as it swung down from overhead.

"What the hell-" His angry gaze locked onto the avid green glare of Julian's.

The two vampires remained locked in a bazaar fresco as each warily absorbed the attitude of the other.

Every sinew strained as Connor held the blade still and skewed his head around to find Gerrard and Birgitta. *She's not here.* "Julian." He looked back at his friend and hissed softly, "I'm free. She did it. Rebekah." Connor knew Julian would know what he meant. It suddenly made sense. The rash act of entering Birgitta's stronghold. *They were trying to save me.*

Julian's jaw muscle twitched. "Did Rebekah survive?"

Connor eased his grip on the blade and withdrew, flexing his fingers where the metal had scored a line in his hard flesh. "I killed her." His features crumpled with genuine despair.

Both vampires froze at a swishing sound coming from the hallway beyond the door. "Later." Connor mouthed, but the fleeting grip on Julian's shoulder transmitted relief and thanks, and Julian smiled.

Birgitta's scent was unmistakable. The door whipped open as Bjorn surged into the room ahead of his regent. Birgitta drifted forward and covered the ground in a fast flowing action.

Sascha and Valdar took up positions on either side of their captain.

Stopping an arm's length from Connor, she laid a hand on his chest. "You killed her?"

Connor inclined his head, confused. "I did. The woman is dead." Disgust rose inside him as the reality of the close call hit home. *I almost lost her.* His face became a tight mask as he met Birgitta's limpid blue stare. His expression slipped when, instead of looking at him, she focused on Julian.

"Is he telling the truth?"

Julian's smile glittered with malice. "He says she has freed him, my queen." He dropped to his knee and bowed his head.

"Julian?" The word grated in Connor's throat.

With the stab of a finger, Birgitta ordered the pair of bondsmen to close in on Connor. He couldn't get the scene playing out before him to add up.

He felt thick steel manacles click around his wrists, but he didn't care, the weight of the chains was just an inconvenience. But then, like Superman reacting to Kryptonite, his hands became blocks of stone as if the dead blood solidified in his veins. *What the hell-?*

Her cool palm covered Connor's cheek. "My Druid Mother has bound you. You drank my blood... no, you won't remember it," she said, when he opened his mouth to protest. "But you did. These manacles were forged beneath the moon at a binding ceremony. The blood in your veins cannot resist the pull of the spell."

As Connor was dragged towards the door, he twisted and kept Julian in his sights. When he saw the principal absently rubbing the back of his hand, the penny dropped. *She got to him when he set foot in the castle.* Julian was entrapped. *Shit. What do I do now?* His only solace was that Rebekah had escaped. *At least she is safe, for now.*

Connor allowed himself to be led away. Although, the force draining his body anchored his feet to the floor, so he could not have walked unaided. The tapestries in the corridors gave way to bare stone as he descended into the bowels of the cold castle. The damp walls were white with frost. He didn't know where he was being taken until he reached a closed iron gate. This was Birgitta's territory. Laughter burst from Connor, and the twins exchanged anxious glances before hurrying onward, dragging the prisoner along with urgency that scuffed his boots across the concrete floor. His head hung down and his shoulders rattled with another burst of ironic amusement. *I didn't choose this place. She put it into my head.* Now, he was free from her spell he realized he was just a pawn in the game... or the prize. What mattered was he had no say in anything, before this moment.

The clang and scrape of the gate being unlocked focused Connor's mind. His escorts pulled on the bars, stepped aside and smoothly swung around until they stood behind the prisoner.

Connor tried to back up, his muscles tight beneath his hardened skin as he fought against the weight of the manacles dragging him down.

Valdar shoved him through the gate and along a corridor which stank of stagnant water and mildew. Connor staggered, almost falling when he ricocheted from the abrasive wall in the tunnel.

Clenching his jaw, Connor closed his eyes. *Julian is a traitor. No, not a traitor.* He knew Birgitta had worked her magic on him too, or a brand of it in any event. He barely noticed a cell door swinging wide until he was grabbed by the back of the neck and pushed inside.

The moonlight pouring in through the high, barred window turned the dew on the walls into a shroud of diamonds.

His new status was clear. *Prisoner.* He slumped down onto the stone seat and taking in a breath filled his lungs with rancid air – he stopped breathing. His mind reeled. He willed his body to leap up and fight his way out of there, but the heavy gate clanged shut and dismay settled in his gut. The key grated in the lock and he stared mutely at the wall.

Chapter 30

In the sudden quiet left by Connor's departure, those inside the blue room exuded tranquility. Birgitta assessed Julian as she arranged the swathe of her white blonde hair to hang down over one shoulder.

"You did well, Principal." She smiled, but her eyes remained dead. The hand she laid on Julian's chest flexed. *He is not Connor, but he is strong.* But she knew it was not about strength. She wanted Connor because he had slain Lars. *I knew he wouldn't kill her, and I have the perfect bait.* The captain of the guard appeared in the doorway and nodded sharply.

"Bjorn, bring the child to me."

"What are you planning?" Julian asked. His voice held an idle tone as his eyes stroked over Birgitta's delicate features.

She smiled. *So much for the might of the London Hive.* I shall enjoy taking their safe world and tearing it apart before I leave this pathetic isle. "I want the child Seren to bring her mother back. Rebekah did not die."

"Ahh," Julian said.

Birgitta knew he had no clue what she intended. His role was to worship and obey.

The soft tread of boots grew louder until they arrived inside the room and Bjorn reappeared. "The girl is here, my lady."

"Good." Birgitta swung around and, as if pulled by a magnet, Julian mirrored the action.

In silence, the pair watched the girl enter and follow the captain's direction on where to stand.

Looking up from her feet, Seren raised her chin at a defiant angle.

"I have news of your mother," Birgitta said.

"Is she dead?" asked Seren.

Birgitta tilted her head. "Yes, and your father is no longer to be trusted." The captain stood behind Seren and settled his hands on either side of her small skull. His clawed fingers spanned her temples and forehead, and he began to apply inexorable force.

Seren appeared not to notice, remaining compliant but unperturbed.

"It is time to decide where your future lies. Here, in strength, or in death."

Despite the pressure of the vise-like grip distorting her features, Seren smiled. "Here, of course. My father is weak. My mother had him under her thumb. He sickens me, now."

The regent stared long and hard at the child. Both knew that a twitch of a finger would deliver the command and Bjorn would snap Seren's neck with a quick twist.

Birgitta stepped forward and when she gripped Seren's chin, Bjorn slowly withdrew his hands. "I have a place for you. The reasons will become clear, but for now, just obey me."

"Very well," Seren tried to nod.

The regent's fingers slid away from the girl's face.

"Come, child. If you prove your allegiance, then I shall turn you. Being a hybrid is an intolerable burden."

"It is the way forward, my Uncle Julian says." Seren smiled into the principal's slack features. "Learn from me, first. After all, the human food you need will not last forever. They will die. I am a hybrid, you should learn from me."

Julian smiled. "It makes sense. There will be other hybrids. They will be an immortal food supply."

The irritation burning in Birgitta's blue gaze faded to contemplation. "Perhaps you are right. There is plenty of time to make you an eternal. You are young. But, if you fail me-" Birgitta left the threat hanging.

"You can rely on me." Seren looked from Birgitta to Julian. "I won't let you down."

"Good. Go back to your room. Principal Julian will be staying with us."

Seren dropped her gaze and bowed her head. "Is Captain Gerrard staying too?" Her smile shone with innocent enthusiasm.

Birgitta turned to where the captain sat on a blue striped seat, his hands braced on his knees. The deep indent in the cushion suggested he had been there days rather than hours. His eyes were unblinking.

"Yes," Birgitta replied, with a dismissive wave of her hand.

Seren dutifully turned and left the room, closing the door after her.

Looking at the wall, as though X-ray vision enabled her to follow Seren's retreating footfalls, Birgitta frowned. "Come, Julian," she said sharply, as she threw open the doors beyond the entrance hall and stepped out onto the moonlit battlements. The wind tore at her ice white clothing, plastering the fabric to her immovable body. She crossed the terrace, rested her hands on the stone wall, and looked down at the harbor. It was now a graveyard of splintered and broken small boats – still moored but the ropes merely stopped the waterlogged wrecks drifting away.

Julian arrived beside her.

Minutes ticked by, with Birgitta staring outward and Julian openly fascinated by her alluring profile, the reflected moonlight fluorescing in the green of his eyes like algae.

Without turning her head, Birgitta said, "What should we do with the girl if she moves against us?"

Reaching out a hand and winding a strand of white silk hair around his fingertip, Julian replied, "Kill her."

Chapter 31

Marius walked along the seaweed covered rocks, the surf crashing around his thighs as the sea did its best to dislodge his heavy frame from its chosen path. Glancing up at the cliff face, he saw the freshly carved track in the chalk and headed towards it. *Rebekah will need a friendly face.* He grinned. Whether she would see him as a friendly face or not, he could not say for certain. He always found speaking to humans a stilted affair, but now, of course, Rebekah was no longer a human.

Leaping easily up over the detritus cluttered at the foot of the precipice, Marius dug his fingers into the chalky rock and scaled the slick surface. As the meadow above came into view, dread filled him when he saw Rebekah. She was laid out on her back. Even though she couldn't be dead – as a vampire no harm could come to her – it rattled him to see her prone form lying so still. The clothes she wore covered enough to be decent, but her legs were bare and so was her midriff – it was easy to see the outfit was created from strips torn from the baggy tunic and pants he had expected. It was an odd thought, but Marius was grateful she wasn't wearing just a fig leaf.

Striding across the grass, he leaned over and stared down into her face.

"Marius, is that you?"

He knew how different he must look to her now – a network of silver threads covered his face and the black pools of his eyes glittered like beaten silver. He smiled. "Yes, it's me."

Rebekah's teeth gleamed in the moonlight as she grinned. Marius studied her, too. When he offered his hand, Rebekah took it even though she didn't need to. Rising gracefully to her feet, she faced the fierce concentration of Marius' expression and said, "Connor is still inside the castle."

He nodded. "Julian, too. I don't like it. Let's get to the ship and find out what Malachi knows about their situation. I hope Osiris is feeding back the information we need to launch a rescue." Marius cocked his head. "At least Connor is awake."

Rebekah frowned. "Is he okay...?" Her fingers grazed the hardened potholes in her healed neck wound. "I know he didn't want to turn me, not like this."

"He still has you. That's all he cares about. That, and getting Seren, Julian, and the others out of the castle in one piece. There is more going on than we can understand. We need to give Malachi the name 'Morrigan' and see if he knows anything."

Swinging around to face the undulating gray sea, Marius located the ship. His words were snatched away by the icy wind. "Are you ready to test your skills, Rebekah?"

Stepping to the edge of the grassy meadow and looking down into the tumbling surf, Rebekah said, "Lead the way. I can do this."

Launching himself forward, Marius ran down the near vertical slope, his boots fracturing rocks to dust as his weight ground craters into the hill. Rebekah followed on behind, embracing the exhilaration. Falling on her ass didn't deter her. *It doesn't hurt.*

Jumping into the icy water, both vampires sank to the bottom. Marius reached back and gripped Rebekah's hand. Together they honed in on the ink black shadow where the ship's hull loomed overhead.

How are we going to get onboard? Frustration hit as she realized speaking was out. She had already learned that letting water into her lungs felt like filling her chest with gelatin. It was best to keep her throat locked down.

She jabbed Marius on the shoulder, pointed up and shrugged.

Marius made an okay symbol, and Rebekah trusted him. Out of the gloom, an ochre brown chain emerged – the rust gleaming like encrusted gold beads – draping in a diagonal across her vision. *An anchor.* She felt foolish. *Of course.*

Marius released her hand, signaled 'stay here' by jabbing his finger at her feet, and leapt up to grab the anchor chain. He appeared to drift upwards until he became a murky bulk hanging overhead.

What the hell is he doing? A dull rhythmic clang vibrated through the water in a series of beats as Marius held on with one hand, stretched out, and banged his palm on the metal hull.

Seconds later, like an Indian snake charming illusion, a rope ladder with metal rungs skimmed down through the water in front of her and a cloud of silt erupted at her feet. Marius swung from the anchor chain to the ladder and vanished above the water line.

Gripping a metal rung and sparing a moment to register it was warm, Rebekah barely noticed her water-logged clothes as she settled into an efficient hand over hand climbing action. When her head broke the surface, instinctively, she gasped. She could understand why vampires hung onto human behaviors.

Looking up the sheer escarpment of slick metal, Rebekah almost laughed at the row of white faces, all registering different degrees of surprise, staring down.

Marius had already made it to the top. When she got close enough, he reached out a hand to Rebekah in a chivalrous gesture. With a smile she gripped his hand and let him swing her in a graceful arc over the rail.

Rebekah stood on the deck and the enormity of her fate stared her in the face as Malachi and Anthony looked familiar, and yet so incredibly different. The salt-peter glow in their eyes and the ethereal gleam to their skin was distracting.

Malachi spoke first. "Is Connor back in the castle? I can't get a connection."

The spell broken, the group of four burst into movement. Heading below deck, they gathered around the table where all the details Malachi, Seren and Osiris shared were ranged out for others to see.

Marius picked up a pen and wrote 'Morrigan' in large letters and drew a thick line that joined it to the list of details they now knew about Birgitta.

Malachi nodded.

"Lars?" Marius studied the display for new information. "We know she was connected to him, then?"

"She was his betrothed. She wears a silver pendant with a glass vial embedded in it." Lost in thought, Malachi drummed his sharp nails on the tabletop putting scratches in the lacquer. "I used to do the same. With my brother Numu. The blood of the ancients is potent. This Morrigan must be Birgitta's maker."

Anthony said, "She's been at sea a long while, and her powers are strong. My guess is that the other presence Osiris detected means Morrigan is somewhere inside the castle now. She was onboard the ship, all along."

"But Julian swept the ship."

"It's not hard to create a secret compartment. I imagine Morrigan is a precious cargo and kept hidden from all but Birgitta's inner circle."

"What do we do now?" Rebekah asked. She looked around the cabin. "Where's Greg?"

"I'm sorry, Rebekah. He didn't make it," said Marius.

As Rebekah's face crumpled, Anthony coughed. "There's an update on that, Marius. I went back to bury him and he wasn't dead... not quite."

Marius' lip twitched and Rebekah wasn't sure if he was glad or angry.

"Please tell me you didn't bring an injured human back here? You might as well light a beacon on our whereabouts to every vampire hunting us."

"Not exactly. I turned him."

Marius' sneer became a smile. "Thank Christ for that."

"He's here?" Rebekah gripped Anthony's hand.

"He's below deck. Restrained. It's still early in the process, he was badly injured and that took its toll, but he'll be fine."

"That is good news. We have Julian and Gerrard inside the castle, so between them and Osiris, a plan of action should play out soon. All we can do is wait, for now," said Marius.

Rebekah looked down at the stained wet rags she wore and grimaced. "Is it okay to wish I could get clean and dry."

Marius' black sweep of hair was frosted with salt residue making him look like an oddly erect elderly gray-haired man. "We both look worse for wear," he agreed.

"I'll go out on deck and wait for Osiris' next update. He seems to have the freedom to move around the castle. You two get cleaned up. Anthony, check on Greg. I'll send for you when I get something." Suiting action to words, Malachi swung around and left the room.

Going below to her cabin, Rebekah dug out black pants and a shirt and washed in a bucket of cold water. No longer being human made simple things more complicated. As if she held a shell to her ear, she could hear the whooshing noise of the ocean and it was distracting. The shushing currents sounded like whispers and she froze mid-action when she thought she heard her name. *Is it possible?* Connor had said he was connected to Malachi and Seren. *Is it possible we are all connected, now?*

The sound of voices died away, and she returned to buttoning her shirt. *I must ask Malachi.*

Leaving the cabin, she spotted Anthony leaning against the wooden paneling in the gangway. She quickly joined him. "Is Greg in there?" Seeing another human going through the same transformation as she was, right now, was a curious thought. "Can I see him? Maybe we can help each other?"

Pushing away from the wall, Anthony smiled, nodded, and opened the cabin door.

Greg lay on a bed. His pallor was gray and lackluster. Rebekah was puzzled. "Why is he like that?"

Anthony laughed. "It is more a case of why aren't you like that."

His eyebrows rose in amusement at Rebekah surprise.

"Becoming a vampire usually knocks the stuffing out of you. The crystallization of the blood cells, the nucleus dying as the vampire DNA infects them... it's usually a downward spiral before the human body recovers. Greg was injured, but you-" Anthony looked her up and down. "You seem to have fast tracked through the fatigue."

"I see."

"Malachi has a theory. He thinks it's because your blood was already inside Connor. It is a unique event and so much the better for you."

Greg groaned and sweat broke out over the granite gray flesh of his naked chest. Anthony walked over to his friend and sat down beside the bed. "Greg is at the other end of the scale. He was pretty near death when I found him. He has a long way to climb back, but he will. He wants to."

With nowhere else to go, Rebekah settled on the bench beside Anthony. She bumped his shoulder with hers. "You and Greg are friends, huh?"

Anthony grinned. "He chose to become a vampire, and he drank from me, so we are brothers now. He was hard as hell as a human. Just think how much grief he's gonna give me as a vampire."

Without opening his eyes, Greg muttered, "Don't you ever stop talking? I'm gonna whip you into shape when I'm up and running."

Anthony punched Greg on the arm. "Bring it on, buddy."

Chapter 32

Waiting in her quarters for the feeding ceremony to begin, and a chance to see Connor again, Seren lost track of time. The room became darker and she acknowledged the truth – no one was coming to collect her. She had walked into the lion's den, and all for nothing. It proved only one thing – *the regent's visit was never about 'the hybrid child'*. The hairs on the back of her neck bristled and a glimpse of her Mama flitted inside her mind, but the image was ghostlike. *Papa?*

She had become used to being alone inside her head, but suddenly, she felt him. Something inside Connor had shifted. *Is Papa free?* Screwing her eyes tightly shut, she tried to 'see' him. *Nothing. What's going on?*

The last thing Osiris had said came back to her – 'If you sense things are going bad, get out of there. Promise me'.

"I should wait, here." Even as she said the words, she circled faster and faster like a missile building up to launch speed. "Damn it," she muttered, and felt a youthful cringe of guilt. Connor would frown at her cursing, but he wasn't here.

Squaring her shoulders, she strode over and gripped the door handle. *I don't know if things are going bad, but something has changed.* Whipping the door open, Seren stepped boldly into the corridor. Sascha – or it could be Valdar, because she really couldn't tell them apart – was not stationed outside, but he could return at any moment. The long hallway was deserted and she expelled a sigh of relief, happy that Sascha was not there. Needing 'human food' was the only excuse she had come up with for leaving her room.

She felt uneasy that the castle was so quiet. A glance through a window looking out over the harbor revealed that the bondsmen who had challenged her out on the quayside had dispersed. *They must be holed up somewhere.* The castle's six feet thick walls offered the regular relief of deep alcoves fitted with padded window seats to hide in. She tried several doors along a carpeted hallway in the search for Connor. The tension in her shoulders bit deeper with every empty room she found. *What am I doing? What if they come for me?* Crippled by indecision, she quickly headed back.

When she turned the final corner and saw a blur of moving figures, she dived into a window alcove and shifted sideways to melt into the thick drapes. She took slow deep breaths and reduced her heart rate to near hibernation, only then did she risk a peep out from where she was hiding.

The 'blur' turned out to be a group of three – the vampire twins dragging Connor away. It explained where Sascha had gone to.

Connor staggered from side to side like a drunk, ricocheting from the shoulder of one guard and bouncing back into the other. *Papa?* Something in his manner gave her hope. Trying to decide if she should follow, she almost missed Birgitta's brittle command of 'bring the child to me' when it rang out.

Her decision was made and she scuttled back to her room. Noticing scattered fragments of glass littering the floor by the window, without stopping to figure out why, she used the hem of her dress to brush them out of sight and closed the velvet drapes. She was standing in the middle of the floor, like a soldier at attention, when Bjorn opened the door.

"Come." The captain remained on the threshold and his blank expression gave nothing away.

"Where are we going?" Seren asked, injecting childlike enthusiasm into her tone.

The captain remained silent, stepped back out into the hallway and waited.

No small talk, then. Seren was relieved she had seen Connor being taken – at least Birgitta couldn't blindside her with that.

When she faced the regent moments later, asking if her Mama was dead felt like betrayal. But, nothing the regent said could shake her resolve. She trusted her instincts. *Mama is alive.*

Her papa was a prisoner, but he had not been distraught with grief.

When the captain's hands framed her head, Seren did not doubt he would crush her skull if Birgitta commanded it. The pressure made the bones creak, and, more terrifying, she felt nervous anticipation vibrating through Bjorn's fingertips. *He wants her to give the order.*

She had said what they wanted to hear, and promised to obey the regent. *What happens now?* The remaining guard in the room shadowed Seren as Birgitta sank deep into silent contemplation. Julian resembled a frozen statue, a hypnotized figure waiting for the magician to reanimate him.

Seren's mind worked overtime as she scanned the still faces around her. As she expected, once she declared her allegiance to the regent, Birgitta's interest shifted and Seren was dismissed.

Under escort, the walk back through the castle brought her no further clues, even though she peered into every open door or hallway.

Alone in her room again, the consequence of Connor being branded a traitor drifted like mist around her – it was there, but unreadable.

She pulled open the drapes and inspected the cracked windowpane. Gazing out at the mainland, she frowned. *Where are you, Osiris?* She had the feeling that, with Julian's enchantment, things were going off the rails. *Papa was taken to the dungeons. Uncle Julian is under her spell, now.* The words rotated around inside her mind and she hoped Osiris could read them. He was inside the castle, but she had no idea how much Birgitta's powers interfered with the process.

Osiris sat up suddenly from his laid out position on the red padded seat of a pew inside the 17th Century chapel. It had been used by the St Aubyn family – having a chapel in a residence was a privilege of wealth – but family services were a thing of the past. The wooden partition separating each pew made it the perfect place to stay out of sight. Since he first took refuge here, no one had come near. Its location up on the battlements meant Osiris could quickly go down into the castle or over the wall at a moment's notice.

Instantly, the psychic jolt he received from Seren sent him out of the door onto the battlements. He crept along with his back to the chapel wall, with the wind screaming in his ears.

He darted across the short open space between two buildings and paused where he could see in through a window. Only Julian and the regent remained in the suite of blue rooms, but he saw everything through the visions Seren had projected and could almost taste her distress. Her scent rode in the air, and part of him wanted to rush into the room and, like her avenging knight, slay the witch who had stolen away everything she loved – *but now Connor has been locked up.* It was more than just a complication, it was dangerous.

He ducked aside, pressing back into the carved brickwork when the door of the blue sitting room burst open and the regent swept away, heading deeper into the castle, picking up a retinue of four bondsmen along the way. A chilled breeze stirred in her wake.

Julian made no move to follow. He lowered himself into an armchair, rested a hand on each knee, and closed his eyes.

Following the regent at a distance, Osiris' attention sharpened when she stopped suddenly. Something about the expression on her face drew his eye. Osiris frowned, not quite understanding what he was seeing as all animation faded from the bondsmen. They didn't precisely slump, but they became less alert, the light behind their eyes fading to black, like a flame in a Jack-o-lantern being extinguished. *What is going on here?*

Birgitta stood still for what seemed an eon. The atmosphere around her shimmered as if the chilled air became a heat haze. Osiris scanned the hallway in the direction from which she had come, checking that the door of the reception room where Julian was waiting remained closed.

Turning swiftly back again, he almost missed the movement. Birgitta disappeared, but the thick tapestry hanging on the wall rippled as it settled back against the hard face of the stone wall. In a smooth flow of muscles, Osiris slipped out of his hiding place.

He kept his eyes glued to the standing bondsmen as he drew closer. They didn't move.

Without touching it, Osiris inspected the tapestry. One vertical side looked more frayed than the other and the whipped edge curled up. Placing his palm flat on the surface beside it, he felt a draft. He gritted his teeth and drew a dagger from the sheath strapped to his thigh. Resting back against the wall, he extended an arm beneath the tapestry. He sidled along, feeling the gritty woven fabric drag across his chest and scrape his hair away from his turned cheek. His outstretched hand folded around an edge where the wall ended. He took another step and wriggled his fingers inside the void beyond. With one more sideward slide, he could reach out and touch the other side of the aperture. It was a narrow space. Cold air poured out from between the two granite slabs. It was pitch-black, but Osiris could see a difference in the darkness. *There's a doorway.*

Excitement flared inside him. *The regent doesn't expect anyone to follow. Could this be the answer?* Instinct told him it was the missing piece of the puzzle. Birgitta's slight frame would have found it easy to pass through the gap, but Osiris had to twist sideways and even then, he cursed silently as the metal plates of his homemade armor scraped along the walls of the narrow passageway. After six feet, it widened and the floor began to slope downward. Ducking under a broken wrought iron lamp holder sticking out from the wall, Osiris moved slowly, pausing every few steps to listen. The air smelled salty. *There must be an exit to the outside.* He pushed the dagger back into its sheath and lengthened his stride, outstretching his arms until his fingertips made contact with both sides of the passage as he advanced. The darkness lifted to a misty gray and the descent continued on.

He reached a 'T' junction where another tunnel joined from the left. Dampness glistened on the walls, and Osiris stood stock still scanning where light gleamed in both directions. *Which one?* Making a decision borne of desperation, he took three steps down one conduit. He suddenly stopped. Something bothered him but he couldn't say what it was. Retracing his steps, he turned towards the other tunnel and as soon as he entered it, he knew. *The smell.* The subtle scent of the regent filled his nostrils and certainty returned.

He moved faster, but silently. The glow at the end of the corridor grew brighter and a whispering voice registered. Osiris put his back to one wall, sidestepping once more until a cavern came into view. The rough surface bore the gouge marks of freshly hewn stone and he recognized it as a vampire excavation. *If the regent had this labyrinth dug out, then whatever she's hiding down here is important.*

The figure of Birgitta faced away from Osiris, the halo of her white blonde hair unmistakable. A shallow copper basin rested on a bed of glowing charcoal, the flames flickering gently. On a stone altar stood a row of glass vials and metal bowls. Beyond the altar, on a platform, rested a stone sarcophagus. *She takes sleep down here?* Her voice rose in an incantation, it hummed through the air as Birgitta picked up the red hot bowl in her bare hands without flinching. "Purify the blood, Earth Mother. Blessing of The Otherworld, bring her to us that we may be strong." Birgitta drifted towards the open coffin shell, and took the three steps up onto the plinth.

Osiris frowned. His nape prickled as unease crept through him. Daring to shift forward one more foot, he gained a clearer view of the regent bending over the coffin. He clamped his mouth closed and concentrated on taking in the details unfolding.

A dry hand slid up over the edge of the sarcophagus and the clawed fingers crackled as they gripped it, the white flesh glowing with an ethereal sheen. Birgitta held out the bowl and a skeletal face framed by crinkled translucent hair rose up, and blackened lips clamped onto the rim. The sucking sound as the corpse drank turned Osiris' stomach. *What is she? Is this Morrigan?*

As the decrepit figure sank back, a scrawny arm extended and Birgitta drew a spike from the woven strands of her braid and pushed it firmly into the wrinkled flesh. Osiris noticed the pendant around Birgitta's neck for the first time. Withdrawing the spike, she let three globules of brown colored blood drop down into the copper bowl. Wisps of smoke rose and the concoction crackled. "I give thanks, Earth Mother. You're power flows through me."

Osiris watched with fascination as Birgitta used the spike to stir the mixture and then filled the glass vial around her neck. As she stepped back from the sarcophagus, she bowed her head in reverence. When she reached the floor of the cavern once more, she lifted the copper bowl to her lips and drank from it. When she turned to replace it on the altar, her beauteous face emitted a brighter glow than it had before. A network of rose crystal threads covered her face and then, almost as quickly as they had appeared, they dimmed once more to her customary translucent complexion

Osiris had seen enough. *Better to leave now, than get caught.* He melted back into the tunnel. Hearing the regent chanting softly reassured him he had gone unnoticed.

As he swung back the way he had come, curiosity got the better of him. *What is down the other tunnel?* Squaring his shoulders, Osiris moved at speed down the opposite freshly cut path. The taste of salt grew stronger.

He heard the sound of lapping water at the base of a descending slope. He traced his fingers along what felt like tracks scored into the walls on both sides, but then he realized they were uniform in depth, and straight. *Almost like rails.* Dropping to a crouch, Osiris peered more closely and confirmed his suspicions. Something had slotted into the walls as a form of moving platform. The floor bore scrape marks too. It all pointed to something heavy being dragged up from the water below, and into a room above. *A sarcophagus, perhaps.* Morrigan must have been unloaded from the ship and brought in via this underwater entrance. It made sense. Osiris suspected many in Birgitta's crew knew nothing about the source of their mistress' powers.

He was about to swing back towards the upper floors of the castle when he heard a noise. A low hiss. Taking slower steps down the suddenly steeper slope, Osiris saw a row of bars. Beyond the bars, a room came into view and shackled to a wall inside it, he found Connor. His manacled hands were stretched above his head and he hung suspended, with his toes barely touching the floor. A human would have deep cuts gouged into bleeding wrists, but Connor's were merely skewed at a hideous looking angle.

Osiris whistled quietly and Connor's head shot up. Osiris smiled and silently raised an eyebrow. Half a dozen feet further down the corridor, the floor was under water, but Connor was dry, at least.

"What are they planning?" Connor asked, thinking the words, but mouthing them for his own satisfaction.

"I have found out who Morrigan is." Osiris answered. "Birgitta is communing with her now. She is an ancient. Just as Malachi suspected."

"If that is where her strength comes from, how can we hurt her?" asked Connor.

"Blessed blood seems to play a large part in the process."

Connor nodded, jiggling his manacle slightly. "I can vouch for the power of the blessing. It's why I can't break out of these." He didn't understand it, but he knew he felt weak. *Something* had transformed the metal into something stronger than a vampire.

Osiris' eyes glinted in the light.

"What?" Connor sensed Osiris' eureka moment.

"What would happen if Morrigan drank contaminated blood? Animal blood perhaps?"

Connor thought about it for a heartbeat. "If her blood is part of the incantations which make Birgitta strong, then introducing a contaminant could do it. Could break the chain."

Osiris nodded. "I'll consult with Malachi, but a rabbit should be easy to find."

"Go," said Connor urgently, "we don't know how much time Seren has, and don't trust anyone. Julian and Gerrard are under her influence. Assume everyone inside the castle is, even Seren."

Osiris raised a hand in farewell and retreated back the way he came. He heard a distant whispered incantation, three words on rotation over and over. 'Purify the blood, purify the blood, purify the blood'. It reminded Osiris of the mindless noises made by someone losing their sanity. As he approached the open mouth of the tunnel which led to the ceremonial chamber – that is how Osiris thought of it, now – he diverted, leaned over and peered inside.

Birgitta's lips moved as the words poured out, but something about the stillness in her awkwardly posed figure made the image macabre. Remembering Malachi's theory of Ovate Druids leaving their bodies, Osiris pulled back swiftly. He felt sure she was still inside her body, but the repeated words felt like they were on auto-pilot, so where Birgitta's conscious thought, and by default, her attention was directed, he couldn't be sure.

Urgency closed around Osiris like a damp chill. Moving fast, he headed back up into the castle and, instinctively following the familiar path, he arrived back at the room he used when he first entered the fortress. Swinging out of the window, he hung onto the outside wall, his black hair snaked around his face in the chaotic currents of air. His eyes remained open against the chilling blast and he focused on Julian's ship anchored across the water.

Malachi? Osiris didn't wait for a response, he knew his master well enough to be sure he'd be listening. *Send Marius out to bring me a rabbit carcass, or fox, something to bleed and use against Morrigan.* As an after thought, he tagged on. *I won't find anything on this rock.* As he climbed back in through the window, just before the invisible cloak blocked out communication, Malachi sent his answer.

In a dark corner of the room, Osiris sank down into a meditative crouch, leaning back against a wall and resting his forearms on his knees. He closed his eyes and concentrated on listening for signs of alarm within the fortress. He stayed in the room for ten minutes, and then scaled the wall down to the footings where, according to Malachi, the sacrificed prey would be waiting.

He found Marius waiting, too. Both the dead rabbit and Marius dripped seawater onto the boulders where they rested.

"What is the plan?" Marius cut to the chase.

"Birgitta takes her strength from an entity she calls 'Earth Mother'. A mummified being. We haven't worked out how, yet, but we plan on infecting her blood."

Marius looked up sharply, rising to his feet. "We? Do you mean Julian and the captain?"

Osiris started talking with a heavy heart. "Birgitta has Julian ensnared by her craft. It is safe to assume Captain Gerrard is also her puppet. Rebekah freed Connor, but Birgitta is not a fool. She used Julian against him. Connor is confined in a dungeon." Osiris smiled. "I've located Connor. He's weak. This Earth Mother has power over him, but he is alert and we are hatching a plan."

Marius nodded his head slowly and rivulets of salt water ran down his face. "That is good news, at least. Rebekah is sensing a connection with Connor, but she hasn't learned how to tap into it yet, so she'll be pleased to know he is still intact."

Osiris frowned. "I get the feeling we are missing something. If Birgitta came to avenge Lars, then why not kill Connor, take Seren and leave? Why wait?"

Marius laughed drily. "Forgive me if I'm glad she hasn't taken such a drastic, straightforward course. Perhaps she is enjoying the power she has over the London Hive."

Osiris stared at Marius' set features. "Or maybe she knows Rebekah isn't dead, or rather, is undead."

"What difference could that make?"

Osiris shrugged. "You're right. None at all." He stooped to pick up the rabbit.

"This plan? It will break Birgitta's hold over Julian?"

"Malachi will know if we succeed. If her power fails her, be ready to breach the castle with a show of man power. We could be setting light to a powder keg."

Osiris pushed the slack carcass inside his tunic and started to scale the wall back up the castle. He heard the splash as Marius entered the water and glanced back to see the charcoal gray surface closing over the juror's head.

In voicing his theories aloud, Osiris had missed out his worst fear. *With Connor imprisoned, Birgitta could just kill Seren and leave.* The speed of his climb increased steadily until he disappeared inside the window above.

Chapter 33

Marius circled around in what had been Julian's cabin, glancing at each intent face in turn. "We don't have time to think about this. Julian and Gerrard are lost to us. Osiris said he and Connor have a plan, and we have to be ready."

Malachi projected an air of calm. "It is not so complicated. Take the ship closer to the castle and weigh anchor. I will join Anthony and you, Marius, as the forward guard the moment I sense the psychic force field weaken." Looking at Rebekah, he said, "You wait onboard until we know how the land lies."

Rebekah stood up, her ethereal pearl tinted complexion drawing every eye in the room. "I'm going with you. I know the layout of the castle. And Seren is in there. I'm going too."

Marius shot a humorous glance Malachi's way and said, "I told you."

"You did." Locating Greg, who stood beside Anthony with his arms folded across his chest, Malachi raised an eyebrow.

"I'm coming, too."

Malachi shook his head. His aged skin creaking with the sudden movement. The expression chasing across his face left no doubt of his feelings. No one listened to anything he said anymore. "Remember, you are both new vampires. Yes, you are stronger than most of Birgitta's guards, but they outnumber you and have experience on their side."

Greeted by stubborn set jaws from both Rebekah and Greg, Malachi snorted with disgust.

"I'll look after Greg," Anthony said.

"I'll look after myself," Rebekah countered.

Taking into account the speed with which Rebekah had adapted to her 'turning' and how she seemed to have honed skills Malachi had seen other vampires take years to master, he could not argue. "Just use your head. Birgitta will not surrender without a fight."

Marius tapped his foot and got everyone's attention. "We are all going, but let's be clear on our purpose. Osiris will find Seren. Rebekah, you find Connor. Greg and Anthony, disable any guardsmen who attack. Malachi and I will focus on finding Julian and Gerrard. Agreed?"

Marius left the cabin and made his way to the bridge. "Daniel, take us around the mount to the seaward side. Get as close to the castle as our draft allows."

The creaking of the hull began almost immediately as the vampire oarsmen took up their stations. Like a well-oiled machine, the long wooden blades cut through the water, each one in perfect synchronicity. They made barely a ripple in the black silk. In complete darkness, the ship oozed like an oil slick across the bay.

Most of the windows of the castle remained black, but the apparently deserted state could not be taken for granted. Malachi could almost see the shroud Birgitta's will cast over the impressive edifice of stone. Invisible to the eye, it refracted a rainbow of colors into his psyche like a pearl-tinted dome.

As they drew close to where the towering walls of the fortress cast a shadow over the gently undulating sea, Marius sent the command to heave to.

When Marius descended to the lower level to where Daniel and Sergeant Hugh waited to deploy the gangplank, he found the rest of the landing party already assembled. Each one watched Malachi closely as the elder vampire concentrated on detecting a chink in the regent's armor.

Chapter 34

Armed with the knowledge that Marius would play his part and a landing party would be waiting to react if Birgitta's powerful grip over the castle faltered, Osiris dropped back into the storage room through the window he had forced.

Not 'if' – Osiris reminded himself – *'when'*.

The crates inside remained in shoulder high stacks. Dodging behind the nearest tower, Osiris shed the makeshift linen tunic and removed the plates of armor, along with his knives, in favor of freedom of movement, and laid them down quietly on the floor. Ready to leave, he inspected the moonlit room from the doorway, checking that everything looked untouched.

He cradled the fragile ribcage of the sleek rabbit carcass in his fingertips, and it swung gently in time with his skimming stride. He listened for signs of vampire movement in the castle hallway before flipping back the tapestry covering the hidden entrance and returning along the descending tunnel.

He moved with swift silent grace, but still found Connor's gray gaze locked onto his when he arrived at the prison cell. The putty colored pallor of his almost father-in-law's face alarmed Osiris. Seeing Connor rendered weak was a harsh reminder of the force they were up against.

Holding onto the bars with one hand and peering across the dungeon, Osiris said, "I have the rabbit."

Connor's chains rattled as he tried to move but was pulled up short. As though continuing a conversation from only moments ago, Connor asked, "You said the ritual 'blessed the blood'?"

Osiris frowned, his recollection racing back over what he had seen. "It seems to be a cycle. The regent feeds the mummified remains, then extracts the mummy's blood and drinks it, and carries it around her neck."

"So, if it's a cycle, we can break it."

Osiris nodded. "With this?" He held the rabbit up by the scruff of its neck.

Connor stared long and hard at the animal, and Osiris waited, frozen like a statue.

"If we can get the blood into Morrigan's brain, that would give us the best chance."

"How do we do that? We need human blood."

"Maybe, maybe not. Osiris, *your* blood can unlock a vampire brainstem."

Osiris grinned. "I told Marius to get a landing party ready."

"Good. Things could happen very fast. Is Morrigan unguarded?"

"Yes. It seems that only Birgitta knows she exists."

"When we were… together, Birgitta would retire to 'meditate' morning and evening. If you go now, the path should be clear." Connor shook the manacles. "I'll be ready to help when I can." The gray light in his eyes glowed with confused irritation. He had never believed in magic. "I don't understand it."

"Be ready, I'll look after Seren," Osiris said, and disappeared.

His bronze-toned skin glistened in the candlelight as he entered the cavern carved out below the foundations of the castle. The chamber with the sarcophagus was empty this time and Osiris found that more unsettling, not knowing what Birgitta was doing at that moment.

The moisture dripping from the low ceiling was creating embryonic stalactites, their milk white appearance resembling fingers of bone reaching downward.

As he crossed the space with the rabbit resting over one shoulder, he gripped the gold armlet around his bicep and eased it down towards his elbow. He felt a quiet sense of confidence. Blood represented the elixir by which the world around him functioned. Stepping up onto the plinth where the open sarcophagus shell rested, Osiris allowed his curiosity to surface as he looked inside.

The gray-colored skin coated the desiccated skeleton like gossamer-thin silver leaf – the cracks in the bones showed through it in a network of dark threads. The cheek bones beneath her skin were like knife blades and the eye sockets were coal black holes.

He guessed it was female by the long almost transparent strands of hair which lay over her thin shoulders. In the depths of the pools of black, Osiris thought he saw a glisten of light.

Taking the waxed stopper from the catheter so deeply embedded into Osiris' bicep it had become part of him, he leaned forward and a drop of blood swelled into a glistening ruby. The dry skin crackled as the corpse of Morrigan shuddered. White threads of saliva bridged the gaping hole of her mouth when it creaked open, and the speck of light in her gaze flickered.

Osiris smiled as he let the droplet fall onto the protruding leathery tongue. Another drop splattered on her thin black lip, and her throat rattled. Osiris didn't notice the clawed hand lifting until the bony fingers scraped over his shoulder blade. He smothered the instinct to jerk back as the taloned nails dug into his shoulder and began to excavate deep holes in his hard flesh. He was grateful the rabbit carcass draped over his other shoulder stayed in place.

Timing would be critical. *How do I know if the brainstem is open?* Connor couldn't help him with that. All he had offered was the advice, 'you will know'. Gritting his teeth against the inexorable force of the wiry strength in the bony limb, Osiris locked his muscles tighter, trying to pull back against the pressure. A nauseating smacking sound echoed from the dry hollow of her mouth and the skin of Morrigan's neck crackled when her head began to lift.

Osiris' stomach rolled over at the thought of those cold slug-like lips closing around the wound in his arm. He tamped down the desperation building inside and tapped into the detached clinical part of his mind. *Is it time?* Everything hung on this moment.

Examining the skeletal features at close quarters, Osiris couldn't find the 'you will know' factor. But then, he detected an odor. It smelled like crumbling bone, and Osiris swallowed the fine dust which coated his tongue. *Where is it coming from?* Focusing on her wide open mouth merely affirmed that, with bare inches remaining between him and the clamoring corpse, time was running out. Deliberately letting five more drops of blood fall in a string of claret pearls, Osiris watched like a hawk as they slid into Morrigan's desiccated gullet, and then he saw it – the mist of dust emitting from the eye sockets.

The flickering glint deep inside them flared.

Osiris wondered if it was the fragile bone of the skull being disturbed by the sudden surge of the brain swelling with hydration. It was the best sign he could hope for. Osiris deftly reinserted the wax plug into the catheter, cutting off the blood supply, and the clawed grip on his shoulder clenched, the nail tips grinding into his shoulder blade.

He could not remember ever feeling desperation. He had been rescued from his mother's womb by Malachi, so weakness was merely a word. But his hybrid heart hitched up a notch and the tendons in his neck became thick cords as he braced a hand on the sarcophagus rim and used all his strength to resist Morrigan's fervor.

Grappling over his shoulder for the rabbit, he dragged it across his chest, and fumbled with the carcass until he had a tight grip on the spine. Taking his eyes off Morrigan for a second, he bit into the thick pelt, his agitation showing as he tore quickly through the membrane of skin and ripped into the muscle. He pressed his face into the delicate bone structure, feeling a buzz of satisfaction when the ribcage imploded.

The rabbits blood began to flow and, still holding the bony rod of its spine, Osiris pushed the oozing carcass into the space between him and the intent skeletal features, emptying the pool of blood filling the animal's chest cavity into the gaping mouth.

Morrigan's eyes widened, the light inside them flared like twin bursts of lit phosphorus and her body shuddered. Instead of releasing, the claws dragged down his back. He had no choice but to stay still. The ridge of the sarcophagus dug into his stomach, his lower ribs creaking under the pressure as convulsions rattled through Morrigan's bones. Even if he didn't survive her crushing strength, he knew he had succeeded.

A keening noise gargled in her blood-filled throat and her free hand flailed until she grasped a fistful of rabbit fur and wrenched the carcass from Osiris' hand. With a wet bellow, she threw it aside.

It hit the wall of the chamber with a wet thump and left a dark red stain as it slid down the wall.

Osiris registered the scamper of approaching footfalls and knew he had no choice. Reaching around, he grabbed hold of the thin wrist pressing against his shoulder and squeezed it in a vise-like grip, but, as fragile as the woman appeared, her bones were like steel rods. Twisting sideways, Osiris clenched his jaw and grimaced at the burning sensation of her nails scything beneath his skin. When he broke away and let go of the powder dry limb, he avoided looking at the bony hand. He didn't want to know what damage she had wreaked, not yet.

Leaping down from the plinth and rushing over to the wall just inside the doorway, Osiris pressed his back into the stone. He couldn't make immediate sense of the clamor of new sounds inside his head, until he realized it was the unfiltered thought processes of combat. *Malachi.* Osiris grinned. *I can hear him. He must be inside the castle.* It also meant Morrigan's force field had fractured. The footsteps became a skimming vibration which betrayed them as a vampire and not human. *Birgitta, it must be.*

A moment later, the regent burst into the chamber, her hair streaming behind her in a cascade of frost-white strands. The gray bony fingers of Morrigan gripped the rough edge of the sarcophagus and Birgitta jumped up onto the ledge.

Curiosity held Osiris still.

"Your blood runs through me. Purify the blood, Earth Mother. Blessing of The Otherworld, bring us together so that we may be strong." Birgitta uttered the incantation over and over as she took a blade and sliced open her forearm. The sound of Morrigan's black dry lips sucking Birgitta's flesh broke through Osiris' fascination. Turning in a blur of movement, he headed swiftly back up into the castle to add his strength to the attack raging overhead.

Birgitta grimaced as her flesh became desiccated and her skin clung to her bones. A hideous smile froze on her face and the chanting incantation became a mumbling rhythm.

Morrigan sat up, and the dried blood which stained her face and chest faded as if her flesh consumed it. The flint-gray hue lifted to pearl white and glistened with a pink glow as Morrigan finally relaxed the grip on Birgitta's arm, and her protégé fell back.

Birgitta crawled across the stone floor, her gown hanging from her thin frame, the fabric slipping from her bony shoulders. When she reached the wall, she slumped against it, dragging her body around to rest back against the hard stone. Her fingers stiffened with spasms as she tried to unlock the vial hanging around her neck. Her blue eyes clouded with cataracts and her hair lost its vibrancy, plastered to her scalp in a dull cap of ochre strands which hung like wet string across her shoulders.

Morrigan sat bolt upright in her coffin and assessed the room. Her eyes gleamed with a reptilian yellow glow. Lifting her chin, she inhaled through her mouth as though, like a cat, she could taste the air. Placing a hand on the stone lip, she leapt from the sarcophagus and stood on the ledge. Looking down at her own feet, she seemed fascinated. Her plump skin glowed with health and if her nakedness registered, she remained unconcerned.

As though drawn by a single thought, like an arrow to a bullseye, Morrigan left the chamber, turned right, and using her hand to steady her whipping stride, headed downwards through the damp salt-soaked air in the tunnel. Her feet splashed in the shallow puddles the tide had left in the uneven floor.

She could smell him.

Swinging into the final fork before the steepest slope took her towards the sea, she headed towards Connor.

Broken chains hung from the manacles on his wrists, and Connor braced every muscle, ready to move. "I've been waiting for you," he said, with a hard smile.

Grabbing the bars and yanking the gate from its hinges, Morrigan lunged forward, shrieking.

Connor dodged the reach of her clawed hands and rushed out through the gate.

Morrigan staggered. Her body glanced from the wall, her shoulder smashing a crater into the stone. As the shards rained down over the ground, she latched on to Connor's scent and, with a much steadier gait, rushed after him.

She kept Connor's broad back in her sights as his black shirt fanned out behind him. *Birgitta, he is coming.* Morrigan knew instinctively where this formidable vampire would go. She already knew he would not run away. He would face his enemies and destroy them. *But not this time.*

Chapter 35

Malachi's body jolted as the tearing sensation Osiris experienced ripped through him, too. With a grim smile, he said, "Osiris has broken the spell. The Earth Mother, her power has been destroyed.

Almost before he finished speaking, the signal was given to lower the gangplank, and the landing party made the crossing, wading onto outcrops of submerged rock. Rebekah left the ship first with Malachi close behind. Marius brought up the rear. The sweeping flat slopes of rock gave way to grass and the overgrown steeply-stepped ornamental gardens leading up to the castle provided cover. The group crouched low and marshalled their thoughts.

"Marius, we'll head towards the west entrance and find Julian. Rebekah, you locate Connor." Malachi's tone held an urgent note. None of them liked the fact that they needed to split up in order to conquer, but there were too many fronts to cover.

Anthony headed to the east side of the castle with four of the Elite Guard following in his wake, and broke a window. Offering a hand to pull Greg in behind, once inside the castle, Anthony beckoned to his companion to stay close – Greg's skittering eyes indicated the overwhelming feedback of acute vampire sensations.

"You'll be okay. Remember to breathe, you can smell them before you see them. They've been on board a ship living in close quarters. Can you smell the salt?" Laying a reassuring hand on Greg's shoulder as he spoke, the realization on the face of the newest vampire made Anthony smile. "You'll be okay. Come."

Anthony kept his protégé in sight as they searched the rabbit run of hallways.

Satisfaction spiked inside Anthony when they crossed a threshold into a cave-like room. He waited for Greg and the escort of hive guardsmen to join him. The deserted hallways suddenly made sense – the silent throng of assembled vampires resembled bats packed tightly into the darkened space.

The bondsmen inside the rough-hewn granite chamber did not seem to notice the arrival of the newcomers. Their lackluster reactions were almost confused. *Malachi must be right. Birgitta controls them.* Taking no chances, Anthony drew two short daggers and nodded to Greg to do the same. Anthony's gesture across his chest reminded Greg of the combat training they had rehearsed. Greg could use his new strength to devastating advantage if he targeted the soft parts of the bondsmen – eye sockets, mouth and throat, and up under the ribcage were the key target areas.

Anthony felt relief when, as if touching them released a spring, the nearby bondsmen swung around, baring teeth and drawing weapons from scabbards at their sides. Back to back, Anthony and Greg fought in spiralling coordination, mowing down the circling opponents as they lunged forward. The cacophony of snapping bones, tearing tendons, and bodies thumping to the ground faded as the casualties began to pile up and fall back.

When four more vampires stepped out of the shadows, swaying from side to side as if trying to remember where they were, Greg and Anthony left the hive guards to ward off the bondsmen who remained. The pair sidestepped in single file up the narrow stone staircase from the garrison room and into the banquet hall above. Its modest size was deceptive – the vaulted domed ceiling created the aura of an amphitheater.

The heavy wooden door at the top of the short flight of steps swung open and revealed Julian. His face wore a stern expression and the residue of bitterness swam in the depths of his stare. Beyond him, inside the book-lined parlor, a pale faced Seren sat with Captain Gerrard beside her. The small retinue of bondsmen in the room stared into space.

Framed in the doorway at the far side, having approached from the west entrance, Malachi faltered as the air inside the library began to hum with a malicious current. The half-smile of recognition fighting for expression on Julian's face dissolved and his green eyes flashed with renewed contempt.

"Take up arms." Malachi's words cut through the air just as the bemused bondsmen shifted to attention and their concentration sharpened to attack mode.

Something is wrong. Birgitta is back in control. Where is Rebekah? A sudden influx of human slaves rushing into the banquet hall caused chaos. Their wardens chased after them and Anthony realized that they had taken the chance to escape while their captors had lost track of conscious thought.

As though it happened in slow motion, a young man wearing only tattered pants made a dash for the open door at the rear. A bondsman accelerated, grabbed his hair and swung him off his feet. The pale undernourished figure flipped through the air like a rag doll. His body landed midway up the plaster frieze and slid down. Blood smeared over the wall where he had crunched into it, and his shattered legs bent back at an alarming angle.

The scent of blood unleashed another level of chaos.

At Anthony's signal, Greg and he pulled soft plastic masks from their belts and pressed them over their mouth and noses. The plan pivoted on an invisible axis. Marius returned to the west door and his whistle signaled to the London hive guards to put on their masks, storm the fortress and engage the enemy.

A dozen hive vampires swept into the castle, some scaling the walls, smashing the stained-glass windows and surprising the bondsmen. Anthony fought to ignore the feasting frenzy as four of Birgitta's vampires tore the young boy's flesh apart. Pulling a handful of vials filled with human blood from inside his jacket, he slammed them against a wall, about ten feet above the floor. When they smashed, the bondsmen circled like vultures as the impulse to feed disrupted the conditioning Birgitta's power hard wired into their brains.

Rebekah had darted away from the battle, dashing along the labyrinth of hallways, looking for the access to the secret corridor. She passed clusters of humans with white bloated features staggering along, and before she could wonder at how they escaped, Osiris came into view. The fierce scowl on his face couldn't disguise the discomfort he felt. It didn't take a genius to work it out, like outlaws in Western movies used stampeding cattle, Osiris was using Birgitta's human stock against her.

As he drew closer, the pink fluid trickling down his chest shocked her. "What happened?"

Osiris grinned. "A story for another time. It's this way." Changing direction abruptly, Osiris darted around a corner and pulled a tapestry aside to uncover the hidden entrance. "Connor is down there. Once I know Seren is safe, I'll come and find you."

Her last sight of him as he disappeared, negotiating the obstacles of aimless wandering humans with ease, was of the oozing claw marks down his back – evidence of the danger Connor must now be facing.

Just as Osiris had, Rebekah side-stepped through the aperture and over the threshold into thicker dank atmosphere, letting the woven fabric fall back into place behind her. The noises from the main part of the castle receded as she hurtled forward, her mind reaching out to Connor. Like feeling for someone in the dark, she searched for his familiar aura. But what she encountered resembled black-hearted rage. *Whose*? Rebekah recoiled at the malignant wall of harsh emotions. Hunger resided inside there, too. Her footsteps slowed as fear of the unknown tried to drive her back. But Connor was somewhere down in these crypt-like caverns. Setting her jaw, Rebekah reached up and pulled a wrought iron lamp holder from the stone wall, and fashioned it into a short spear. Being armed renewed her determination.

Walking faster, and not allowing thoughts of how Seren, Julian and the rest were fairing, she followed her instincts.

The ground vibrated and the noise of battle raged in the chamber up ahead. If this was a weakened Birgitta, then Rebekah felt scared that Malachi had underestimated the Druid's power. Light flickering through a distant doorway projected hideous forms onto the rough-hewn stone wall of the tunnel. *Two shadows.*

Rebekah rushed into the room in time to see an enraged Connor hurtle through the air. An explosion of grit kicked up when he landed on his back. His contorted features were unrecognizable. Waves of ruthless spite radiated from him. *Connor?* The stare which turned her way revealed pupils dilated to fathom deep caverns. She sensed the electrical storm inside Connor's head and suddenly understood. *He's using grave sleep to fight.*

Nanoseconds elapsed before Rebekah shifted her attention to Connor's adversary. *Birgitta.* Her long hair covered her shoulders in blonde silk, her satin skin gave her graceful figure a healthy glow, but she was naked. Rebekah stood stock still, shocked at the sight of the warrior regent. A worm of jealousy stirred inside her. Rebekah watched the ruthless figure hone in on Connor's prone body. The penetrating gaze he levelled at Rebekah's frozen form sparked with ice gray clarity. He was back, and he feared for her safety.

The naked female form lost its softness as she pinned Connor to the floor, the sinews and tendons carving troughs into her smooth skin. An odor of arcing electricity hit Rebekah and Connor's body went into spasm, his limbs rattling and convulsing uncontrollably before they suddenly went slack.

Finally, Rebekah jolted forward and raised her sharpened spike, confronting the scene playing out in terrifying slow motion.

The muscles bulged on the regent's back as she lifted Connor's arm and bit into it. His muscle tone collapsed as she sucked his congealed blood. Disgust knotted Rebekah's stomach as Birgitta's throat gargled and she dribbled regurgitated blood into Connor's mouth.

A movement in a darkened corner made Rebekah freeze. Another thinner, emaciated woman with blonde hair smiled at her, revealing blood-stained teeth. Her bony fingers shook as she replaced the lid on a vial around her neck and, before Rebekah's eyes, as the figure rose to her feet, the aging process rewound and her skin became smooth and succulent. *Birgitta.* Rebekah frowned, dropping her hand until the metal spear pointed to the floor as she tried to process what she was seeing.

The figure crushing Connor into the ground turned the black abyss of her gaze on Rebekah. "Ah, at last." The dry fibers of her vocal chords creaked.

Birgitta, now disconcertingly younger than her naked counterpart, said, "Rebekah, we have been waiting for you. This is Morrigan."

Morrigan stood slowly and lithely stepped away from Connor, leaving him lying on his back, motionless on the ground. Her smile tightened every muscle in her face.

The air in the room rushed into Rebekah's lungs, and the voice invading her head rose in pitch to female tones. It was not Connor's voice, but Morrigan's.

Birgitta moved to stand beside the elder Druid.

The whispering inside Rebekah's head became a constant stream. Without knowing why, she lifted the metal spike, silently crossed the floor and hammered it into Connor's palm, pinning his hand to the ground.

His eyes closed and his vitality drained away.

"Revival sleep will not save you." Birgitta planted her foot on Connor's chest as Morrigan surged forward and stopped mere inches from Rebekah.

"Now we have our ring of three. The coven is complete; I am earth, Birgitta is water, and you, my dear, are fire. You felt it, even before he turned you." Morrigan's scathing glance took in Connor. "He has stolen enough from you. Now, take your destiny in your hands." Morrigan's razor sharp nails lifted Rebekah's chin. "To survive in this world, female vampires have to be strong, and, now we are three, no-one can take it away from us."

Morrigan's bony digit pointed accusingly at Connor's prone body. "Your heart has been soiled by him. He has to die if you are to ascend to your power."

Connor's ribcage creaked beneath the weight of Birgitta's foot and his eyes opened, glazed with delirium.

Rebekah forced a smile. "He is pathetic. What have you done to him?"

"Us?" Birgitta laughed. "Not us. He would be too strong, even for our potions. *You* weakened him. He thinks he's in love." Birgitta shook her head. "Vampires cannot love, but he truly believes it."

"I know that, now." Rebekah's heightened senses focused on the cold stone inside her own chest and she grinned.

Taking a sidestep, Birgitta slid her hand into a deep crack in the wall and pulled out a sword slotted between two blocks. Rebekah felt the weight inside her chest grow heavier as the gleaming steel emerged in a seemingly endless blade. In a smooth silent action, Birgitta swung the sword up over her head, poised in a two-handed grip.

"Please-" Without registering the thought, Rebekah found herself already across the room, gripping Birgitta's wrist.

The regent's ice blue glare flashed above a curled lip.

"Let me do it," Rebekah whispered.

Surrendering the sword, Birgitta withdrew slowly and backed away. She stood beside Morrigan and watched Rebekah test the balance of the blade and line it up on Connor's throat.

His eyes fluttered open and, when he looked into Rebekah's face, their distended pupils snapped closed. He clenched his fist over the head of the nail skewered through his palm and muttered, "Now."

Rebekah lifted the sword, shifted her weight away from Connor and swung it around, aiming the slicing blow at Birgitta. The shockwave shuddered up her arms as she made contact with the slender porcelain column of the regent's throat.

Stone grated beneath his boots as Connor sprang to his feet, flew across the space towards Morrigan and with a swiping back fist, buried the nail protruding from the back of his hand into her cheek, grinding her cheekbone to dust and crumbling her teeth. The screeching sound pouring from Morrigan's gaping mouth made Rebekah recoil. The sword clattered onto the floor as she shrank back and put her hands over her ears.

The gash in Birgitta's neck closed to a scratch, and disappeared altogether as her blue eyes glittered with rage. "You could have had it all." Rebekah fell back step by step. The shrill noise still vibrated through her, but now she realized it was the least of her problems.

When a cold stone wall blocked her staggering retreat and chilled her spine, Rebekah started praying. She wanted to screw her eyes shut, but couldn't. Digging her fingers into the gaps between the blocks, she hung on tightly, watching the battle rage between Connor and Morrigan.

The ancient Druid possessed strength that matched Connor's. Her snarling face crumbled away more with each puncture wound Connor drove into her flesh, but still she struck out, clawing at his chest and throat, and shredding the fabric of his shirt.

Birgitta gripped Rebekah by the neck and her new vampire flesh creaked beneath the crushing pressure. She felt as though she was choking, but it was human panic.

Glancing over Birgitta's shoulder, Rebekah smiled. "Seren," she croaked, relief ringing through the word.

Birgitta's eyes narrowed – she didn't want to look, but had to. When her grip on Rebekah's throat faltered, using strength she didn't yet understand, Rebekah broke off a lump of stone as if it was a loaf of bread and slammed it down onto Birgitta's skull. When Birgitta staggered back, Rebekah hit her again and again until, through her blonde hair, she saw dough-like gray matter. The glass vial around Birgitta's throat glinted, the light glowing inside it pulsing. Rebekah yanked on the chain and gripped the vial in her fist until the glass crumbled and blood oozed over her palm.

The copper bowls and vials on the stone shelf rattled as Morrigan let out a bloodcurdling screech and dropped to her knees. The keening pitch reached a crescendo. Covering her head with her hands, she yanked her thin brittle hair out by the roots. Morrigan's skin tightened, her fractured cheekbones sawing through the thin parchment.

The wall of silence arrived abruptly. Morrigan's fragile skeleton crumbled into piles of gray dust, like a sandcastle drying out in baking sun. Birgitta's decomposition took longer, but Connor and Rebekah shared a stunned moment, just staring at each other.

First to recover, Connor closed the distance and took Rebekah into his arms. His kiss dragged gently over her lips as though he was tasting her for the first time.

"Are you alright?" Rebekah pushed her hands into Connor's dishevelled hair and stared into his face.

"I'm just glad you trusted me."

"Why did I do that. Put that spike in your hand?" Rebekah frowned.

Connor laid a palm over her cheek, and ran his thumb over her bottom lip. "You trusted your instincts. Their theory on love was wrong. It didn't make me weak, because you love me too."

"I thought you were dead. I mean worse than dead."

"They knew Morrigan's blood would enchant me. But, she did not know her own strength, and she gave *that* to me, too. I willed you to join in my gamble. I turned you, and your blood is part of mine. We were of one thought. Thank goodness."

Taking her hand, Connor said, "Let's find Seren. I'm sure she'll be waiting."

Chapter 36

Anthony felt as though the plastic mask he wore smothered him, even though he didn't need to breathe. His pride in Greg reached new heights. Ex-Marine and vampire was proving to be a devastating combination which Anthony almost envied.

The stampede of humans scampering in through doors died away from a pouring stream to a trickle of befuddled stragglers and, once the initial surprise of the young boy dying subsided, Greg and Anthony worked as a team to herd them into the vestibule – a place where gentlemen once drank brandy and smoked cigars, leaving the ladies to retire to the parlor – and posted guards on both the exit out onto the terrace and the entrance into the banquet hall.

Birgitta's bondsmen, scattered around the room like marbles tossed across the floor, appeared to be riding a rollercoaster of emotions. Deciphering where their impulses came from and what they would do next created unbearable tension. Some ran headlong towards the broken stained-glass windows and threw themselves out. *Are they the enemy, or victims of brainwashing?*

At Anthony's nod, the hive guards lined up and picked off only the bondsmen who launched an attack.

Julian and Captain Gerrard displayed the same unstable swings in behavior – both slipped in and out of consciousness.

Malachi guessed the truth. "It's a waiting game," he told Marius. The real battle is happening in the dungeon below us, between Connor, Rebekah, and Birgitta. If the regent is defeated, then Julian will be restored."

Marius' grim smile spoke volumes. Both vampires agreed that Julian's self-recrimination would be hard for him to bear if he remembered the part he had played.

From the corner of his eye, Marius saw Julian jolt forward and shunt an elbow into a guardsman's sternum. The vampire's face folded with confused shock – killing the hive principal carried the death penalty, so the dilemma was clear. Defend himself, or die? With a sigh, Marius pulled a syringe from his belt. He jerked his chin at the guard, who offered himself up as the target for Julian's driving uppercut. Coming up from behind, Marius buried the needle into the side of Julian's neck, twitched his thumb on the plunger, and stepped back as the principal toppled like a felled tree.

In the split second it took for Julian to hit the floor, Marius checked the amber fluid remaining in the syringe chamber and calculated the dose he'd given. The signal of five fingers he held up to Anthony made his companion grin. *Five minutes should be enough.*

The vampire guardsman switched from combatant to support, instantly dropping down to lift Julian's slack body and lay it out on a couch in the semblance of comfort.

Marius turned his attention to Captain Gerrard who was penned in a book-lined cubby hole by four guardsmen. The scene reminded him of hyenas badgering a lion. Satisfied he wouldn't need to stab the captain with muscle relaxant, Marius felt easier.

Anthony kept an eye on Captain Bjorn, who still stood in front of the fireplace, remaining detached throughout the process. *Is his connection to the regent more deep rooted? Or less?*

Osiris, as soon as he strode into the parlor, gravitated towards Seren and remained within arms' length of her the entire time. He exuded relief and satisfaction that they had both survived.

"Connor will succeed, I know it," Osiris said, deflecting Seren's attention from the wounds on his shoulder. He had pressed the flap of flesh back into place and pink oozing fluid filled in the scored scrapes. He would bear new scars, but nothing he wouldn't suffer a hundred times over to save Seren and Connor from harm.

Like magnetic filings, the bondsmen corralled in the banquet hall, after circling aimlessly, unable to locate the stone stairwell which led below to their 'bat cave', gravitated towards each other, creating huddled order of a kind. Their blank expressions remained, but Anthony could see the confusion, like a human with concussion, going on behind their stares.

The thirty disoriented vampires became a herd of placid sheep. When they abruptly looked at each other and started muttering, Anthony focused his attention on the hallway down which Rebekah had disappeared. He felt the rush of compressed air like a train arriving at a station before he caught sight of the two approaching figures.

His clenched fists relaxed when the dark sleek form of Connor emerged, with Rebekah tucked into his side, and Anthony smiled.

Gerrard's hands dropped to his sides and the snarling tension dissipated, leaving him looking stunned and confused. The shield of four guards relaxed too, waiting for *Captain* Gerrard to surface again and end the moment of uncertainty.

"Did I hurt anyone?" the captain asked, growing in stature and exuding authority.

"Good to have you back, Captain. What is the last thing you remember?" asked Malachi.

"Meeting the regent..." Gerrard frowned.

Marius dropped to one knee beside Julian. He lifted an eyelid and Julian stirred – the world turned on its axis, becoming a sane place once more when his green gaze became alert. Swinging his legs around, he sat up, labored in his physical movements but in control of his mental faculties.

Like a drunk who feels bad about things he couldn't quite remember, Julian sought out Gerrard as the last person he clearly recalled. He struggled to join the dots of his memory from that point. The principal turned like the hub of a wheel and ranged his attention around the room, apparently taking stock and confirming the different factions of 'Operation Connor' were present and accounted for.

"Connor, Rebekah." He walked forward, but faltered at Connor's narrowed gaze. Julian froze mid gesture, with his hand inches away from his friend's shoulder.

Silence seeped through the room like a gas which made every occupant stop breathing. "I did something." Julian's voice grated in his throat and, as if searing pain cut through his head, his features cramped and he pulled his hand away and covered his forehead.

Connor sliced a glance at Rebekah, and the trust in her eyes reminded him of what *he* had done, too. "*You* didn't. It was her, Birgitta. Let's move forward."

Julian's shoulders dropped and his half smile exuded relief before he leaned in and thumped Connor on the back in an awkward man-hug.

From across the room, where he stood beside Greg, Marius said, "Let's just agree things didn't go quite as planned, but we got there in the end."

Julian's attention turned to Greg and the flawless luminescence of his vampire skin. "I can see your sacrifice was greater than we bargained for."

Greg shrugged and replied in his typically laconic fashion, "I'll live. *Forever*, apparently."

Julian chuckled.

"The regent? Let's be clear, she is gone?" Malachi voiced the thoughts on the tip of every tongue. "How did you do it?"

Connor nodded soberly. "She has been neutralized, as has her 'Earth Mother'. But how? That will take a bit longer to answer."

"But this *attention* from the regent was revenge for Sentinel Lars?" Malachi pressed.

Anthony watched Connor's expression closely. Knowing his mentor well, he knew there was more to it than that.

"I believe it began there, yes. But she sought other things too." Connor's grin was tainted by bitterness. "We'll never know for certain, but I think she used us all to get Rebekah here, and most importantly, to get me to turn her." At Julian's sharp look, Connor said, "I'll explain it all later."

"The important thing is, the regent was destroyed," said Julian.

With an angry roar, Bjorn broke from his frozen sentinel stance. A dozen stunned faces turned towards him as he flung aside the flap of his cape and drew a curved blade from its sheath. The blade glittered, and for a nanosecond, no one moved, not sure of his intended target. Connor jolted into a run to shut Bjorn down before he could act, but too late. Bjorn lunged forward. Connor gripped the captain's flaring cape, tearing a strip from the hem as Bjorn snarled with crazed ferocity.

Arcing around, Bjorn headed straight for Julian – he was unarmed, but raised his forearm and braced his weight to take the impact. Marius appeared from nowhere. Bjorn swung the blade in a devastating arc as Marius' black-clothed figure obscured his target. Stepping in fast and driving the sword downwards, Bjorn cut into Marius' throat just above the collarbone and the juror's body dropped to the floor, his skull hitting the marble fire grate with a sickening crack.

Anthony, Connor, and Greg dived in and grappled with Bjorn, whose wrist broke when Greg wrenched the blade free, shoved him to his knees and clamped his arm around the Swede's neck. Even the constriction of his throat didn't smother the harsh laughter, or the globule of spit he directed at Julian, who had dropped to the ground beside Marius, his hand clenched over the wound which oozed thick blood.

It was a reflex, even though bleeding to death could not happen. The real damage lay in the interruption to Marius' blood network. The veins and arteries were the pathways for rehydration. The heart, although not beating, acted as a reservoir.

"Connor," Julian barked.

Leaving Bjorn to Anthony and Greg, Connor joined Julian and prized his fingers away. Staring into Marius' coal black gaze was the hardest thing Connor had done in a long time. "Marius, why?"

With his vocal chords severed, Marius' reasons would die with him. Doing the opposite to Julian, Connor opened up the wound, used the fabric of his jacket to absorb the leaking blood, and delved his fingers inside. Connor met Marius stare head on. "I'll do what I can, but I need to get you back to London." Looking over his shoulder, Connor called out, "Osiris, go aboard the ship with Marius. He'll need constant infusions of blood until I get him on the table."

"Of course." Osiris came forward, already loosening his gold armlet. "What about him?" Pointing at Bjorn, Osiris' curled lip clearly illustrated his opinion.

"Julian?" Connor threw the question over to the principal, concentrating on sweeping a lamp from a side table and onto the floor. Upending the table and snapping off two of the legs, he dropped to his knee and lifted Marius' shoulders. He pushed the tapered end of the turned-wooden posts underneath him – they dug into his shoulder blades, but the patient felt none of the pain a human would – and lined them up to frame the back of Marius' head. He bound the splints into place tying strips torn from his shirt around Marius' forehead and securing two leather belts donated by onlookers around the patient's shoulders.

Between them, Captain Gerrard, Hugh, Daniel and another guardsman lifted the fallen juror with care and bore him away to where the ship had been moored.

Greg and Anthony's eyes remained locked on Julian. Their vised grip on Captain Bjorn made it impossible for him to move, but, the grin on his face they could not prevent.

Julian assessed the aftermath of Birgitta's demise. He had the safe transportation of Birgitta's human herd and their adjustment to a 'free range' existence to think about.

Then there were the rudderless bondsmen – they were victims, too. They would have to choose between repatriation or becoming part of the London Hive. And finally, there was Marius. How many problems did Julian need on his plate?

He asked himself if the captain should be spared, but he saw only undiluted hatred on Bjorn's face. *For his loss of power, perhaps? Or did he really care about Birgitta?* Julian's eyes narrowed as he searched for one iota of regret.

The silence of those around him told him more than any voices could have.

"Finish him." Julian's cold expression didn't falter when, in concert, Greg and Anthony applied opposing pressure, and a loud crack rang out.

Chapter 37

Lining up the trolleys of instruments, mole-grips, grinding tools, glue and packing gauze, Connor prepared the theater for Marius' procedure. He always considered Marius to be a juror with gravitas and an ability to tackle each situation in a careful and measured way. But now the impressive figure was laid out on the metal operating table, Connor realized that somewhere along the way, Marius had become a friend.

Marius remained conscious throughout the operation, but restraints on his arms and at his thighs made sure that if the worst happened and he descended into grave sleep, he couldn't hurt Connor. Not feeling pain had advantages, but Connor, knowing the procedure would still be harrowing, talked to the patient. Marius could not answer, of course.

"Tap your fingers if you want me to stop, Marius." Connor unbound the padding from the wound and adjusted the table so Marius' head dropped back and extended his throat. Pressing his fingertips along the tendons in the neck, he quickly confirmed they were severed on one side. Pushing his fingers inside the gash, Connor prayed the blade had not penetrated too deep.

"The carotid artery is only nicked. The blade got stuck in your collarbone. That is good news," Connor said, distractedly. *More than just good news.* Repairing the carotid artery meant the blood network between the juror's brain and body were still connected. "The bad news is your vocal chords have been cut."

Pausing to make eye contact, Connor tried to gauge his friend's reactions. The dark eyes wore an expression of resignation, but not defeat. Connor didn't think so, anyway.

"Okay. Let's clear out the wound and see what we have left." Using mole-grips, Connor broke up the damaged tissue. Hardened vampire flesh resembled gravel and the noise as it crumbled put even Connor's teeth on edge.

Marius tapped the table and Connor stopped.

This time the dark eyes were sharp with unspoken words. Connor put the tools down and braced his hands over Marius' temples and closed his own eyes. The electrical signals in Marius' brain were erratic and the pictures projected kept melting and changing, but in the end, as though it was too much effort, Marius settled on a single image of himself with his head and body separated, clearly 'dead'.

Connor withdrew. "I'm saving you, whether you like it or not."

Marius screwed up his eyes and his arms rattled in the restraints.

"I am saving you," Connor repeated stubbornly. "You know, not being able to speak is not the end of the world. Sign language is an option."

Marius growled.

"Please, old friend. You went to the ends of the earth for me and Rebekah. Well, the end of England, anyway. Let me do this for you. I'll make you a deal. If, after one month, you want to die, I'll do it."

Marius nodded as sharply as his awkward position allowed.

Connor completed his repairs in silence. After clearing out the cavity and preserving as many tendons and veins as possible, Connor inserted nylon rods to give Marius' neck the tensile strength to support his head. He mentally crossed his fingers that the range of movement would be enough to make Marius feel normal.

After the surgery, Connor injected Marius with muscle relaxant and emptied two vials of human blood into his mouth. "Rest now. The blood will rehydrate the traumatized area and then we'll get you up and about."

Connor wheeled the examination table out of the operating theater and into a dimly lit side room. With a firm pat on Marius' shoulder, he left him and went out to where Julian, Anthony, and Malachi waited like anxious relatives.

"Well?" Julian looked as though he'd been standing in one spot staring at the door where Connor would emerge for the entire operation, and he probably had. Alexander had joined the waiting party. His young handsome features were clouded with concern. As the youngest juror, he was often left to hold the fort when the hive responded to a threat, but remaining behind could be tough, too.

"Well, he's not just a bodiless head," Connor quipped. The gallows humor caused a ripple of laughter that unified the gathering in relief.

Julian frowned. "I don't understand why Bjorn's blade did so much damage."

With a bitter laugh, Connor said, "That is down to us. Escorting Rebekah across country, he covered his skin against the sun – he literally began to get soft."

It was a sobering thought. Vampire skin would always be impervious to humans but, as the group exchanged glances, they acknowledged that they had all neglected the air exposure that maintained their hard shell – a vital survival weapon when fighting their own kind.

"Will he recover?" Julian asked grimly.

"I've done what I can, but he won't be 'good as new'. He can't talk," said Connor.

"Is that a final prognosis?" Julian's guilt pulled his features tight and his green eyes became dull.

Connor decided honesty was the best policy. "He wants to die. I've made a bargain with him, but he'll never talk again."

Julian swayed on the spot, digesting the information. "I see. Not being able to talk is not the end of the world. It is up to us to make him see that. Is his mental state in question?"

"Not at all. You know Marius. He is a thinker, a deliberator." Connor was sure of one thing, it wasn't a promise he wanted to keep, so he'd do everything to change his friend's mind.

"It's my fault," Alexander muttered. The young vampire raked his hands through his sand-colored hair and screwed up his face.

Both Connor and Julian looked stunned. "You weren't even there, how can any of it be your fault?" Julian laid a hand on Alexander's shoulder. "Marius would never stay behind and let you go in his place. You have no reason to blame yourself."

"You don't understand. The regent. I set the wheels in motion with Lars. It's all my fault."

Julian let his hand fall away. "What are you talking about?"

"I-"

Before Alexander could continue, Connor held up his hand. The anguish in Alexander's face convinced Connor there would be consequences to whatever he had to say. "Wait. Marius should be here to hear this first hand." Connor looked at Julian for confirmation.

"Are you admitting to a crime against the hive?" Julian's voice was heavy.

"Yes."

"Guard." Julian kept his attention on Alexander as the youngster's shoulders slumped, his body in danger of crumpling.

A guardsman wearing the purple robes of the council appeared in the room, the door still swinging shut as he stood to attention in front of Julian.

"Take Juror Alexander to the court anteroom and hold him there." As the guard moved towards him, Alexander raised his hands in surrender and cooperated to being ushered out. At the doorway, he stopped. "Tell Marius, I'm sorry."

"You can tell him yourself," replied Connor, "he'll be up and about in an hour or so."

The door closed behind the young juror and Malachi said, "Why didn't you let him explain? It could just be irrational guilt."

Julian shook his head. "I know him better than you. Whatever is eating at him is big. To be honest, I don't want to know and hide it from Marius. Better we all learn his dark secret together."

"What do we do now?" asked Malachi.

"We wait for Marius, for the muscle relaxant to wear off."

Connor looked at his watch and Julian shoved his shoulder. "Rebekah will still be there when you get home. In fact, she'll be with you forever. That's a wonderful thought, I should think."

"You could-"

Julian's second thump was harder. "No, I couldn't, and neither would you if you'd not been driven to it."

Connor considered his first sane moments with Rebekah, down by the shore when he turned her, and smiled. "I don't know what I was so scared of." He felt as though he occupied a room inside his head and could choose which door to open. Seren, Malachi, and now Rebekah, were all just a thought away.

"I'll do things in my own time. Leizle is young. I will wait."

"Until she chooses you? She already has, Julian, you know that won't change. She loves you, and you love her."

Julian's jaw muscle twitched and his closed expression forbade Connor to go on. "Okay, okay." Connor raised his hands in submission. "No more pressure. We will wait for Marius."

In a decisive rush, as though Julian needed to offload a heavy weight, he said, "There will never be a good moment, but I have to tell you something about Councilor Serge."

Connor sneered as though Julian had spat poison into his face, and folded his arms. Anthony shuffled his feet and looked uncomfortable.

"Really? You too? What is going on?"

Inhaling for an insanely long time, Julian finally said, "He's in the hospital chapel."

Chapter 38

Staring up at the night sky filled Rebekah with childlike wonder. Even the light pollution from the circle of thirty foot tall flood lamps, marking the perimeter boundary where vampire territory became human, could not drown out the scattered pinpricks of diamonds. There were so many more stars than she realized, and they created a rainbow of colors. *Human eyes really are half blind.* The blindfold had been torn from her eyes, and now the world was filled with a thousand distractions.

"Eh hem, Rebekah."

She turned to Captain Gerrard and almost laughed at the awkward expression on his face. He stood ramrod straight.

"Yes, Captain?"

"We really can manage from here. The regent's humans have all being given clean clothes and our herd, sorry, I mean human community, have taken them under their wing."

Even though the captain didn't say it, Rebekah knew he welcomed the addition of fifty humans because it eased the strain on the blood rations of the London Hive. It occurred to Rebekah that she too, now had to consider where her daily dose of human blood would come from. She turned to look along the street which formed part of the newly constructed human village – 'farm' no longer fit with the hopeful relationship Connor and Julian had fought for.

The glow of electric lighting behind the glazed window frames were things she, as a survivor of a post-apocalyptic world, could barely remember. Her reality was a subterranean dwelling where using light was treated with the same respect as brandishing a hand grenade.

The gray steel shells of the siphoning sheds still reared up in the background, but visiting them and giving blood no longer happened under guarded escort and restraints. Now, tentative friendships were developing, although trust remained fragile. Most of the vampire community still stayed away – not drinking from a warm human was more than some could resist. They were still hunters, after all. Vampire guardians still patrolled the ground between the fences and the village, just in case an intruder chanced their arm.

Blood donations formed part of a barter system. Humans possessed a commodity the vampires needed, and vampires provided housing, food, and helped their charges in any way they could. Humans quickly saw the advantage of having beings with unlimited strength who never required rest or sleep to call upon. It was early days, but bumps along the road made life interesting.

Rebekah had spent almost twenty years on one side of the equation, and now understood the whole picture. Hunger gnawed like a rat inside her gut and she acknowledged her own weakness. The welcome glow of the human habitats bled into the heavens like a halo, to her new vampire sight, and although she longed to see them up close, to see how far removed they were from her own home, she dared not go any further.

Looking out over the 'village', Rebekah asked, "Do I make you uncomfortable, Captain Gerrard?"

Rebekah expected a stilted reaction, but she got laughter. She glanced at the tall well-groomed vampire. His uniform was buttoned up to his throat, the folded collar ready to flip up and cover most of his face on sunnier days, but expressive creases in his smooth skin transformed his stiffness into warmth.

"Yes, you do. But only because you are unpredictable."

Rebekah's brown eyes glittered mischievously. "I think Connor would agree."

"Thank you for helping with the human flock. Things went much smoother with a female to ease their worries. I think they found you less intimidating."

"It is good to feel useful. But now, you are right, I must go home." Rebekah glanced back towards the gateway in the sweeping fence – the twelve foot barrier would remain in place for now, but its primary purpose was to keep hungry vampires out. "Charles is getting twitchy, I think. He won't leave me to go home alone, so I better take pity on him."

"Good night, my lady."

Rebekah's eyebrows rose. "Goodness, you'll be tugging your forelock next, Captain."

"I'm an old fashioned man. You are a lady. The regent certainly was not. You deserve a title."

Rebekah whispered, "How about you call me Miss Rebekah? I think that's as formal as I can bear."

"Very well, miss." The smile Gerrard flashed bode well for a future friendship.

Turning to go, Rebekah waved. "Good night, Captain." She skimmed across the sea of rippling grass to the metal-mesh door in the perimeter. She tried not to tease Charles when it whipped open and his face lit up with relief.

Passing through the gate he held open, on a serious note, Rebekah said, "Do you think we should feed before I go home? Just in case."

"Good idea."

Rebekah surrendered herself to Charles' care as they left behind the floodlit setting of the human village.

She may be a new vampire, but her close association with Connor had been the best training ground. When Charles ducked through the hedgerows which lined the country roads winding through the South Downs of Kent, and into the cover of the woodlands, Rebekah could already guess what the menu contained. Rabbit, stoat, weasel, foxes, and badgers sprang to mind. Charles knew Rebekah would rather avoid deer. They fascinated her as a child and she couldn't imagine killing one – not yet.

Charles came to a halt in the thickest part of the woodlands, where the dense canopy made the still air warm. He nodded at Rebekah and waited. It was a test. She knew he was observing, at the ready to correct her mistakes.

Rebekah stared into the patchwork of shadows. She counted five sets of glinting mammalian eyes, each frozen by the sudden appearance of a predator. Leaping left, her shifting weight made a boot shaped crater in the soft earth as she easily caught a rabbit by the neck when it tried to run. Using a tree trunk as a springboard, she doubled back to grab a fox by its tail. The animal unleashed a keening growl and its sharp teeth skated over Rebekah's arm and tore her combat jacket. She swore gently. Stopping dead, she dropped the rabbit carcass at her feet and with a quick twist of her wrist, the fox didn't suffer. Feeding was a swift affair and she didn't waste a drop. Sweeping away the mulch of fallen leaves, she laid both her kills into a shallow grave. The circle of life would take care of the rest. Dehydrated animal flesh was not fit for human consumption. *Oscar wouldn't even want to put it in a stew.*

Thinking of Oscar, led onto thoughts of Leizle, and to a feeling of homesickness. "Let's go home," she whispered, and Charles set the pace as they headed past Swanley and crested the undulating hills beneath which lay the human eco-town. The newly formed chimneys venting clouds of steam did not exactly shout out their location, but they no longer had to hide.

Rebekah turned to Charles. His small terrier-like appearance often led to him being underestimated, but he ruled the hospital blood dispensary with an iron will. Connor said he made even the fiercest vampire toe the line with one look, and Rebekah studied his gentle face and wished she could witness that. *Maybe, one day, I will.*

"Thank you, Charles, and good night. I can manage from here."

Charles reached inside his coat and pulled out a flexible jelly-like mask. He held it out to Rebekah. "Connor should be back tonight, but take this. It will help with the blood fumes if you find your will power is weakening." In his other hand was three vials of blood. "Human," he said, "just in case."

Rebekah grinned. "You think of everything. Thank you."

She tucked the mask into her utility belt, took off across the meadow towards the camouflaged entrance to the habitat, and waved again before she ducked inside.

Even in the pitch-black of the entrance tunnel, she could pick out rocks and the glint of beetle shells and studied those in fascination. She began to wonder how vampires got anything done, with all the distraction nature threw at them. *Will I bump into Leizle or Thomas first?* She knew they would both be waiting for her.

Flipping back the black out curtain, she shied away at the all-encompassing wall of human odors. Her mouth watered and she swallowed it down. The earth seemed alive with a thrumming sound, and she realized it was the accumulation of human heartbeats echoing through the chambers and tunnels.

The flames of the torches on the walls were slowly being replaced with bulk head lamps. Another benefit of liberation had been the vampire workforce who had excavated a larger generator room.

As the gradient became steeper, Rebekah's question was answered. Near the bottom of the slope Leizle and Thomas sat on the ground side by side, resting back against a wall. They struggled to their feet as if they were in their forties rather than late teens.

Rebekah grinned. "I take it, judging by the stiff legs, you've been here a while."

"Where were you? Greg got here ages ago. He said you'd be back tonight, but we were beginning to give up hope."

Even as Leizle spoke, both youngsters rushed forward and entangled Rebekah in a clumsy group hug.

Standing strong in the center, Rebekah became the anchor which stopped them all toppling over. "Woah there, gently does it."

Loosening their grip and peering at her in the lamp light, they both scoured her features.

"You look so pretty," said Thomas, wriggling an arm free and touching her cool pale cheek. "What is it like?"

Leizle's green eyes sharpened with envy and curiosity as she waited for the answer.

"It's like being an onion. Just when I get used to something, the speed, the strength, the brighter sharper vision, another layer falls away and I discover something else. It also feels like I'm living on a knife edge, well, not living exactly, but you get the idea."

Rebekah looked from one intent face to the other. "If I disappear on you, please forgive me." When they both nodded solemnly, Rebekah tugged the see through mask from her belt and waved it in front of them. "This is another of my survival tools, but as you can see, it's a scary piece of kit. What girl wants to be seen in this?" Rebekah pulled a comic grimace.

Thomas and Leizle's laughter evaporated the tendrils of tension.

"Let's go and find the others. Are Seren, Osiris and Malachi back?"

"Yes, they are all in Malachi's chamber."

I wonder if everything is all right? Much as Rebekah wanted to go and find out, she needed to reconnect with her human family first. They all knew her fate, and part of them would be scared about how much she must have changed.

The group walked along the tunnel until they reached the dining cavern, and another onion skin fell away as Rebekah realized two things; going slowly was becoming more challenging each day and, if she closed her eyes, she could tell which human was Leizle and which was Thomas. Sorting out the indicators themselves would come later, she felt sure, but for now, the cocktail comprised of smell, the sound of their heartbeats, and a color to their emotions – an aura.

Stopping on the threshold of the dining area, a smile radiated from Rebekah. Even though the engagement party decorations had been stowed away, it couldn't wipe out the joyous feeling of the occasion before it was cut short by Birgitta's arrival. Seren was a grown woman, and now, thanks to a bizarre chain of events, Rebekah felt she was part of her daughter's life, completely, for the first time.

Rebekah registered the scene in the dining cavern in a sweeping glance. Greg sat at a bench one side of a table, with Oscar, Seth and Adam sitting like birds on a wire facing him. The scene screamed penitentiary tension – with elbows set down on the table, their hands were used as chin rests or their arms were folded, as though accidental touching of 'the prisoner' would get them ejected. Greg, of course filled the role of the prisoner. Others in the eco-community radiated out like the debris of a hand grenade blast, all facing in Greg's direction but further away.

In the lightning fast moment of vampire communication, Greg looked over at Rebekah and smiled, but his steady gaze revealed sadness. The gray strands in his hair now appeared more like shards of crystal and his skin had the same quartz-like beauty. Connor explained it was the crystalline structure of vampire flesh which made them almost light refractive. In Rebekah's mind, it translated into the oxymoron of 'delicately strong'.

Rebekah had good reason to want this transformation. For Greg, although the alternative had been death, the consequences meant losing the close camaraderie of fellow Marine, Seth. His relationship with Oscar, Adam, and other human survivors of the pandemic and the vampire uprising was like a deck of cards tossed into the air; some would land face up and be part of his hand, others would land face down and be lost to him. Greg realized which human fell into which category would be their choice and not his.

In a preternatural whisper, Rebekah said, "You have new friends, too. Anthony, Daniel, Isaac, even Brynmor and Charles. Think of it as a caterpillar and butterfly transformation. Different, but not all bad, hmm?"

Greg paused, frozen in place for a nanosecond, and then a smile lit his face like a sunrise.

"It just takes time." Rebekah smiled, too. "C'mon, Marine. You can do this. These are still your friends and you've got their backs."

"Even if there are days when I look at them and see a Christmas turkey on legs?" Greg chuckled.

Rebekah shook her head in agreement. "Now *that*, I understand. I guess there'll be days when we both will have to stay away. Are you okay right now?"

Greg nodded carefully. "It's why I'm here. Apparently, the human blood residue still in my system, *our* system, makes it easier to resist them."

Rebekah brandished her mask and contraband vials of human blood. "Whatever gets us through the day, my friend. Don't forget, we don't have to pretend. These people love us and they'll understand." Glancing at Leizle and Thomas standing close beside her, she said, "Okay, we are the sword of Damocles hanging over their head, but we all know the score."

Greg nodded. Flipping back his coat to show-off his own mask. "The best friendships survive rough seas and near disaster. Seth, Oscar, and the rest are fighters. We'll be okay in the end."

Effortlessly switching gear, Rebekah and Greg let the humans into their world once more, both making a huge effort to slow down their thoughts and actions until the other occupants of the room began to move again.

"Rebekah," Oscar called out, pushing up to his feet. He did well to smother the stunned expression at her sudden appearance. "Greg told us you were changed, too." His voice shook a little.

Inhaling gently, trying to discern his emotion via human pheromone cues was something Rebekah had inside knowledge of, as the mother of a hybrid. Oscar smelled of relief and joy, and maybe a tinge of nerves, but that was to be expected.

He crossed the room and as always, his bear-like dimensions dwarfed her. He enfolded her in his arms and hugged tightly.

Rebekah obliged him with the response he always got in this situation. Huffing out as he squeezed, she muttered, "Okay, broken bones here."

They both knew she was faking it, but he released her and peered down into her face. "Well, lass, you look beautiful. Much too pale, but a real sight for sore eyes." He winked with genuine warmth.

With Oscar's arm lying across her shoulders, Rebekah waved and nodded at the sea of familiar faces. With Greg also in their midst, and nothing terrible having happened yet, a collective sigh drifted up into the upper limits of the domed ceiling.

"Leizle, sit with me, let's talk." Rebekah would need to have lost all sense of empathy not to know that barely contained questions boiled inside the younger girl, but personal ones.

Grabbing a cup of coffee from the serving table, about to get two, but then abandoning one cup and leaving it empty, Leizle sat opposite Rebekah. This time, it was less about keeping a barrier between them, and more about Leizle wanting to look Rebekah in the eyes when they spoke.

"Where's Julian?'

Even Rebekah had a whiplash moment at how fast Leizle cut to the chase."

"He's with Connor. There are loose ends to tie up. Freed human slaves, bondsmen to process into the London Hive, or house until they board a ship for Europe and repatriation."

Leizle drummed her fingers. "What does Julian think about you? Being a vampire, I mean? When did Connor do it? Was it an accident? Did it hurt?"

Rebekah raised her hand to stem the verbal assault, and Leizle fell silent.

"Where do I start? Yes, it hurts like hell, white hot burning pain, and you're trapped inside unable to move. It was necessity. Connor saved my life." Rebekah grew very still. "He did it after he'd killed me. He drank my blood and it broke the spell. And Julian? What does he think? The same as always, I imagine. Humans are a dying species and should remain human."

Tears welled in Leizle's eyes and Rebekah reached for her hand. "It doesn't mean Julian won't turn you, sweetheart. It just means he won't be pushed into it. Connor wanted me to be twenty-four, the same age as him when he was changed. I'm not saying Julian thinks the same, but you are only nineteen. Just have a little faith."

Leizle swiped away the tears. "You're right. I'm just jealous. There, I said it." Her smile was small but determined. "I have a fantastic man. He moves slower than a glacier, but even glaciers thaw, eventually. I have faith."

"Good." Rebekah smiled.

"Get out of here. I know you are dying to see Seren. Go, for heaven's sake."

Chapter 39

Julian, Connor and Marius walked three abreast down the central corridor of the council building. Marius' footsteps were loud, deliberately so. If Connor needed more evidence that the dark juror felt angry, it came when they reached the door to the jurors' anteroom and Marius slammed it open with such force a cascade of plaster hit the polished wood floor.

"Juror Marius." Julian's patience wore thin. "We don't *know* what Alexander wants to tell us. We aren't keeping you out of the loop. Now we are here, we three will hear what he has to say for the first time." Julian's glance said 'God help me Connor, I wish I'd left him sleeping and saved myself a load of trouble'.

"He's frustrated at not being able to talk. Give him time."

Marius stalked across the room and took his seat at the conference table. He rested his clasped hands on the polished surface and it appeared the display of irritation had burned itself out.

Julian took his place beside Marius, with Alexander's empty seat on his other side. Carefully, as though sliding a raw steak across to a lion, Julian edged a pad and ballpoint pen along the table in Marius' direction. Ignoring the steady beat of Marius' drumming fingers, Julian signalled to the council guardsman. "Bring in Juror Alexander."

Connor rested against the back wall and watched Marius closely.

When Alexander entered, escorted by two guardsmen wearing the purple garb of the Elite Guard, his round-shouldered subdued demeanor did not bode well.

Connor didn't like it. Anger, or indignation at being detained, would be more encouraging.

"Alexander." Julian inclined his head. "Thank you for waiting. Now, let's return to why you are here." With the photostatic memory of every vampire, the comments Alexander made earlier were reiterated in a toneless voice. "You said, 'The regent. I set the wheels in motion with Lars. It's all my fault.' Is that correct?"

Alexander nodded and Marius stopped tapping and sat up straight. His attention fully engaged for the first time, he picked up the pen and pulled the paper closer.

"Yes."

"Please elaborate." Julian laid his palms down on the table and waited.

"The regent coming here is my fault, and-" Waving a hand in Marius' direction, he said, "by default, I am responsible for Marius' injury."

"You mention Lars. As I recall, Lars' attack on the eco-town and Seren's kidnap came out of nowhere. Tell me what wheels you set in motion." Julian epitomised calm, but the glint in cold green eyes told a different story.

Alexander swallowed. "I didn't know what would happen."

Marius tapped his pen on the paper.

"But you knew *something* would happen?"

"Yes."

"*How* did you know this?" Julian asked.

"It was Councilor Serge."

Connor, frustrated with his view from the back of the room, darted around the table and leaned back against it, directly in front of where Alexander usually sat. "Councilor Serge?" As irate as he was at learning of Julian's deception, he suddenly felt pleasure the slimy old snake was within strangling distance. Connor had an urge to go to the chapel, disturb Serge in his coffin shell, and rattle him until his teeth fell out, but he wanted to hear Alexander's story, too. "When?"

"When he was in the Loch Glascarnoch Hive. I went to see him, remember? Rumors of the hybrid birth were piling on the pressure. We suspected Serge."

"You were on council business and reported back that Serge was still securely imprisoned and no real threat. Don't tell us you were lying. No, you can't have been, we had him escorted down from Scotland when Matthew went missing," said Julian.

"Perhaps you should tell us what you did?" said Connor quietly.

Alexander exhaled and then loaded up with a deep breath. "It was very vague. I met Lars on my journey back to London. Serge told me about him and I decided to find out what he was up to. What plan against Connor they were hatching."

"And did you?" Julian's level tone cut through the air. The two guardsmen shifted slightly, they sensed the gathering menace thickening the atmosphere.

"Discover the plan? No, I swear."

"What then. Why are you to blame?" Connor blurted.

"He, Lars, told me I had to do something. He said if I didn't, just the fact I met with him would hang me as a traitor. It seemed to be a small thing. I fell for it. All I was told to do was keep Doctor Connor busy."

The table screeched as it shunted back when Connor shot to his feet. "Busy? Busy so he could steal my hybrid child?"

Alexander held up his hands as though Connor's words were stones. "But I didn't know that. I swear. Keep you busy. That is all he said."

"If that is what you were told, why did Supervisor Matthew not just keep me busy, but almost kill me?"

Alexander shrugged.

Marius' hand banged down on the table and the sharp crack made everyone in the room jump.

Julian grinned. "Marius is right. That answer will not do. Answer the question."

"I let Matthew make his own decision on the 'how'." Alexander looked Connor in the eyes. "I swear, I never told him to hurt you. When I found out what he did, I was disgusted. Appalled. Angry."

Marius scrawled a note and passed it to Julian. Glancing at Marius' rigid profile, Julian said, "Marius wants to know why you feel so guilty, if all you did was 'talk' to Lars and Matthew?"

"I feel guilty that Lars took Seren, and Birgitta avenged him. I started the domino effect. That's all I mean."

Julian shook his head. "Even decent people make unwise choices. You can't stay on the council, of course. I can no longer trust you."

"I understand that." Alexander dropped his head. Every line in his body screamed relief.

Marius scribbled another note. His script large and angular.

Again, Julian took it, looked at Marius and then across at Alexander. "Where is Supervisor Matthew?"

"I don't know."

Connor folded his arms and rested back against the table.

Marius stabbed a finger at his note. "Where is Supervisor Matthew?" Julian too, sat back and waited.

The young ex-juror stared at a spot on the wall above Julian and the minutes ticked away. Marius began rapping his nails on the table, adding a new cluster of scratches to the varnished surface.

The silent stand-off continued, each vampire knowing the one who broke would be the weakest link.

Alexander's chin lifted another inch. "I killed him."

Julian stood up. "You *killed* Supervisor Matthew? Why?"

"Because I was angry about what he did to Doctor Connor."

Marius shook his head. He opened his mouth, made a whistling sound, and thumped Julian's shoulder.

"Why?"

"I was angry."

"I remember that time, clearly." Julian grinned. "As though it was yesterday, in fact. I remember you being subdued. I'll ask you one last time. Why did you kill Matthew?"

In a flat dead tone, Alexander finally said, "He would have talked. And I regretted everything I did. He deserved it for almost killing Connor." The young vampire looked to Connor for support.

"If he deserved punishment, it was not yours to dole out. What he *deserved* was a trial, and to serve a sentence where he would spend decades in Storage Facility Eight." Connor rubbed a hand down over his face. "I'm disappointed in you, Alexander."

"You did it because you didn't want to join him in the storage facility," said Julian.

Marius scribbled a jagged sentence. Julian read it. "How did you kill him? Is he at peace?"

The second part drew a sharp look from Julian towards the dark silent vampire beside him.

Is there honor among thieves, Connor wondered.

Resigned to revealing the worst, Alexander said, "I used a skewer into his neck. Into the brain stem."

Connor's brows rose. *Brutal. Final.*

Marius smacked Julian on the arm with the back of his hand. "And then?" Julian asked, but not before shooting Marius a waspish glance which said 'stop doing that'.

"I buried him."

"You buried him?"

"Where?" Connor tagged Julian as his reactions took over.

"At his house."

"At the farm?" Julian frowned.

"No," Connor muttered. "He had a bolt hole, a house, didn't he, Alexander? So, you planned his death?" *What did it take to do that?* Connor looked at the mild mannered Alexander with new eyes.

"You followed him home, killed him, crushed his skull, and then buried him? Is that correct?" Julian wanted to tick the boxes and make sure he had it all straight in his mind.

"Yes."

The shadows skittering behind Alexander's eyes, the color of a rain-soaked sky, chilled Connor. "No, that's not correct, is it Alexander?"

The jury sat stone still, once again.

Finally, Alexander said, "I buried him in his garden. No, I didn't crush his skull. I know I should have, but I didn't."

"You left him to rot, knowing he could be conscious for weeks? You left him to die and broke the hive code of conduct. Guards-" At the same time as he snorted the words, Julian lost sight of Alexander's horror struck features when Marius' broad back appeared suddenly between him and the accused.

"Juror Marius, sit down. Juror Alexander will be tried and convicted through the court."

Marius swept swiftly around behind Alexander, his large hands framing the young vampires throat. His victim clawed at Marius' forearms, shredding the black cotton shirt he wore. Marius met Julian's indignation head on and jerked his chin downward, once.

Confused and frowning, Julian looked down at the table and saw a much longer, more measured note written in a neater hand than the others.

Picking it up, Julian read aloud. "Honor is non-negotiable. I do not lay blame at your door for my misfortune. I acted to save Julian, our principal, and would do it again. What I can lay at your door is 'behaviour unbecoming a gentleman', and the callous act designed to save your own skin will not go unpunished. You cannot be allowed to live." Julian looked into the coal black abyss of Marius' cold anger as he finished reading.

"No, Marius," he said, and looked into the faces of the two vampires he had hoped would sit beside him for decades.

Marius shook his head, the anger cooling to sadness as he put an arm around Alexander's throat and, with a sharp twist, snapped his spine. Marius braced his hands on the young vampire's skull. Alexander's knees buckled. His hands swayed at his sides. Marius' grip was all that held Alexander's slack body upright.

Alexander's final expression exuded acceptance and relief. It was the first indication that the young juror had been in his own kind of hell since he took Matthew's life.

Perhaps Marius was right to end it now, thought Connor.

The sound of crumbling bone whispered into the atmosphere. Marius applied inexorable pressure to Alexander's skull until the structure imploded and his features turned to dust.

"Guards," Julian barked. "Take Juror Marius into custody."

The guardsmen stalked forward, like hunters cornering a wild animal.

Marius raised both hands – his clothes were smothered in bone fragments and dust, which he made no effort to brush off. Alexander's body lay at his feet.

A reflex of distaste surprised Connor, it was a similar feeling to human disgust if the scattered ashes of a cremated loved one caught the wind and blew back into your face.

The lead guardsman slipped a steel garrotte from his belt, dropped it around Marius' neck and primed a ratchet mechanism – a practice reserved for vampires who executed their brethren in 'calculated rage'. If the prisoner tried to run, the ratchet would activate and the victim's head would be cut cleanly from their shoulders.

"Julian, is that really necessary?"

Without taking his eyes from the dark juror, Julian replied, "I've known Marius a long time, but I would never have thought he would do this. Yes, it is necessary."

Marius' flurry of forceful hand signals told Connor, 'I understand Principal Julian has procedure to follow. However, Alexander killed a weaker vampire for his own gain, in cold blood. He planned it to save his own skin. I too, thought I knew Alexander, but I won't accept corruption in a juror on the council. A protocol exists for execution without trial'.

Connor nodded. "I understand, Marius, but did you not exercise revenge, too? Blame Alexander for your loss of speech?"

Marius grinned, replying in sign, 'Not in the way you imagine, Connor. If I could talk, then I could add the weight of my opinion. Make sure Julian understood how I felt about Alexander's betrayal. I would have activated 'juror execution'. Alexander admitted his crime. He killed for his own gain and withheld mercy. But I can't speak, and after what we have just come through, my impulse was to end this farce. I regret that now. But I'm not a loose cannon. Please convey my regret to Principal Julian'.

Marius looked at a bemused and irritated Julian. "I got some of that Marius. Makaton sign language has been around a while, although, I didn't know you and Connor were so fluent. The raised brow of Julian's skeptical look scoured Connor's face.

He shrugged and, in Makaton, replied, 'I dug out a book on Makaton after the operation. I wanted to ease Marius' frustration'.

Julian picked up Marius' notes and waved them in Connor's face. "And these? These were an amusing joke?"

Connor replied calmly, "No, *those* were for you. *You* don't speak Makaton, and, the mood you were in, I didn't think you'd be best pleased if I suggested you learn it before the trial."

"Well, it looks like you should've tried harder to make me listen. Teach me now."

Pulling the small Makaton handbook from his back pocket, Connor held it out. "It's easy enough. Pictures and instructions for words and simple concepts. Knock yourself out."

Resembling an unhappy headmaster, Julian took the book, hitched back against the juror table, and proceeded to take his time to flip through every page, twice. "Okay, I've got it."

"Marius, explain what just happened here."

Marius' fingers flew through a dialogue twice as long as the one he had with Connor. Connor caught references to Burma, to Hitler's Reich and more personal references to situations which were common experiences to Marius and Julian as jurors, but were before Connor's time.

At the end of the communication, Julian said, "Guards, release Juror Marius."

While the guards did as they were told, Connor asked, "What changed your mind?"

"He said 'sorry'," Julian replied, deadpan.

Marius approached, rubbing a hand over his nape as if his nape was sore. The thump he landed on Julian's back underlined the feeling that they were back on an even footing.

Connor felt relief. "According to Alexander, Councilor Serge is up to his neck in this. More than that, he is the point of origin for much of the shit that has hit the fan. If Alexander has met his justified fate, it seems only right and proper that Serge pays for his part," said Connor, evenly.

"And you'll take no pleasure from that, of course," said Julian.

"I'll admit to taking a great deal of pleasure." Since they transported Serge down from the Loch Glascarnoch Hive, Isaac had shouldered the task of keeping the councilor hydrated, subject to new instructions from the hive jurors. Isaac was about to be liberated from the task.

The journey from the council building was accomplished in mere seconds. When the three vampires breezed through the plate glass front doors of the hospital, half a dozen heads turned in their direction.

Charles and Brynmor paused in the task of overseeing the blood delivery from the 'donor village', as the human farm was now called. Both vampires took a step toward Connor with smiles on their faces, but they faltered at the intent radiating from the trio of elder vampires.

With a conciliatory wave, Connor took charge of the procession through what was, after all, his territory. As quickly as the blur of three appeared, a swinging door which headed into the surgical wing was all that remained to mark their passing.

Connor experienced a buzz of excitement at finally having proof of Serge's vendetta which would allow Julian to sentence the councilor to death. The night he protected Rebekah and his unborn child and wrenched Serge's arm from the shoulder sealed their path as 'enemies to the end'.

And Connor could almost taste the moment. All humans and hybrids would be safer with Serge gone. The councilor still championed his agenda to use hybrids as a captive food source which, because they too were immortal, would allow full-vampires to continue to live forever.

The grin on Connor's face became fixed as after three turns and pushing through two more sets of doors, he entered the mortuary.

Julian and Marius arrived a second behind him, and Isaac appeared as though a rang bell announced their arrival.

In busy times, Isaac notified the blood dispensary and in an odd chimera of triage and a delicatessen counter, vampires were given tickets numbered in order of urgency. Although, some took their blood rations and sought out other secure locations, be it deserted transport containers at the docks or a freezer in a derelict abattoir – the choice was theirs.

On the wall of cadaver drawers behind Isaac, very few of the metal tags hanging on the handles were turned to white, which meant 'available'. It was a busy night. On the occupied drawers the red tags vibrated chaotically, winking in the light like a warning sign. Connor did not need to hear the faint screech of nails scoring over metal to confirm the confined vampires were in grave sleep.

"Doctor Connor, Principal Julian, Juror Marius." As Isaac acknowledged each of the prestigious potential clientele, his eyebrows rose higher. He knew all three vampires from the London Hive high echelon would not take grave sleep at the same time. A quick check of their hands, in which they should be holding vials of human blood to rehydrate their brain, confirmed his opinion. They were not looking for him in his role as morgue attendant. "What can I do for you?" he said, with a dry smile.

"Hello, Isaac, we're here to interview Councilor Serge."

Isaac's dark eyes burned with curiosity, but all he said was, "Certainly."

Serge's detainment in the chapel broke new ground. Isaac used creative dosing of a muscle relaxant/animal blood cocktail to keep his charge's flesh fully hydrated, which meant the human blood feed required by Serge to retain full brain function when, and if, he resumed normal life, was reduced to every other day.

"You are in luck, I haven't visited the councilor yet today." Turning to his cold store of vials and tools of the trade, Isaac selected a syringe, a ruby red vial of blood, and one with the clear fluid of anticoagulant, and blended them expertly before loading the syringe with the concoction – the fastest antidote to muscle relaxant therapy.

Leaving the morgue, the group of four raced along the corridors as Isaac led the way to the chapel. The wood lined walls smelled warm and immediately, the rows of pews and the thought of the decades of tears shed here in praying for loved ones made all four vampires move slower.

Serge's steel coffin shell glimmered in the dim light at the far end of the chapel, where it had been tucked into a corner.

As he primed the syringe, and approached the steel box, Isaac froze. "He's gone."

Stepping closer as if, maybe, Serge could be hiding, despite the mirror slick finish of the steel, Connor said, "Where is he?"

Isaac replied, "I don't know."

Connor expected to feel anger, but ironic laughter burst from him.

Julian said the words which went with Marius' puzzled expression. "I don't see the humor, Connor."

Connor shook his head. "It just doesn't surprise me that Serge has hit us with the unexpected. The man is so slippery he should be covered in scales."

The relief on Isaac's face dissolved when Julian turned to him and said, "How the hell can this have happened? He must have an accomplice." The inference was clear.

"I swear I had nothing to do with it, Principal."

"Then who? You managed his muscle relaxant dose, so he didn't walk out. Someone helped him."

"I honestly have no idea. I should have come here earlier today, but I took my eye off the ball. We are all human-" Isaac shot a look at Connor. "Doctor Connor's disappearance caused a lot of concern. And, with so many high ranking vampires away, there was some unrest to deal with."

"Unrest?" Julian reacted to Marius' explosion of sign gestures. "You're right. Taking Captain Gerrard and Hugh along was a risk."

"Charles asked Brynmor to ride shotgun on the dispensary sessions. He needed his muscle to keep order more often than he liked. I know he has made a report for when Doctor Connor visits the hospital."

"The vampires in the frame? Do we know them as trouble makers?" asked Connor.

Isaac frowned. "It was more about unusual periods of high demand. As though whole clusters arrived to stretch the facility to the extreme, but then their urgency evaporated just as quickly. The super tanker nomads visited twice instead of their usual once, and their group was larger than Charles expected. Supplies had to be sent for from the donor village. It took time. They hung around making many vampires edgy."

"I see."

Neither Connor nor Julian believed Isaac was involved in Serge's escape, but equally, they had no suspects and nowhere to start the search.

Marius looked regretful and signed his apology. If he hadn't been rash and executed Alexander, they might have had a starting point.

"You are right, Marius. But what's done is done. Connor will talk to Charles and Brynmor, and I'll send a messenger to the England hives to report any sightings of Serge." Julian grinned. "A seventy-year-old vampire with a missing arm should be easy enough to spot. In the meantime, let's focus on restoring order to the hive."

"Isaac, let Charles know what has happened, and I'll talk to him tomorrow. For now, I'm going home to check on Rebekah and Seren," said Connor.

"I'll walk with you," Julian replied.

Both vampires made it as far as the main entrance to the hospital in silence.

Eventually Connor asked, "What are you thinking, Julian?"

"I want you to join the council. With Alexander gone and Marius under stress, I need some solid support."

Connor shook his head. "I have the blood substitute product to develop. We have to iron out the inconsistencies. Work out why some batches don't work."

"Who then?"

"Anthony. You can trust him and he has combat abilities you can count on in a tight spot."

Julian nodded slowly. "Can you spare him?"

"Brynmor has potential beyond his lab skills. He can fill in for Anthony in theater when needed, I'm sure."

"Very well. I'll talk to Anthony." Julian slapped Connor on the shoulder. "I'll see you, later. I'll be along soon to see Leizle."

Chapter 40

Connor entered the eco-town and began his usual reassuring ritual of locating Rebekah by her scent and heartbeat before he remembered she no longer had one. Instead, he headed straight for the chamber he shared with Rebekah. At the threshold, he scanned the room and frowned. Usually, she would be here, sleeping, but of course, things had taken a detour. *She doesn't sleep anymore.* He paused to absorb the regret – the loss of the old routines and details he loved so much. Tapping into the stream of her thoughts involved a switch in the cerebral process, like opening the door at one end of the corridor which now connected them.

What he didn't expect was to find her door shut. But he knew where she could be found, at least. Changing into clean clothes, he inhaled the familiar scent of her which still hung in the air. It was recent. If he had a suspicious mind, he'd think she was hiding from him.

He left their cosy den and headed for the dining cavern. When he arrived there, intending to pass straight through, he found Oscar, Seth, Adam and Greg sitting together. The empty jug of mead and three half full pint glasses told the tale, even if the scent of alcohol accented blood fumes weren't immediately obvious to Connor's vampire thirst. It created a pleasant high, feeding from an inebriated human, and for a moment Connor enjoyed another memory.

The plastic face mask which flattened Greg' features made the scene surreal.

"Guys," Connor nodded in greeting, keeping his expression serious.

Oscar jumped up, tottered dangerously, and sat down again fast. "Hello, laddie, we're celebrating you're 'ome safe."

"Cheers, Oscar. We're all glad to be back." Connor was more thankful that none of the humans had witnessed the depths into which he had sunk.

Greg seemed to know what he was thinking. Beyond the detection of Oscar, Seth and Adam, the two vampires spoke with preternatural speed.

"Great sacrifices were made, Greg. I'm grateful."

Greg lifted his mask an inch away and grinned wryly. "I'm beginning to understand the pain you went through to be there for us, too."

"I'll help you adjust in any way I can, although-" Pointing at the mask Greg still held poised near his face, Connor said, "judging by things, you're finding your way through."

Greg chuckled. "Let's just say, I've been out and hunted in the woods three times already. I'm sure, by morning, there'll be no rabbits left within a two-mile radius. As for human blood. Osiris has generously offered his services as my 'last resort'."

Dipping into his pants pocket, Connor produced a vial of human blood and tossed it across room. "Here. Tomorrow I'll take you into London and get you registered at the dispensary with Charles." It occurred to Connor, Greg could be useful in the search for Serge, so 'killing two birds with one stone' came to mind. But that would wait. *Let him enjoy suffering with his friends, tonight.*

"Thank you." The Marine nodded.

With a wave, Connor left Greg to replace his mask and pocket the vial of blood, and went into the kitchen.

There he found Seren, Osiris and Malachi, all standing as though they were mannequins on display in a shop window. The complete lack of animation made Connor wonder again at how hard it had been, throughout the century of his existence, to blend in. *But, no Rebekah.*

Connor began to feel like he was being led down a garden path. He frowned, but his thoughts were interrupted by Malachi's. *I have news.*

Even though the group of four shared a psychic connection, Connor blurted, "Is it bad news?"

"I have received a report from Egypt. From Imhotep."

"Osiris' father? How did he send news?"

It was only then Connor tuned into a thick slow heartbeat in a cavern below. "Is he here?" Connor's eyes gleamed with excitement. If the enigma of Osiris fascinated him, then the man who made him was equally intriguing.

Malachi grinned. "No. He sent a warrior priest. There are reports of vampires on killing sprees – decimating the humans stock of settlements in Sakha. There are rumors of the same in the Vladivostok Hive and in the Northern China territory. Imhotep is concerned. He needs me to go into the Cairo Hive and find out what is happening in the Far East."

"Vladivostok? That's more than 5,000 miles away? Should he be concerned?" Even though the entire continent of Europe and Asia lay between England and the 'problem', Connor felt a shockwave of unease.

"I can see by your face, you already know the answer to that. 5,000 miles, in vampire terms, is not so very far. But maybe not. It is why I must go home."

Malachi wasn't yet dressed to travel. Connor detected tension between Seren and Osiris.

"What else?"

"Osiris is insisting on escorting me. We can travel faster if I don't need to register for human blood rations along the way."

Connor could see why this would upset Seren. "So, once you're home, Osiris will return? That doesn't seem so bad, squirt." He used his childhood nickname as he ran a hand down over the black silk of his daughter's hair.

Seren nodded. "I want to go, too."

"No," Connor said.

"Papa, after all we've been through, how can you say no?"

An ache in Connor's gut made him grimace. His own foolishness had forced his child to grow up fast. If he could turn back the clock, he would. "What does your mother say?"

"Coward," whispered Seren.

"You better believe it. If you knew what *she's* been through, you'd know that her word is final."

"We have spoken to Mama. Malachi has agreed to perform our binding ceremony, here, tomorrow night. Mama says, if you agree, we can go, but she wants to see us married first."

Connor silently digested the information. He shut all the doors inside his head so the thoughts he battled with were only his own.

He had expected Rebekah to refuse, but she was always stronger than he realized. *I am a coward.* The engagement had been a large celebration. A wedding in twenty-four hours would be a very quiet affair.

"If, when I talk with your Mama, she says yes, then you can go." Still studying Seren and Osiris, Connor opened the cerebral door and spoke to Malachi. *If it gets too dangerous, promise you'll abandon your quest and bring them back.*

The elderly vampire smiled his assent.

"So, where is your Mama?" Connor asked when, once again he failed to pick up a scent strong enough to help him.

Seren looked innocent. "Mama said only to give you this clue. "She is at the place where you first realized you loved her."

Connor's photographic memory took a lightning fast trawl through the years of torment that being with Rebekah had put him through, and couldn't single out one precise moment. *Women.* He turned and headed towards the panic room – the converted walk-in freezer which made human scents almost undetectable, provided they kept calm. *Maybe she's here.*

As he pulled open the door, he knew he was wrong. When he stopped racking his brain, closed his eyes and just inhaled her scent it came to him – a night, three years ago drifted in a cloud of colors and delicious emotions. It was their *first* night, when he surrendered to the truth and admitted he could never be happy without her.

Closing the panic room door and retracing his steps, Connor's preoccupied satisfaction piqued Seren's curiosity. "Where is she, Papa?"

Connor grinned. "Our glade," was all he said before, even to vampire senses, he became a gray clad blur of movement.

Chapter 41

Connor made his way across the lush meadow grass beneath a moon which shone with ethereal brightness. *A full moon.* The precise opposite to how it had been at the time that Rebekah wanted him to remember.

He easily recalled the heightened emotions rampaging through him when he saved her from her own human stupidity. She had chosen to walk across a field in full sunlight thinking it would protect her from hunting vampires. All it did was whet a predator's appetite. Hunting resembled revenge, it was a dish best served cold. The sun always sets, eventually.

Of course, she wasn't thinking straight after the rollercoaster ride of meeting Connor and the dangers they had faced together.

Without her even knowing, Connor had fought to save her from a feral vampire attack, and then protected her from within the cover of the woods. Each rash move she made, he had witnessed and become more incensed.

When he eventually snatched the opportunity to swoop in and pluck her from the field, his anger was incandescent. Rebekah had known, before he did, that he cared too much for it to be anything other than the deepest of connections. *Love.*

He hadn't experienced that for over a century, so it was no wonder it made him angry and confused.

Entering the woods now, and skimming between the trees, Connor headed unerringly to the small flower-littered glade where, in moments of respite, he used to take the human Rebekah. So many poignant milestones in their relationship were played out here and it drew them like a beacon of sanity in an insane world.

He chose to bring her to this place of refuge when Douglas drugged her and forced her to marry him. Luckily, Connor did reach her *before* Douglas could force her into the marriage bed. A fierce frown creased Connor's features, his lip curling in disgust, as if the event had occurred only yesterday. But no, he and Rebekah had survived many trials since then.

Connor stopped in his tracks. *But, everything is changed now.* He owed his existence to her stubborn strength, and he had ended up turning her before he wanted to. He smiled. *She won this battle.* Rebekah would have become a vampire years ago, except he refused to cooperate.

He started to move again, slowly. Seren was flying the nest. He still reeled from the news that she and Osiris were heading out into dangerous waters alone, but he should be used to headstrong women by now. *But Seren and Osiris are joined.*

His speed accelerated in time with his resolve.

Absorbed in his own thoughts, he ploughed trenches into the ground beneath his feet when he came to a sudden stop, worthy of the funniest cartoon character. If an artist brought Connor's reaction to life, his eyes would have popped out on stalks and heat blasted from his ears.

In a re-enactment of the moment when Rebekah had figuratively reached inside his chest and taken his heart, she stood quietly, resting back against a broad trunk of an oak tree. She wore the same clothes he had taken from a department store when they made their escape from London on that first day.

The cotton shirt skimmed over her curves. The blue denim jeans clung to her lithe figure. Her eyes remained closed but he knew she noticed his arrival when a soft smile exposed white teeth. As though drawn in to play his part in a scene, just as he did all that time ago, he crossed the rough grass and leaned against the tree, placing one hand either side of her head, and said, quietly, "Are you insane? Do you want to die? There are some dangerous monsters out there." He would never make a good actor, he frowned fiercely, but couldn't keep the smile on his face, or the joy in his heart, from infecting his words.

Still without opening her eyes, Rebekah replied, "I often think, in some way, I *was* insane. Oh no, that's not what I said. I said, 'I thought you'd gone. Are you alone?'." Her dark lashes swept up and her amusement melted when she looked into his preternaturally beautiful face, and saw it with her own vampire enhanced vision. He stole her breath away. Her mouth dropped open.

"I know exactly how you feel," he murmured, tracing a fingertip down her throat. He was surprised she remembered her exact words on a night so long ago, after all, she was only human, back then. With a predatory smile, he added, "Oh no, that's not what I said, either. I said, 'Of course, I'm alone.'. And then I did this-" His cool index finger traced the contours of her clavicle, coming to rest in the V at the base of her throat. Looking into the glittering pools of her brown eyes, Connor enjoyed feeling the excitement race through her body as his finger traveled downward and dipped into her cleavage.

It wasn't the human excitement of that night – the thunder of heartbeats and fragrant perspiration, this time it was an arcing of electricity as though a set of jump leads were discharged inside his head. It sent a lightning fast bolt of warmth which dropped through his center and warmed his heart, gut, and that part that men often took too much direction from. He leaned in to kiss her and her body moved into his as though a magnetic force pulled her towards him.

Rebekah pushed her hands into his hair, winding the silken strands around her fingers and pulling him in closer. The play acting was forgotten as Connor lost himself in another first, for him. Birgitta's blonde image solidified on the fringes of his mind, and tension locked his muscles as guilt tried to douse the fire he wanted to embrace.

As though she knew, Rebekah said, "Come back. She drugged you, you never gave her your heart."

His gray gaze bored into hers as he lifted her thighs to frame his hips.

"Love me, Connor." The words were meant to be another revisiting of those she had said so long ago, but there was anxiety laced through them.

He laid her back on the bed of lush grass and with nimble fingers, undressed her. He wanted to feel her cool smooth skin against his, and moments later, he sighed as, resting on his elbows, he gently brushed the feathered strands of her hair back from her cheeks and said, "I'll always love you."

She lifted her face and kissed him. "I know-"

"But it's not enough," Connor said.

Rebekah became very still, the same electricity burning between them arced with a biting tinge of pain.

Resting his forehead on hers, Connor said, "Marry me."

Her smile lit up the night sky, as far as Connor was concerned, but he waited, frowning a little and saying, "I'm dying, here."

Rebekah giggled. A delightfully musical sound which entranced him.

"Is that a yes?"

"Yes, yes, yes. Now, will you make love to me?"

Connor looked thoughtful, his long finger stroking his chin. "Should I ask Uncle Harry for your hand? I don't want to sully your virtue."

"Beast," blurted Rebekah, as if her virtue was not already long gone.

With a wicked smile, he kissed her and looked into her eyes, again. Returning to the script of their first intimate moment, of seemingly a lifetime ago, he murmured, "Beautiful." His tongue flicking over the pink bud of her nipple. "Trust me, I'm a doctor."

Her husky laughter stuck in her throat.

Absorbed in relearning every nuance of her body, which was the same and yet so alluringly different, Connor's face reflected the tension radiating through him. The usual fear which lurked beneath his ardent gaze evaporated as she blossomed beneath his touch.

Rebekah's fragile human form had bruised easily, and that had cluttered his mind with so many fears. The vampire revival sleep he always had to cling to clouded his senses. Now, the moonlit night became a burning supernova as Connor unleashed his inhibitions, chased the tingling trail of pleasure through his own body, and took her with him. In contrast to the breathlessness of human pleasure, the vampire silence of the moment was an illusion as, in a tangle of limbs and stroking fingertips, they floated in a world of wonder.

Chapter 42

Julian arrived at the eco-town and headed towards the cluster of human heartbeats. Like Hansel and Gretel following a trail of breadcrumbs, he focused on each one in turn until the brighter orb which belonged to Leizle made him smile.

Connor had felt the same connection to Rebekah, as if her heartbeat also vibrated inside his chest. Julian, in those early days of Connor's apparent madness, couldn't understand it. But then, Leizle's green eyes and burnished copper hair caught his attention. Even if she had not had those dramatic embellishments, he knew he would still have fallen in love with her. In a trait she shared with Rebekah, it was the fire inside her which captivated him.

He slipped beneath the blackout curtain and picked up speed. Julian registered a flurry of movement at his shoulder, where Marius and Anthony moved along the tunnel with him as though they shared the same mind. *Connor was right, Anthony is a good fit.* The three achieved an effortless dynamic, and the space left by Alexander was quickly filled, like the shifting of sand. Julian felt regret in one sense, but living for two hundred years had taught him one thing; change is important. *Adapt or die.*

Anthony's physical strength – honed as a human pugilist – complimented the deep waters of Marius' intellect. Not to say Anthony lacked intelligence, but rather, Julian had a profound sense that historic events Marius had lived through marked his soul in ways no one could imagine. His execution of Alexander proved that Marius would remain an enigma.

Julian glanced at Anthony's profile, assessing his tight features behind the clear plastic mask he wore, and received a thumbs up. Anthony's control around humans no longer caused concern, but inside the eco-town, like Dumbo and the magic feather, he took extra precautions.

Further along, a break in the tunnel wall marked the entrance to the meeting cavern. Light spilled out and soft music haunted the air. Along the passageway approaching the cavern from the opposite direction, lanterns filled with clusters of fairy lights lined the route in another trail of breadcrumbs, enticing the humans to come and join in the fun, not that they needed much encouragement.

Taking the sharp turn into the room, Julian stopped on the threshold. This was less of a party, and more of a ceremony than the last celebration. All twenty humans residing in the habitat occupied rows of chairs.

The fairy light explosion gave way to an array of tall church pillar candles. On the gold satin draped altar sat a gold goblet. The hieroglyphs decorating it looked Egyptian, as did the beautiful engraved frame supporting a foot-tall hour glass.

Leizle was sitting in the front row of the almost silent gathering and, as though she felt his gaze on her skin, she turned and bestowed a dazzling smile on Julian. In a silent graceful movement, she rose and walked up the central aisle between the chairs, framed his face with her hands, lifted up on tip toes, and kissed him chastely.

"I've missed you," she said.

Her gentle wistful tone sliced into his soul. "I missed you, too, Red." Her touch felt hot on his night chilled skin. He slipped his hand around her waist, savoring the heat which scalded his palm, lowered his head and tasted her kiss once more. "I'm here for a day or so, at least."

The flush of pleasure his words brought her was all the reward he needed, but she said, "That's wonderful, my love." With a squeeze on his fingers, she withdrew, and she and her scampering heart returned to her seat.

Taking a place at the rear of the cavern, resting back against the wall beside Marius, he noticed Anthony was no longer there.

"Where did Anthony go?"

Marius' response was less a Makaton sign, than a rueful stab of a finger.

Blending in as if he belonged, Anthony sat in the back with Greg, Seth, and Adam forming the remainder of the row. Anthony and Greg – their friendship forged in battle – radiated calm solid reliability. *A good team.* And that set Julian speculating on possibilities.

Marius nudging his arm interrupted his thoughts. Malachi's appearance created an aura of awestruck silence. The gilded edges of the white robe he wore swept the floor as he made his way forward. Stepping up onto the dais and stopping in front of the altar, Malachi turned to face the gathering. An ethereal glow took the edge off his usual jaundiced complexion, and his skin seemed smoother, softening the angular planes of his skull. The imperial effect of the Egyptian headdress framing his face bestowed a hypnotic sense of gravitas.

His entrance signalled that the waiting was over.

Julian assessed the room with interest. He knew Osiris held the position of Wenuty Priest in the Earth Walker tribe. The watcher of the hours. As though Malachi read his thoughts, the elderly figure gripped the heavily embossed frame of the hour glass in his hands and turned it over. White sand flowed with a reverent whisper through the narrow waist, and at the same second, Osiris appeared in Julian's peripheral vision.

The Egyptian warrior wore a crisp white skirt which hugged his hips and molded to solid thighs. The wide band of gold framing his torso and those gripping his right bicep were both engraved with Egyptian Gods in hieroglyphic profile. A medallion resting in the center of his broad naked chest depicted an eagle entangled with a serpent. It signified strength and cunning.

The humans peered back over their shoulders and watched, entranced as Osiris paused, turned and stretched out his hand. Seren's shrouded form joined him and rested her fingers on the back of his. The gauze of the veil could not mask the ebony sheen of her bejeweled hair or the joyous glitter in her eyes. Her dress flowed down her body, moving like a river of ice as the pair made their way to where Malachi waited.

In the perfect timing Julian expected, Osiris arrived with his bride at the precise second the last grain of sand settled in the bottom chamber of the hour glass.

"My son, the moon and stars bless you." Malachi turned to Seren. "The sun in all her splendor bows down to you both."

He gestured them forward, and both Osiris and Seren knelt on padded cushions on the edge of the dais, bowing their heads before the altar.

In a musical chant, Malachi repeated the words three more times. Taking a bowl fashioned from beaten gold, he dipped his fingers into it and marked Osiris' cheekbones with what looked like pearl white teardrops.

Osiris turned to Seren and said, "The moon and stars bless you, and I, your Lord, bow to your splendor." Lifting her veil, he dipped a fingertip into the bowl Malachi offered, and marked Seren's cheekbones with the same shimmering teardrops.

Taking her hand in his, Osiris turned towards Malachi.

Pulling a thin length of bronze colored silk from around his waist, Malachi bound their joined hands in an intricate figure of eight pattern. "I bind thee. Moon to sun. Eagle and serpent. Strength to strength."

Osiris repeated the words, looking into Seren's eyes as he did so.

At his nod, Seren responded. "I bind thee. Sun to moon, serpent to eagle. My strength to your strength.

Malachi turned away and when he swung back, he held a gold ring, its spiral design resembling a coiled serpent. One eye glinted with an emerald.

Lifting the couple's joined hands once more, Malachi slipped the flattened coil of gold onto Seren's wedding finger and pushed it up until the serpent's head rested smoothly against her knuckle. Using his fingernail as a blade, Malachi cut the spiral in two and slid the lower half down, leaving one completed circle around Seren's finger.

With a deft movement, Osiris re-aligned the coil into an enclosed band below the snake's intricately decorated head. "I bind thee to me," he said. "The serpent protects thee from all harm." And then he pressed his lips to the back of her hand.

From the remaining spiral, as though the gold were soft dough, Malachi fashioned a rounded end which, when pressed into an intricate mold became an eagle's head, with feathers and a smooth golden bright eye. As he had with Seren, he pushed the spiral onto Osiris' finger, until the eagle's profile fit snuggly over his knuckle, and the coil formed a band which Seren pressed into an enclosed circle. "I bind thee to me," she said. "The eagle protects thee from all harm."

Malachi clasped their joined hands in his once more, and said, "The moon and stars bless you both. Strength to strength, none can break your bind." With the mystical skill of a magician, Malachi touched the binding of silk ribbon and it fell away. "You are 'one soul'."

Turning to face the assembled witnesses, for the first time, Osiris smiled. The silence lasted a moment longer, before the human tension broke with a sea of sighs and sniffles.

"Osiris raised Seren's hand to his lips and said, "My heart, my love, my wife."

Everyone in the room moved at once, clapping and cheering.

"So, my little girl has grown up," Connor said quietly at Julian's shoulder.

Julian's head shot around. He had been so absorbed in the spectacle, he'd missed Connor and Rebekah's entrance.

They both radiated subdued happiness, and Julian smelled a rat for the first time.

"What aren't you telling me?"

The expertly cut suit molded to Connor's shoulders shifted as he shrugged. "She is leaving us. Seren."

"What?" Julian darted his attention to Rebekah's tense face. She looked beautiful with the network of glistening quartz threads enhancing the contours of her skin. "Where is she going?"

"Not for good. But Osiris is escorting Malachi to Egypt. She will go too."

"Why?" Julian watched the young couple accepting congratulations from the gathering across the room. "Never mind. That is a stupid question. They just got married."

Connor laid a hand on Julian's shoulder. "We'll talk in a while. But for now, let's celebrate-" His dark brows rose over twinkling gray eyes. "And let's hope the sirens stay silent, this time."

Julian took his place beside Leizle just as Adam and two others began an impromptu jamming session. Mimicking a skiffle band, they used items from Oscar's kitchen as percussion instruments. Their feet tapped in time with the descant chorus of pots, pans, and spoons, both wooden and steel. Soon, others in the group started to dance.

Seren approached. "Uncle Julian." She smiled.

"Let me see the ring," said Leizle, capturing Seren's deceptively delicate looking fingers in hers. The serpent's emerald eye twinkled in the light.

"It's beautiful."

Julian realized where he'd seen it before. Or something like it. Malachi wore a ring – the serpent head rested on the back of his hand and the coils encircled his finger three times. But *that* ring had a ruby for an eye. Julian frowned, trawling through things he knew and those he had heard about. *Numu. Malachi's twin.* Connor had fought Numu in 1910. Noticing the emerald eye on the snake was what saved him. Made him realize in time it was not Malachi, but an imposter, and Connor killed Numu, instead of the other way around. It seemed fitting somehow, that Malachi had passed it on to Seren and Osiris. *The bond between twins is very strong.*

Watching Leizle's admiring glance taking in both Seren and Osiris, even Julian admitted the truth. She wasn't envious of the ring, but of their declaration of commitment. As they joined the ebb and flow of the socializing current, Julian, pretending to look in another direction, observed her from the corner of his eye.

Her smile became a brittle mask at times, while her mind traveled into realms of fantasy. The number of occasions she unconsciously circled back to gaze at Rebekah gave Julian the key to where her thoughts were. Rebekah gave the impression of being illuminated from within. A preternatural glow made her breathtaking. Julian gazed into Leizle's eighteen-year-old face and knew exactly what pressure he would come under later in the evening.

Will I have the strength to refuse her, when all she wants is to be with me forever? Julian hoped he could buy her another year of human maturity. He lied to himself every day, but today, he shook his head at his own transparency. He wanted to give her time for her infatuation to burn out, if that's what it was. He loved her enough to let her go, but he had waited two hundred years to feel like this, so he *knew* it was love.

He gently stroked his fingers over her wrist. When she looked up, he smiled. Her green regard held a thousand questions.

"I am so happy to share these moments with you. I love you, Red."

Her shoulders slumped for a moment. She knew him well, and read the battle going on inside him, but, a moment later her chin came up in a 'bring it on' gesture.

He chuckled. Catching sight of Greg across the room, Julian whispered, "I'll be back in a moment." And he set off to intercept him.

"Greg," said Julian. "How are you?"

The question was loaded with many levels of enquiry. Greg still wore his familiar combat gear, almost as though he used it to remind the humans he had not changed *that* much.

Greg pulled a metal hammer from his utility belt, and Julian theatrically shied away like Dracula from a priest wielding holy water. When Julian refocused, he saw what Greg was showing him. The hammer head was distorted into a fist imprinted clump of metal.

"I carry this to remind myself that everything around me is as fragile as spun glass nowadays." Greg grinned.

"It must be tough having a foot in both camps." Julian gestured to Anthony's figure, fingers flying as he talked to Marius. The newest juror expression was earnest as he practised this new form of communication.

"You know," Julian said slowly, "there is a place for you in the Elite Guard, if you want it. Gerrard would welcome you as a deputy."

"Thank you, Julian."

"You aren't finding it hard being enclosed with so much temptation?" Again, Anthony's security blanket of the mask came to mind. But, Julian knew it had taken *him* a while to find control, too.

"I don't know if it's because feeding from them would be like hurting my own children, but I can resist them." He grinned. "I enjoy the sensation of appreciating their heartbeats and the pulse which makes their complexions alluring and pink, but I can resist them."

It hadn't occurred to Julian that perhaps he found it easier to visit the eco-town because the humans here were now friends, not just food. But even friends were in danger sometimes. "Remember, once the residue of your own human blood diminishes, then grave sleep can come on fast. Learn to recognize it and 'get the hell out of Dodge' when it happens. You don't want to carry the guilt of killing your best friends around for decades. Loads like that get heavier."

"'oorah," muttered Greg, acknowledging Julian as his commanding officer.

Patting Greg on the back, Julian prepared to move away, saying, "If you change your mind, the guard slot is always there."

"Thank you, Julian, but I'm hopeful Connor will find a way to mass produce his blood substitute and then guards won't be so important."

Julian raised a brow. "You surprise me, Marine. You should know better. If vampires no longer *need* human blood, that won't stop those who still *want it.* Deep down, just like the human race waged wars, vampires are hunters."

Greg laughed harshly. "You're right. I'll guard my friends for now, the rest is for the future."

Knowing when he was being dismissed, Julian raised a hand in salute and tracked down his next target. He had news which Connor was going to find frustrating.

He found Connor in his chamber dressed for a night expedition. Wearing his favored greatcoat – newly repaired, but the pattern of stitched seams ran down the fabric like battle scars – he had leather gloves in his hand, about to shove them into his pocket.

"Going somewhere?" asked Julian.

"Riding shotgun to the coast," Connor replied as though he was saying 'going to post a letter'.

Julian absorbed the tightness in Connor's shoulders and dark clouds in his friend's gaze, and he wasn't convinced by the casual attitude.

"I suspect your news is as challenging as mine."

Connor stopped in the process of buttoning his coat. "Your news?"

"All in good time. First, why are you 'riding shotgun', and for whom?"

"Malachi is leaving us. As I said, Seren and Osiris are seeing him safely back to Egypt."

"And?"

"What do you want to hear? That I'm worried sick? That I wish I could go with them, but sadly, I'm no good as fast food?"

"Well, I *was* wanting to know why Malachi is rushing off, but I can see you have a lot more on your mind."

Connor ran his hand over his jaw. "All I know right now is that Malachi had news about disruption in the vampire hives in the Far East. It could be disease or just a revolt. Malachi needs to protect the Earth Walker tribe."

"And he needs Osiris in case there is no food when he gets there? I can see why you're worried." Understanding suddenly dawned for Julian. "That is why the binding ceremony was held so quickly. And Seren will meet her father-in-law, Imhotep. The Great One." Julian's gaze glittered with excitement.

"If it is safe." Connor inclined his dark head. "Now, your news."

"It appears that releasing Serge might have been Alexander's last act."

"But why? And how do you know?"

"We'll never know for sure, the 'why' at least. A last act of rebellion? Covering his tracks again? Who knows? But, he *was* seen by two porters entering the chapel."

"No one challenged him?" His expression said 'were the guards asleep on the job'.

"He's a juror. The Defcon level had dropped down a notch once we got you home." Julian shrugged.

"He was obviously stressed," Connor mused. "Maybe his conscience got to him and his drive for answers took him there. Serge could have already escaped. Alexander would not raise the alarm. He was in a shit storm already."

"Isaac managed Serge's blood dosage with muscle relaxant. How could Serge escape without help?" Julian's skeptical expression said it all. "You're clutching at straws."

Connor could only agree. "We will never know it was Alexander though, as you say."

"I've yet to hear anything back from the British hives. But, being seventy human years and only having one arm, I'm sure when he surfaces looking for rations, he'll be noticed."

"Unless he has more friends than we know about. What if-"

"Hard to believe." Julian was thoughtful.

Rebekah appeared at the cavern door wearing combat khaki and an impatient expression. "Hello, Julian. Sorry to be rude, but Malachi is ready to go, and," Lifting an eyebrow, she said, "I'm sure Leizle is wondering where you are." With a stern look, she disappeared.

Connor forced a laugh. "That's us put in our places."

"Looks like you've got company on the 'riding shotgun' journey. She's a force to be reckoned with."

"You better believe it." Connor patted his coat pocket, checking his leather gloves were still there, then swung towards the doorway.

"Connor?"

With one foot already outside in the tunnel, Connor stopped and looked round.

"Do you regret it? Turning Rebekah?"

Connor ducked back into the room. "I regret *how* it happened. In anger. But no. You know the saying 'you don't know what you've got 'til it's gone'? Well, the other is just as true, 'you don't know how wonderful something is, until it finally happens'. This 'Rebekah' falls into that category. Wonderful."

Julian stayed silent.

"Does that answer your question?"

He cleared his throat. "Yes. Yes, it does."

With a twinkle in his eye, Connor said, "Good luck with Leizle." Then he disappeared.

Julian circled the cavern, gathering speed, as though taking a run up at a tough obstacle. When he left the chamber and hurtled along the corridor, skimming up the walls on each turn like a toboggan, he still had no idea what would happen when he saw Leizle. *Maybe, we are ready for 'wonderful' too.*